SOFI AND THE BONE SONG

Also by

ADRIENNE TOOLEY

Sweet & Bitter Magic

SOFI
AND THE
BONE
SONG

ADRIENNE TOOLEY

MARGARET K. McELDERRY BOOKS

New York   London   Toronto   Sydney   New Delhi

MARGARET K. McELDERRY BOOKS
An imprint of Simon & Schuster Children's Publishing Division
1230 Avenue of the Americas, New York, New York 10020
For information about special discounts for bulk purchases, please contact Simon & Schuster Special Sales at 1-866-506-1949 or business@simonandschuster.com.
The Simon & Schuster Speakers Bureau can bring authors to your live event. For more information or to book an event, contact the Simon & Schuster Speakers Bureau at 1-866-248-3049 or visit our website at www.simonspeakers.com.
Interior design by Irene Metaxatos
The text for this book was set in Caslon 540 LT Std.
Manufactured in the United States of America
First Edition
10 9 8 7 6 5 4 3 2 1
Library of Congress Cataloging-in-Publication Data
Names: Tooley, Adrienne, author.
Title: Sofi and the bone song / Adrienne Tooley.
Description: First edition. | New York : Margaret K. McElderry Books, an imprint of Simon & Schuster Children's Publishing Division, [2022] | Summary: After losing everything to an undeserving rival, a sixteen-year-old musician sets out to expose that her rival's newfound musical abilities stem from an illegal use of magic—but what she discovers will rock everything she knows about her family, music, and the girl she thought was her enemy.
Identifiers: LCCN 2021015408 (print) | LCCN 2021015409 (ebook) | ISBN 9781534484368 (hardcover) | ISBN 9781534484382 (ebook)
Subjects: LCSH: Lute—Juvenile fiction. | Magic—Juvenile fiction. | Music—Juvenile fiction. | Fathers and daughters—Juvenile fiction. | Friendship—Juvenile fiction. | CYAC: Lute—Fiction. | Magic—Fiction. | Music—Fiction. | Fathers and daughters—Fiction. | Friendship—Fiction. | Lesbians—Fiction.
Classification: LCC PZ7.1.T6264 So 2022 (print) | LCC PZ7.1.T6264 (ebook) | DDC [Fic]—dc23
LC record available at https://lccn.loc.gov/2021015408
LC ebook record available at https://lccn.loc.gov/2021015409
ISBN 9781534484368
ISBN 9781534484382 (ebook)

For Katie, because

IN THE KINGDOM OF

AELLI

NORTH

N
W E
S

❋ MAP KEY ❋

◆ TOWN

═ BORDER

• • • • MUSIK TOUR ROUTE

≈ RIVER

♫ TAVERN/THEATRE

ODDSLOW
never again!!

JUURI

Saint Ogden's Theatre

TROGG
"Song of St Swithin's" heavy drinkers

The Fourth Horse

SKAAL

The Beast's Belly

"The Weary Wayfarer" 2x encore. good brandy

Jambor

OHRE

The Passing Breeze

girl with apples??

wastelands

"The Ballad of Sir Ellis" only one encore...

RUSHAM

no ballads

The Fair Fellows

VISC

ELGAN

The Surly Saint

crowd as surly as tavern name suggests. next time more wine??

THE KING'S CITY

The King's Theatre

don't forget to finish "Ya Love a King"

The Gate

THE
QUEENDOM OF ROTH

SOFI AND THE BONE SONG

ONE

THE KING came to Juuri on a third day, which meant that upon his arrival, Sofi was otherwise engaged. While her father welcomed King Jovan and his attendants in their parlor, Sofi pressed her knees against the firm floor of her closet and called out to the Muse.

"Sing to me, O Muse, for without you I am lost. Pray for me, O Muse, for without you I am empty. Let your notes be played, let your song be sung. I will hear you, if only you will speak to me. Let me be worthy—" Her voice broke on the word, as it did each time she spoke the prayer. "Let me be heard."

Even though Sofi knew her father was downstairs, she could practically hear him on the other side of the door, commanding her to repeat the prayer: *"Again."*

She obeyed. Even when Frederik Ollenholt was elsewhere, his voice still echoed in her head, as sharp and cold as a fresh layer of snow.

"Sing to me, O Muse, for without you I am lost."

Sofi's father was not known for his kindness, but then, kindness and talent were not one and the same. What Frederik Ollenholt lacked in niceties he made up for in his command of the Muse, in the intricate, complex music that poured from his fingers to his lute. As one of the five members of the Guild of Musiks and the only lutenist licensed to cross the border of their Kingdom of Aell into the wider world, her father didn't need to be kind. He needed *talent*. So if Sofi ever wanted to become her father's Apprentice—which she desperately, gut-wrenchingly did—she needed to ensure the Muse was on her side.

Sofi fumbled in the darkness for the dress nearest to her, tugging it from its hanger and pulling it tightly around her shoulders like a blanket. "Pray for me, O Muse, for without you I am empty."

For ten of the sixteen years of her life, Sofi had prayed to the Muse every third day, yet there was something about that exact moment—the scratch of wool against her cheek, the muted echo of the royal party downstairs—that made the prayer's words ring differently in her ears. This time, her voice echoed around the closet like Sofi was at the bottom of a well, the prayer reverberating against ice and stone, hollow and sprawling.

Sprawling. That was it.

Sofi got to her feet so quickly she nearly smacked her head against the top of the closet. She had long grown out of the small, cramped space, but the dark helped her focus. Concentration was especially important on third days.

Third days were for praying.

Sunlight flooded into the small space as Sofi pushed open the closet door and spilled into her bedroom, heading directly for her desk. She rifled through the endless sheaf of papers littering its surface until she found a scrap that wasn't covered with words she liked or the fragment of a concept or the sketch of a song. She fumbled for a pencil that had not yet been sharpened all the way to its nub, one that was long enough to still fit between her fingers.

Sofi scrambled to put down the lyric that had sprung fully formed into her head, her left hand smearing her words as it hurried across the page. She'd been working on a song about Saint Brielle, but the final line of the chorus had eluded her for days.

Now the Muse had offered Sofi the missing piece, laid it out as neatly as a carpet unfurled at the feet of a king: *Until death's final, sprawling song called them back where they belonged.*

She shivered gleefully. This line was further proof that Sofi's devotion to the Muse would always be rewarded. Proof that she was the clear choice to be named her father's Apprentice, the first step toward becoming a Musik in her own right.

Sofi wasn't the only one who knew it, either. Only yesterday, another of Frederik's students, a girl called Neha who had been studying with Sofi's father for nearly five years, had walked in on Sofi composing in the parlor and sighed dramatically.

"I almost don't know why I bother," she had grumbled as Sofi put the finishing touches on the thirteenth verse of "The Song of Saint Brielle." "The words fall out of you so effortlessly, it's almost like magic."

While to a non-musician, it might have sounded like a compliment, to Sofi those were fighting words. Using magic in music went against the highest tenet of the Guild of Musiks. It was a crime that could get a musician-in-training Redlisted, losing them the right to ever perform again.

"It's because I *practice*, Neha." Sofi had scowled from the settee. "You should try it sometime."

"Someone's testy." Neha had *tsk*ed. "They *do* say that using too many Papers makes a person mean. Of course, *I* wouldn't know," she'd said smugly, tucking a strand of long black hair behind her ear, showing off the backs of her hands. Her brown skin was clearly absent of the words that identified a Paper-caster. On Neha's dark shade of skin, the words would have gleamed as white as snow.

By then Sofi had removed her lute from her lap and rested her hands on her knees. Had she been employing Paper magic, the words would have shone black as ink on her white skin. "Why don't you come take a closer look if you're so concerned about the *integrity* of my music?"

"No, thank you." Neha had rolled her eyes. "I've heard enough stories of your famous temper. I don't need firsthand experience. Now, if you'll excuse me, it's time for my lesson." She had flounced away, leaving Sofi stewing.

The implication that she was using magic in her music was insulting. The Papers Neha had mentioned had been published thirty years prior, after the Hollow God's gospel spread throughout the world. To escape persecution from his fanatical followers, witches fled north to Aell, whose aging, greedy King Ashe had offered the covens safety and security within his borders in exchange for some of their magic. The desperate witches worked with his men of science to make magic accessible to all. Thus the Papers were published.

Now, for a price, anyone in Aell could purchase a piece of parchment, offer it a drop of blood, and reap the rewards of that particular spell. A Paper for "sketch" would allow the Paper-caster to draw a perfect rendering of the king. A Paper for "chignon" would guide the Paper-caster's hand to pin their hair into a perfect twist. A Paper for "warmth" would start a fire, and a Paper for "blush" would turn the Paper-caster's cheeks as pink as a sunrise without the aid of face paint.

Overnight, the Papers had turned the extraordinary ordinary. And if there was one thing Sofi Ollenholt refused to be, it was ordinary.

The implication that she was using magic in her music was also damning. Musiks were musicians who lived, composed, and performed without the assistance of magic— Paper or otherwise. Any student hoping to ascend to the rank of Apprentice had to keep their hands clean and their art pure.

Even the rumor of a musician using magic was enough to destroy their career entirely—and hers hadn't even begun.

Sofi shook away the memory of the interaction. Neha had always been jealous of Sofi's innate ability, her natural talent. Sofi would not let the other girl's baseless accusations get to her. She had never even *touched* a Paper, so strongly did she eschew magic, so hard did she work to keep herself clean. Deserving. Worthy of one day becoming a Musik herself.

Sofi grabbed her lute from its place on her pillow and brushed the strings lightly, patiently adjusting the tuning pegs. Aell's perpetual cold meant her strings tended to tense, and if she wasn't tender with them, the catgut would snap. The body of her lute pressed gently against her stomach, held in place by the crook of her right arm. That hand plucked the strings while her left hand fingered the notes up and down the instrument's neck.

That shiver returned, the hair on her arms standing at attention as Sofi coaxed sound from her instrument, notes ringing out soft and sincere in her small room. While sometimes the more familiar pieces of her training routine felt tedious, this part never got old: the playing. Piecing her words and her melodies together. Using her hands and her voice and her mind to create something entirely new, something that would not exist were it not for her.

When Sofi played, she had power.

"Did bright Brielle put forth the snow, from where death's sweaty hand would go," Sofi sang, her left ring finger pressed tight upon the two strings of her lute's fourth course.

"The devil's hot, candescent glow did urge her boldly on."

Sofi played her way through the story of Saint Brielle, the woman who ended the devil's scorching summer nearly two centuries ago. As Sofi sang her praise for the saint who commanded winter's wind, the snow outside her bedroom window turned to sleet, hammering against the glass and displacing the crow that had been roosting beneath the slats of the roof. Ice collected in the window's corners as the view of the snow-capped trees was blurred by wretched, unending white. Sofi sighed bitterly, her fingers falling from her instrument.

Lingering seasons weren't uncommon in Aell. The Saint's Summer, when Saint Evaline brought forth the harvest from the icy ground, had come after six years of cold. Saint Brielle's winter ended ten agonizing years of summer. But Aell's current winter was pushing seventeen years, longer than any in the history books or the epic tales sung by Musiks.

Sixteen years of snow. A season as old as Sofi.

The cold was all she'd ever known.

She pressed a hand to the frigid windowpane above her desk. Heat from her fingertips leached onto the glass, leaving marks that disappeared almost instantly. Sofi was afraid of fading away that easily, of leaving not a single visible mark on the world.

It was why she worked so hard. Played so often. Practiced so frequently. Why she obeyed her father's orders and followed the training routine he'd set for her. So many years after its creation, it now held the monotonous familiarity of a lullaby: The first day was for listening, the second for wanting, the third for praying, the fourth for feeling, and the fifth for repenting. But sixth days were special.

Sixth days were for music.

It was a routine more extreme than the methods required of her father's other students. But that was by choice. Sofi had always been willing to work harder. Push herself further. She would do whatever it took to become her father's Apprentice and finally be able to perform publicly. Without the Apprentice title, musicians could only play and compose within their own homes. Sofi was far too talented for her songs to be confined within the four walls of her bedroom.

She placed her fingers back on the lute's strings, picking the song up from its second chorus.

"That's new."

Sofi yelped, nearly falling off her chair as Jakko, her best friend and her father's only live-in student, smiled at her from the doorway, his glossy black curls tumbling dramatically into his eyes.

"What are you doing in here?" Sofi settled her lute carefully back into its case. "The king's downstairs. Shouldn't you be groveling?"

Jakko sighed dramatically and flung himself onto her bed, hugging a pillow to his chest. "Jasper didn't come this time. What's the point of making an appearance if the prince can't see me?"

Sofi rolled her eyes as she swept the papers littering her desk into a haphazard pile. "I still think that the alliteration is a little showy, even for you." She threw her bare foot onto the mattress, nudging Jakko's side. "I mean, Jasper and Jakko?" She wrinkled her nose in mock distaste. Jakko reached out a hand to tickle her, his golden-brown fingers warm against her toes. She kicked his hand away playfully.

"What are you wearing tonight?" Sofi cast a glance at the dress form that held her ruby-red gown for that evening's performance. Most days she opted for shapeless, gray wool shifts. Function rather than form. It was a shock each time her father performed publicly: the jewel-toned dresses that appeared in her bedroom; the paint Marie, their housekeeper, would smear on her lips and cheeks; the way Sofi was flaunted about. That public display of self was a different sort of performance entirely.

"Well"—Jakko ran a hand through his curls—"now that Jasper's not here, I have half a mind not to attend the performance at all."

"You are," Sofi laughed, "the least devoted student my father has ever had."

"Untrue," Jakko volleyed back. "Remember Thea?"

Sofi put a hand to her heart in mock pain. "Low blow." Thea had been Sofi's first crush. Luckily, there had never been any awkwardness or competition between the two of them because Thea was so useless at the lute that Sofi's father had refused to teach her any further after only three lessons.

Frederik Ollenholt had quite a lot of what he called "artistic integrity" and what other people called "impossible standards."

"All my blows are low." Jakko wagged a finger at her. "I should've been a flautist."

Sofi snorted. "You should have. There wasn't any competition for *that* Apprenticeship. The only musician that showed up to audition was Therolious Ambor's own son, Barton." She made a face her best friend didn't return. Jakko had suddenly become very interested in her duvet cover.

"What's wrong?" Sofi moved onto the bed, sticking a finger under Jakko's chin and tilting it up, forcing him to meet her eyes.

"I'm almost eighteen, Sof." His voice was soft like a swaying breeze. "If your father doesn't take his Apprentice in the next few months, I've got nothing." His eyes flitted away from hers again.

"And?" Sofi prompted, even as her stomach squirmed guiltily. She knew Jakko well enough to know when he had more to say.

"And . . . ," he started, looking pained. "If he chooses me, what does that mean for you?"

It was Sofi's turn to look away.

While anyone could—for the right price—take lessons from a Musik, the position of a Musik's Apprentice was both highly coveted and highly competitive. Each Musik took on only one Apprentice in their lifetime. That Apprentice was granted their mentor's treble clef pin, which allowed them to inherit the title of Musik when the reigning Musik retired or passed on. If Sofi wasn't chosen as her father's Apprentice, she would lose the chance of ever becoming a Musik, and the talent she had spent her life honing would become nothing more meaningful than a party trick. Without the title of Musik, Sofi would never make her mark on the world.

"I'd figure something out." But Sofi's lie fell flat. There was no other option.

Not for her.

Not every musician had the willpower or discipline to become a Musik. But Sofi, with a dead mother and a father who spent most of his life on the road, had nothing but time. She had dedicated her entire life to ensuring the Muse was on her side. She had been handed a lute at four years old and could read music before she could write her own name. She whiled away hours studying theory, poring over lyrics and rhyme schemes. By the age of eight, she was performing works that tripped up her father's most seasoned students. Once, when she was ten, she taught herself to play a song holding her lute upside down, just to prove that she could.

But beyond her hard work and dedication, and perhaps most importantly, Sofi was *good*. Her technical skill was unparalleled; she could play even the most complex melodies after hearing them only once. Sofi was so focused on perfection that any mistake she made—missing a note or striking an errant string, falling out of time or taking a beat too long to make a transition—became a learning experience, an obsession, the same phrase played over and over until she was certain she would never waver again. Even her father, with his signature scrutiny and painfully expressive features, found less and less to criticize as the years went on.

Sofi adored Jakko. He was a good lutenist and an even better friend. But the title of Apprentice would one day be hers.

It had to be.

"Liar." But Jakko's voice held no anger, only familiar resignation. He rolled onto his stomach, cheek pressed against her pillow. "Do you ever wish we loved an art that wasn't so competitive? One that allowed us to use Papers?"

Sofi made a face, thinking of Neha. "Of course not." She flopped over, nuzzling up next to Jakko. "Anyone can use a Paper to pen a poem about the queen or paint a picture of the king and call themselves an artist. But we create freely, with clean hands and talent alone."

She offered her hand to Jakko, who pushed her unmarked skin away with a roll of his eyes. There was never any speculation as to which spell a Paper-caster had chosen to employ. *Heartbreak,* a hand would read, if a poet used a Paper to conjure the feeling necessary to write a poem of longing and loss. *Flame,* it would warn, if the caster needed fire. It was not uncommon to see Paper-casters whose hands were covered with so many words they appeared to be wearing gloves.

When the Paper's power faded, so too would the word. The hand that had once flawlessly sketched the face of a king would go back to barely being able to draw a straight line. The fire that had been conjured would begin to dim. If an artist wanted to finish their sketch, if an innkeeper wanted to restoke the flames, first they would need to purchase another Paper.

Sofi shrugged. "What can I say? I love feeling superior."

Jakko pushed himself up onto his elbows and frowned. "Do you love to feel superior or do you love to *suffer*? Because, Sofi, those bruises look nasty."

Sofi swiftly rearranged her skirt to cover her knees. "I do what I have to for my art." Her voice was hard.

"Of course." Jakko's tone was too casual. "Still, don't you find it odd that your father never included anything like that in my training routine? No praying? No repenting?"

"I suppose," Sofi said. But what she meant was no. Sofi had been practicing advanced training methods since she was a child. Methods her father's other students weren't privy to. Rather than making her feel isolated or alone, this distinction was further proof that becoming a Musik was her destiny.

Sofi reached for Jakko's hand, twining her fingers in his. His palm was sweaty in that overheated-teenage-boy way. Jakko had been studying with Frederik since Sofi was thirteen and he fifteen. Three years later, they were practically inseparable, no dream too sincere, no competition cutthroat enough to keep them apart. It wouldn't always be this way, but Sofi knew all too well what it was like to be alone. She would hold on as long as she could to his bright laughter, the way he lit up every room. The way he trusted her.

The way she *almost* trusted him.

"How come Marie never puts satin sheets on *my* bed?" Jakko rubbed his cheek theatrically across Sofi's pillow.

"Because you steal her cheese." Sofi giggled, squeezing his hand. She wished there were a way for them both to play music, together. That Jakko would not be relegated to nothingness when she was named her father's successor.

Jakko made an affronted noise. "That's true," he finally conceded. "I do."

"I knew it," Sofi gasped, gripping Jakko's wrist.

"Ow," Jakko whined. "Your calluses are so rough."

Sofi let go of him, waggling her fingers in his face. "I have the prettiest hands you've ever seen."

"That's not necessarily what I'd call them." Jakko swatted at her, finally pushing himself up and off her bed. "Now, come on, Lady Ollenholt." He offered her his hand. "Let's go greet the king."

By the time Sofi and Jakko arrived in the parlor, the pastries had been reduced to crumbs and the tea had gone cold. Marie tutted beneath her breath as she met them in the doorway. The housekeeper reached up to tuck one of Sofi's unruly brown curls tenderly behind her ear.

"There you are." Frederik's expression was pinched despite the light bravado of his voice.

"Jakko. Sofi." King Jovan's voice was a deep bass that resonated warmly within his chest. He got to his feet, unmistakably royal, his brown skin flawlessly smooth, his beard closely cropped, his clothes perfectly tailored, his penchant for gold striking against his warm complexion and his glittering brown eyes. "Give your king a hug, then." He opened his arms to Sofi, looking for all the world more fatherly than Frederik.

Sofi moved to him, inhaling the scent of sap and pine and the sweet sharp slice of perfume. Her father wasn't a hugger, and Marie, despite her mothering tendencies, preferred to fuss rather than to envelop. It was not lost on Sofi how absurd it was that the most consistent embraces she received were from the king of her country.

"How are you, Your Majesty?" Sofi asked as they broke apart. Up close, there were shadows beneath his eyes.

"I look a sight, don't I?" the king asked humorlessly. "I've just come from a meeting of the Council of Regents. Twenty years a king, yet I'm still paying for the sins of my father."

Sofi's brow furrowed sympathetically. The Papers commissioned by Jovan's father, King Ashe, had generated incredible wealth for their country. But that power had increased Ashe's greed tenfold, and he'd soon set his sights beyond Aell to the countries who served the Hollow God. The Hollow God's followers lived by the pillars of piety, simplicity, hard work, and suffering. Unregulated magic had no place in their world.

So King Ashe was careful to position the Papers as everything witches were not: careful, contained, and controllable. Yet once the deals were done, the new Papers he'd sold hadn't worked as the originals had. This magic turned volatile and downright dangerous. Instead of a Paper that commanded water buckets to carry themselves, the Kingdom of Tique faced a slew of slimy newts that sent a sickness through the country's waterways. Heinous burns cropped up on the faces of Dolgesh citizens who had used glamours to polish their appearances. And when the Queen of Roth's personal chef used a Paper to speed up the simmering of a stew, the monarch found herself suddenly and violently ill.

The Council of Regents—made up of rulers from those neighboring monarchies—began to suspect that Ashe had been using the power of witches to expand his empire by weakening theirs. In retribution, they built the Gate, which closed their borders to all citizens of Aell, keeping Aellinians alone. Contained.

"Of course," the king continued, his hand heavy on Sofi's shoulder, "you wouldn't know anything about that. I cannot wait for your father to transport us all with his performance tonight. I do believe the entire Guild will be in attendance." His eyes fell tenderly on Frederik like a mother bird to a hatchling.

The five members of the Guild of Musiks were King Jovan's peace offering to the Council of Regents—proof that Aell held no ill will against its neighbors. That its citizens could create even when their hands were clean of magic. The instruments of the Guild—lute, lyre, drum, flute, and accordion—were the only ones allowed to be played in public. Musiks were the only Aellinians allowed through the Gate.

King Jovan had high hopes that it would be the Guild who would ultimately convince the Council to reopen the border and let Aell rejoin the world.

"Yes," the king continued, "it's shaping up to be a most exciting evening."

Sofi could feel Jakko's eyes on the back of her neck. These days, gathering the entire Guild in one room was a feat. When Sofi was younger, she had accompanied Frederik to many a performance, traveling by coach to towns all across Aell to see his fellow Musiks perform in gilded theaters. But those performances had been fewer and farther between as of late.

Tonight was already a significant occasion. But as the king's eyes glittered mischievously, reflecting the roaring fire in the hearth behind him, it was clear something greater was afoot.

"Certainly, Your Majesty," Sofi agreed, curiosity mounting. "A most exciting evening indeed."

TWO

TWENTY MINUTES before Frederik was set to take the stage, a member of the Kingsguard opened the front door of Saint Ogden's Theatre, and Jakko and Sofi stepped into a wave of sound. The lobby smelled like a greenhouse, oversaturated with conflicting floral perfumes emanating from the delicate skin of ladies' wrists. A cacophony of voices echoed off the ceiling, where a sprawling mural depicted summer—a season that had not been seen in sixteen years.

Saint Ogden's Theatre had been constructed hundreds of years before the Papers were published. Sofi didn't have much of an eye for architecture, but the building had its tells—specifically the lush green of the plants and the vividly rendered flowers twisted around trellises painted above the crowd's heads.

If she squinted, Sofi could see the careful brushstrokes, the places where the artist had poured their soul into the painting. The lines weren't eerily straight, the colors not overly smooth like the paintings of Paper-casters. There were no frantic swipes, as though the magic guiding the artist's hand was running out and the artist hoped to complete the work without having to purchase another Paper. It had been painted by an artist with nothing but time—something increasingly rare these days.

The artistry spoke to her. Jakko called her a snob for preferring art made without Papers, but Sofi disagreed. What was art if it did not come from hard work and devotion? If it was not tended to and grown in the careful pockets of one's heart?

Jakko tugged on Sofi's sleeve. "I think I see Braeden standing underneath the sconces. How do I look?"

Sofi laughed softly at Jakko's mention of the mayor's son and straightened his gray suit jacket. "Prince Jasper really doesn't know what he's missing."

Jakko ran a hand through his curls, making them look perfectly disheveled. "Meet you at our seats." He winked, then disappeared into the throng.

Sofi hummed softly to herself as she moved through the crowd toward the theater's marble staircase. She caught pockets of conversations as she darted around bustles and ducked beneath tuxedo-clad elbows.

"—haven't been to the theater for ages," said a gray-haired woman clutching golden opera glasses to the bridge of her long nose. "I've been looking for a reason to break out my silks." She ran a hand tenderly down the side of her skirt, rubbing the violet-hued fabric between her gnarled fingers. Sofi caught a flash of several words written on the woman's skin.

Sofi rolled her shoulders back, fidgeting with the collar of her own elaborate gown. The long red sleeves were skin-tight—she had almost no range of motion beyond lifting a hand to accept a greeting or reaching into her pocket to produce her ticket.

"I purchased a new Paper for tonight," the gray-haired woman's companion replied. "Even though it was far more expensive than I recalled. Ah well," she said airily. "I never could have done this hairstyle on my own." She put a hand lovingly to the expanse of complicated swoops and sparkling pins that made up her elaborate bouffant. Not a single hair was out of place. Her skin read *chignon*.

It was eerie how casually people donned the level of polish the Papers offered. Where others fawned over the results of Paper-made glamours, that level of calculated, pristine perfection made Sofi uncomfortable. Humans were messy and complex. It pained her that magic disguised that potential for failure with a fleeting sense of flawlessness.

"Now, children, you must promise to sit still." A father knelt on the plush carpet beside two young children. "This is an incredible opportunity. Perhaps one day, if you're lucky, it will be you upon that stage."

The children's eyes widened with awe even as they fidgeted in their finery. Sofi stifled a snort as she left the family behind. Luck had nothing to do with musicianship. Hard work and dedication, now, those were the real factors. One could not *hope* and make music. One could not rely on *luck* to pen a song. Music was about tenderness, care, and devotion—things Sofi had not often been on the receiving end of from her father. She had instead learned to love and be loved through music.

"The carriage ride was *terrible*. So many potholes this far north," came a pinched voice to Sofi's left. "Saints, I miss the summer." She winced as the speaker hacked a loud cough into a handkerchief.

Before she could take another step forward, her ears perked up at the reply from his companion: "No one *demanded* you attend, Tambor." A woman's voice, soft and warm as a crackling fire.

"I am a member of the *Guild of Musiks*," came the affronted reply. "My presence is requir—ouch!" The speaker gave a furious yelp as Sofi barreled past the simpering figure of Therolious Ambor and flung herself into the arms of Denna Mab.

Denna did not miss a beat, but then, she was a Musik, and keeping time was one of her specialties. She lifted Sofi into her arms and planted a giant kiss on her cheek.

"I'd know those curls anywhere." Denna laughed as Sofi inhaled her familiar scent of jasmine blossoms and cedar—the same wood that made up the body of her famous lyre. "How are you, Sofi-girl?"

Sofi grinned up at Denna, the woman's dark brown skin glowing in the warm light of the lobby, the reflection of the crystal chandeliers twinkling in her brown eyes. Her long braids were twisted up in an intricate topknot.

"Better now," Sofi said honestly. Denna hadn't been to Juuri in nearly three years. "You haven't been avoiding me, have you?" she asked, suddenly stricken by the thought.

Denna was her favorite of the five Guild members, always making time to ask about Sofi's study, the only one beyond Frederik who seemed truly invested in her dream of one day joining the Guild. But it wasn't just her kindness—which, as Sofi knew from personal experience, was not necessary to become a Musik—that left an ache in the center of Sofi's chest.

It was Denna's playing.

Her songs were like a drink of water after a deep sleep, like being tucked into bed by someone who loved you. Sofi wept at the end of each performance when Denna's fingers lifted from the strings of her lyre. It wasn't until she'd heard Denna play that Sofi realized music could take a heart apart and put it back together again. It wasn't until she'd heard Denna sing that she'd learned to love music, not just as something that connected her to her father, but as something that gave her an identity of her own.

"Darling," Denna laughed, using her thumb to wipe away the smudge her lip paint had left on Sofi's cheek, "if there's anyone in this town I'm avoiding, it certainly isn't you."

Sofi couldn't blame her there. She herself had gotten quite good at avoiding Frederik Ollenholt, and they lived in the same house. "Well, at any rate"—Sofi clutched Denna's arm—"I'm so happy to see you. Please tell me you'll be taking the stage in the second half?" It had been years since Frederik had allowed Sofi to attend one of Denna's performances.

"If the Muse allows it." Denna grinned. "She knows I'm a terrible audience member."

"*I* will *not* be performing," came the reedy voice of Therolious Ambor. Sofi turned to give him a tight-lipped smile. She had never particularly cared for Tambor, as the Guild members called him. He was a flautist, and, according to her father, *skilled at blowing air up everywhere.* Tambor and Frederik had always had an intense rivalry, despite the fact that they were both Guild members and therefore frequented the same circles and performances. Sofi had never been quite as taken with Tambor's music as she had been with her father's or Denna's, but then, she was rather partial to stringed instruments, which allowed the musician to write lyrics as well as melodies. Without words, Tambor's performances always felt a bit lacking.

"What a . . . shame, Master Tambor." Sofi dipped her head in faux reverence to hide her smile. When she had regained her composure and returned her gaze to the Musiks, Tambor was staring at her suspiciously.

He opened his mouth to speak, no doubt to insult Sofi's father in some new, creative way, but he was interrupted by the theater chimes signifying that the performance was about to begin. The lobby fell to a hush as the sweet tinkle of silver filled the air. Then, all at once, the roar returned as hundreds of people rushed to find their seats.

"I'll see you soon, Sofi-girl." Denna squeezed Sofi's elbow. "Got to head to our seats. Yve and Raffe are probably already in the front row waiting to chastise us for our tardiness." She smiled softly at the mention of the final two Guild members. Sofi bade Denna farewell. Tambor merely grunted at her. Then the Musiks were swallowed by the crowd.

Sofi stood a moment, alone, watching the lobby empty. There was an energy that filled a theater before a performance, a rumble deep in her chest that hit almost as hard as when Raffe, the Guild's percussionist, whacked their largest drum with a mallet. She wanted to drink in every moment.

"Excuse me, miss." A green-vested usher who looked to be about Sofi's own sixteen years hovered nervously next to her. "Do you need help finding your seat?"

"No, thank you." Sofi smiled, patting the ticket in her pocket. As family of the performer, her seat was in a private box at the top of the theater, nestled between the royal box and the other curtained boxes sold to the highest bidders. "I know exactly where I'm going."

"Better hurry." The usher nodded toward the marble staircase. "The show is about to begin."

Sofi headed up the stairs, clutching her giant skirt in one hand, her shoes slick against the polished marble. Halfway up, she slipped, her feet flying out from beneath her. Sofi tensed, waiting for the bright burst of pain as her temple hit the stone below. Instead, a strong hand closed around her arm and yanked her upright, steadying her on the stair that had nearly been her undoing. Sofi caught a glimpse of the letter *F*, midnight black against white skin.

"All right there?"

Sofi looked up to thank her savior, and her stomach did a somersault. The girl before her was beautiful, all blushing cheeks and silky white-blond hair in perfect ringlet curls. Her lips were stained the color of a summer berry, and her eyelashes were so long they practically touched the sky. Sofi swayed slightly, heart skipping a beat as the girl steadied her again. Her long, perfect hands held fast to Sofi's arm. Even the curling words that signified the use of Papers looked elegant and seductive on her skin: *curve, flush, poise*.

Heat flooded Sofi's cheeks. She had never been so grateful for Marie's skill at face paint and hairstyling. She would have otherwise faded hopelessly next to this girl, who was the cherub in a chapel painting, the subject of a poet's meandering profession of love. This girl looked like magic, but for the first time in her life, Sofi didn't care.

"Thank you." Sofi curtsied awkwardly, stomach sinking as she realized exactly how ridiculous she likely looked. Why had she *curtsied*? Pretty girls had always made her a bit silly, but usually she managed to keep herself upright, at least.

"Of course." The girl removed her hands. Sofi's arm burned where her touch had been. "This is a special occasion. No reason to ruin it with a black eye." Her eyes lingered on Sofi's, sending her stomach again into a spirited flutter.

"Much obliged," she managed. "I'm Sofi."

"I'm Lara." The girl's lips quirked into a smile as she offered her hand. "It's a pleasure." Sofi's cheeks flushed warmer still as their fingers met.

They stood on the steps, hand in hand, until a sharp voice

called out from above. "Laravelle," it barked. Lara flinched. A tuxedoed man at least ten years Lara's senior glowered down at her from the top of the stairs.

"That's me." She pursed her lips. "Unfortunately, my full name makes me sound like a piece of furniture."

Sofi bit back a grin. "Or at the very least, a pink satin pillow."

Lara looked down at the rose-colored silk of her dress. "I don't just sound like one." She giggled. "I look like one, too." She gestured to the bows on her sleeves, which were tied so perfectly no human hand could have done it. Above them, the tuxedoed man cleared his throat. "Bye, then." Lara hurried up the steps and disappeared through a curtain to the right.

Sofi gripped the railing, steadying herself. Then she barreled up the stairs to the left and slipped through the forest-green curtain of the Musiks' Box.

"Where have you been?" Jakko blinked up at her through his thick eyelashes. "Your father's already tuning. Normally you're hanging over the box by now, imagining what you'll look like one day on that stage." He squinted at her through the darkening theater. "What's the matter with you? You're all flushed."

"I'm fine," Sofi insisted as she settled herself in the plush green-velvet chair, spreading her skirt around her carefully to avoid any wrinkles. "I just . . . got caught up."

Jakko looked at her skeptically but mercifully didn't push. Sofi leaned forward, resting her elbows on the box's railing, scanning the crowd, telling herself she wasn't looking for Lara.

Unfortunately, the patrons in the private boxes were cast in shadows, so Sofi moved her gaze to the level below. There was not an empty seat in sight.

Performances by Musiks were rare enough for the event to be considered a veritable who's who of Aell society. Ticket prices were high—the going rate for box seats like Sofi's was enough to feed a family of four comfortably for half a year. But the Guild of Musiks held the fate of Aell's trade embargo in their calloused hands. Such a high price kept them comfortable, allowing them to create uninhibited by earthly woes. They could devote all their time to the Muse and to their work. That freedom inspired greatness.

Sofi's father spent his days composing new works that would be canonized, new songs to enter the history books, to be learned and performed by other musicians the whole world over. Words immortalized. Melodies memorized. It made Musiks immutable. Permanent. Everlasting.

Sofi's mother, on the other hand, had left no mark on the world. She featured in no stories told by Frederik or Marie, had penned no diaries recounting her days, had not even left behind a portrait that revealed her face. In fact, were it not for her daughter, Sofi's mother might not have existed at all. Sofi had spent countless nights mourning that emptiness and contemplating that absence. She refused to go out in a similar way. Sofi would not spend her life playing music for only herself. Her words warranted an audience. Her songs deserved to be sung long after she'd returned to dust.

She *had* to become a Musik.

A spotlight blinked to life, bathing Frederik, who stood center stage, in warm golden light. His instrument sparkled like a gleaming smile, for Frederik Ollenholt's lute was made of bone.

Sofi had always coveted her father's instrument. The careful construction of its round body, which tucked perfectly into the crevice of her father's arm. The gleaming snow-white neck with glittering silver frets. The lush sweep of the strings that hummed against his fingers. It was the finest lute Sofi had ever seen. And one day, when she inherited his title of Musik, it would be hers.

On the stage below, Frederik struck a careful note, plucking the first, then third, then fifth courses as he started the familiar melody of "The Ballad of Sir Ellis," a tense, ninety-minute epic detailing the life and death of one of Aell's most famous knights. The tune was bright like the early hours of morning as Frederik sang Sir Ellis's early life, the ships he sailed and the swords he forged.

Twelve verses in, the melody turned windy, like a ship in a storm, as Frederik sang of the loss of the knight's true love, Lord Ackles, who was captured during an enemy raid. After an hour, the song turned sharp and staccato as it recounted the way Sir Ellis had tended to battle and led his army to reclaim Castle Lochlear.

Even though the audience knew how the story ended, Sofi could see them leaning forward in their seats, the rhythm of her father's careful fingerpicking mimicking the seconds ticking down on a clock. And finally, at the end of the song, great, wild smacks loosened and shook free the notes that followed Sir Ellis to the end of his life, as he returned to the ground from whence he came, his sword ready for the next who would free it from the earth below.

Frederik never wavered. His fingers flew and struck and plucked and brushed the strings, jumping from note to note. It was a dizzying dance, one that Sofi tracked diligently. Her father did not even break a sweat. Even after bearing witness to so many of his performances, Sofi still found it inspiring, how calm and collected Frederik was as he sang, so proficient at his craft that it seemed as though he had nothing in his hands at all.

When the final note rang out through the theater, the crowd leaped to their feet. That a person could carry them through the ever-changing emotions of human life in the span of ninety minutes, that one could compose a ballad that so neatly encompassed a legacy . . . that was the true gift of a Musik.

A slew of ruby-red roses sailed through the theater and landed at Frederik's feet. Sofi scanned the upper circle for the source of such opulence. To grow anything in Aell required a greenhouse and constant upkeep to prevent the snow from stealing the fragile blossoms. As she surveyed the crowd, her eyes caught on her savior giving a standing ovation in a box to the far right of the theater.

Lara was openly weeping, kohl streaming down her cheeks like a river, hands clasped to her heart. Even from a distance, she was beautiful. But more than that, Sofi was touched by her reaction. The story of Sir Ellis was beautiful, yes, but it was familiar. No one would be reduced to tears solely because of the content. No, Lara's reaction had something to do with the performance, which made Sofi's heart skip another beat. Someday, perhaps Sofi might inspire that same level of emotion in Lara with *her* performances.

She quite liked the idea of that.

As she daydreamed of one day being the Ollenholt who knelt down to gather roses from an adoring audience, the applause faded to a whispered hush. Sofi startled as King Jovan took the stage. She and Jakko exchanged a curious glance. This wasn't in the program. Usually another Guild member would play while the show's featured Musik took a moment to tune and prepare for their second song. Instead, the King of Aell smiled out at the crowd.

"I do apologize for the interruption," he said, "but I have a bit of news I wish to share with you all." Sofi frowned down at her father, who looked just as uncertain as she felt. "The Guild of Musiks began, as you all know, as a way to repair our relationship with the rest of the world due to some"—the king paused—"unfortunate circumstances with the Papers."

Beside Sofi, Jakko rolled his eyes. That was certainly one way to describe the plague of moths that had descended upon the country of Eruth, or the well water that had turned to blood in the Republic of Kip.

"But I am pleased to announce that our efforts are finally beginning to pay off. In fact, our offering has been met with such support that the Council of Regents has requested a new generation of Musiks. Once the newest Guild members have completed their tour, the Council will begin the destruction of the Gate."

The crowd began to buzz in earnest. When the Gate had been built to keep citizens of Aell out of the wider world, the country had not panicked.

At first.

But when Aell fell into a seemingly endless winter while the rest of the world remained unaffected, its citizens could not flee. Crops withered. The piles of gold in the treasury dwindled. The supply of original Papers, unaffected by rogue magic, was limited. And those Papers that did still exist couldn't conjure food, or water, or the seasons. Despite the Papers' ability to make fire, the warmth never lasted long enough for anything to grow. After sixteen years of winter, people had begun to believe the Hollow God had cursed their country for still worshipping the saints. In hopes of changing their circumstances, some of the country's citizens had begun to quietly convert.

"Which means," King Jovan continued, "that it is time for the Guild members to pass on their titles."

Jakko gasped. Frederik looked stricken. Sofi leaned so far forward over the railing of the theater box she threatened to fall onto the orchestra seating below. Every other Musik had already named an Apprentice. Frederik alone had yet to pass along his pin. Sofi hardly dared to breathe as the king continued to speak.

"Master Ollenholt has served his country diligently," the

king continued, "always postponing his own retirement for the good of the Guild. But, Frederik," the king said, squeezing the Musik's shoulder jovially, "it is finally time to name your Apprentice." King Jovan winked cheekily up at Sofi and Jakko, who were hyperventilating in the Musiks' Box. "Your king demands it."

THREE

THE AUDITION was to be held at Saint Ogden's Theatre on a sixth day, a coincidence so fortuitous that Sofi assumed it had been planned by the Muse herself.

For three days she holed up in her bedroom and practiced, eschewing everything but the plates of biscuits and pitchers of water Marie placed outside her door. The housekeeper was all too familiar with the ways of the artist, having served the Ollenholt family for more than twenty years.

Sofi refused to emerge from her room for anyone, not even Jakko, who, on the fourth day, while Sofi was in the fetal position, *feeling*, had pounded on the door with the palm of his hand. On the fifth day he rapped seven times, employing the secret rhythm they'd invented for emergencies. But Sofi was repenting, rocking back and forth on the floor, calling out to the Muse.

On the sixth day, Jakko did not knock at all.

Sofi's hands shook as she buttoned up her gray wool dress. She had opted to wear something simple for the audition so as to let her skill speak for itself. She brushed her hair back into a messy bun and examined herself in the looking glass. Her dark curls had already gone rogue, threatening to escape from her bun. Her face was pale. Sofi pinched her cheeks until small blots of red bloomed.

"Well then." She spoke matter-of-factly to her reflection as though this wasn't the most important day of her life. As though all of her training, her suffering, her sacrifice, had not been building up to this one pivotal afternoon. "I suppose this is it."

She tore herself away from the mirror, from the damned *hope* reflected in her eyes. Hope, Sofi knew, was inconsequential. Today was about talent, nothing more. This was exactly what her father had been preparing her for, the reason for the careful, purposeful restraint that his training routine had built within her. Sofi had to stay in control. Of her body, her heart, her mind. Her instrument. She had to guard her performance from anything that might interfere. No flicker of nerves, no spark of hope. Just Sofi, her lute, and the music.

Tenderly, as though tucking a baby in for a nap, Sofi settled her wooden lute into its case. The velvet lining had torn in two places, stuffing spilling out like snow, and there was a crack on the neck of her instrument, which her father had refused to let her repair. *If you always fix a thing, then you will not understand the consequences of breaking,* Frederik had said, which Sofi thought unfair given that she had inherited the lute with the mar already on it.

Once she was named her father's Apprentice, however, she would finally be permitted to play his bone lute. And when she inherited his title of Musik, the instrument would be hers. Should her father wish to come out of retirement to perform, it would be Frederik who would have to ask *Sofi* for permission to play the bone lute.

Securing the strap of the lute case over her shoulder, Sofi emerged into the hallway. The house was oddly still. On such an important day, Sofi had expected more bustling about. But the hallways were silent. No footsteps echoed up from the entryway below. Frowning, Sofi headed to the east wing toward Jakko's bedroom. There was no sound from behind his door. Sofi didn't bother to knock, she merely flung the door open. But the room was dark and cold. The curtains were drawn, and no embers lingered in the hearth. Jakko, who was the messiest person Sofi had ever known, appeared to have tidied up. *His bed was made.* It was all incredibly strange.

Sofi told herself that Jakko was merely nervous. Nerves could do a lot to a person. Only that morning, she had stumbled over the words in the Muse's Prayer, something she'd had memorized for over ten years. When she descended the stairs, she'd find Jakko pacing the entryway, his brown eyes alight and his black curls glossy. He'd squeeze her arm, and all would be well.

But when Sofi reached the front door, there was no sign of her best friend.

Her heart leaped when she heard soft footsteps on the mahogany floors, but it was only Marie bringing Sofi her traveling furs.

"Where's Jakko?" Sofi asked as the housekeeper blanketed her in a heavy brown cloak.

"You're late, dear," Marie said, ignoring her question as she pulled the furs tightly beneath Sofi's chin. "Your father's already in the carriage."

"But—" A blast of cold wind burst forth as Marie wrenched open the front door. The wind howled like the scrape of a bow across untuned violin strings. Sofi stumbled through the storm toward the dark outline of the carriage and the team of restless sleigh dogs. The footman, Vaun, whose irritated expression was mostly hidden behind his gigantic scarf, yanked open the door and practically shoved Sofi inside. She landed ungracefully at her father's feet, sprawled beside his lute case.

"Nice of you to join me." Frederik Ollenholt was dressed all in black as though in mourning. Not a single snowflake clung to his furs. His beard had been freshly trimmed to a sharp V, which only stood to make him look more disappointed than usual.

He was alone.

"Where's Jakko?" Sofi struggled with her furs as she attempted to remove her lute case from her shoulder.

"It appears that Master Lang no longer hears the calling of the Muse," Frederik said evenly. "When I woke this morning, his room was cleared out, and he'd left his lute behind."

The carriage lurched forward, sending Sofi sprawling backward onto the opposite bench. Her blood had gone cold, icy dread filling her veins. "That isn't possible," she said shakily. "Jakko loves music. He wouldn't just . . . leave before the audition."

"And yet"—Frederik stroked his beard—"it appears that he has."

Sofi tore at the furs tucked tightly around her neck. She was starting to feel suffocated. "He wouldn't just *go*." Her voice cracked. "He wouldn't leave without saying goodbye."

Frederik made a soft noise in the back of his throat. "Are you certain?"

Sofi shook her head uncomprehendingly, trying to fight back the burn of tears threatening to spill from her eyes. "He's my best friend."

"Best friend," Frederik scoffed. "You cannot be *friends* with the competition. Surely you know that. Success is a green-faced monster, Sofi. People become jealous. Vindictive. No." Her father's gray eyes were dark. "When you are a Musik, you must trust no one but yourself. Do you understand me?" His voice was urgent. Rough.

"I . . ." Sofi was having trouble forming words. Her best friend had abandoned her. But her father had also said *when* she was a Musik, not *if*. "I do."

"Good." Frederik slumped back against the carriage wall, suddenly drained of all intensity.

The storm continued as they flew toward the theater, the

silver runners of the carriage slicing neatly through the banks of snow. They passed a copse of firs cloaked so thoroughly in white they offered not even a hint of green to the endless, monotonous landscape. Flurries of snowflakes tapped a rhythm against the frosted window. Sofi began to play a counterpoint on her thigh, the steady beat of her fingers helping to calm her racing mind.

With Jakko gone—confusingly, inexplicably . . . *gone*— there was not a single lutenist Sofi knew of who would pose even the slightest challenge. She had of course observed her father's other students diligently, sometimes even resorting to crouching beneath his desk or hiding in the study's closet in order to better study their abilities. There was Braeden, who had spent months devising a fingerpicking method that Sofi taught herself in a manner of minutes. Neha had the singing voice of a saint but never seemed to do anything other than brush her lute's strings lightly, as though she were afraid of hurting the instrument. There were others, of course, who held some skill. But there were many, many more who had only made it through a handful of sessions before their names were scratched off her father's student roster.

While Frederik did not require his other students to obey Sofi's routine of days, he was still strict with them, offering more critique than comfort, more disappointed sighs than rounds of applause. But that had never bothered Sofi. She did not seek anything other than the truth. She wanted to be the best, which meant she had to work the hardest, grow the fastest, want it the most.

Across the carriage, Frederik's arms were crossed, his right fingers tapping chaotically on his left shoulder. Sofi tried to identify the pattern—it was a game they sometimes played, trading rhythms back and forth in subtle ways while the world carried on around them. Music was its own language, and for Sofi and Frederik it had always been easier to speak through notes and sounds and songs than it was to exchange words.

But the longer Sofi studied her father's flying fingers, the clearer it became that there was no reason or rhyme to his fidgeting.

"Everything all right, Father?" Sofi chanced a glance at his face, which was, as expected, rather pinched.

His fingers stopped moving. The sudden stillness was unsettling. "I am not ready to retire," he said simply. "I don't understand what a new generation will bring to the world that the current Guild members cannot offer." He sniffed. "I'm sure they cited all the usual reasons: new voices, new perspective. Well"—he turned his face to the window, which was now almost completely frosted over—"I don't know what's wrong with *my* perspective. I have offered a mere five hundred epics to the canon since I took my title twenty years ago. I am only just about to enter my prime." His gaze remained fixed on the foggy glass.

Sofi pulled her furs more tightly around her and flexed her fingers, which had gone stiff with cold. The chill inside the carriage wasn't just from the snow outside. There was a storm brewing within her father, too. She was relieved when she heard the driver shout, when the carriage began to slow, when the door was wrenched open and her father and his bone lute disappeared into the flurry. Sofi gathered her own lute, steeled her nerves, and followed.

Saint Ogden's Theatre was different in the daylight. Without the warm glow of lit sconces and flames dancing from the crystal chandeliers, the forest-green carpet and curtains looked black. The mural on the ceiling cast summer into shadow, and the bright flowers jeered down at Sofi's snow-matted fur and damp curls.

Luckily, Sofi wasn't being judged on her appearance.

She shrugged off her outer layer, the snow leaving wet spots on the carpet, and offered it to an usher who was darting frantically about. It was the same boy from the performance who'd sent her up the stairs where she'd nearly tumbled to her death—or at the very least, embarrassment. To have fallen fully on her face in front of Lara, the glittering girl who'd come to her aid, would have been devastating. Not that she stood a chance with a girl that clever and quick, regardless.

Sofi was quite proficient at pining—she'd harbored affections for girls before, caught up in their smiles or singing voices or silky curls. But she'd never moved beyond yearning. Any time she got too close, her father's voice would echo through her head: *A true musician never loves anything more than the music.*

Anyway, it wasn't as though Sofi was ever going to see Lara again.

Wind howled as the front door flew open and the remaining four Guild members overtook the lobby, stamping snow loose from their boots, shaking off their furs and piling them into a heap in the tiny usher's arms.

"Well, then." Yve, the short, spry accordionist with straight black hair and bangs that fell across her forehead like a curtain, clapped her hands, and the lobby fell silent. Sofi finally registered that she wasn't alone. Figures littered the perimeter of the room, clutching lute-shaped cases to their chests. A quick count revealed that there were ten hopefuls vying for the title of Frederik's Apprentice. "Show me your clean hands, and then we'll get you all on the list. Your name acts as your signature—agreeing to accept the responsibilities of the Guild, should you be chosen." Yve's eyes met Sofi's. She winked. That settled Sofi's nerves, some.

One by one, the hopeful students sauntered forward to add their names to Yve's list. Sofi hung back, watching as each of them offered their hands for Yve to examine before picking up the quill. Some were accompanied by fussing parents, others by partners, their fingers intertwined.

When Sofi stepped forward, she did so alone, Jakko's absence more glaring than ever.

"Good luck, Sofi-girl," Denna whispered as Sofi held quill over parchment.

Sofi scrawled her name in thick black ink, each scratch of the nib echoing in her ears. "I don't need luck." She handed the quill back to Yve, who tucked it behind her ear.

Denna grinned. "I know you don't." She gave Sofi's arm a

squeeze, and then she followed the rest of the Guild members into the auditorium.

Frenzied whispers broke out among the assembled auditioners as instruments were gathered and a procession paraded into the theater. Sofi noted Braeden and Neha both trickle past her without so much as an acknowledgment. Her eyes registered a few younger students, likely there for the experience more than anything. It wasn't every day a musician got to perform for the Guild of Musiks.

In the theater, the lights were low. One lone beam of light shone on the stage, illuminating the spot Frederik had stood three days prior. During the first few auditions, Sofi slumped in a plush velvet seat in the back row of the theater, eyes closed as she measured their performances. She kept waiting to feel her chair shake, courtesy of Jakko's excited, restless energy beside her. He was always fiddling. Fidgeting. *Forward momentum*, he always said. *Annoying*, Sofi always corrected.

But the seats stayed still.

The first lutenist was too stiff, fingernails clanging against the strings as they moved from course to course, leaving a sharp ringing through the empty hall that sounded like the strike of a hammer against steel. The second was too loose, taking great sweeping strokes on the strings with their right hand so that the lute rang out like the lazy snores of a drunk uncle.

The third performer was good enough that Sofi opened her eyes. Neha stood on the stage, her shoulders tense, but her fingers were smart and fluid. She was a different player than she had been the last time Sofi had bothered to spy on her lesson. Her voice was pure as she sang "The Song of the Last Summer," which had been penned by Frederik Ollenholt himself. The performers before her had stuck to simple harvest songs. Neha was taking a risk, performing a song written by the Musik she hoped to one day replace. It was a bold move—one Sofi respected.

She was planning to do the exact same thing.

As the verse took the double-time turn into the chorus, Neha's fingers slipped. Her voice wavered. The song fell to pieces. Neha began to weep. "Thank you," called a sharp voice from the audience. It was clear from Frederik's tone that there would be no second chance. Her former teacher's dispassion served only to make Neha cry harder. Sofi's heart very nearly went out to the girl as she stumbled off the stage. There was nothing more devastating than a final note left unplayed. Still, if Neha had practiced more diligently, as Sofi had suggested only days before, perhaps she would not have faltered.

The next player who took the stage was shaken from Neha's quick downfall. He strummed his lute several times softly, then started the song. On the wrong note. Beads of sweat formed on his brow. Tambor coughed loudly into his handkerchief. The player's ring finger fumbled, throwing off his plucking pattern. As he attempted to correct himself, he accidentally increased the song's tempo. Fingers flying, he managed to strike four incorrect strings, the smallest letting out a sharp squawk that echoed through the room.

"Enough," Frederik roared. Even from the back row, Sofi could see the vein throbbing near his temple. The musician on the stage fell silent. The whispering in the auditorium stopped. Sofi's father got to his feet. "This is *not*," Frederik roared, words clipped, "Apprentice material. Nothing I have seen today tells me anyone is even slightly ready. So *please*," he emphasized, "if you are planning on performing at a similar caliber, get out. *Now*."

He surveyed the remaining six musicians. "Now," he roared. Three people gathered their lutes and rushed from the theater, their companions hurrying behind.

Frederik sank slowly back into his seat in the fifth row. Sofi watched his shoulders sag. "Next," he called, sounding defeated.

As Braeden took the stage, Sofi got to her feet. The energy in the auditorium had shifted into something sour. She refused to let it infect her playing. She took the long way to the wings, heading through the lobby down a long hallway, the comfortable weight of her lute slung across her shoulder.

While Sofi was acutely aware of the significance of her audition, she was not fearful or flustered like some of her father's other students. There was no place in Sofi's training routine for nerves. Each day was laid out, the intention clear. Each day, Sofi gave herself over to the instruction her father had set for her. Now the training was simply a part of her. So long as she kept herself calm, careful, and focused, there was nothing she needed to fear.

She had proven herself to the Muse. She had given in to

the experience of suffering, had practiced until her fingers bled and prayed until her knees bruised.

She had done everything that she had been taught. Being named her father's Apprentice was the inevitable conclusion.

Braeden's playing was muffled by the theater's thick curtains. He performed a perfectly adequate rendition of "O'er These Fields of Gold." The applause was smattering at best. She didn't hear the penultimate performer. Cloaked in shadow in the wings of the stage, Sofi clutched her lute to her chest. She whispered a silent prayer to the Muse. *Grant me steadiness*, she begged. *Grant me surety. Grant me strength.*

She adjusted the tuning pegs, plucking the strings so lightly the notes were audible only to her ears. When the lute was in tune, she took a deep breath. Rolled her shoulders back. The performer exited the stage with a soft after-performance glow.

I will destroy you, she thought as she offered him a small smile.

Then Yve called her name, and Sofi took the stage.

THE FIRST DAY

Sofi was four years old the first time she laid hands on a lute. At first, all her stubby fingers could do was move slowly up and down the neck, traveling carefully from note to note, tongue tucked between her teeth the way she saw her father do when he was concentrating on a particularly tricky lyric.

Sofi thought she ought to have an impressive *concentrating face*. Denna, the Musik with the big smile who always snuck Sofi sweets when she came to call on Frederik, creased her brow when she played her lyre. Tambor, who played the flute, never smiled when he played, but then again, Sofi hadn't ever seen him smile offstage, either.

Once or twice, Sofi accidentally bit down on the tender pink of her tongue when her fingers fumbled, causing her to cry out. But soon, as her fingers found purchase on the lute's six courses, she became more confident. Dared to hum softly as she practiced transitioning from note to note with her left hand, plucking carefully with her right.

Her father wasn't home much during her early days of study. He was off with the Guild, exploring the world beyond the Gate, sharing songs of Aell's triumphs. Her father's job was very important; that was clear from the way Marie always sang his praises. The King of Aell had even been to Sofi's house. That, her father had told her, meant that their family was *very* special.

Sofi had been on her best behavior the day of the king's first visit. She'd worn her prettiest dress in the king's color of ruby red. She had even been forced to sleep in rollers so that her hair would curl perfectly around her shoulders. When she'd met King Jovan, Sofi had curtsied and called him "Your Majesty," and the king had smiled at her, had offered her a cake made of pears and spice, so sweet and warm it tasted like a hug.

Yes, Sofi's father was very special. It was no wonder she wanted to be just like him—wanted people to bow to her, to bring her presents. Wanted to make it so that even Frederik Ollenholt had to pay attention to her in a way he never had before. Sofi's father was on the road so often, and when he *was* home, he shut himself away in his study, composing his next masterpiece.

No, Sofi knew—even early on—that the only way to speak to her father, to really get him to see her, was through music.

And so, two weeks shy of her fifth birthday, Sofi composed her first song. Her father was home for three whole days, his footsteps tolling against the marble floors like church bells, announcing his presence.

While he was home, Sofi was always underfoot. He allowed her to sit beneath his desk while he taught students, and Sofi would lean her cheek against the rough wood of the under-side, dreaming of the day she might be the Ollenholt taking the stage.

The day before Frederik departed again for the King's City—a first day—Sofi had burst into his study, wearing the same dress she'd donned for the king. Tulle puffed up beneath the red skirt, making her look like a beet. Her father stared at Sofi bemusedly as she settled herself, not beneath his desk, but in the straight-backed wooden chair reserved for his students, and sat her lute in her lap.

"When the church bells sing their song," Sofi sang without any introduction, tucking her tongue between her teeth as she moved from course to course, "ding-dong, ding-dong."

As she sang the words she'd painstakingly scrawled on a spare piece of staff paper, there was a flutter in her chest, like the hummingbirds that sometimes darted outside her window, their wings beating almost faster than her eyes could see. That flutter made her warm, the way she never was in the Ollenholt manor with its high ceilings and marble everywhere. That warmth spread from her heart to her hands to her toes.

So powerful was her belief in the music that she could almost hear the church bells that she sang of, despite the fact that the nearest chapel was half an afternoon's carriage ride away.

Sofi glanced up from her strings, hoping to gauge her father's reaction. But Frederik wasn't looking at his daughter. His attention was fixed on the ceiling. He frowned, seemingly flummoxed.

Almost like he could hear the bells too.

"When the brothers speak their psalms . . ." Sofi began the next line, but before she could complete the rhyme, Frederik snatched the lute from her. One of the tuning pegs scraped her hand, leaving a sharp red streak in its wake. Sofi opened her mouth to protest, to cry out, but her father held up a finger, his expression dangerous.

"Be quiet," he whispered, and it was scarier than if he'd shouted it. Disappointment was written across his face. Sofi, who had only wanted to please him, to be close to him, fought back tears. She had ruined everything, and worse, she wasn't sure exactly *what* she'd done.

They sat together in suffocating silence. No bells chimed. No sound came from her father. Sofi hardly dared to breathe. Finally, Frederik blinked rapidly and shook his head as though to clear it.

"Sofi," he finally asked, voice soft, tender in a way it had not been moments ago. "How did you make those bells ring?" It sounded as casual as asking her if she'd seen the snow falling outside their window.

Sofi, eager to regain his favor, answered quickly. "I didn't do anything. I only sang the song I wrote for you. Only played my lute."

Frederik pursed his lips, considering.

"Did I do it wrong?" If she was going to be a Musik one day, she needed to make sure she knew the right way to compose. This, clearly, was *not* the right way. "Is there something I could do better?"

Frederik stared down at his daughter. He opened his mouth, then shook his head. "I shouldn't tell you. It's a much more advanced training technique than you're ready for."

Fire burned in Sofi's chest. She wanted to be the best. If her father treated her like a baby, she would never get good enough. "I can do it," she insisted. "Tell me."

Frederik knelt in front of Sofi. "Think of it like a game." He smiled. Sofi leaned toward that kernel of affection like a moth to a flame.

"I like games."

"I know you do." Her father nodded, almost as though he was trying to convince himself. "In order to win this game, you have to give me your voice."

Sofi frowned, trying to understand. "My voice?"

"Ah, ah, ah," Frederik reprimanded her. "I have your voice now. You cannot use it. Cannot speak. Cannot sing. Do you understand?"

Sofi opened her mouth to answer, but when her father's face fell, she quickly corrected herself. She nodded.

"Very good." Frederik clapped a hand on his daughter's shoulder. "You're a natural. Now, there's much you can do with this silence. Listen to the world around you. Find melodies in everyday actions. Suppress the urge to speak without consideration. This will help you grow as a musician." He looked suddenly worried. "That *is* what you want, isn't it?"

This time Sofi didn't slip up. She kept her lips pressed tightly together and nodded.

"There's my good girl." Frederik squeezed Sofi's shoulder. The weight of her father's touch was so encouraging. He only wanted to help her grow as an artist. To make her a better musician. "This will be good for you." Frederik nodded resolutely. "Yes." He nodded again, sounding even more certain. "The first day is for listening."

FOUR

THE WEATHERED floorboards creaked beneath her feet as Sofi strode across the stage, lute tucked neatly beneath her arm. With each step she became even more sure of herself. This, *here*, was exactly what she had been working toward. She easily found her place center stage, the light warm across her face.

The audience was silent—the spotlight so bright she could not make out the expressions of her adjudicators; nor could she tell if any of the other musicians had lingered to watch her play. But Sofi was not bothered. In fact, she preferred it.

Music was personal. Up to this point, every performance had belonged only to her. It was a comfort to know that even once she became a Musik, she would be able to maintain that level of intimacy with her instrument and the Muse.

"State your name," Tambor barked before delving back into a coughing fit. It was a wonder the man had any oxygen left to play his flute.

"Sofi Ollenholt." She resisted the urge to roll her eyes. All five Guild members had known her since she was a baby.

"And what will you be performing, Miss Ollenholt?" Even though Sofi could not see her, she could hear the smile in Denna's voice.

"I have chosen to perform 'The Weary Wayfarer.'"

That got the room's attention. "The Weary Wayfarer" was one of her father's most difficult songs. Some days, when Sofi practiced the dizzying plucking and striking patterns until her fingers went numb, she wondered if he had penned it specifically to prove his incredible prowess. Most songs that Musiks offered to the canon were songs celebrating famous rulers or saints, songs to call forth the harvest, and songs to celebrate the Muse.

But "The Weary Wayfarer" was a song *about* a song—the titular wayfarer, Elane, was a musician from a time before the Guild who traveled from town to town performing for her room and board. Each verse not only told the tale of the village visited, but it also contained a couplet from the tune performed *by* the musician.

Frederik's composition work was bafflingly tight, sewing the multiple melodies together with the musical equivalent of silver thread. It was, in Sofi's opinion, a masterpiece.

It was also nearly impossible to play, between the constant shift in tempo and rhythm, the melodies that bled into one another, and the harmony line that the voice sang over the lute. Lesser players than Sofi had been reduced to tears after attempting the first verse. One of her father's students, a young boy named Gareth, had actually abandoned lessons altogether after simply hearing Frederik perform it.

Playing "The Weary Wayfarer" was like flying down a mountain on a sled. The ride was made even more frightening by the knowledge that with one wrong note, it would all come crashing down. To play this song flawlessly had been Sofi's greatest challenge to date. It had required her to use every single skill she had ever learned to keep her emotions in check, her instincts carefully coiled—to focus only on the technical and leave the rest behind.

Raffe cleared their throat. "Are you . . . sure?"

Sofi bit her lip to keep from smiling. Raffe, the Guild's drummer, knew perhaps best of all how tricky the rhythm in "The Weary Wayfarer" was, as they were used to the constant shifting of complicated rhythms in their own work. Sofi appreciated Raffe's concern, but it was unwarranted. She had been preparing for this performance in earnest for more than five years. *Scrambling is for eggs,* Frederik had once told her. *A true musician is always prepared for what's to come.* And so Sofi had scoured the songbooks, looking for the piece that would prove, without a doubt, that she deserved to be a Musik, not just because it was her destiny but because she had *earned* it.

"Yes." Settling her fingers onto the opening notes, she swept her hand across the strings. "I am."

She launched into the introduction, the notes bright and

lively as Elane began her journey. At the top of the tune, the bard was young and full of hope, her songs soaring and sharp. Sofi picked the notes spryly, her left hand wandering up and down the neck of the lute. But as Elane traveled the world, gathering stories from all ends of the earth, her load grew heavier. The song picked up momentum as she carried her tales from town to town, opening the villagers' eyes to what lay beyond their borders. Sofi's left hand raced from course to course, her right hand alternating between plucking the strings and tapping on the hollow body of her lute, adding a new layer of percussion.

The song turned languid, like running water, as Elane began to age, songs spilling from her fingers faster than she could sing them, attempting to set free all her stories before death returned her to the ground for good.

Sofi sang: *"And Elane said, 'There's far to go,' but weary were her gentle bones. 'It's always darkest, this I know, before the morning comes.'"*

It was this verse of the song that put a lump in Sofi's throat each time she sang it: Elane's fear that she was running out of time, that she had so much left to tell and sing and write. It was the way Sofi felt every time she clutched her lute close and coaxed notes forward, each time she found the right string of words to pair with a melody. Life was so fragile and imper-manent. She needed as much time as she could get. Enough time to create and offer her mark on the world.

But this sort of emotion, this *feeling*, was exactly what her father had trained her to push past. These were the kind of thoughts that belonged to fourth days, reserved for the quiet, private moments alone. Those thoughts, those feelings were not for the world. Not for her music. And certainly not for the stage.

Sofi was stronger than that. She'd been trained to be.

So she swallowed the lump in her throat, tucking the flutter of feeling behind the wall she'd built in her brain. She focused only on the notes, on the shape of the words that tumbled from her tongue.

Not a finger slipped. Not a string buzzed. Not a word wavered.

Sofi's wall did not crumble.

She was perfect.

When her fingers stilled, the theater was silent. But Sofi did not fret. It was not the strained silence of embarrassment but the quiet of a breath being held, of handling a piece of porcelain with great care. The quiet of acknowledgment. Of perfection.

It was Sofi who broke the silence. It was she who said: "Thank you." Then, just as swiftly as she had arrived on the stage, she left, the wall she'd so expertly built crumbling, releasing every ounce of excitement and certainty she'd been withholding.

Sofi pressed herself against the wall of the wings, the cold stone refreshing against her neck. She had worked up a sweat, damp pools spread beneath her armpits. But it didn't matter. She was too busy riding the thrill of a job well done. Of hard work paid off. Not even the Muse could have found fault with her form. As she replayed her performance and Frederik announced the end of the auditions, Sofi almost missed the sound of a new voice calling out: "Wait." Sofi peeled herself away from the wall and peeked out from behind the curtains. The theater had emptied of performers. Only the members of the Guild remained. The Guild, and . . . a girl.

Although Sofi was no longer squinting into the spotlight, it was still difficult to make out the newcomer's features from where the girl stood in shadow beside the final row of seats.

"Am I too late?" she asked, rushing toward the stage. "Our carriage hit a snowbank and one of the dogs ran off, but I couldn't miss this. Musik Ollenholt," she panted as she ascended the steps to the stage, "I saw your performance three nights ago, and I had never witnessed art so beautiful. I simply had to have the chance to learn from you."

The girl had not yet stepped into the spotlight, so Sofi could not discern much of her other than the white-blond sheen of her hair.

"You're here to audition?" Sofi could hear the skepticism in her father's voice.

"Yes," the newcomer said breathlessly, crossing center stage. "I am."

In the wings, Sofi gasped as the light glittered off a girl she had never expected to see again.

"What's your name?" Frederik asked.

"My name is Laravelle Hollis." When Lara fidgeted, her gown of silver reflected the light, casting a thousand tiny glimmers around the room. Her hair fell in a soft curl down her shoulders. Her cheeks and the tip of her nose were pink from the cold. She looked like a saint.

"Sign here, Miss Hollis." Yve had run the roster up to the stage, her eyebrows pinched as she examined the hands of the girl before her to ensure they were clean.

Sofi couldn't look away, either. When she'd met Lara on the stairs, she hadn't noticed the instant kinship she often felt with other musicians. While her grip had been strong as she steadied Sofi, there had been no calluses on Lara's fingers that tugged at the fabric of Sofi's sleeve. Words had shouted up from Lara's hands proclaiming her use of Papers. She could not have been a serious musician.

No, Sofi had been drawn to Lara for another reason entirely, which made it even stranger to see her standing onstage. What business did a girl Sofi had never seen before have auditioning for the role of Frederik's Apprentice?

"I have prepared a song," Lara said once the ink had dried on her name and Yve had returned to her seat. "I'm a soprano, so I've chosen 'Where the Lilies Lie.'"

"Do you need time to retrieve your lute, Miss Hollis?" Denna's voice floated across the theater.

Sofi, too busy staring at Lara's face, had failed to notice that she didn't have an instrument on her. She slapped herself lightly on the cheek in an attempt to pull herself together.

Lara's face went as pale as her hair. "My *what*?"

"Your instrument," Denna clarified politely. Beside her, Tambor giggled.

"Oh," the flautist chortled, "now, this is *rich*."

"Therolious," Yve hissed.

"She's auditioning for an Apprenticeship and she didn't bring her instrument?" Tambor cackled. "Frederik, this showing has been *quite* illuminating as to the caliber of the students you teach."

"At least I *have* students, Tambor." Sofi peeked through the curtains just in time to watch her father shift in his seat. "But this girl is not one of them. I would not teach a student who was so ill prepared they would forget their instrument for the most important audition of their life."

Back onstage, Lara cleared her throat. "Actually, I, um, don't own a lute?"

Sofi and her father nearly had matching heart attacks.

"Then how," Frederik asked, when the vein in his temple had settled back into his skin, "do you intend to audition?"

Lara tugged at the end of her hair. "I didn't realize—" she began, just as Therolious Ambor said, "Why don't you offer the poor girl your lute, Frederik?"

Sofi gasped. The other three Guild members went perfectly still. Even Lara, who was clearly in over her head, stayed silent. The air in the theater was tense.

"What an *interesting* suggestion, Therolious." Frederik's voice was as sharp as a knife. "Alas, you know that it wouldn't be proper for a Musik to share their instrument with a student. Someone find Sofi," he snapped. "She can offer up her lute." He got to his feet, the seat of his chair slamming up against the backrest noisily. "I'll go find her now."

Sofi slunk back into the shadow of the wings, clutching

her lute tightly to her chest. She would do almost anything for her father, but she would *not* sabotage herself by aiding the competition, no matter how beautiful the competition might be. Yes, she found Laravelle's face to be conventionally attractive, and it was true, her stomach *had* fluttered when Lara had touched her three days ago and then *again* today when the light hit the curve of her cheekbone, but a silly crush would *not* be her undoing. After all, Jakko was—or at any rate, *had been*—her best friend, and Sofi had been prepared to beat him handily.

"Sofi!" Frederik bellowed from the aisle, his voice echoing eerily about the empty theater. "Sofi, show yourself *at once*."

"Don't be ridiculous, Frederik," Tambor snapped, rising to join Sofi's father in the aisle. "She already signed the page. She's on the roster. She has to audition. It would be such a shame if she came all this way from—" He turned his attention to Lara. "Where did you say you were from, dear?"

"Oddslow," Lara offered, as though her hometown half an afternoon's ride north might save her. "My father, Antonin Hollis, is actually the second cousin of King Jovan twice removed." She shrugged as though it didn't really matter either way, but of course, it absolutely did.

King Jovan had created the Guild of Musiks. If Laravelle Hollis wanted to contest the fairness of the audition process, her signature on the roster would be damning. Of course the Guild was grateful for their patron, but they were dependent on him, too. None of them could afford—creatively or monetarily—to anger the king.

"Is that...so?" Frederik's voice sounded far away, although he had not moved from where he stood.

"Oh yes." Lara nodded eagerly, pleased to have resparked the conversation. "They correspond quite frequently."

Sofi could not figure out if Laravelle Hollis was a manipulative, calculating genius or the most ignorant person who had ever existed. Even though Sofi's instincts pointed toward the latter, her stomach still twisted as Frederik gathered the bone lute and headed slowly toward the stage.

"SOFI!" Her father's fury was nearly enough to coax Sofi from the shadows, but a single thread of uncertainty held her back. Her father was prone to tests, and with the title of Apprentice hanging in the balance, Sofi could not afford to fail. She thought again of her father's words in the coach, warning her not to trust the competition. And so Sofi stayed hidden.

Still, a lump formed in her throat when her father offered the bone lute to Lara. The girl flinched away from it as though it were a rabid dog, her brow creased with worry. That alone was proof enough that Laravelle Hollis had absolutely no idea what she was doing.

Sofi had handled the bone lute three times, but she had never been allowed to play it. Had it been offered to her so easily, she would have embraced it. After all these years, she felt as though she knew it. On sixth days, she would sit at her father's feet in his study as he played, his fingers flying across the strings, coaxing out the purest of tones, his voice swirling as he wrote songs about saints, sinners, and all those between. It was always then, watching her father building melodies from silence, spinning stories like silk, that Sofi was especially grateful that music was separate from magic.

Magic was easy.

Music was its own impossible feat.

What would music be like in the hands of one less worthy? Of a person who had not patiently prayed to the Muse, who had not grown accustomed to the pain and the hurt in their pursuit of perfection? What would their songs sound like? What use would it be to listen?

As Lara took the lute, fumbling to find a way to grip its bulbous body and its lithe neck, it was clear Sofi would finally learn the answer.

Lara cradled the instrument awkwardly in her arms. Her face was curtained by her curls. She swept her fingers tentatively across the strings. The first string of the middle course was out of tune.

Sofi let out a sigh of relief. When Lara had first stepped onto the stage, Sofi had feared that she was one of those absolutely infuriating people who were skilled at everything they tried their hand at. The sort of person who opened their mouth and sang like a nightingale. The sort of person who was not only talented but also saved strangers from tumbling down the stairs. But if Lara attempted to play a song—even a simple one—with a course half a tone sharp, her audition would be over before it began.

Lara brushed her right hand across the strings again. She frowned. Adjusted the tuning peg almost absentmindedly. The note fell back into tune. It was an action so simple most people might not have noticed it. But it made Sofi's blood run cold.

There was no way that a girl who did not even own a lute had perfect pitch. Yet Lara had thoughtlessly corrected the string with a twist of the peg, without the aid of a tuning fork. Sofi didn't use a tuning fork either, but it had taken her years of practice to be able to abandon it.

Dread crept its way up Sofi's spine as Lara took a deep breath. The girl closed her eyes, and then she began to play.

It was a common melody, a midsummer song, the words nonsensical but heartfelt. *"Lay the lilies down,"* Lara sang. Her voice was warm and lovely, and she navigated notes with ease, her tone soaring, like the flutter of butterfly wings.

Her fingers danced between frets, hammering on the strings and plucking careful rhythms. The lute sang a counter-melody, gentle enough that it did not overpower her voice. She played with the skill of a seasoned musician. Even when she closed her eyes to sing the verse about the tall summer grass, her fingers did not waver.

It shouldn't have been possible.

Sofi peered around the curtain, hoping to see her incredulity reflected on the faces of the Guild of Musiks. But to her horror, they did not seem suspicious in the slightest. Yve and Raffe had misty eyes. Tambor wore a smug smile, as though his suggestion to offer up Frederik's lute had birthed a prodigy. Denna frowned the way she did when she was concentrating deeply, but even that proved that she was intrigued by Lara's performance.

And it was a *performance.* Lara's face reflected every word she sang, smiling sweetly as she sang about the soft breeze blowing through the petals, eyes blazing as a stem was plucked from the soil, and at the end of the song, as a daughter lay the lilies at her mother's grave, Lara's voice broke, and a single tear rolled down her face.

Sofi had been taught that a great performer valued perfection and control above all. That was *not* how Laravelle Hollis played. But instead of deterring the audience, it only seemed to encourage them. Four of the Guild members were now leaning forward in their seats.

The only hope Sofi saw was the discomfort written across her father's face. Surely Frederik would convince the rest of the Guild that the unusually emotive performance of a harvest song was nothing compared to his daughter's navigation of one of the most complex ballads in the modern canon. Surely Frederik would fight for Sofi's right to inherit his title. After all, it was *he* who had created Sofi's routine, *he* who oversaw her training. This was his legacy too.

Still, there was a pit in her stomach as she surveyed the enchanted expressions of the adjudicators. Once Sofi had believed the title of Musik was hers to win. Now, she saw, it had only ever been hers to lose.

FIVE

SOFI TOOK her time emerging from the wings.
She waited until Lara had untucked the bone lute from the crook of her arm, eyes wide with wonder as she examined the instrument in all its glory. She watched as her father took the stage, all but ripping his lute from the girl's arms. She waited until Lara curtsied and Frederik said brusquely, "We'll be in touch," as he ushered her off the stage.

"Sofi!" her father roared, but still she did not reveal herself.

It was less that Sofi did not want to move and more that she *could* not. She was rooted to the spot, stuck amid the shadows of the theater, a statue frozen in time. Sofi had lived her entire life with a singular purpose. Every thought, every word, every action had been in pursuit of becoming her father's Apprentice, and then, one day, a Musik. That her future was now in jeopardy—thanks to a girl who did not even own a lute—was unfathomable.

Sofi searched for the feeling of accomplishment that had bubbled to the surface after her own performance, but it was like trying to recall a memory from long ago. Gone was her steadiness. Gone was her surety. This wasn't how the auditions were supposed to have ended. Success belonged to those who worked for it. Not those who rushed in, panting heavily, grasping at the tail of the moment.

Sofi had done nothing *but* work, had spent long days practicing and praying and feeling and suffering because that was what her father had said the Muse demanded. Hadn't she given everything to her music? Hadn't she done more, even, than had been asked of her?

When Sofi's fingers slipped while practicing "The Weary Wayfarer," she had flung her lute aside and pressed her neck against the frozen pane of her bedroom window in punishment. As the goose bumps crept down the nape of her neck and her skin screamed, she told herself: *I deserve this*. She'd let the cold settle in her bones even as she stared longingly across the room at her shawl lying on the bed. But she did not go to it. She had not earned its comfort.

When the cold from the window had been thoroughly extinguished by the heat of her skin, Sofi had moved away, idly tracing her fingers across the icy patch at the back of her neck. She had promised herself she would not forget—she would not fumble on the fifteenth verse again.

Today, she hadn't.

That discipline, that commitment, was what a Musik demanded from their Apprentice. The knowledge settled Sofi's stomach some. She had spent every day beneath her father's roof proving to him that she alone could take up the title and preserve his legacy. She alone knew what it took to create unparalleled art.

She had spent hundreds of sleepless nights warring with words, wearing pencils down to their nubs, covering page after page with lyrics and couplets and rhymes. She was ready for what the role of Apprentice—and then Musik—demanded. Laravelle Hollis was not. Surely that would be taken into consideration. Surely that made Sofi the only real choice.

Emboldened by her renewed surety, Sofi finally drew herself out of the shadows and back onto the stage. The auditorium was empty, save for Frederik and Tambor, who were huddled in the aisle, whispering furiously. Frederik had his finger in Tambor's face, and Tambor had drawn himself up to his full height, his face an impressive shade of puce.

Onstage, Sofi cleared her throat. The absurd tableau froze.

"There you are, Sofi." Tambor sounded positively tickled.

"Am I . . . interrupting something?" She glanced pointedly between her father and the flautist.

"Of course not." Frederik clapped a hand tightly on Tambor's shoulder, his knuckles ghostly white with effort. "Everything's fine here, isn't it?"

Tambor shrugged out of Fredrick's grip. "Yes, of course." He coughed mightily into his handkerchief. "If that's all?"

"Yes," her father said stonily. "We're done here."

"You've made your decision, then?" Sofi descended the steps from the stage quickly, lute case smacking against her leg.

"It took some deliberation, thanks to that mysterious Miss Hollis." Tambor coughed again. "The girl without a lute . . . You should have heard her play, Sofi." He grinned wolfishly. "She was divine."

Sofi glanced quickly at her father, hoping he would offer some insight into their decision. Surely Tambor was just taunting Frederik—and by extension, Sofi—by complimenting Lara's performance. But Frederik offered his daughter nothing. He had turned away and was striding up the aisle.

She hurried after him. "Have you chosen your Apprentice?"

Her father did not answer as he entered the dimly lit lobby. Yve and Raffe were already wrapped in their traveling furs and spilling out the front doors to their carriages. Denna brought up the rear, wrapped in furs of vivid red. Sofi wanted to call out to her but feared witnessing pity written across the Musik's expressive face. As though she could hear Sofi's thoughts, Denna turned and caught Sofi's gaze. Their eyes locked, and Sofi tried desperately to glean something from Denna's guarded expression. But then the young usher hurried forward, offering Frederik's gigantic black fur and Sofi's smaller brown one. When Sofi looked up, Denna was gone.

The world went wobbly as Sofi wrapped herself tightly in her cloak, which was still a bit damp from the morning's storm. This wasn't at all what she'd expected from the day

Frederik Ollenholt named his Apprentice. She had expected a bit more . . . fanfare.

But the Guild members were walking away from Sofi rather than congratulating her. Did that mean her father had gone in a different direction? He couldn't have . . . could he? Sofi couldn't take the anticipation. She couldn't handle the waiting.

"Father!" she called, following Frederik out into the afternoon, but the wind blew her words away as they struggled toward their carriage, snow falling in sheets, soaking Sofi's already wet furs until they were so heavy they threatened to topple her over.

She needed Vaun's help to clamber into the coach. But even once she had settled herself on the bench across from her father, the door shut tightly against the elements, she did not feel at ease. Silence hung between Sofi and Frederik, as furious as the storm that raged on around them.

"Tell me," Sofi said, as the carriage lurched forward, sending her stomach roiling. She hated how small her voice sounded, but she could not bear the ache of not knowing even one minute longer.

"Tell you what?" Frederik's gaze was fixed on the frosted window.

"You can't be serious." Sofi wanted to scream. Her father was being purposefully obtuse, and she could not fathom a reason why he would be so evasive if it were she who he was planning to name as Apprentice. "The legacy of Frederik Ollenholt is going to be passed to a girl who practically *stinks* of petty glamours and enchantments?" Sofi did not mention that she knew from experience the stink was rose scented. "I mean, her *hair?* Those *teeth?* Again, I say, *you can't be serious.*"

That got Frederik's attention. "You *did* see her, then?"

Sofi, who didn't see the point of lying, nodded. "I was watching from the wings."

Something primal flashed across her father's face. "Didn't you hear me call your name?"

Unease squirmed in Sofi's gut. She had been so certain it was a test. One final opportunity to prove her self-restraint and control. "I don't see why that matters."

"It matters," Frederik said through gritted teeth, "because you could have *brought her your lute to play.*"

Sofi shook her head uncomprehendingly. "Why would I have done that?" She clenched her fists in an attempt to ebb the fury that was flowing through her. "You told me only hours ago, right here in this very carriage, that I was not to be friends with the competition. Surely offering up my instrument to a stranger competing for the same position as I was counts as a friendly favor." The challenge was bright, like salt on her tongue.

To Sofi's surprise, her father did not take the bait. Instead, he slumped back against the carriage wall, all the fight seemingly gone from him, his body jerking as the carriage jostled from side to side. "It appears I may have trained you *too* well," he finally said.

Sofi wasn't certain how to respond. That was the *point* of her training—to mimic Frederik's mindset so that her instincts were as sharp and reactionary as his, both onstage and off. Sofi had done absolutely everything that her father had demanded of her. She had fasted through many a second day when she was commanded to *want*. She had spent fifth days decrying every glimmer of negative thought, every flicker of unworthiness because she had been told to repent.

And each morning, regardless of the day, Sofi would press the soft flesh of her fingers deep into a string block, one of her father's inventions. The string block mimicked a lute's neck, but was portable, so a student could practice their finger positions without hauling around the entire instrument. It was strung with four courses, and Sofi, already fully in control of her fingers, used it instead to reinforce her calluses, the tips of her fingers smashed against its strings for as long as she could bear until finally, the skin stopped breaking and bleeding. To play the lute, one needed fingers that could withstand any pain. Often her father had to play for hours on end. Never once had Sofi seen his fingers falter or his skin crack. Until she could say the same for herself, Sofi had kept the string block close. Pain then had meant glory to come.

Or at least it had, before *her*.

But Laravelle Hollis didn't even own a lute. It didn't make any sense. If she didn't have the Muse on her side, what *did* she have?

The answer was so obvious as to be offensive: Laravelle Hollis owned Papers. Sofi had seen the words on her hands during Frederik's performance. If she found no fault in using magic in her everyday life, who was to say that Lara had any qualms using it in her music, too?

A person who showed up to an audition—arguably the most important audition of their life—without a lute was not a person who respected process. Therefore, who was to say that she hadn't found a way to utilize or manipulate a spell she owned into something that gave her unwavering stage presence and startling charisma? Who was to say she hadn't cast a spell on the audience, making them believe that her standard offering of a harvest song was good enough to win herself the title of Frederik Ollenholt's Apprentice?

Who, really, was even to say that she wasn't a *witch*?

The carriage lurched again, slamming Sofi's shoulder into the wall as they crossed a particularly hilly patch of road. It shook some sense into her. No one in Aell had seen a witch since the Year of the Reaping, when the new Papers had traveled beyond the country's border and turned volatile and violent. King Ashe had blamed the disastrous results on the witches in his employ, and rather than face the charges, those witches had fled. Several others turned up dead.

As the supply of original Papers continued to dwindle, the king sent the Kingsguard scouring the country looking for the lost witches to make more. As Aell's winter raged on, the need for witches only increased. But it had been nearly twenty-five years, and no one had seen hide nor hair of one.

No, Laravelle Hollis was likely not a witch. But there had been something suspicious about her performance all the same, and Sofi could not believe she was the only one who had noticed. She could not be the only one curious as to *why* Lara had gone to such lengths in hopes of being named Frederik's

Apprentice, not when the punishment for using magic to perform was so severe.

"Father," she tried again as the carriage began to slow, the metal runners gliding smoothly across the carefully frozen driveway of their manor.

She was interrupted by the door opening. Vaun reached in a hand to help Frederik to the ground, but Frederik waved him away. "Shut the door," he commanded.

The driver's frown was visible only in the furrow of his thick, snow-dusted eyebrows, which peeked above his gigantic scarf. "As you wish, sir."

The door closed, sealing Sofi and Frederik back inside. Sofi hadn't thought the coach could grow quieter, but without the rush of the runners cutting through snow, the yelps from the team of dogs, or the clatter of the world around her settling, it was almost as though sound no longer existed at all.

"The decision has been made," Frederik said casually, like they were discussing the weather. "I will be taking on Laravelle Hollis as my Apprentice."

Sofi's stomach plummeted. Although she had been trying to brace herself for the worst possible scenario, the ice flooding her veins proved how ill prepared she had truly been. "You can't be serious."

"She will be here in the morning to begin her instruction." The resignation in her father's voice was enough to send Sofi spinning. Waves lapped against her cheek; the salt of the ocean dripped onto her tongue as she stared across the carriage into the eyes of the father who had betrayed her.

She opened her mouth, then shut it again, her brain stopping and starting the way it did when she got stuck constructing a particularly tricky lyric. "Why?" she finally managed.

"Your performance was excellent—" Frederik began, but even a compliment from a man who was stingy with them did nothing to alleviate Sofi's sorrow.

"My playing was *perfect*," she interrupted. Her father looked up from the corner of the coach, and nodded, quick and sharp.

"There was no fault in your playing," Frederik allowed. "But there was something about the way Miss Hollis performed— something that cannot be practiced nor taught. Something that comes not from hard work but natural prowess."

"You told me *nothing* was more important than hard work," Sofi snarled, smacking her lute case in anger. Her palm began to throb. "You told me that if I obeyed your rules and practiced and prayed that I would become a Musik one day." The tears stopped falling, burned instead in the corners of her eyes, in the back of her nose, in the top of her throat. "I bled, I bruised, I broke myself ten times over because you told me that was what I had to do. And now you tell me that perfection wasn't *enough*?"

Her father looked down at his hands, which were uncharacteristically still. "It came down, as it always does, to a vote." Frederik was full of movement, no part of him more active than his fingers. But now they did not fidget, drum, nor tap. His hands were folded simply in his lap. "I argued your case, but in the end you did not receive enough support from the Guild."

"This is wrong," Sofi shouted, her voice reverberating around the small space. "You know that I deserve to be your Apprentice." She ran a hand through her hair, forgetting it had been pinned back into a bun. Her fingers tangled in her messy curls, and she began to struggle through a fresh round of tears. "She had to have been using magic."

Frederik flinched. Alarm bells clanged nauseatingly in Sofi's head, and she braced herself for her father's impending fury. But instead, silence hung between them, thick as smoke and just as suffocating. When Frederik finally spoke, he offered only a terse, "Her hands were clean."

Sofi could not believe how calm her father was. It was almost as though he didn't care that his legacy was going to be left in the hands of a girl without a single callus. "Then she's using something stronger than the Papers," Sofi spat, heat rising in her cheeks. She wielded her anger like an iron poker, hoping to stoke similar flames of fury in her father. "You saw it too." She shoved a finger in her father's face. "Don't tell me you didn't. Don't you dare lie to me."

Frederik, whose reflexes had always been impeccable, slapped her.

"I saw nothing," he said coldly, rapping on the window for Vaun to let him out, "but the performance of someone who was better than you. Now control yourself before you disappoint me again."

Sofi sat in the freezing carriage long after her father had departed, clutching her cheek. But really, it was her pride that hurt. She stayed slumped against the wall, her nose and fingers slowly growing colder and colder, and just when she decided that she might as well sit until the rest of her froze over too, the carriage door was wrenched open by Marie, shivering in the snow.

"Your father returned over an hour ago. What are you still doing out here?" The housekeeper tugged at Sofi's frozen hands, making a fuss over the way the tips of her fingers had begun to turn blue. She led Sofi inside, sat her on a wooden stool before the roaring fire in the kitchen, and fetched her a bowl of cold water to begin the treacherous process of combating frostbite. Sofi let herself be poked and prodded. It didn't really matter what happened to her fingers anymore now that she would never be a Musik.

Marie, who had been the closest person to a mother Sofi had ever known, tried her best to cheer Sofi up. She brewed her favorite herbal tea and even let her have an extra pat of butter with her biscuit. But the third stool, tucked neatly beneath the table, made Jakko's absence even more obvious. If Sofi was to have lost the title of Apprentice to anyone, surely it should have been her best friend. But just like her dream of becoming a Musik, Jakko was gone too.

Frederik did not join them in the kitchen for tea; nor did he appear for dinner. Marie loaded up a tray of soup and sausages to take to his study, but before she could bustle off with it, Sofi got to her feet.

"Let me."

The dark wood banister and bright marble floors took on

new importance as Sofi carried the tray through the house toward her father's study. The manor had always been a place where she suffered—praying endlessly in closets, cowering on the floor of her bedroom while she repented, playing until her fingers cracked and bled.

The punishment had been purposeful, this Sofi knew. *A relationship with the Muse has to be tended to slowly and steadily,* her father had explained early on, *the way drops of water freeze into an icicle. Not every musician has the willpower. The discipline.*

But Sofi had never wanted to be like "every musician." She'd wanted to be special. So she'd invented her own little hurts, the pain pushing her forward. Making her *better.* That word had once been vast in its possibilities. She'd often traced it in the air with a finger, imagining it imprinted on her skin the way the Papers seared words onto hands. Were her finger a pen, Sofi's body would have been covered with the word, pale skin peeking through the loops of the *e*'s. But now the word was worthless. *Better* than nothing was still, essentially, nothing.

She wanted to know *why* she had been relegated to nothingness. She deserved to know. And her father held the answer.

When she reached the study door, Sofi shifted the tray, balancing it on her left hip while she knocked with her right hand. She waited a moment, but there was no sound. No movement.

Sofi knocked again, louder. Still nothing. So Sofi pushed her way into the wood-paneled room. The curtains were drawn, the shadows so thick that at first she didn't notice

Frederik Ollenholt slumped, facedown, upon his desk. He didn't look asleep.

Sofi screamed. The tray clattered to the floor, scalding soup splattering her ankles. Sofi hardly felt it as she hurried toward her father, shaking him roughly. Desperately.

He wasn't breathing.

Called by the cacophony, Marie rushed into the room. At the sight of Frederik's lifeless slump, she screamed louder, even, than Sofi. It was Marie who confirmed that the master of the house had no pulse. But it wasn't until the doctor arrived that the truth was spoken aloud.

Frederik Ollenholt was dead.

SIX

THE GIRL in the mirror was a mess.

She hadn't slept—that much was obvious from her bloodshot eyes, the bags beneath them as black as the mourning dress she wore. Her curls were as limp as her posture. Her hands were still. The girl in the mirror was devastated. Defeated. Entirely and completely alone.

Sofi twisted her hair into a bun at the nape of her neck. The girl in the mirror did too. Immediately, strands of hair slipped from the safety of the pins and stuck to her tearstained cheeks. She swatted at her face, struggling, each fruitless swipe sparking fury so white hot that she nearly tore the hair from her head just so that she would finally know peace.

Her anger caught on the reflection of her parchment-littered desktop. Sofi had once done all her best songwriting at night. The darker the hour, the freer her mind, the house quiet save for the creaks and groans as it settled. It was then that Sofi had been her true self: not just Frederik Ollenholt's daughter but a musician—and a good one, at that.

But now she was neither. She was not a Musik. She was the daughter of a dead father.

It wasn't a fourth day, but Sofi felt anyway. She wanted to burn it all down, to unleash her impossible pain on the proof of twelve wasted years of study. She wanted to sweep an arm across the top of her desk and send the contents crashing to the floor—shards of glass from inkwells embedding themselves in her bare feet, black ink staining the bedspread, lyrics she'd called forth with blood, sweat, and tears lost to the flickering flame in the hearth. What use was it, really, to hide those feelings away when the worst possible outcome had already come to pass?

But before Sofi could do any real damage, there was a tentative knock on her door. "Sofi?" Marie's voice was tender, which made it that much more difficult to keep her composure. "Are you dressed? Brother Bertrand is here with the . . ." She trailed off. Sofi couldn't blame her. Brother Bertrand was a cleric—if he was here, it meant the ritual burning was complete and her father was now nothing more than the dust from which he'd once come.

"Send him away." Sofi put a hand to her bedroom door but did not open it. "Please."

Silence. Then Marie's voice, even gentler, if that was possible: "He asked to see you specifically. He found something in your father's pocket." Sofi shook her head uncomprehend-ingly. Surely the contents of her father's pocket couldn't have been more than a spare lute string and the nub of a pencil.

"It has your name on it," Marie added.

Sofi opened the door.

Marie looked nearly as broken as Sofi. Her cheeks were hollow, her eyes red. She'd run the Ollenholt manor since before Sofi was born, before Frederik had even taken a wife. Sofi flung herself into Marie's arms, and they held each other tightly. It was a comfort to touch another person who knew the loss that flowed from Sofi's head to her toes.

"My girl," Marie whispered, her voice hitching like a scrubbing brush caught on a particularly rough spot of floor. "It's going to be all right."

Sofi wasn't as certain.

She allowed Marie to lead her down the stairs and into the parlor, where, only days ago, her father had met with the king. Now all that remained of her father was an urn, gold and gleaming in the candlelight: Frederik Ollenholt's final resting place.

Sofi thought of her father's hands. Some men had only one instrument, but her father had three: his lute and his two hands. That two of those fine instruments were now nothing more than ash in a container small enough to shove in the back of a cupboard was impossible to comprehend.

The room swam before Sofi, her lungs desperate for a breath that would not come. She blinked wildly, but the tears were in her mouth, as salty as the sea and just as sad.

Brother Bertrand, in sweeping robes of black, nodded solemnly at Sofi as he got to his feet. Sofi and Frederik had never been churchgoers, but, like most children, Sofi had belonged to her parish's choir—an a cappella group that sang the songs of saints before the brother's sermon. But with no instruments allowed, original songs strictly forbidden, and a lack of consequences for her off-pitch peers, Sofi had quickly grown bored. She hadn't seen Brother Bertrand since she'd abandoned her place in the alto section.

The brother pulled a thick envelope from the folds of his pocket. It was the signature crimson of her father's stationery, the same color that covered the parlor—the thick velvet curtains that hung about the wide windows, the lush rug that covered the hardwood floor.

Even through her tears, Sofi recognized her father's seal, the gummy, gold beeswax and the indent of a treble clef from the pin he always wore on his lapel. The pin that now belonged to his successor.

Someone who wasn't Sofi.

"This was found in your father's pocket." Brother Bertrand's voice was gentle as he nudged Sofi's attention back toward him. He was uniquely familiar with death and spent most of his time with the grieving. "I wanted to see that it reached you safely. I thought it might be important."

"Thank you, Brother." The envelope was heavy—clearly it contained more than words. Sofi turned the crimson envelope faceup. Her father's spidery scrawl spelled out her name, a splatter of ink smudged atop the letter *i*, as though it had been written in a rush. What could her father possibly have to say to her in death that he had been unable to share with her in life?

"Please let me know if there is anything else you require from the brothers, Miss Ollenholt." Bertrand inclined his head. "We are always here to ease the transition from life back to the earth. For both the dead *and* the living."

Sofi offered him a tight smile. "Thank you for your assistance, Brother." Her eyes ached from crying, her throat was hoarse, her shoulders tense. She did not want to cut her heart open for a clergyman. She wished there were a polite way to ask the brother to leave so she could open the envelope in private.

Marie, ever intuitive even in her grief, offered an arm to Bertrand. "Let me show you out."

It wasn't until the hem of the brother's robe had disappeared into the hallway that Sofi sank onto a settee and tore into the envelope. Something hard tumbled onto her lap: a small golden key. It was simple enough, with a long, thin body and two fingernail-size teeth. But it left Sofi stumped. There were no locked doors in the Ollenholt manor.

She returned her attention to the envelope, hoping to find some sort of clue. But when she unfolded the thick sheet of parchment, she found only six words written in the same hurried scrawl as her name on the envelope.

I hope you can forgive me.

Sofi turned the page over, but there was nothing else. No clue as to what her father wanted to be forgiven *for*. Was it his decision to grant Lara the title of Apprentice? Was it for leaving Sofi parentless? Or was it something else entirely?

The words swam before her exhausted eyes. All Frederik had left for his daughter was a key with no lock. A plea with no apology.

Sofi was so tired of not knowing things.

The front door closed, followed by the bright click of the lock. Marie's footsteps echoed down the marble entryway. The housekeeper paused in the parlor doorway. "Tea?" Marie's eyes were bright with fresh tears. "I need something to do with my hands."

"Please." Sofi tucked the key and note into her pocket and got to her feet to accompany Marie into the kitchen. But before she'd even left the parlor, there was a knock on the door. Brother Bertrand must have forgotten something.

Sofi changed course, trudging down the long hallway to the front door. She struggled with the lock and swung the door open to the snowy afternoon. But it wasn't Brother Bertrand who stood on the doorstep.

It was Laravelle Hollis.

She was dressed in a deep-purple gown, wrapped in a stylish snow-white fur. Snowflakes dusted her perfectly curled hair and clung to her long eyelashes. One gloved hand clutched the strap of a smart traveling case, and another, larger trunk was settled beside her. There was no sign of a coach or carriage amid the falling snow. It was as though Lara had simply appeared on Sofi's doorstep. Almost like magic.

"What are you doing here?" Sofi asked roughly, just as

Lara's eyes widened and she exclaimed: "It's you!"

In another life, Sofi might have been flattered that Lara recognized her even without her face paint and fine dress. But it only served to further illustrate the divide between them. Lara looked like a painting, all pink-cheeked and bright-eyed, while Sofi was sunken, shriveled, and sad. It was hardly fair to face someone as beautiful as Lara when Sofi was fully made up. It was cruel that she should have to stand before her in her current state of grief.

Lara was still smiling hesitantly. "Am I . . . in the right place?"

"That depends on where you think you are," Sofi said, more sharply than she meant to. Lara's smile slipped slightly.

"I'm looking for Musik Ollenholt." She eyed Sofi warily. "He sent a letter saying I'm to begin my training immediately."

Sofi tensed. While Marie had sent word to the Guild the night before, clearly the news of her father's death had yet to be made public. "Musik Ollenholt is dead."

"But . . ." Lara looked stricken. "I saw him yesterday. I *performed* for him."

"Well, obviously it happened after that," Sofi snapped, shivering. The afternoon air was frigid, a chill creeping through the flimsy fabric of her mourning dress, but still she did not invite the girl inside.

"I . . ." Lara looked around uncertainly. "Should I go?"

"*Go?*" Sofi asked incredulously. "You can't go." Lara blinked at her blankly. Sofi sighed at the indignity of the conversation. "As my father's chosen Apprentice, the law states his title will be passed to you in the event of retirement or death." Her jaw tensed. She didn't know if she could bear to speak the words aloud. "You are now a Musik."

Lara began to laugh, high-pitched and slightly hysterically. "No." She shook her head. "I'm not."

"*Yes.*" The word sliced through Sofi's heart like Marie's paring knife through an onion. "You are."

"But I was only meant to learn from him—wasn't that what the auditions were for?" Lara tugged her white fur even more tightly around her shoulders. "I wasn't auditioning to be an *Apprentice.*" She laughed a little, but the sound was short-lived when she realized Sofi would not join in. "The closest I've ever been to music is singing soprano in the church choir. I can read notes, but I'd never played an instrument until yesterday."

Sofi wanted to scream. This girl had stolen her future *unintentionally*? Not only had Laravelle Hollis never played a lute, but she didn't even possess the sort of cutthroat aspirations that might have allowed Sofi to begrudgingly respect her victory.

That this was all just some horrible misunderstanding only served to cut deeper. Lara's signature on the roster had been binding—had said she would accept the role of Apprentice were she to be selected. And she knew not the slightest thing about being one. She probably didn't even know that she was now the rightful owner of Frederik's bone lute. That she could don his treble clef pin and perform in public.

"Sofi?" Marie's voice rang down the long hallway. "It's time for tea."

Sofi wanted nothing more than to shut the door in Lara's face and huddle in the kitchen in front of the fire with Marie, clutching a hot mug of tea. Surely Lara would figure out what she needed to know about being a Musik, or . . . she wouldn't. It wasn't *Sofi's* responsibility to teach her all the things Frederik no longer could.

But Lara's expression was so earnestly pained. Her teeth had begun to chatter, and the trunk at her feet was covered with a fresh dusting of snow.

"Come on, then." Sofi cursed herself even as she opened the door wider and ushered Lara inside, shouting for Marie to make the tea for three.

Marie made up the room that had once belonged to Jakko, and Sofi helped Lara lug her trunk up the stairs.

"What do you have in here?" Sofi panted once they'd finally set the trunk down beside the bed. Lara opened the lid to reveal several brightly colored gowns and a stack of thick books. Nestled amid the fabric and the leather-bound covers were small glass bottles, some filled with herbs, others with various liquids or face paints. Beside the bottles lay several scrolls tied with silver string. Although Sofi had never purchased one herself, she recognized them immediately for what they were.

"Are those . . . Papers?" Sofi asked innocently, as Lara began to unpack, hanging her dresses carefully in the wardrobe. It was strange to watch this girl invade the space that had once been Jakko's, to display her colorful clothing on the same hangers that had once held pants and tunics in her best friend's preferred aesthetic of muted earth tones. Sofi squeezed her eyes shut, hoping that when she opened them, Jakko would be back where he belonged, and Laravelle Hollis would be nothing more than a passing memory of a girl on the steps of a theater.

"Hmm?" Lara's voice destroyed Sofi's hoping. Sofi opened her eyes to find Lara looking at her trunk. "Oh, yes." She smiled softly.

Sofi leaned casually against the doorframe, watching her flit about like a moth. "What sort of Papers do you own?"

"Oh, silly things, mostly." Lara's lips quirked upward self-deprecatingly. "To light my way. To keep me warm. To keep my hair glossy in a world of endless snow."

"Nothing you can't live without, I hope?"

Lara frowned. "What do you mean?"

Sofi wasn't certain whether to laugh or cry. "You're a Musik now, which means your hands must remain clean from this moment onward. No Papers. No magic of any kind. Surely you know this?" She struggled to emulate the brisk, impersonal tone her father had used when instructing his students.

Lara's eyes flashed with horror. "Of course I did," she said quickly, pulling the sleeves of her aubergine dress over her hands to hide the word "curl." "Do."

"Of course you do," Sofi repeated soothingly. "Although"— she glanced over her shoulder conspiratorially—"if you *did* use any Papers the day of your audition, you *can* tell me. It's okay."

Yve's examination of Lara's hands had been perfunctory at best. Surely there had been something the Musik had missed. If Sofi could get Lara to confess, she might be able to petition the Guild to hold another audition.

Lara tugged her sleeves even higher over her hands. "Actually . . ." She looked nervous. "I *did* use a Paper for my hair and my face paint. There were two words upon my hands when I left my house."

Sofi's heart fluttered. This was it. She had her.

"But then my carriage hit a snowbank, and when I went to help Hans, the snow seeped into my chignon and washed the paint from my face. The marks were gone from my hand by the time I reached the theater."

"That's what you looked like *without* glamour?" Sofi thought she might be sick. Lara was the most beautiful person she'd ever laid eyes on, and it wasn't even an illusion.

Lara blushed, which only served to make her prettier. "I guess so?"

Sofi exhaled sharply. "So you just walked into an audition without a lute and still managed to perform perfectly?" She rearranged her face in a desperate attempt to look kind. "Surely you understand my skepticism. You used no magic at all?"

Lara shook her head. "I didn't, I swear. Even when I *do* use Papers, I don't do much more than cosmetic glamours. I couldn't . . . I can't . . ." She looked dazed at the thought. "I don't have that kind of power." She shrugged. "Maybe I'm just a natural?"

Sofi scoffed. She had spent countless hours practicing

scales, her fingers so accustomed to the spacing of the frets on her lute that she could play even the trickiest turns with her eyes closed. She had spent nights dutifully rubbing walnuts into the nicks on the lute's neck, oiling the fading wood carefully with one of Marie's stolen pastry brushes. Some nights when she was especially lonely, she even slept with her lute on the pillow beside her, long ago trained not to toss and turn so she would not disturb it.

Her talent still took effort to maintain. Lara's should have, too.

Lara picked up another dress, a navy blue gown with a matching cape. "Were you at the theater the day of the auditions?"

"Mm-hmm." She tapped her knuckles against the wooden doorframe in three-quarter time.

"Were you there helping your father?" Lara fumbled with the clasps on the cape.

"I was auditioning," Sofi said flatly.

Lara stopped fumbling and looked up at her. "You're . . ."

"A lutenist." Sofi smiled thinly. "Yes."

"Oh." To her credit, Lara looked flustered. "I'm so sorry, I should have realized . . ."

"That I'd been training my entire life only to lose my chance of becoming a Musik to a girl who doesn't even own a lute?" Sofi tried to laugh, but it came out more like a bark. "It's okay. You didn't know."

Lara looked even more horrified than she had when she'd learned Frederik was dead. "Sofi," she breathed softly, her voice unbearably tender. "I had no idea. I—"

"Nothing to be done." Sofi's throat was so tight she had to choke the words out. "I don't need your pity, Lara. I've plenty of my own already." She clenched her teeth, trying to fight back the tears that threatened to form. "I do hope you will be comfortable here. My room is down the hall if you need anything." She offered Lara a weak smile. "But as it's been a rather trying day, please try not to need anything." With that, she left, closing the door behind her.

Sofi slumped against the wall and sank to the ground, no fight left in her. Her line of interrogation had offered nothing—had only served to give Lara a reason to pity her. Grief was exhausting—both the mourning of what had been and the uncertainty of what was to come.

She shifted where she sat on the floor, the key in her pocket pressed awkwardly against her hip. She fished out the accompanying parchment that held her father's final words.

I hope you can forgive me, Frederik had pleaded with his daughter.

But her father had granted Sofi's dream to another. Had nullified every note she'd ever played, every prayer she'd ever spoken, every feeling she'd ever contained. Had left his daughter alone, her life irrevocably altered.

Sofi would not forgive what she could not understand. And so, once she had retired to her bedroom, she flung her father's note into the fire.

THE SECOND DAY

Sofi was five and a half the next time the king came to call. In the six months since his last visit, she had grown older. Wiser. Well versed in listening. In fact, to prove to her father how seriously she took her training, on most first days Sofi never spoke at all.

At first this had concerned Marie. She tried to bribe Sofi with sweets—offering bowls of hand-whipped cream in exchange for a full sentence, sprinklings of powdered sugar on her morning bread for the price of a single syllable. But her father was Marie's employer. Sofi was certain he was using the housekeeper to test his daughter's devotion while he was away from the manor.

So Sofi always refused.

As her father had promised, she was rewarded for her silence. Sofi now heard melodies everywhere—in the creak of floorboards, in the thunk of an axe, in the swish of a skirt. Music was in everything, and therefore, the most powerful art.

Sofi wanted to be that powerful too. Wanted to prove to the world that she was strong.

Unfortunately, on the day of the king's visit—a second day—Sofi didn't look strong. Marie got Sofi dressed, pulling the fine ruby-red dress over her head with a bit more force than Sofi thought necessary. But Marie needed the momentum to tug it over Sofi's shoulders. Sofi had grown since the last time she'd worn it—both up and out.

She scowled at her reflection in the mirror. Despite the dress's long sleeves, her wrists were exposed to the cold air. The stitches of the bodice pinched the soft flesh of her underarms. The skirt's tulle wilted like the snowdrops that lined the manor's backyard path, the once-white petals turned brown and drooping mere minutes after being plucked from the ground.

Sofi couldn't get over the dress's pinching and poking, the fabric prickly against her skin. She wanted something new to wear.

Frederik liked his daughter best when she was quiet, so she couldn't go to him with her woes. Marie, anxious to return to polishing the marble entryway, was too busy to spare Sofi's appearance a second glance.

So, as Sofi often did when she was lonely, she turned to music.

"Let me be a sight to see, in a dress that's long and green," she sang, fingers picking a plucky tune on her lute. She was picturing a dress she'd seen only once when she'd snuck into the South Wing where her mother's clothing still hung in a closet.

Sofi didn't know much about her mother. Her father never spoke of her, and Marie—overly superstitious and pious as she was—refused to dwell on thoughts of the dead.

"All I want, it must be said, is to be free this dress of red," Sofi continued, her heart pounding like the deep, resounding smack of Musik Raffe's mallets on their bass drum. The pounding was complemented by a warmth that spread from her fingers to her toes. A dress that fit would make it easier for her to stand still, to be the picture-perfect daughter she knew her father wanted. Her fingers flew across the strings desperately.

Then the clock struck midday. Her presence was required downstairs.

Sofi set aside her lute and moved to close the closet door, which Marie had left ajar. Her gaze caught on a flash of green. Sofi rubbed her eyes. It couldn't be. But even though she blinked, the dress remained. Forest green and long-sleeved, just as she'd pictured. A garment she'd never seen before hanging in the back of her closet. Perhaps Marie had purchased it as a surprise, overlooking it in the frenzy of the day.

But, Sofi figured, as she tugged the dress from its hanger, if it was in her closet, that meant she could wear it. She shed the red dress and stepped into the green one. It fit Sofi perfectly, as though it had been tailor-made for her.

She felt free. Comfortable. *Powerful.*

Marie frowned as Sofi descended the stairs. "What are you wearing?"

Sharp footsteps slapped against the floor. "Didn't you dress her?" Frederik's voice was high and pinched, the way he sounded just before he took the stage. His bone lute was tucked beneath his arm.

"In the ruby-red dress you purchased in Visc," Marie insisted, voice trembling. "I've never seen that one before in my life."

Frederik turned his attention to Sofi. "Well, I certainly didn't buy it. I would never dress her in green. It's garish."

Sofi's stomach squirmed. She didn't know what "garish" meant, but judging by her father's expression, it wasn't good.

"I wanted it." Sofi's voice was no more than a whisper, but

Frederik, whose ears were attuned to even the slightest sound, heard her.

"*You* did this?" His gaze flickered to Marie, who was clutching a rag and floor polish, looking a bit helpless. "Marie, why don't you go prepare the tea?"

"Oh, but the floor—" Marie gestured to a patch near the front door that did not gleam as brightly as the rest of the white marble.

"The tea, Marie," Frederik snapped.

The housekeeper nodded, collecting her cleaning supplies from the entryway, casting a worried glance over her shoulder before disappearing down the hall.

Frederik knelt down on the just-polished floor so that he was level with his daughter. "Where did you get this dress?"

Sofi's stomach fluttered with nerves, but Frederik didn't sound angry, only curious. "I found it."

Her father raised an eyebrow. "Where?"

"In my closet."

Frederik frowned. "Yet neither Marie nor I have seen it before. Help me understand." Sofi shrugged. But her father was not satisfied. "You said you wanted it? What did you mean by that?"

Sofi didn't like the intensity of her father's gaze and wanted to please him rather than make him angry. "I didn't like the red dress. So I sang a song about wanting a green one."

Frederik's gray eyes flickered with something Sofi could not place. Fear? But no, as her father often said, fear was an emotion for weaker folk than he. "Did the old dress fit?"

Sofi shrugged again. It was uncomfortable, but technically with enough maneuvering, she could wear it, even though it pinched the soft flesh of her underarms and made it difficult to breathe.

"Yes or no, Sofi?"

She squirmed. "Yes."

"So you didn't need this new dress, did you?" It was clear from his tone what her answer should be.

"No?"

"That's right," he said, smiling proudly. Sofi wanted to sink to the floor in relief. This, here, was how she wanted her father to always look at her. "There's a difference between wanting and needing. You may want things you don't need. It's incredibly important to know the difference."

"Why?"

"Just because you think you want something," Frederik said slowly, "doesn't mean that you do."

Sofi was confused. "But I *did* want the dress."

Frederik sighed. That hitch of disappointment sent worry flooding through Sofi. She was upsetting her father. She needed to work harder to prove herself. "Tell me," she urged, winning herself a half-hearted smile. "I want to understand."

"Getting what you want can be dangerous," Frederik explained. "When you receive, you become contented. When a musician is contented, they lose the strength and yearning necessary to compose songs that please the Muse. You don't want that, do you?"

Sofi shook her head quickly.

"That's my good girl." Frederik offered her a full smile this time, bright as the morning sun. "Now, the only way to prevent complacency is to never speak your wanting aloud. You must bury it deep inside, where only you can see it. Hold it close, but do not give in to it. Do you understand?"

Sofi considered this. "So I should want, but . . . inside?"

Her father rose to his feet, adjusting his grip on his lute. "Exactly, my girl. That's exactly right. You see now that I'm only trying to protect you, Sofi. I'm only trying to make you great. You know that, don't you?"

Sofi nodded eagerly. She *did* know that. Her father loved and respected music above all. If he saw Sofi's potential to become a great musician, she would do everything she could to prove him right.

"Now, go upstairs and put on that red dress," her father commanded. "Oh, and, Sofi?"

Sofi paused on the first step.

"Let's add this to your training routine. Yes," Frederik said, nodding to himself. "The second day is for wanting."

SEVEN

LETTERS CAME for Sofi and Lara the next day, both stamped with the king's seal.

Sofi tore into her letter as soon as she bade farewell to the windswept royal messenger, scanning for any comment on the selection of Laravelle Hollis as Musik. Surely Denna, at least, had noticed something suspicious about Lara's impossible success and shared it with the king. But Sofi's hope sputtered and died as she reached the end of the page. It was merely a kind message from King Jovan sending his condolences for Sofi's loss.

It was thoughtful, of course—surely the King of Aell had much more pressing matters to attend to than writing sympathy cards. Still, it left Sofi wanting. She supposed that was apt. After all, it *was* a second day.

She crumpled up the letter and shoved it into her pocket. She wasn't sure how many more disappointments she could handle. An unfamiliar flutter of laughter rang out from the kitchen. It had none of the sharp edges of Frederik's cackle, nor the round warmth of Jakko's guffaw. It was surreal, knowing that the two constants in her life were no longer around, while Laravelle Hollis suddenly . . . was.

Sofi could already feel a headache clustering behind her left eye. She took a deep breath, steeling herself before pushing her way into the kitchen. She paused in the doorway, struggling to make sense of the scene before her. Lara was elbow deep in one of Marie's mixing bowls, flour coating the table like snow on the ground. There was a streak of white in Marie's hair and a smudge across Lara's cheek.

"You have to autolyze first," Lara was saying. "It's my gran's secret method, and it's never failed me."

Marie scribbled something in the margins of her cookbook, then pulled a tea towel from a drawer, offering it to Lara to cleanse her hands.

"Sorry to interrupt." And she was—Marie had been so despondent the last couple days. It was nice to see her smile, even if it was Lara who brought her happiness. "There's a letter for Laravelle."

Lara stopped peeling dough from her fingers. "Lara, Sofi. I beg of you." She grimaced. "*Please* call me Lara."

"There's a letter for Lara," Sofi acquiesced. "From King Jovan."

That got their attention. Lara hurried forward, using a

thumbnail to expertly slice open the seal. She rubbed the parchment absently between her thumb and ring finger as her eyes roved across the page. Halfway down, her smile wavered. "There are so many rules." Her tongue worried at her cheek as she continued to skim the parchment. Sofi moved forward to read over Lara's slumping shoulder, the king's words scrawled in a loopy, black script:

Dear Musik Hollis,

The Guild of Musiks announces a celebration of the life of Frederik Ollenholt planned in a fortnight at Castle Lochlear. Due to your accelerated progression from Apprentice to Musik, you must fulfill the following requirements in order to participate:

1. Complete five public performances in the Kingdom of Aell. The following taverns await your arrival: The Fourth Horse in Trogg, the Beast's Belly in Skaal, the Fair Fellows in Rusham, the Passing Breeze in Ohre, and the Surly Saint in Elgan.

2. Each performance must consist of an original epic composition.

3. Upon your arrival at Castle Lochlear, you will perform your entire catalog of original songs for myself and the Guild.

4. At the conclusion of this final performance, you and the new class of Musiks will set off beyond the Gate on your introductory tour.

We await your contribution to history. Do not dally.
In the Service of Your Majesty,
Jovan, King of Aell

Sofi wasn't certain what, exactly, Lara found objection to. It was all aboveboard. If anyone was to object, it should be Sofi, whose father was being celebrated at an event his daughter had not even been invited to.

"Each performance must consist of an original epic composition." Lara read the second rule aloud. She looked from the letter to Sofi, who was leaning in the doorway, trying to appear uninterested. "What does he mean, 'original epic'? I can't just play songs that have already been written?"

Sofi's eyes went so wide she was certain her eyebrows had disappeared beneath her bangs. "No. You absolutely cannot."

What did Lara think a Musik did if not *write* the music they played? No one would be remembered for repeating another's words. It was bringing new music to light that let a Musik leave behind a legacy.

"Oh." Lara chewed on her thin bottom lip. "Well. I should probably start writing songs, then, shouldn't I?" It was as though she was waiting for Sofi's permission.

Sofi's heart clenched. *Wanting* on a second day was usually much more difficult, but today it was as though the Muse had orchestrated her suffering. "That would make sense."

"Right. Of course you're right," Lara mumbled, folding the tea towel into thirds and placing it tenderly on the countertop. "That's fine, then. Surely it can't be too difficult to write a song, can it?"

Sofi started to giggle, so absurd was Lara's question. Only a person who had never tried their hand at penning couplets, at finding the perfect words for a line of melody, would ask something so obtuse. Jakko used to complain that writing songs was like trying to gather water from a frozen well: *frustrating, time-consuming, and impossible without a little fire.*

"Sofi," Marie chided, recognizing the vindictive edge in Sofi's laughter. Like father, like daughter.

"Apologies." Sofi was not the slightest bit sorry.

"You'll have to forgive her." Marie clapped a flour-coated hand on Sofi's black dress. "She tends to forget that not everyone was born with their fingers wrapped 'round a lute." She squeezed Sofi shoulder a bit harder than Sofi thought was altogether necessary.

Lara looked at Sofi curiously. "How long have you been writing songs?"

"Forever," Sofi answered instantly.

Marie chuckled fondly. "When she was five, she burst into the kitchen singing a song she'd written about the 'broken birds' outside her window. 'Broken birds, baby birds, what do you see?'" the housekeeper sang, off-key.

"And then a crow flew right into the kitchen window," Sofi said darkly, squirming out of Marie's grip. The thud of its little bird body hitting the glass still haunted her to this day.

"Ah." Marie adjusted her apron, eyes cast downward. "That's right. That it did."

"Life imitating art," Sofi said flatly. She turned to Lara. "Come on. Let's make some art of your own. Hopefully with less bird carnage." She led Lara out of the kitchen and down the long marble hall toward Frederik's study.

The room was musty, the curtains drawn. Marie had clearly skipped over the study during her daily dusting. Sofi wasn't surprised. Marie was a superstitious woman—she would not have wanted to revisit the room where the master of the house had died. It was the same reason she never entered the bedroom in the South Wing where Sofi's mother had died and why she had refused to tell Sofi—no matter how much she begged—anything about the woman at all.

Sofi's footsteps were light on the carpet as she moved to her father's mahogany desk. She sank into the leather chair, choking on its familiar scent of pepper and pipe tobacco. It made her father feel too close.

It made him feel too far away.

"Are you okay?" Lara lingered in the doorway. "Your eyes are shiny."

"I'm fine." Sofi knocked a paperweight from the desk with her elbow so she would have an excuse to duck out of Lara's sight and brush her tears away. There, tucked beneath the desk, sat the bone lute. Without thinking, Sofi reached for the case, hoisting it onto her lap and releasing its clasps with a soft *kthunk*—the whack of a broom against a dusty rug.

She lifted the lid to reveal the bone lute, gleaming and bright as snow reflecting the sun. She ran a hand carefully across the bone lute's strings, shuddering even as the notes rang out as bright and sharp as a knife against a glass goblet.

Despite having coveted its sound for the majority of her life, it was the first time Sofi had ever touched the bone lute's strings. They moved like water beneath her fingers, glossier than the catgut strung upon her own wooden instrument. The bone lute's body vibrated, thrumming like a steadily beating heart. She lifted it from the case and settled it in her lap.

Had her father been alive, Sofi never would have dared to touch his instrument. But Lara, who was still hovering uselessly in the doorway, likely had no idea the bone lute even belonged to her. Sofi had half a mind not to tell her, to continue to cradle the beautiful bone instrument and never let go. But even if Lara didn't know who the bone lute belonged to, the Guild of Musiks did. The line of succession—both of title and instrument—were very clear: When the title of Musik was passed to the Apprentice, so was their instrument.

The bone lute now belonged to Laravelle Hollis, so Sofi clutched it even closer. She positioned her fingers on the neck of the lute and struck the strings again, falling easily into the opening of "The Song of Saint Brielle." A persistent buzzing began in her ears. Her limbs had gone thick and slow, almost as though she no longer commanded them.

Still, she played, moving from course to course. Note to note. Tried to ignore the churning in her stomach.

Sofi told herself that playing the bone lute was honoring her father's memory.

Instead, it felt like betraying him.

Sofi stopped, the melody falling to pieces at her feet. For

so long, she had dreamed of her hands upon the bone lute. She had pictured the way the notes she coaxed from its strings would resonate within her heart. Instead, she felt it in her teeth, sharp and bright and painful.

It was the grief, she knew.

It was all too much.

"Can I try?" Lara had moved toward the desk excitedly, her cheeks flushed, eyes bright.

Sofi offered the bone lute up wordlessly. She had expected giving up the instrument to hurt. She hadn't expected the lute to hurt *her*.

Lara's hand closed around the lute, holding it tentatively, like an uncertain parent cradling their newborn babe. Rather than sink into the wooden chair on the opposite side of the desk, Lara chose to settle herself on the floor.

Batting her curls away from her face with one hand, Lara clutched the lute carefully with the other. Each time she dipped her head forward to look at the strings, her hair fell back around her shoulders, framing her face and making her look irritatingly angelic.

Stop getting distracted, Sofi told herself. *But . . . the second day is for wanting*, herself said back. And as loath as Sofi was to admit it, she had been wanting since that moment in Saint Ogden's Theatre when Lara's hand had wrapped around her arm.

"Who was that man you were with at my father's performance?" Sofi demanded, her reverie spoiled by the memory of the tuxedoed man at the top of the stairs calling Lara away. "Your brother?"

"Willem?" Lara grimaced. "My betrothed."

Sofi froze. That was certainly not the answer she'd expected. "Your what?"

"He's from an excellent family," Lara said darkly. "And willing to pay a premium for my hand in marriage."

Sofi frowned. "You're not a goat."

Lara let out a surprised giggle. "No." Her expression grew somber. "I suppose I'm not. But when your family needs money, it makes it difficult to turn down a man with a pedigree. Besides," she said, "he can afford to attend the performance of a Musik. Before I saw your father play, the only music I'd ever known was singing in the church choir."

Sofi snorted derisively. "That isn't real music."

"What do you mean?"

Sofi laughed again. "Just what I said. Singing is . . . fine, I suppose. But without an instrument, it's only words. That isn't the true form of the art."

"A voice can be an instrument." Lara insisted, twirling a curl around her pointer finger.

"Not really." Sofi made a face. "Anyone can sing, even if it's off-key. Not everyone can play the lute or the lyre. That's what takes real skill. Being smiled on by the Muse. Putting in the long hours of training. Devoting yourself fully." She looked at Lara pointedly, hoping her intention was clear.

Lara was silent for a moment. "Sometimes a voice is all you have."

Something in her tone sent shame flooding through Sofi. It was the first time she'd heard Lara sound truly vulnerable.

She twirled in her chair, breaking their eye contact. By the time she'd made a full circle, Lara had returned her attention to the bone lute.

When her fingers brushed across the strings, Lara's face opened like a flower to the sun. Her left hand moved boldly across the frets, her right hand swimming across the strings like a fish through water. A *magical* fish, Sofi reminded herself. There was still something suspicious about Laravelle Hollis.

Lara happened upon a tune, letting it open up like a river to a stream. But it quickly solidified into a familiar melody— the bridge from "The Ballad of Sir Ellis," written by Frederik Ollenholt himself.

Sofi cleared her throat. Lara looked up from the lute, and the song shuddered to a halt.

"What?" She raised her eyebrows.

"It's just . . . you . . . didn't write that?" The desk chair creaked as Sofi leaned backward sheepishly. She felt strangely guilty, exposing Lara to the anguish that it was to be a musician, happening upon a perfect melody only to realize it already belonged to another song.

Lara frowned, her lips dipping almost theatrically. "You made it look so easy. I got overconfident, I suppose. I'll try the lyrics, then."

Sofi tried to stifle her grin. Crafting lyrics was a deceptively difficult process. Anyone could chance upon a good line. But to do so often and consistently, that was nearly impossible without practice.

Lara placed the lute carefully back into its case and pulled her knees to her chest with a swish of satin. "Let's see." She tapped her lips with a pale finger.

The room fell into silence. It was almost peaceful—the study's picture window was fogged with the girls' body heat, and outside, snow was falling as it always did. Sofi's mind began to slow, her focus shifting to the rhythm of her heartbeat. There was something steadying about the constant beating. It was as though she were her own metronome—she could always count on herself to keep time.

Across the room, Lara was murmuring quietly. "Sir Stanlon said, the dragon's dead. He hit his head. And went to bed. Forever."

Sofi laughed so hard she nearly fell out of her chair. The rhyming was so rudimentary as to be insulting. Listeners wanted to be able to know what came next, but a rhyme should be met with an anticipated welcome, not with an eye roll.

"Oh, worms eat your eye," Lara snapped.

Sofi was impressed. She had not expected Laravelle Hollis, with her glossy curls and her satin gowns, to swear like a sailor. "I'm sorry," she said, and she found that she was. "I'm just being honest. The ability to take a note will serve you well as a Musik. The Guild are not always the most tactful of folk."

"Right," Lara muttered. "Well, you don't like my words and you don't like my melodies; what *do* you like?"

"Very little, to be honest." The leather creaked beneath

Sofi as she readjusted her position, pulling her legs up and over the arm of the chair. "Don't take it personally."

Lara sighed heavily. She ran a hand through her hair. "Maybe my father was right." Sofi had never heard anyone sound so sad. Lara's emotions took up so much space.

"When I received word I'd been accepted, my father sneered at me. Told me he didn't know who I thought I was. My duty was to our family, not to my whims. He had invested in me. My Papers. My gowns. Fattening me up like a calf for the slaughter. But I just . . ." Lara looked at her nails, bitten down to the skin. "I wanted to know what it would feel like to *love* something."

Sofi cocked an eyebrow at her. "You've never loved anything?" Lara seemed like the sort of person who had a fluffy cat that she coddled endlessly.

Lara jutted her chin out defiantly. "Have you?"

"I love music," Sofi answered instantly.

Lara's expression softened. "I want that too." Sofi snorted, and defensiveness spread across Lara's face. "What?"

"Well, you've only owned a lute for a matter of hours." Sofi shifted again, planting her feet back on the floor. "You've never written a song, and the first time you ever performed was two days ago. I've been playing the lute since before I could walk. Singing before I could speak. So you'll forgive me for finding that divide a bit amusing. Our feelings are not the same."

"I own a lute?" Hope spread across her face like butter on warm bread. Sofi rolled her eyes. Lara had completely missed the point.

"My father's lute is yours," Sofi said dully. "All your dreams are coming true."

"They are, aren't they?" Lara plucked the bone lute's strings idly, looking thoughtful. Then she looked up at Sofi. "What will the Guild do to me if I enter the King's Court and perform a song with lyrics like the ones I just spoke?"

"Honestly?" Lyrics that childish would get Lara laughed off the stage.

"I was under the assumption you had always been honest with me. Laughter of that nature is hard to fake." Lara's expression was sour.

"I was merely caught unaware. There is a certain . . . delicacy required in songwriting. Your rhymes were as heavy as a sack of stones."

Lara sighed. She did not appear angry so much as resigned. "I thought as much. So?"

"They . . . will not be pleased. But why would you want to write a song about Sir Stanlon anyway?"

"He slayed a dragon and married a queen. Isn't that what regents care about?"

She wasn't wrong. But what regents cared about usually made for poor songs.

"Okay, how would you have written it, then?" Lara reached for the bone lute, tucking it back into the crook of her arm.

"A song about Sir Stanlon?" Sofi grimaced, shoving her hands into her pockets. "I wouldn't have." Her fingers closed around the crumpled parchment from King Jovan. She pulled it out, smoothing it across the corner of the desk.

A flash of ink on the backside of the page caught her eye.

PS, the postscript read. *The Guild is hosting a celebration of your late father's life. I would love nothing more than for you to be the guest of honor. I will save you the seat beside me.*

Lara plucked the lute's second course. "What should I do, then?"

Sofi clutched the page tightly. "Take me with you."

She could practically hear the Muse above frowning. Second days were for wanting, but she was not supposed to speak her wanting aloud.

But then, keeping her wanting quiet had not served her either. Sofi had *wanted* to become a Musik, and now she would never be. Her songs would never reach the ears of listeners. Her life would not leave a single mark on the world. All the music that lived within her, music that begged to burst forth, would remain unplayed and unsung.

"Why?" Lara didn't sound angry, the way Sofi would have if someone had deigned to intrude upon her own tour. Instead, she sounded intrigued.

"Because I have spent my entire life preparing for the title you now possess." The truth of it crashed through her like a cymbal. "I am an exceptional songwriter. I can help."

Lara's eyes narrowed suspiciously. "Why would you help me?"

Sofi ran a thumb over the parchment that held King Jovan's signature. If she traveled with Lara, she would be able to keep an eye on the newly christened Musik. The two of them would spend every waking moment together. Surely, in such tight quarters, Lara's perfect shield would slip, allowing Sofi to uncover the truth behind her sudden skill. Then, when Sofi had the ear of the king, she would be able to reveal Lara for the fraud she truly was.

The king would be so grateful that no magic had been allowed to pass through the Gate, putting the reopening of the country's border at risk. That would surely be enough to convince the other Musiks to name Sofi as the Guild's lutenist instead.

"I will travel with you on the road and write your songs. Then, before you embark on the tour beyond the Gate, you will grant me the title of your Apprentice." Sofi hoped it would not come to that. But if she was unable to locate the source of Lara's success, she still needed to secure her own future.

Second days were for *wanting*, after all.

To Sofi's surprise, Lara did not laugh; nor did she look distressed. Instead, she sized Sofi up. "And these songs you write on the road, they will be *mine*? None will know you authored them?" Sofi nodded. While she had penned nearly one hundred songs, all in various stages of completion, she would not give them up. No, those were too personal. Instead, Sofi would spend her time on the road pushing her abilities as a songwriter even further. She would find a new voice, would make Lara's songs *just* good enough to please the masses without offering her anything truly masterful. Sofi had so little left that she wanted to keep as many words as she could for herself.

"And you promise not to kill me by your own hand?"

Sofi blanched. *"What?"*

"I know how the line of inheritance works." Lara shrugged. "I would really rather prefer you not try to kill me and ascend to Musik immediately." She tapped a finger pointedly on the desk. "No. We'll wait until I have a canon of songs and the world knows my name, at least. I'd like to leave behind a legacy." She smiled wryly at Sofi. "Now, if you'll excuse me, I need to check on my dough."

"Of course." Sofi could be patient. Her father had instilled that particular trait in her early on. This, now, was just another test of her self-control.

"Lara," she said, the other girl's skirts swishing as she headed for the door. Laravelle Hollis turned back, one eyebrow cocked pointedly. "Do we have a deal?"

"Yes." Lara offered a pale hand for Sofi to shake. "We have a deal."

EIGHT

LONG AFTER Lara had disappeared through the doorway, Sofi stayed sitting behind her father's desk, watching the shadows move across the walls of the study as the sun sank in the sky. It grew dark in Aell so early—it wasn't even teatime yet. Sofi and Lara would have to keep a constant pace on the road to ensure they didn't spend all their time in the dark as they moved from town to town.

Sofi closed her eyes and bit her lip. This wasn't the way things were supposed to go. *Sofi* was supposed to be the one touring, following the same path her father had walked all those years ago. Touring was an Apprentice's rite of passage. It *made* the musician.

Tugging open the desk's top drawer, Sofi rifled through a stack of papers, frowning as she failed to find the map she sought. Frederik's study was filled with maps of the world he'd seen beyond the Gate, but his map of Aell was special.

Her father had first shown Sofi the map when she was eight years old. Her finger had followed his as he traced the great road that led from their village of Juuri to the King's City, sharing stories of each town along the way. *One day, this journey will be yours, my girl,* Frederik had said, and Sofi's heart had burst. It would be a way for the two of them to bond.

Their relationship had always been imbalanced, her father not only her parent but her instructor, too. Sofi had wanted to please him, often more as a musician than as a daughter. But the lines were hazy. She had hoped that one day, when Frederik had bestowed his title to her, they would finally be equals.

Alas, it was never to be.

Having rifled through the left drawer to no avail, Sofi moved on. The center drawer contained leaf after leaf of blank staff paper—pages that would never be filled by Frederik's hand. Sofi gathered a stack for her own use before sliding the drawer shut.

The top right drawer was a veritable archive of programs, playbills, and newspaper articles that spoke of Frederik's musical prowess. Sofi filtered through clippings that called her father a "silver-tongued songwriter who makes every story seem worth singing," a "master of all things string," and "able to coax tears from even the stoniest observer." The articles all commended his songwriting, but in the end they focused on his playing: "the sort of skill that cannot be taught, an inherent ownership of the instrument that left this reviewer aching."

Sofi frowned. That was almost verbatim the way her father had described the Guild's reaction to Lara. Although, she supposed, judging by the way the ink had faded and the parchment had yellowed, her father had returned frequently to these quotes. Surely the phrases had simply settled themselves in his repertoire.

It was in the bottom right-hand drawer that Sofi found her father's map of Aell. It was easily identifiable, its edges worn, the parchment soft and yellowed, tied with a ruby-red ribbon. Sofi pulled it out and spread it across the desktop. Her finger traced the familiar road, snaking like a serpent from the north of the country to the south before landing on Castle Lochlear in the King's City.

There she would be able to share her suspicions about Lara with the king. King Jovan knew Sofi. He had always recognized their shared appreciation of music, the way they valued the art above all else. Surely he would want to investigate the reason for Lara's quick ascension in an effort to preserve the sanctity of the Guild.

This was, after all, much bigger than Sofi's jealousy. It was a matter of international importance. For Aell to be once again accepted by the Council of Regents, no magic could be present in the Guild of Musiks. That Sofi might be able to become a Musik once Lara was removed from her position, well, that would merely be an added benefit.

Sofi squinted down at the map, which was covered in notes scribbled in her father's spidery hand, his faded words describing the villagers or the epic ballad he'd performed. She brushed her fingers across the aged, almost-leathery page. In a way, she supposed, her father would be taking the journey with her, only not the way she'd hoped.

She had taken for granted that they'd have more time together, although she wasn't certain *why*. Even alive, her father had been absent most months out of the year, leaving Sofi to absorb as much as she could from the air around her, stealing scraps of his sheet music to study in her room. She'd spent hours analyzing the way her father plotted his tablature, the way he formed his notes, the trick of his melodies. His talent was a lock, and Sofi had tried to form herself into the key that would open his abilities so she could access them herself.

In the time Sofi had taken to snoop, the study had descended into true darkness. She fiddled with lighting the oil lamp that sat on the desktop as the scent of baking bread wafted down the hallway. Sofi knew she should make an appearance in the kitchen—she needed to tell Marie she'd be leaving with Lara. It would take quite a lot of convincing to assuage the housekeeper's fears, to reassure her that they would be fine out in the world alone.

Sofi pushed the chair away from her father's desk. She had what she needed from the study, but it still didn't seem like enough. She wanted answers. She wanted understanding. But her father had taken it all with him, leaving behind nothing for his daughter but an empty plea.

And a key, she remembered suddenly. He had left her a key.

Sofi knew the Ollenholt manor like the back of her hand. There were no locked doors or forbidden drawers. But then, Frederik had never been one to hide his secrets in plain sight. Surely anything he wanted to keep hidden would be here, in his study.

Sofi started with the shelves, tugging at the spine of every book in hopes of revealing a secret passageway. Next she searched behind the curtains, scouring the wall for a piece of wallpaper ready to be pulled away to expose a hidden door. She tested every floorboard for creaks and groans, and when she still came up empty-handed, she turned her attention again to her father's desk.

She removed all the knickknacks from the desktop, running her hands across the smooth wooden surface, searching for flaws. She stuck her stubby fingernails in the cracks and crevices, hoping to find some give. Then she slipped to the floor, scooting beneath the desk to search the underside.

It had been several years since Sofi had folded herself up into a tiny ball of a girl, spying on the students her father instructed, running her fingers absentmindedly underneath the desk, fingering the groove that sat beneath the bottom drawer while the musicians practiced their sonatas. Her entire childhood, she had assumed the groove was just weathered wood or shoddy craftsmanship, had never had a reason to investigate further. But now, as she ran her fingers across the desk's underside, she realized that it wasn't a warped knot or even an error in construction.

It was a keyhole.

With shaking hands, Sofi pulled the gold key from her pocket. She turned it with a soft click, and the desk shook slightly. Sofi scooched out from beneath the desk only to find a slim drawer, no thicker than the neck of a lute, sitting open.

At first glance, there didn't seem to be anything of note. A few unfinished songs Sofi had never heard her father discuss. A gold pen. A leather folio. Sofi spread the staff paper and folio across the floor. She hummed a few bars of the song her father had entitled "The Suffering of Saint Eru and His Sword." The melody needed some work, but the lyrics were quite sharp.

She moved the song aside and untied the leather straps of the folio. But instead of more music, as Sofi had expected, she came face-to-face with the portrait of a woman. Although Sofi had never seen this woman before, she recognized her instantly. The slope of the woman's nose, the curl of her dark hair, her thin lips and square chin . . . Sofi had seen them all before.

On herself.

Sofi's vision swam as she looked upon the face of her mother for the very first time. She had cried so frequently in the last couple days that she should have been out of tears. But each one of her hurts had been so distinct that each layer of grief peeled back and exposed her heart in a new, completely unique way.

The woman who stared up at her had soft eyes. A careful smile. Sofi's fingers brushed her mother's cheek. She wondered what her voice had sounded like—if it was deep and warm like a fire or high and lilting like a bird. She wondered what her touch had felt like—if she was tender, like the brush of fingers across strings, or firm, like the strike of a mallet against a drum.

These were questions Sofi had never allowed herself to ask before. She'd always kept thoughts of her mother tied carefully up, like the portrait in the folio, just far enough away from her heart that her imagination could not get the best of her.

A true musician did not have room for distractions. *Music is only mastered by those who devote themselves entirely,* her father had liked to say. There was not room enough in a heart for both love *and* craft.

But, of course, that had left Sofi lonely—and even lonelier now that her craft had failed her too.

She turned the portrait over, hoping perhaps to find some sort of inscription, any sort of insight into the person her mother had been, or perhaps where she had come from. But there was no illuminating message, only two words penned in a looping script: *Delphine Lail.*

Sofi stared at the letters, trying to decipher what they might mean, her brain so desperate for an answer that for a brief moment she could not see them for what they were: a name.

For so long, her mother had been only a concept. But now Sofi could finally see her as a person with a face and a name and a life no longer lived.

Now that Sofi was able to picture who exactly she had lost,

it was almost like losing her mother a second time. *I hope you can forgive me,* Frederik had written. But knowing that this portrait of her mother had existed so close to where Sofi had lived with a shadow in her desperate heart, she wondered if she ever could.

Sofi crept toward the South Wing. It was an ingrained habit, that creeping. No one else ever seemed to set foot in the room where the lady of the manor had died. Frederik, who hardly spoke of his late wife, had moved his things into a small room in the West Wing immediately following her passing. Marie, ever superstitious, always skipped over that particular wing of the house while cleaning.

White sheets covered the furniture, the dark wood of the room colder still amid the drawn curtains and the thick layer of dust that covered the floor. The tracks from Sofi's last pilgrimage had all but faded. It had been nearly a year since she'd made for the closet where her mother's final earthly possessions remained.

There wasn't much. A few dresses. A brooch with a tableau of a horse-drawn carriage carved into ivory as white as her father's bone lute. A pair of pink silk slippers too small for Sofi's feet. When Sofi was eight, she'd rifled desperately through the pockets of her mother's brightly patterned dresses, fishing out small scraps of paper, couplets written in her father's spidery hand, waxing almost poetic about blushing pink cheeks and long raven hair.

Sofi had tried to piece together a picture of her mother

through the words her father wrote about her, through the full, floral-patterned skirts, through the impossibly delicate brooch. But the portrait from her father's locked drawer was proof she'd never gotten it right.

She glanced in the streaked, dusty mirror, catching sight of her own square chin, the slope of her nose. She held her mother's portrait up, her brown eyes meeting her mother's painted ones in the looking glass. She shut her eyes, trying to memorize the shape of her mother's face. She tried out her mother's name on her tongue. *Delphine.* It tumbled from her lips like a melody.

That the truth of her mother had been so close, the final piece of the puzzle ready to snap into place, was hard to reconcile. She carefully placed Delphine's portrait facedown beside the silk slippers. She ran a hand across the soft fabric of her clothing, the short sleeves of a dress her mother would have worn in spring and in summer—in seasons Sofi had never seen. The ache was tangible, like her heart had been stabbed with an iron poker. She was filled to the brim with wanting. With missing.

With loss.

Sofi exhaled wearily. She was always losing. First a mother, then a best friend, then a title, then a father. It was beginning to seem as though there was nothing left for her to win.

Perhaps that meant she had no choice but to start taking.

Before she could talk herself out of it, Sofi reached for a dress—blue with delicate white flowers in bloom. It slipped from its hanger the way water fell from cupped hands. Sofi wrapped it carefully around the portrait of her mother and clutched the bundle to her chest. If she concentrated, she could almost smell something earthy and floral. Warm and comforting and lovely.

The grandfather clock chimed. It was time for tea. Marie would be looking for her.

Sofi swallowed the lump in her throat and left the bedroom as quickly as she'd entered. She stowed the dress and the portrait beneath her pillow and headed down the stairs. The manor was quiet. No one called her name.

When she got to the kitchen, she paused at the swinging door.

"Now, I'm not superstitious, mind you," Marie was saying. Sofi rolled her eyes. Marie was the most superstitious woman Sofi had ever met. "But I did find it odd the way the minute that little girl was born, the summer turned to snow. Great white flakes floated down outside the window as I bathed her and swaddled her, and I thought it was my imagination. Her mother had a hard labor, you see. We'd been up for nearly three days. I was sure I was hallucinating."

Sofi squirmed as Marie laid out a story she had relayed only once before, thanks to relentless goading by Jakko and too much apple brandy. Yet here she was, offering it freely to Laravelle Hollis. There was something about that girl's face that made people trust her.

It made Sofi suspicious.

"When Lady Ollenholt died, the winter inside this house was matched by the weather outside of it. The ground froze, and the snow kept falling. It's falling still." Marie sighed. "You're probably too young to remember the seasons, isn't that so?"

Sofi edged closer to the crack in the door and caught the tail end of Lara's nod. "I'm only just seventeen. So while I was born during the spring, I don't remember it, I'm afraid."

"Shame." Marie tutted the way she did when she was distracted. "I miss it. My bones, especially. Can't get warm these days, no matter how large the fire or how thick the blankets. People get meaner too." She pushed back her chair. "Now, where is that girl?"

Before she could call, Sofi straightened her shoulders and pushed her way through the door, panting slightly as though she'd run from the other side of the house. She didn't want Marie to know she'd been overheard.

"Sorry." Sofi pulled the map from the pocket of her skirt. "I hope you didn't wait on my account." The table was laid with three cups of tea and thick slabs of the golden bread that Lara had baked. Between bites, Sofi unrolled the map of Aell and pointed out their route to Lara, her finger slithering down the main road. The only stories that she wanted to offer Laravelle were tales of the road. Stories that didn't belong directly to Sofi.

"We'll need to leave at dawn if we hope to make it to Trogg before sundown," Sofi told Lara as she added an extra knifeful of butter to the still-warm bread.

"We?" Marie's chair scraped the stone floor, one eyebrow raised. "Where do you think you're going?"

"With Laravelle." Butter ran down Sofi's chin. Underneath the table, Lara kicked her. "Lara, I mean."

"You will do no such thing," Marie snapped, getting up to pour them all more tea from the white ceramic pot in the center of the table.

"I most certainly will." Sofi frowned, dropping the crust onto her plate. "My father is dead. She has no one to train her on the finer points of musicianship. Who better to do so than I?"

Marie's frown became even more pinched. "I don't like it." She shook her head. "A person shouldn't travel so soon after a death. It invites in the darkness."

"It's Aell," Sofi pointed out, shooting a glance at the window, where despite the early hour, the sun had all but disappeared from the sky, a slice of orange just barely visible on the horizon. "It's always dark."

Across the table, Lara giggled. Sofi shot her an appraising look. At least the girl had a sense of humor.

"Anyway," Sofi continued, "I couldn't possibly let Lara travel on her own. It will be a long and potentially treacherous journey."

"Exactly why I don't want you going." Marie shook her head. "Haven't I been through enough?"

Sofi's argument died on her tongue. Even Lara looked uncomfortable by the silence.

"It's okay." Lara sounded uncertain. "I'm sure I could manage on my own. Besides, I'll have the carriage driver."

Sofi nearly spat out her tea. "What carriage driver?"

It was Lara's turn to frown. "Won't there be . . . a coach? How else will we get from town to town?"

Sofi wanted to laugh, but it wasn't polite to revel in another's misfortune. "An Apprentice takes their induction tour on foot," she told Lara gently. "An homage to the troubadours of old. And a troubadour is, quite literally, a wandering musician. One cannot *wander* in a coach."

Lara blanched. "But it's . . . freezing. And . . . snowy. And . . . and cold."

Sofi nodded. "I'll pack a tarp. And I think we have an extra pair of snowshoes somewhere."

"That's all you have to say to me?" Lara clutched her mug so tightly her knuckles turned white. Clearly, that was not the level of reassurance she had been hoping for.

"Yes." Sofi took another sip of tea. "See?" She turned her attention back to Marie. "I *have* to go with her."

Marie, who had resumed her place at the table, put her head in her hands. "I always knew you would be the death of me, Sofi Ollenholt."

"We'll be careful, Marie, I promise." Sofi patted the housekeeper gently on the back. "But I have to do this."

From across the table, Lara smiled weakly at her. Sofi took her final bite of bread, chewing slowly. If she'd been granted the title of Apprentice, if her father had still been alive to accompany her, the conversation would have gone differently. Marie would have already been fluttering about, packing food enough to feed a regiment—preparing salted fish and pickled eggs and perhaps even tucking away some of the dried meat

Sofi loved so dearly. She would have knitted Sofi a new pair of mittens. She would have sent her off smiling rather than wringing her hands with worry and disappointment.

Well, Marie wasn't the only one who was disappointed.

Sofi had always dreamed of how she'd spend her time on the road—the way she would listen to the melody of the world around her, feel the ache in her legs and the spark in her heart, carrying only the hope for her long, prolific career as a Musik.

There were different things Sofi would carry now. Anger. Regret. Curiosity. Suspicion.

She hoped they were enough to keep her warm.

NINE

SOFI HAD never owned a pet, but she imagined caring for one would require the same amount of energy needed to travel on foot with Laravelle Hollis.

"Why's the inn called the Fourth Horse?" Lara peered down at the map in Sofi's hands, wiping a bead of sweat from her brow. After much urging, she had traded her thin, brightly colored gowns for a gray wool dress from Sofi's collection, topped with her cloak made of soft, white fox fur.

"Saint Evaline is the patron saint of the north." Sofi kicked one of her wooden snowshoes against a fallen tree trunk to free the chunks of ice from the leather lacing. "She loved her horses."

"Hmm." Lara made a soft noise as she stared out at

the road ahead, taking in the same white snowscape they'd been walking for hours. "How do you know so much about the saints if you don't go to church?"

Sofi rolled the map back up and shoved it in the pocket of her cloak. "Source material." Lara looked confused. "For my songs," she clarified. "It gets rather tedious writing about knights. They do so much dithering about."

Lara snorted and sank down onto the tree trunk, not bothering to brush away the snow.

"Lara," Sofi groaned. "We have to keep this pace the rest of the afternoon if we want to arrive before the sun goes down."

"I know." Lara tightened the laces on her snowshoes. "I just need to catch my breath. We've been walking all morning."

Rather slowly, Sofi wanted to add. But she held her tongue. Instead, she sank down onto the log as well and pulled out a piece of dried meat from the checkered tea towel Marie had pressed into her hands before they'd departed that morning. She offered some to Lara.

Lara accepted the food gratefully, tearing off a bite with her back teeth. "Do you want me to carry the map?" Sofi shot her a bemused look. "I'm feeling a bit useless." Lara wrinkled her nose. "You have to write all these songs, and I'm just here . . . walking."

"Oh"—Sofi struggled with her own bite—"don't worry. I haven't written anything yet."

Lara stared up at her from the trunk, wide-eyed. "But . . . I have to perform tonight."

Sofi nodded. "I know."

Lara's forehead creased. "Are you trying to sabotage me?" But she didn't sound angry, only curious.

Sofi laughed like the idea hadn't already crossed her mind. "No," she admitted. "I want to be a Musik much more than I want to sabotage you."

It was Lara's turn to laugh. It was a pleasant sound, like the tinkle of theater chimes. Surely that was the reason Sofi's heart fluttered. Not because of the way Lara threw back her head and exposed the curve of her pale throat. "That's"—she bit her lip—"not comforting, exactly, but it is . . . reassuring? I think?"

Sofi glanced upward at the sun, which had settled itself firmly in the center of the sky. "As long as we reach Trogg by sunset, there will be plenty of time. Once I have a melody, I just need enough story for . . . fifteen, sixteen verses, tops?"

Lara choked. "Sixteen verses?"

Sofi nodded. "The letter said 'epics,' which is about that length, yeah."

"But . . ." Lara trailed off desperately. "If the song is an hour long, it'll take me even longer than that to learn it."

"We'd better get moving, then," Sofi agreed, offering Lara a mittened hand.

Lara didn't take it. "But . . . what if I don't have enough time?"

"Well, it's a good thing all the verses will have the same melody, the chorus will repeat, and all the lyrics will be written out on sheet music for you, then, isn't it?" The words were like vinegar on her tongue, made even sourer by the confusion on Lara's face.

"I thought a chorus was a group of singers?"

Sofi bit her tongue so hard she tasted copper. *"Saints and sheep,"* she swore. "I cannot work in these conditions. Get up."

Lara shook her head uncomprehendingly. "What?"

"I can't believe I have to do this, but I am going to explain to you the most basic, most important piece of being a Musik: the structure of a song." Sofi fought the urge to roll her eyes. She could not believe she had to revert to such rudimentary teachings. But she needed Lara to trust her. She needed to get them both through this tour. And if explaining the difference between a verse and a chorus to Laravelle Hollis was the way to do that, then so be it. "Up."

Lara got to her feet. Their snowshoes crunched against the ground as they made their way back onto the path to Trogg. Wind whipped at them, blowing Sofi's untamed hair into her mouth. She batted it away with her mittened hands, trying to grasp how to articulate truths it seemed she had always known. For so long she had been a student. It was strange to find herself the one leading the lesson.

"The first thing you need to understand is structure." That was the proper place to begin. Without it, a song would fall apart, or listeners would grow bored, unable to follow the thread the musician wove. "Every song is inherently the same."

Lara's brow wrinkled. "But they all have different melodies and words."

"Perhaps so, but every song you've ever enjoyed follows

a pattern. You wouldn't begin to sew a dress without first preparing the pattern, would you? That's how you get a left sleeve longer than the right and a bodice sewn for a girl half your size." Sofi had wasted quite a bit of fabric in her youth.

Lara frowned thoughtfully. "You mean the way a tailor takes measurements?"

Lara's hands were soft. Sofi should have known she'd never used them to create a thing in her life.

"Yes," Sofi said wearily, "like that." Perhaps the dress metaphor wasn't a terrible way to continue the lesson. "So what does the tailor do after he takes your measurements?"

She grimaced as the words left her mouth. It sounded too superficial when reduced to such a comparison. But sewing was, Sofi knew, an act of artistry, even though on most garments available for purchase, every stitch was eerily uniform thanks to the Paper for *sew*. There was not a single skipped stitch in the bunch, which made for carefully tailored clothing but a sincere lack of garment identity.

It took Lara no time at all to answer. "Choose the fabric." She began to babble about silk versus satin, crinoline versus taffeta, and though Sofi was unable to follow her train of thought, there was something quite endearing about the passion with which Lara spoke. Apparently, Laravelle Hollis *had* spent her life devoted to an art. That art simply hadn't been music.

"Wait." Lara stopped midsentence about the benefits of lace in a layered garment. "What do textiles have to do with a song?"

Sofi rubbed her mittened hands against her ears, which had started to ache from the winter's chill. "That's the subject, isn't it?" She raised her eyebrows challengingly.

"The fabric." Lara's eyes were wide with understanding. "What you choose to work with makes the song. A satin gown will turn out differently than a woolen one." She dispassionately pinched the sleeve of the borrowed dress she wore. "The material really does make quite a bit of difference."

"Don't insult my style," Sofi snapped.

"What style?" Lara snickered.

"Shut up." Sofi swatted her lightly. "But yes. Exactly. The subject of a song is the fabric. And the fabric makes or breaks the song."

She squinted out at the endless snowscape. Everything was white, the afternoon sun reflecting off it in blinding pockets. There was no reprieve in sight.

"Hence why you know so much about Saint Evaline and her horses?" Lara was looking at Sofi a bit too knowingly.

Sofi had always leaned toward famous female figures. Whether the hours she spent poring over their accomplishments had anything to do with the mother-shaped absence in her life was something she refused to consider. Whether the accomplishments of women made for better songs was simply an inarguable truth.

"It has nothing to do with horses," Sofi insisted. "She single-handedly called forth the harvest for the entire country after Sir Stanlon slayed the dragon who served as summer!" She stopped walking and wheeled around to face Lara, who had fallen several steps behind her. "Tell me that coaxing food from the ground to feed an entire populace isn't a better tale than slipping and falling sword-first into a lizard?"

Lara stopped walking and appraised Sofi with a soft smile. Her cheeks were flushed with pink spots the circumference of a silver coin. "I wish someone would do that for us *now*." She looked thoughtful. "I would love to witness a summer."

"Exactly why Saint Evaline is worthy of a song." Sofi picked up her pace. "She's an excellent piece of fabric." Lara's snowshoes swished as she hurried to catch up. "Okay, so the tailor has the measurements, they have the pattern, and they have the fabric," Sofi continued. "What's next?"

"Constructing the dress," Lara exclaimed.

"Exactly," Sofi said. "We have everything we need. So now we create. Let's say we start with the bodice. Then we make the sleeves. Those are our verses. They're necessary to the construction. But what it all comes back to is the skirt. That's your chorus. Because without a skirt, we don't have a dress, do we?"

Lara looked scandalized. "Without a skirt, it's just a shirt."

Sofi smiled despite herself. "Precisely. And what a listener craves more than carefully constructed rhymes is predictability. They want to know what to expect. If you promise them a dress, they want a skirt that swishes."

"Obviously." Lara's tone made it clear this was not up for discussion.

"So, when you write a chorus, you want to make them feel comfortable. Give them a rhythm they can follow. A dress they want to wear again." Sofi adjusted the rucksack she had slung over her shoulder. "By the time you reach your second chorus, the audience should be singing along. If they can't, your dress doesn't fit. And if you keep selling poorly constructed dresses, your customers won't come back to your shop, will they?"

"Absolutely not." As though to illustrate Sofi's point, Lara tugged at the sleeves of the wool dress she was wearing. She was taller than Sofi, so her wrists were exposed to the frigid air. Her fingers were nearly purple. She had refused Sofi's offer of gloves. She hadn't said it was because they were lumpy and dirt-brown, but Sofi had her suspicions.

"Why don't you just use a Paper to warm your hands if mittens are so offensive?" Sofi watched Lara's teeth chatter with raised eyebrows.

"You know full well you made me leave all my Papers behind." Lara pursed her lips, which continued to tremble. "Brat," she grumbled quietly.

"You're a Musik," Sofi said incredulously. Before they'd left the Ollenholt manor, Sofi had rummaged through Lara's entire pack. *For your protection,* she had insisted, plucking a single scroll from the bottom of the bag and tossing it into the fire, where it sparked purple. "If I find any other secret scrolls, I'll have no choice but to report you to the Guild."

"You're kind of intense, you know that?"

Sofi wanted to scream. She wasn't *intense*. She simply cared deeply about the sanctity of the art form that she'd been raised to love. The one thing over which she'd always had control, even when the rest of her life had been empty and cold. That Lara was so flippant about the Papers and the rules of the Guild only served to make Sofi more suspicious about her "inherent ability" with the lute.

"Will you please just take the mittens?" Sofi sighed. "No one is going to see you wear them. But you can't play the lute if your fingers fall off. At that point you might as well use Papers and get yourself Redlisted."

She shivered. Any musician found to be using magic was branded by the Kingsguard, the truth of their betrayal burned red onto the skin of their hands, so they could be instantly recognized for their transgressions. Redlisted musicians were forbidden from ever owning an instrument again.

"You're so dramatic." Lara sighed heavily. "But I do like my hands as they are." She flexed her fingers. "Fine. Give them to me."

Sofi rolled her eyes as she rummaged through her bag to pull out the gloves. They had been one of her first knitting projects, back when Marie had tried to tempt her away from her father's strict instruction. The housekeeper had tried her best to make Sofi fall in love with a craft that wasn't songwriting. To embrace a life that wasn't dictated by music.

But Marie—like Sofi's attempts at knitting—had been unsuccessful.

Sometimes she wondered if Frederik had instructed Marie to try to pull his daughter away from the music as a test of Sofi's devotion. She had been kept on her toes every moment of her sixteen years, never fully trusting anyone but herself. Never truly loving anything but her music.

"So." Lara rubbed her newly mittened hands together as though trying to spark a flame. "A song is like a dress, but a Musik is both the tailor *and* the dress form. They model their own creation and hope they've done enough to get someone to buy it."

Sofi frowned. "Yes, actually." She examined Lara, walking in step with her, who was beaming with understanding. "That's exactly right."

"Well, you don't have to sound so surprised." Lara laughed just enough to wrinkle her nose. It was frustratingly endearing. Sofi made a noise in the back of her throat.

"But, of course, in this situation, you're the tailor and I'm the dress form," Lara continued. "So, tailor, what will you create for me?" She held out her arms and spun in a circle, the thick wool of the dress she wore barely moving despite her momentum.

Biting her chapped bottom lip, Sofi took Lara in the way a tailor might examine a customer. "Something simple to start. The people of Trogg are humble folk, who battle with the frozen ground and icy lakes to farm and fish to the best of their ability. They do not care about court politics or heroic knights. They care about their saints."

Lara stopped twirling. "Saint Evaline!" Her eyes

sparkled with excitement. "If we're playing at the Fourth Horse, we should sing about their patron saint."

"*You're* playing at the Fourth Horse." Sofi failed to keep the bitterness from her voice. "*You* should sing about their patron saint."

For one blessed moment, she had forgotten the true nature of her relationship with Lara. While teaching her about songwriting, Sofi had maintained the upper hand. But the truth fell down around her like the snow that tumbled from the sky. Lara was still the one with all the power. The one with Frederik Ollenholt's bone lute slung across her shoulder. The one allowed to perform original music without consequence.

"Yes," Sofi finally agreed. "Saint Evaline is the perfect subject. I'll keep the melody straightforward and the rhymes simple so you can commit them to memory. It may be the songwriting equivalent of a wool dress, but you look nice enough in that one. I'm sure no one in Trogg will mind."

Lara looked at her curiously. Sofi's face flushed. She had only been extending the metaphor. She hadn't meant anything by it. She cleared her throat sharply, and Lara looked away.

Sofi spent the rest of the walk muttering softly to herself, twisting words to fit her meaning, spinning melodies that would serve Lara's trilling voice. When the sun started to slip slowly down the sky, casting pink shadows across the unturned snow, Sofi and Lara paused at the lip of a hill, taking in the sweeping valley and the town of Trogg below.

Tiny cottages dotted the square, the thatched roofs thick with snow, the windows blurred with condensation. Chimneys pumped out clouds of gray smoke that curled in the cold evening air. Lara stared at the little hamlet with trepidation, so Sofi led the way dutifully through the snow, trudging down the steep incline of the hill into the arms of the waiting inn.

They stopped beneath the swinging wooden sign, complete with a painting of a majestic white mare, tugged off their snowshoes, and leaned them carefully against the stone wall of the inn. Lara sighed and rubbed her neck, wincing as she removed the bone lute from her shoulders.

The wind roared, the hint of a melody running through the air, soft and wavering, changing so quickly Sofi barely had time to catch the notes. She hummed frantically, adding to the tune swirling about her brain. The notes fell perfectly into place, as though the melody had been saving them seats.

The tune was inarguably catchy, the lyrics simple yet memorable. Although it was not Sofi's finest work, this song still had lasting power. It was a pity all the credit would go to Lara.

"Coming?" Lara asked as the front door opened and a small bell trilled a welcoming ring.

"Go on ahead," Sofi told her. Lara shrugged, disappearing inside.

Alone for the first time in what felt like weeks, Sofi let out a feral scream, her breath emitting a giant cloud that hung in the freezing air. The inn's front door swung open, the bell jangling merrily.

"Everything all right?" Lara asked, poking her head back out into the rapidly darkening afternoon. "It sounded like a cat was dying."

"Fine," Sofi lied.

Sofi was always lying.

TEN

THE INTERIOR of the Fourth Horse was small but lively. A cheerful fire flitted in the hearth. Long wooden tables lined the perimeter, crude benches cut from thick logs rested neatly beneath. A few men were drinking from pewter tankards, steam rising from the depths and warming their red noses. The barkeep was an old man with kind eyes, stirring a pot of something that smelled spiced and sweet. He was shouting at a person Sofi couldn't see, but even his shouting sounded amicable.

Sofi's frustration faded as warmth spread across her fingers and face. She'd always had a soft spot for taverns. The energy, the roaring fires, the way the insides seemed to look the same no matter which town a person found themselves in. There was something comforting about that consistency—knowing that no matter how far a person wandered, they could always end up sitting before a roaring fire, surrounded by the scent of cider and the spice of mulled wine.

When Sofi had been very young, her father had taken her along on one of his tour stops in Aell. Frederik had been in wonderful spirits—had even paid for two rounds of drinks for the entire room before he'd taken the stage. Sofi had sat with a hot mug of cider and watched the way the patrons' eyes widened as her father's fingers danced across the strings. Afterward they had showered him with compliments, turning Frederik's usually pinched face red and glowing. That was always when Sofi liked her father most: reveling in a job well done. That glow that hung about him after a performance, the way he came alive onstage and after, had been another reason Sofi was drawn to music. If she worked hard enough, practiced diligently enough, one day she might be able to inspire that sort of joy.

A short woman placed a steaming bowl on the table in front of a bearded man, then spotted the two girls in the doorway. "Hello, travelers!" She wiped her hands upon her apron and held them both out to Lara, her green eyes twinkling brightly. "Welcome to the Fourth Horse. How may I be of service to you today? A room? A meal? Both, perhaps?"

"I—oh!" Lara was interrupted as the innkeeper pulled her forward, reaching for the sack slung across her back.

"Let me take that for you." Lara opened her mouth to protest, but the woman had already hoisted Lara's bag across one shoulder and was reaching for the bone lute's case. Lara shot Sofi a desperate look as the woman buzzed about her like a honeybee.

"What's this?" The innkeeper squinted at Lara's lute case. "It's heavy."

"I'll hold on to that, thanks." Lara pried the case gently away from the woman. "It's a lute. I'm, um"—she glanced uncertainly at Sofi, who nodded encouragingly. They'd been over this. Twice—"I'm the Guild's newest Musik, here to play tonight in exchange for room and board. I'm sure the king sent word."

The woman stopped fluttering and clasped her hands over her heart. "Saint Evaline heard my call. I got the letter from the king, but I still didn't believe you'd actually *play* here. Horace!" she bellowed to the man behind the bar. "Ring the bell. There's a Musik in our midst." She clutched Lara's hand even tighter. "I can't tell you what an honor this is. We're simple folk here. Can't afford to attend fancy performances in theaters, and no musicians tend to stop here despite the fact that I make the best deer-heart stew in all of Aell. I'll get you the finest room, of course, and dinner's on me. My husband will drum up your crowd." She stopped, laughing, "Drum . . . get it?" Lara shot Sofi a wide-eyed look of alarm.

Help me, she mouthed.

Sofi bit back a grin as she bustled forward to save Lara. "The Musik will need a few hours to prepare," she interjected quickly. "Her performance will begin after supper."

The innkeeper did not even look at Sofi. "Of course, of course. The people of Trogg are always much kinder after they've been fed, anyhow. Now come with me, come with me. I've got just the room for you, Musik . . ."

"Hollis," Lara finished for her. "Musik Hollis."

Sofi's polite smile slipped. The title sounded wrong paired with Lara's name. When her father had been alive, it had always been a thrill, hearing him addressed with the honorific. It let Sofi live vicariously through him as she imagined her future.

The future that now belonged to Lara.

The innkeeper led them down a long hall with brightly colored doors, unlocking a door green as a fir tree and ushering the pair inside.

The room was dark—the one window filtered in the fading light of the afternoon. The canopy of the bed brushed the beams of the low ceiling. The innkeeper heaved Lara's bag onto the foot of the bed, then bustled toward the candelabra that sat on the bedside table. She plucked a box of matches from her pocket, and a flame burst to life. She took her time lighting the tapers. A few words were written across the woman's hands, their color lackluster, which meant the Papers' power was fading. *Flame*, one read. *Help*, read another.

"Now you make yourselves comfy—there's a pallet beneath the bed for you." The woman nudged her chin in Sofi's direction. "And, Musik Hollis, just holler if you need anything at all. I can't wait to hear you play." Her eyes turned misty. "It's been too long since anyone came to our little town, Musiks being as important as they are. You are a *gift*." She squeezed Lara's shoulder, pressed the candelabra into Sofi's hands, and departed.

Lara flopped onto the bed, one hand to her heart. "That's so kind. She nearly made me cry."

Sofi, who had returned the candelabra to the bedside table and was kneeling on the floor, searching for the pallet beneath the bed, grunted.

Lara leaned over the side of the bed, her face mere inches from Sofi's. "What are you doing?"

"Finding myself a place to sit." Sofi tugged at the pallet with such force she nearly toppled over. She batted away a strand of hair stuck to her lip. "I have a song to compose."

"No, no," Lara insisted, sitting up. "You're the one doing the important work. Sit here." She tapped the mattress beside her.

Sofi hesitated. At home, she was used to composing with the structure of the hardback chair at her desk. But their walk had been long and all of her ached, so Sofi pulled a stack of fresh staff paper from her bag, stuck a pencil between her teeth, and settled herself across the foot of the bed. The tune that had been swirling about her head began knocking on her brain, begging to be let out. Sofi scrawled down the notes on two separate stacks of paper—one copy for her records and one for Lara to follow during the performance.

Her left hand moved furiously, smudging the lines in several places, yet Sofi selfishly kept the neater copy for herself. If Lara couldn't read the lyrics or fumbled a note at the turn to the bridge, well, that certainly wouldn't be *Sofi's* fault.

Once the song was committed to paper, she pulled her lute out of its case, adjusting the tuning pegs, her entire body relaxing as her fingers found the strings. She began to build the walls inside her mind, the careful control required to offer a perfect performance.

She struck the opening notes, allowing her concentration to take hold. But she'd barely made it through the introduction before she was interrupted.

"Are you okay?" Lara was looking at her with concern.

"Yes?" Sofi had absolutely no idea what she was talking about.

"Oh, sorry." Lara shook her head. "It's just . . . you looked like you were in pain."

"No?" Sofi shifted on the bed, trying to catch a glimpse of her face in the window. She felt fine. She'd merely been focusing.

"Oh. I guess that's just your face when you play, then." Lara shrugged, looking embarrassed. "Sorry. Carry on."

Sofi replaced her fingers on the lute's strings, but she did not strike them. Instead, she frowned. "What did I look like?"

Lara shifted on the bed beside her, cheeks tinged pink. "It's nothing. I'm sorry I said anything."

"No," Sofi demanded. "Show me."

Lara exhaled sharply. Then she screwed up her face so that her nose wrinkled and her eyebrows creased. Her lips were pursed and her eyes unfocused. She looked rather monstrous.

"You're exaggerating."

Lara's expression smoothed out to its usual serenity. "I'm not. It was eerie. And despite the expression, you looked . . . empty? If that makes sense?"

"It doesn't," Sofi said flatly, but in actuality, it did.

That was the reason for the walls, after all. The carefully placed stones that held back the flood of emotions that made her music too unpredictable and flighty. Her instincts needed to be reined in. The Muse demanded complete and utter control of the craft.

But surely there was no need to look like an angry rodent when she played. Certainly not when she sat so close to someone as beautiful as Laravelle Hollis. It only stood to deepen the divide between them. So before Sofi started the song again, she took a deep breath. She rolled back her shoulders. And she tried her best to knock the wall down.

"Through the ice and cold hard ground, Saint Evaline she sends the sun," Sofi sang, the melody carrying the steady hope of harvest season, of full bellies and stocked pantries. *"Here the roots go way, way down, till the time when next she comes."*

It was a firm, certain song, the lilting rhythm sure to delight the hardworking folks of Trogg. She was especially proud of the chorus, the notes from the whistling wind draping themselves across her tongue, as long and languid as she envisioned the bright nights of summer once had been. Without the familiar wall that kept her focused only on the technical aspect of playing—the transition from course to course, the shape of the words in her mouth—Sofi lost herself in the melody, in the story of Saint Evaline and how she saved her people. The warmth, the care, the *love* that went into such a selfless action.

As she played, she could almost feel the soft, warm breeze sent by the saint, saw it ruffle the ends of Lara's hair, watched the other girl, who only moments ago had been clutching her shawl close, shed it and lift her face up as though to greet the sun.

By the second chorus, Lara could sing along. By the third verse, she had pulled the bone lute from its case and found the song's pulse, her middle finger and thumb plucking out the soft, rolling rhythm. When the song ended, they simply sat in the room, the final notes hanging between them.

"Whoa." Lara looked a bit dazed. "That was . . . incredible. Truly, Sofi, I *felt* the warmth. That breeze. How did you do that?"

"Music is sensory." Sofi shrugged, trying not to let on how pleased she was. "It can make you feel all manner of things, if you let it."

"I want to do that," Lara said breathlessly, eyes bright. "I want to make people feel the way that song made me feel."

"See, even with a terrifying expression on the face of the musician, a good song can work wonders on an audience."

But Lara shook her head. "You didn't look like that this time. You looked entirely different. Happy, even. Free." Her eyes lingered on Sofi's. "You should always look that way."

"Don't tell me what to do." Sofi scowled, but the words came out softer than she'd intended them to. She had liked losing herself in the melody. Letting loose the flutter in her chest, letting her heart lead rather than her head.

But she refused to tell Lara that.

"You've got it, then?" Sofi asked, shoving the sheet music toward Lara. "No questions?"

Lara scanned the staff paper, frowning as she muttered softly to herself. "Will you play the fourth verse for me again? I want to make sure I nail the turn into the chorus."

Sofi did, trying not to notice the way Lara swept her glossy hair behind her shoulder to reveal her long, pale neck. Laravelle Hollis was still her rival, no matter how pretty her face or how kind her concern. She was still the girl who'd stolen Sofi's future.

Sofi would do well not to forget that.

The inn's front room was packed. Tables were crowded with broad bodies, and people lined the walls, leaning against the stone and one another. A serving boy bobbed and wove through the crowd, drinks balancing precariously on his tray. No one noticed him.

Every single eye was fixed on Lara.

She stood in the corner beside the hearth. She had changed out of the gray wool and into a simple dress of forest green that complemented the brown of her eyes. Her white-gold curls were piled into a messy bun at the top of her head. She fiddled with the lute, adjusting a peg here, testing a string there, the flickering flames from the fireplace casting a soft glow across her pale skin. Her hands were clean.

She looked like a painting, but one that had been made without magic. Rare and beautiful.

Lara looked up from her strings. Spotted Sofi. Smiled.

And then she began to play.

"Through the ice and cold hard ground, Saint Evaline, she

sends the sun," Lara sang, her voice soft but certain. *"Here the roots go way, way down, till the time when next she comes."*

The crowd leaned forward, hoping to get closer to the source of the song. As Lara continued to play, even Sofi found herself drawn to the girl, as though she had cast a spell. She *was* casting some sort of magical spell, Sofi reminded herself, but then, her hands were clean. Papers left a mark, and Lara had none.

But her performance was still impossibly endearing. Incredibly sincere. As she sang, her face was open and honest, reflecting every moment of the music. While no warm breeze whipped around the room, she still drew in the audience, transporting them to a time when winter was vanquished. And because it was clear that Lara so truly believed it, her performance offered hope that one day summer would return to Aell again.

It was intoxicating.

It was infuriating.

There was nothing technically impressive about Lara's performance. She hit all the right notes, but it wasn't her playing that was the star. *Lara* was. It was exactly as Frederik had said: There was something about Lara herself that made her performances so intriguing.

But Sofi could not put her finger on *what*, which only served to irritate her more. Sofi was the best living lutenist in Aell. She should be able to perform circles around this girl. The fact that she couldn't made her more certain than ever that Lara was hiding something. That the root of her success was not authentic.

That she was employing magic to cheat her way forward.

When Lara's fingers finally came to rest, the room was silent, save for the crackling of the fire. Then the cheering began, loud and earnest, all banging tankards and good-natured shouting. Lara blushed, her face as pink as the dress she'd worn the first day Sofi met her. The longer the applause lasted, the more flummoxed she looked until finally she giggled, waved her hands, and the noise stopped.

"Thank you," Lara said to the room. "This was my first official performance as a Musik, and you all made it one that I'll never forget." She smiled that smile that put the sun to shame. "Now please, eat, drink, and be merry."

The room roared with approval. Lara bent down to return the lute to its case. The audience started to speak, the inn buzzing like a hive of bees.

"She's a natural." A figure slid onto the bench opposite Sofi, clanking two pewter tankards onto the table. "Timely, too. Wish we had ourselves a Saint Evaline right about now. Saints, I miss being warm." Long, thin, skeleton-like fingers pushed one of the glasses toward Sofi. She recognized those hands.

"Yve." Sofi blinked up at the Guild's accordionist, her tiny frame completely out of place amid the tall, broad-shouldered locals. "What are you doing in Trogg?"

Yve took a long sip of the brown liquid in her tankard before setting it down with a smack. "Checking up on the Guild's newest member, of course." Her eyes flashed to Lara, who had been swarmed near the hearth by adoring listeners, a crystal glass of honey wine pressed into her hands. "But I must admit, I'm glad you're here, too. I was"—she clanged her fingernails against the pewter tankard—"ill at ease after the audition."

Hope shuddered in Sofi's chest. Had Yve, too, noticed something amiss with Lara?

"The animosity between your father and Tambor was concerning," the Musik said instead.

Sofi shook her head uncomprehendingly. "What do you mean?"

Yve pursed her lips, thinking. "The timing of your father's death feels . . . strange. I only wondered if he said anything on the carriage ride home."

Sofi frowned. "Just that he had chosen Lara as his Apprentice. That, to me, was a bit suspicious." Her gut churned with her own daring.

But Yve only frowned. "Nothing odd there." She shrugged almost casually, which sent the insult crashing into Sofi like stone. "She has a spark. She'll bring out the best in the new Guild members." She glanced guiltily at Sofi. "You understand, of course. She's a natural. Her composition, I mean . . ." Yve hummed a few bars of the chorus.

Sofi thought she might be sick.

Yve reached across the table, her long fingers curling around Sofi's. "I can't imagine how difficult the loss of your father must be. The Guild was hit hard by the news. Of course, we expected to move on from our titles, but not like this. It's why I wanted to be here tonight. You know how chaotic Castle Lochlear can be. I didn't want to overwhelm her." Yve's eyes flickered back to Lara, who was now chatting with a dark-brown-skinned man who was gesticulating wildly. Lara clutched his arm for support while she laughed. Something suspiciously like jealousy flickered in Sofi's stomach.

"I see she's met Luk." Yve smiled like a proud mother observing her offspring. "My Apprentice." She took another swig from her tankard. "It'll be strange to pass on my straps to another." She licked her lips absentmindedly. "Very strange, indeed."

Before Sofi could say anything, Luk led Lara to the table where Sofi and Yve sat. Yve burst into a flurry of applause, leaping to her feet to offer Lara a hand in greeting. Sofi watched it all, almost as though she were outside her body. It was unnerving to witness Lara's induction into the Guild Sofi had always believed *she'd* be a part of. Watching the only life she'd ever known move on without her.

"Sofi?" Lara was looking at her expectantly.

Sofi blinked wildly as though awaking from a dream. "Sorry, what?"

"Luk is headed to the bar. Do you want anything to drink? The honey wine is quite good."

Sofi shook her head, reaching for the tankard Yve had placed before her. "I'm fine." She took a large gulp, spluttering as the spice hit her tongue. She had been hoping for just one moment of dignity. She could hardly bear the collective looks of pity. "I'm afraid I'm a bit weary from the walk. You all enjoy your evening. Yve." She nodded at the Musik. "Luk.

Pleasure to make your acquaintance." Her eyes met Lara's. "Musik Hollis." She dipped her head.

Sofi could feel Lara's eyes on her. Her mouth twitched as though she wanted to say something or perhaps even stop her. But, to Sofi's disappointment, Lara merely nodded.

Sofi retired to the room behind the green door. She tossed and turned on the thin pallet, her mind stewing. She had known that watching Lara play would not be easy, but she had not expected to have to face the Guild—nor the circumstances of her father's demise—so soon after they took to the road.

Raucous singing floated down the hallways from the main room. Sofi rolled onto her side, shoving her head under the pillow as Yve's voice snaked beneath the crack in the door. Yve was leading the crowd in one of her famous drinking songs. Depending on how drunk both Yve and the company were, the singing might continue until sunrise.

It wasn't until Sofi was on the very edge of sleep that she remembered what day it was. In any other situation, she would have fallen to her knees and begged forgiveness for her oversight. After all, she had spent her life groveling, begging, and demeaning herself in the name of the Muse. Perhaps it would have been different if she'd been rewarded for her efforts. But instead, when Sofi had needed her most, the Muse had turned her back.

And so, rather than flinging herself from the lumpy cot and rebruising her knees in service of someone who did not want her, Sofi merely buried herself deeper beneath her blanket and, for the first time on a third day, did not pray.

THE THIRD DAY

For Sofi's sixth birthday, Marie made strudel.

Frederik was home, back from beyond the Gate, and he'd brought fresh apples. Sofi, who had only ever known apples in cider, wondered at the fruit's brightly colored skin, how it faded from green near the stem to dappled reds that dripped down the fruit like paint. The skin was waxy beneath her fingers and the fruit crisp and juicy between her teeth, sloshing rhythmically as she crunched.

Sofi couldn't remember the last time her father had been home on her birthday. He would bring her belated gifts, of course—soft fabrics and gold chains from the world beyond the Gate—but it wasn't the same as having him there.

Birthdays were usually spent in the kitchen with Marie, stools nestled in front of the hearth, playing card games and eating flaky shortbread cookies dusted with powdered sugar. But when her father was home, dinner was served in the dining room. The silver candelabras were lit, the fine china laid out. Marie did not eat with them.

The housekeeper's absence was obvious—the silence in the room was as cold as the icy wind that howled outside the dining room's windows. Sofi was so wildly overtaken with nerves that she could hardly stomach her squab. She sat up extra straight, careful not to scrape her knife across her plate, to not disturb her father in any way as they shared their meal.

He had been home from the road only a handful of days

since the dress debacle. Sofi wanted to prove to him that she had corralled her wanting. Was excelling in her silence. She'd even found a way to sneeze on first days without making a sound.

But her father was more focused on his food than on his daughter.

"Father?"

Across the long table, Frederik looked up from his fork. "Hmm?"

Now that she had his attention, Sofi wasn't certain what to do with it. She couldn't outright tell him the ways she was excelling at her study. She'd heard him speak disdainfully about Yve for doing something similar, calling her prideful. Sofi didn't want him to speak of her with that same furious tone.

No, it was too risky to center herself. If Sofi wanted to keep her father happy, she should focus on his favorite subject: himself.

"I heard a new melody this afternoon from your study. What are you working on?"

At the subject of his work, Frederik brightened considerably. "Yes, I've started writing an epic about King Jovan. It will be called 'To Love a King' in hopes that it convinces those Council members to do just that. It's up to the Guild to repair the image of Aell and its king after what his father did with those Papers. Nasty things, those." He shivered as though snow had slipped through his collar and down his spine. "Be wary of those who take shortcuts, Sofi. Hard work and dedication are the only way." His fork scraped against his plate, and he grimaced. "Yes, the only way. But you know that, don't you, my good girl?"

Sofi beamed, flushed with her father's favorable attention and his compliment. "I do."

Frederik returned to his squab, breaking apart the bird's tiny bones with a sharp crunch.

It was then Marie came in with the strudel, the golden-brown pastries like pillows on the plate, bringing along the bright spice of cinnamon and the warmth of the stewed, sugared apples. Atop was a fine dusting of powdered sugar, Sofi's favorite, just like the soft snow that blanketed the Ollenholt estate.

Marie set the plate of strudel on the table, winking at Sofi as she wiped her hands on her apron. "Now, mind you it took me ages to roll that dough thin like paper, so you'd best appreciate." She laughed, ruffling Sofi's hair. Warmth flooded through Sofi's chest at the housekeeper's fondness. Unlike with her father, it wasn't difficult for Sofi to win Marie's approval. All she had to do was be herself. "When you sing to the saints, tell them how much you appreciate these gnarled hands of mine."

Across the table, Frederik looked up with alarm. "When she what?"

Marie looked a bit sheepish. "Sings to the saints, Master Ollenholt."

His face darkened. "Why would she do that?"

Marie's hand stiffened where it rested on Sofi's head. "It's a birthday tradition in my family, adapted for your daughter's penchant for melody. Before diving into dessert, the birthday-haver speaks to the saints. Just a quick conversation. A way to connect. Our Sofi has always preferred to sing."

Frederik made a soft noise, his expression twisted. "Let me hear it, then."

Sofi's throat had gone dry. She tried to swallow and nearly choked on the cottony consistency of her tongue. Sofi wished that her father hadn't come home, that she could have spent this birthday like the ones before, warm and cozy before the fire, singing to Saint Evaline, imagining herself as the bringer of spring, laughing with Marie at the loftiness of such dreams.

Instead, the dining room was cold, her stomach sour. Still, she didn't dare disobey her father. So she began to sing.

"*Bring me hope and keep my health,*" she started, her voice shaky, her eyes fixed on her dinner plate. "*I turn to you for all things else.*" She grimaced as her father frowned at the shoddy rhyme. The song had been written when she was younger and possessed less skill. She thought she ought to prove to her father that she had grown as a songwriter, so instead of singing the next line, Sofi made one up on the spot.

"*Keep our plates full and our goblets unending,*" Sofi sang, a bit more certainty in her voice now. Her father's brow had relaxed, so she allowed herself to give in to the warmth that glowed in her chest. "*Keep my talent unfurled and my voice unpretending.*"

Marie, who had reached for a pitcher to refill Frederik's glass, accidentally knocked the goblet over, water spilling across the tablecloth. But then, almost in slow motion, the water retreated, back into the goblet, which righted itself as though nothing had happened.

All three of them stared at the glass, unbelieving. Frederik clutched the table with white knuckles as Marie rubbed her eyes. Sofi sat stoically. She wasn't certain how, but she felt as though this was her fault.

It was Marie who finally broke the silence, offering a shake of her head and a laugh much too loud for the room. "I must be losing my mind," she said, clutching the pitcher to her chest. "I would have sworn that goblet tipped. . . ." She laughed again, the sound wild. "I think I might need a lie down. If you'll excuse me, Sofi. Master Ollenholt." Marie cleared their dinner plates and returned swiftly to the kitchen, muttering under her breath.

"What was that lyric you sang?" Frederik asked once the door had closed behind the housekeeper, his voice careful. "Keep our plates full and . . . ?"

Sofi wrenched her eyes up from the tablecloth to meet her father's inquisitive gaze. "Our goblets unending." Her voice was no more than a whisper.

Frederik frowned theatrically. "This is what I was afraid of. The wrong saints are attuned to you, Sofi. It doesn't help your music much if Saint Thomas hears you on your birthday, now, does it?"

Sofi shook her head accommodatingly, despite not fully following her father's train of thought.

"That's right," Frederik said. "It is the Muse who should be worshipped above all else."

Sofi's trepidation lessened. That made sense. "So I should *sing* to the Muse?" she clarified.

"No." Frederik shook his head. "You are not ready to sing to her. You haven't yet built up the necessary relationship. The proper connection. No, to start, you must *pray*."

Satisfied, Frederik reached for a strudel. The pastry flaked as he bit into it, powdered sugar settling in his beard, making him look older. "I was going to gift you a new doll for your birthday," her father said after he'd sucked the sugar from his fingertips, "but the Muse's preferred prayer is the proper present for one who hopes to become a Musik. Surely that's more important to you than yet another thing?"

Sofi nodded, because that was what she knew she must do.

"Very good." Frederik clapped his hands together. "I'll teach you the Muse's Prayer." He got to his feet and moved around the table, pulling out the chair next to Sofi's. Instantly, she was warmer, basking in the glow of his attention. "Now, you're getting a bit of a late start here, so you'll need to pray to the Muse a bit more frequently to make up for lost time. This will ensure she smiles down on you and is always ready to give you strength, steadiness, and sureness when you perform. That is a gift that keeps giving."

Sofi nodded. It would be nice to have someone to turn to in her uncertainty. Sometimes, when she played or composed, she found herself stuck. With her father on the road and Marie so unversed in the ways of music, the Muse could be her support system. Her stomach slowly unraveled as her father smiled down at her.

"We'll add this to your routine, I think," he said, tapping a rhythm in six-eight time on the table. "What day is it?"

"A third day," Sofi answered quickly.

"Yes." Frederik nodded. "That seems right." He turned toward his daughter, eyes fire-bright. "The third day is for praying."

ELEVEN

SOFI WAS up before the sun, the darkness sweeping the small room in all directions. The pallet swished as she struggled to her feet, her back and neck aching from a night that might as well have been spent on the ground. Her stomach twisted nauseatingly as she remembered going to bed without praying the previous night.

Sofi's routine had never been something she'd had to work to maintain. It was like breathing—something that simply *was*. She'd never been tempted away from her training before. Had never defied the Muse for fun. Yet one night on the road with Laravelle Hollis and Sofi was already giving in to childish envy. Showing weakness when she needed strength more than ever. She would have to work harder than ever to redeem herself in the eyes of the Muse.

The fourth day was for feeling. And Sofi did feel, guilt draped over her like a veil. Still, it was not enough. She cast a glance at a sleeping Lara, shrugged on her furs, and crept out of the room into the silent, dark hallway. The colorful doors all looked gray in the early-morning hours. In the main room, the fire had fallen to embers, the serving boy slumped over a wooden table, fast asleep.

Sofi fiddled with the front door before managing to maneuver the metal latch open. She slipped out into the early morning, the horizon glowing a soft blue even while stars still twinkled in the sky.

The searing pain of her bare feet sinking into the snow made her gasp. She covered her mouth with an ungloved hand. She would not whimper. She would stand, feeling, until she no longer could. It was funny, the way that snow was like fire, the bright, burning heat consuming her until her teeth chattered and her littlest toes began to turn blue. Her hands locked up—though she tried to furl and unfurl her fingers the way she often did for dexterity, her limbs rebelled. Her body screamed and her heart shouted in sympathy, but her mind refused to waver.

Sofi needed to *feel*. And wasn't that exactly what she was doing? With this sort of control, Sofi would be unflappable, prepared for anything. She could not be defeated.

The inn's front door opened, and a familiar white-blond head appeared, blinking the sleep out of her brown eyes.

"Sofi, what—" Lara took one look at Sofi's bare feet

before tugging her inside, slamming the door behind them so loudly that the serving boy startled awake.

"What were you doing?" Lara's voice was hoarse, but her horror was palpable.

"I—" Sofi trailed off, frustrated. Lara did not know about Sofi's routine. It was going to be difficult to get her to understand the necessity of suffering for art. "What are you doing awake?"

"I heard the door open." Lara looked pointedly at Sofi's toes. "Come on." She grabbed Sofi's wrist and dragged her toward the dying embers in the hearth. "Sit," she commanded, pushing Sofi down onto the floor.

"You," Lara called to the groggy serving boy. "Do you have a Paper for fire?"

The boy nodded, hurrying to the hearth. He pulled a scroll from his pocket and a pin from his lapel. He offered the Paper a drop of blood, then placed it on the silent logs in the fireplace. A flame roared to life as the word "warmth" spread across his hand. Sofi grimaced at the casual display of magic. Still, she couldn't help but shift, putting her legs in front of her so her toes could soak up the heat emanating from the fireplace.

"Now"—Lara took Sofi's hands in hers and rubbed them together in an attempt to warm them—"do you want to tell me what you were doing?"

"It's a fourth day," Sofi mumbled, not wanting to admit how much better she felt now that she was inside.

Lara stared at her blankly. "I know my days, Sofi. That

doesn't explain why you were standing barefoot in the snow."

Sofi sighed, feeling a bit embarrassed. She'd never had to explain her routine to anyone before. Jakko had known only the pieces she'd been willing to share, and even then, Sofi had downplayed some of its harsher components in an attempt to avoid his well-meaning judgment. He hadn't faced the same impossible pressure from Frederik.

"Fourth days are for feeling."

Lara blinked uncomprehendingly at her. "What are you talking about?"

"The first day is for listening," Sofi recited softly. "The second for wanting, the third for praying, the fourth for feeling, the fifth for repenting, and the sixth for music."

Lara's bemused expression did not change. "What kind of twisted nursery rhyme is that?"

"It's a routine." Sofi pulled her hands from Lara's grasp. "Yesterday was a third day, and I didn't pray. I need the Muse to forgive me my transgression."

"That . . . doesn't make any sense."

"Of course it does." Sofi was just as flummoxed as Lara looked. "To be a truly great musician, you have to maintain a close relationship with the Muse. Sometimes that requires suffering for your art."

Lara frowned. "The things you love shouldn't hurt you, Sofi."

"I'm not . . ." Sofi trailed off, looking at her blue-tinged toes. But she *was* hurt. Had been, over and over again, all in the name of music. She'd lost Jakko, her best friend, to the pressure of competition. She'd lost hours to the Muse, begging to be made worthy of carrying on her father's legacy. She'd lost her future to Lara. And she'd lost any chance of knowing her mother, thanks to her father's penchant for secrets.

Each of those losses added up to their own hurts. Hurt she was too afraid to feel, so she invented other ways to feel instead—like standing barefoot in a bank of snow.

Sofi *was* hurt. But how was she to tell Lara that it wasn't just music that was hurting her? She, herself, was doing the hurting.

You must be sharp, Frederik had always told his daughter. *Do not dull your edges for the benefit of anyone. Not even me.*

And so Sofi had always been defensive. Had prepared herself to cut and slice through the criticisms and judgments that might come her way. But no one wanted to get too close to a knife. Which was why Sofi often found herself alone.

"We missed you last night, you know." Lara's voice was light, changing the subject as casually as opening a window.

"Hmm?" Sofi asked, pulling her eyes away from the fire.

"Yve and Luk and I. It was so kind of them to come see me perform. And they had such complimentary things to say about the song." She smiled tentatively, as though hoping that might be enough to cheer Sofi up. "I especially missed you when they asked where I found the inspiration for the three lines in five-four that mimicked the fall of rain on a field of wheat. I had to spill my honey wine on Yve's lap to get out of answering."

Sofi snorted, imagining the pinched expression on the accordionist's face as she had to sop up the sticky-sweet liquid from her lap.

Lara grinned at her. "Thought you might like that. You looked a bit ruffled when she first sat down."

Sofi worried her tongue in her cheek. "It was nothing." She didn't want to let on exactly how much Yve's words had truly affected her. "I'm just not very good at accepting condolences."

"Well, then"—Lara grinned—"I shan't give you any. No apologies for knocking a beverage across the lap of one of the most famous women in the world. Do you think she'll still let me see her play? I'm not sure I even know what an accordion is, to be quite honest with you."

Sofi laughed despite herself. Lara was trying to distract her, and, rather annoyingly, it was working. The girl really was incredibly charming.

"Come on." Lara pushed herself to her feet, offering Sofi her hand. "Let's get you some socks. I imagine we've got quite the walk ahead of us today. You're no use to me if your toes fall off," she said, winking.

Sofi put a frozen hand in Lara's warm one and let herself be led back down the hall and into their room. As she pulled on thick gray socks and stepped into her boots, for the first time on a fourth day, what Sofi felt was *grateful*.

The road to their next destination—the city of Skaal—was straightforward, back up from the valley of Trogg, through farmland, and past a small wood. Sofi set a brisk pace, keeping her eyes fixed on the morning sky, which was a bright, new blue. The feeling had fully returned to her toes, but the crisp air that tousled her hair and caressed her cheek left a malicious, lingering chill. A sharp reminder of her morning. Yet Sofi could not stop remembering Lara's insistence that love did not also have to hurt.

It was a tempting possibility. But one of Sofi's most valuable traits was that she could not be tempted. She had maintained a singular goal for so long. Had refused to stray from the course her father had set.

And where did that get you?

She grumbled as her snowshoe smacked against a step of uneven ground. Those were the sort of questions she tried to avoid—questions that frightened her. Made her take a long look at her choices.

Questions that might leave her with regret.

No. Suffering mattered. This Sofi knew. She just needed to find a way to remind herself of it.

As she walked, hands tucked beneath her armpits for the extra warmth, Sofi asked the Muse to make her steady. She asked the Muse to make her sure. Sofi could not turn her back on the only piece of her old life that had ever truly served her. She would not lose sight of the reason she was on the road: to expose Lara for the fraud she surely was and to inherit the title of Musik. A few kind words from Laravelle Hollis would not be enough to knock her off course.

By the time they reached the top of the hill, Sofi had settled on a subject for the evening's song: Lady Wildmoore's patience.

Skaal was a larger town than Trogg, home to a chapel with a stained-glass window that Aellinians traveled for miles to admire. Skaal's citizens considered themselves cosmopolitan. They were sure to appreciate a song about the most famous lover of Oleg, the second king of Aell.

Lady Wildmoore had lived more than three hundred years ago, but still the story was often told about the wide-eyed woman who had sealed herself away in a tower, far from the sun and the flowers and the fresh air, all to prove that she would love Oleg more than measure. When the king learned of her self-imposed suffering, of the lengths of her sacrifice, he went to the tower and called for her to turn her face to the sun. Upon hearing his voice, Lady Wildmoore left the tower, and King Oleg was enchanted by her. They were married the very next day.

Through her song, Sofi would prove that suffering was not only necessary but good. It created love. It elevated art.

She hummed and whistled as they walked, tapping the rhythm on her thigh with her middle finger. She took in the swish of Lara's skirt, the crunch of the snow, the slant of the sun across her own cheek, and spun them into her melody, the rhythm of the world rising to meet her song.

He loved the lady laid in wait, her earthly world abandoned.

Who wouldn't be flattered by the sort of sacrifice Lady Wildmoore had made?

The sun it called to see her face, but shadows she commanded.

So, too, was the Muse flattered by the lengths Sofi went to create. Certainly without her many years of suffering, she would have been unable to compose lengthy songs so deftly, finding rhythm in the crunch of her snowshoes, the flutter of Lara's eyelashes, the whisper of the wind.

Oh, lady, why are you so sure the sacrifice is golden? The colors fade, but he remains beloved and beholden.

"Stop." Sofi flung out a hand and caught an unsuspecting Lara in the gut.

"What the—" She gasped desperately for air while Sofi grimaced guiltily.

"Sorry, but there's a log." She pointed across the road to a felled tree, its light bark dappled with gray.

Lara shook her head uncomprehendingly. "So?"

"So it's the perfect place to learn a song. Come on." Sofi darted across the road, wooden snowshoes slapping the ground packed hard as stone. She cleared a space to sit and settled her lute case in her lap, running a hand fondly across the top of the fraying leather.

Lara took her time getting there. "Sofi," she said, when she reached the tree trunk, "it's freezing. My fingers will fumble."

"Exactly." Sofi's eyes were bright. "If you can play the song in these conditions, imagine what you'll be able to do in a tavern beside the fire."

"That makes no sense." Lara planted her hands on her hips. "I can't play at all with frostbite."

Sofi rolled her eyes as she pulled her lute from its case. She wouldn't keep them out in the snow for long for fear the moisture would warp her lute's wood further and the chilly air would cause a string to snap. But she wanted to give Lara the thrill of pushing through the discomfort. The power that came from existing beyond limitation.

"The days they passed as thread it spools from weavers to their spindles," Sofi sang, her voice soft amid the world blanketed in snow. She tapped into the feeling she'd had in Trogg, the freedom she'd felt without the wall, allowing the flutter in her chest to take wing. Her words hit the air like puffs of smoke from a chimney, warmth radiating from the source. *"And she would mourn those thoughts unt'ward, as daylight surely dwindles."*

A cloud rolled in front of the sun, bathing them in shadows as the light dusting of snow turned into thick, sticky flakes. Sofi sang the longing and the woes of Lady Wildmoore, the woman's suffering sitting sweetly on her tongue. Lara, who had started her listening with skepticism, moved closer to Sofi on the tree's trunk as the song continued, her eyes wide.

"Well?" Sofi asked once she had reached the end, flexing her fingers, which had started to cramp from the cold.

"Saints, Sofi." Lara clutched her heart, looking pained. "How did you do that? You made me *feel* her suffering. Her fear and uncertainty and longing." Lara got to her feet and shook out her hands as though they'd fallen asleep. Then she stopped and stared at Sofi. "Wait, is that how you feel *all the time?* Like your heart is broken and you're hanging by a thread?"

"I . . ." Sofi stopped, flummoxed. "Is that . . . not how you feel?"

Lara looked at her incredulously. "Not *all the time.*"

It was Sofi's turn to look incredulous. "No wonder you can't compose, then." Each day of suffering served its own purpose. Each day peeled back her layers, cured her skin the way Marie preserved their meat, ensuring Sofi stayed impenetrable. Without the feeling, the praying, the longing, she would never have been able to create and compose so quickly.

"That's . . ." Lara looked unbearably sad. "Sofi, that's not what makes you a good songwriter. You don't have to suffer in order to create."

"Of course I do." Lara was so ignorant of the true process of a Musik that it was almost laughable.

"*No.*" Lara's voice was hard in a way Sofi had never heard from her. It took a moment to realize that the endlessly patient girl was *angry.* "Earlier I thought maybe it was just a one-off thing, and I worried it wasn't my place to say anything. But now . . ." She ran a hand through her hair, which glinted in the weak sunlight. "Your father encouraged you to do punishing, vile things to yourself. He made you believe that standing barefoot in the snow would make you a better musician." Her eyes flitted to Sofi's feet, now carefully encased in socks and boots and snowshoes. "Sofi, that isn't training. . . . That's abuse."

"He was just pushing me to be the best," Sofi replied automatically. "To ensure the Muse found me worthy. It was the only way to overcome my instincts. The only way to . . . to become a Musik."

The words hung awkwardly between them, wide as a ravine.

"Well, clearly that wasn't the case." Lara's voice was soft, as though the truth spoken quietly would dull its edges.

"Maybe I just didn't do enough," Sofi mumbled, fidgeting with her mittens.

Lara looked like she was going to cry. She sank back onto the log next to Sofi, staring out at the road rather than at Sofi herself. "Sofi, you don't have to hurt yourself to be worthy of pursuing your dream. You don't have to deny pieces of yourself in order to be good. Your songs are never better than when you let yourself go. You're a different girl when you offer yourself the freedom to merely play. No grimaces, no frostbitten toes. Just your love for the music."

"Can we not talk about this right now?" Sofi could barely hear herself. It was hard to listen to Lara, who didn't know what she was talking about. It was terrifying to hope that maybe she was right. Maybe Sofi *didn't* have to hurt. Maybe she could be enough as the person she was rather than the person she kept forcing herself to be.

She pinched the soft skin of her wrist. That was the sort of hope she was supposed to ask the Muse to forgive. It was proof of her uncertainty. Evidence of her insubordination. Thoughts like those were the entire reason Frederik had created her routine of suffering. To prevent his daughter's resolve from being infiltrated by weaker people—people like Lara, who resorted to magic rather than hard work.

Art was about discipline. It was about commitment. It was about devotion.

If that wasn't true, then Sofi didn't know what was.

TWELVE

THE CITY of Skaal was best known for its cathedral, but it was a tavern Sofi headed for instead.

The church's stained-glass windows depicting Saint Edritch and the Beast were the subject of many a pilgrimage. The first panel showed the white-furred monster's snarling snout and the frightened, cowering children. The second depicted Edritch playing the tune on his flute that soothed the Beast and saved the babes. But Sofi wasn't interested in the artistic interpretation of music. She was here for the real thing.

"An hour of music for room and board." Sofi leaned her elbows on the long mahogany bar as she negotiated with the owner of the Beast's Belly. While King Jovan had alerted the tavern owners to Lara's arrival, he had failed to outline any performance stipulations. If there was anything Sofi had learned from her father, it was the necessity of ideal playing conditions.

She was grateful to have something to focus on that had nothing to do with her routine or the squirming, squishy feeling sloshing in her stomach.

"Two hours." The innkeeper picked up a rag to polish an already spotless bottle.

"Ninety minutes, and she gets to drink all the honey wine she wishes." Sofi jerked her head at Lara, who was lingering uncertainly behind as negotiations took place.

The barman squinted at Lara. "Honey wine, eh?" He placed the bottle back in its place with a soft clink. "I'll allow it." His eyes slid back to Sofi. "You have to pay for your own drinks, though."

Sofi snorted but offered her hand. "Deal."

"Very good." The man clasped Sofi's hand tightly. "It's been ages since we had a proper Musik in these parts."

"Six years?"

The barkeeper frowned. "How'd you know that?"

Sofi grinned. "Because I was there."

She had been ten years old the last time a Musik had performed in Skaal. On the pulpit of the famous cathedral, Raffe had put on a show that sounded like the saints themselves sending thunder down to earth. Raffe's percussion created music from rhythm and math and sparked in Sofi the understanding of how *personal* music could be. Sofi couldn't create the sort of sounds Raffe could, but of course that made it all the more alluring to find her own voice.

"People will be very pleased you're here, Musik Hollis. They're tiring of the poet." He grumbled to himself. "I'll have to tell him he's got the night off."

"Yes," Sofi said, as Lara said, "Oh, I wouldn't want to put him out."

"Yes," Sofi repeated through clenched teeth, "you absolutely would."

Poets are like roaches on a wharf, Frederik Ollenholt used to say. *Plentiful, and just as useless.* Jakko had often regaled Sofi with his renditions of "poetry," which had mostly been him listing as many rhyming words as he could think of in a row.

"At least let him go on after me," Lara pleaded with the tavern's owner, her brown eyes wide and earnest.

"Well, you did only offer me an hour and a half." The bartender shot a look at Sofi. "I'll let him take the late slot."

Lara squealed delightedly. Sofi hung her head in her hands. "When he does the one about how his heart is 'as wide as the ocean and just as blue,' I'm blaming you."

"I don't know that one," Lara mused, slipping onto the barstool next to Sofi.

"Don't worry," Sofi exhaled loudly, "you will."

Sofi sat at the bar, watching excited patrons filter in, squeezing themselves onto the long wooden benches, ordering steaming bowls of root vegetable soup and chalices of mulled wine, the cinnamon and cloves sharp in Sofi's nose.

Lara had taken their things to the room on the second floor in order to freshen up, so Sofi was alone, observing. Listening.

Burning her tongue on too-hot tea. She studied the profile of a woman leaning against the bar. Sofi's heart skipped as the woman glanced to her right and revealed her face in full. Sofi's mother's image swam before her eyes—Delphine Lail in all her glory. But when Sofi blinked, the woman had turned back to the side, and her chin was too pointed, her nose too small. There was no resemblance there at all.

Wishful thinking, nothing more. A weakness, Sofi knew.

She took another sip of tea.

A hand clapped Sofi's shoulder. Her teacup clattered to its saucer as she turned, expecting to see Lara, but she found Raffe instead, a dusting of snow clinging to their eyebrows and their long dark hair, which was pulled back with a black ribbon. Sofi grinned broadly. She'd always had a fondness for Raffe, with their quiet, steady demeanor so diametrically opposed to their music, which bellowed and beat and howled.

"What are you doing here?" Sofi got to her feet to greet the Musik, who sported a dark vest, white shirt, and black cravat. Behind them was a person with broad shoulders and a shaved head who looked about two and twenty, dressed in well-worn traveling trousers and a long, structured wool coat.

"Cass and I are here to see Lara play." Raffe looked almost apologetic. "Have you met Cass? She's my Apprentice."

Sofi held out her hand. "Sofi Ollenholt." Cass's eyes widened at Sofi's last name, but only for a second, before taking Sofi's hand.

"Pleasure."

"All mine." Sofi wished she meant it—that they were

meeting under different circumstances: as equals.

Raffe took up the barstool next to Sofi, Cass claiming the one beside them. "I have to admit," the Musik said, "I'm a bit surprised you're traveling with Musik Hollis. All things considered."

Sofi chewed on her cheek, wondering how candid to be. "Lara needed guidance," she finally said. "As my father can no longer advise her, I felt that the responsibility belonged to me."

"That's incredibly big of you." Raffe raised their hand to get the attention of the bartender.

"Yes, well," Sofi grumbled, "that's me. Ever adaptable."

That got a smile out of Raffe. "I *am* very sorry for your loss," they said quietly.

"Which one?" Sofi searched for anything in Raffe's eyes that might give credence to her misgivings about Lara's talent. But like Yve, Raffe seemed oblivious to Sofi's suspicions.

They sighed heavily. "You know we had to do what was best for the Guild, Sofi."

"And *all* of you believed it was her?" It was undignified to fish for compliments, but Sofi didn't care. Surely at least *someone* had voted for her over Lara.

The barkeep tapped his ring on the bar, stealing the Musik's attention. Sofi scowled into her tea. She didn't want the answer anyway.

"Why the long face?" Lara's touch was a butterfly on Sofi's shoulder. She looked elegant in a long-sleeved white dress with a silky ruby-red cloak, its thick ribbon tied in a perfect bow beneath her chin.

"My tea's gone cold." Sofi dipped her pinkie finger into the dregs.

"We can fix that, silly."

As Lara waved for the barman, Raffe cleared their throat pointedly. Sofi went down the line making introductions, watching Musik and Apprentice light up in Lara's presence. Lara had that effect on people. Sofi herself felt it in the way her shoulders were no longer hunched. She was lighter, somehow, after Lara's teasing. The attention warmed her, like she had been standing in the sun. Or maybe it was just the hot water the barkeep poured atop her tea leaves.

At the innkeeper's signal, Lara knelt to release the bone lute from its case, then strode to the front of the room, settling herself before the fireplace. The flames reflected off her glossy cloak, making it appear to be threaded with gold.

"He loved the lady laid in wait," Lara sang without introduction, and the room hushed instantly, holding on to her every word. Sofi watched her from the stool, eyes narrowed. There was something about Lara she still did not understand. Sofi didn't know *how* Lara was able to captivate an audience so easily, how she could stand before the room as though she deserved their attention.

The longer Sofi watched her, Lara's fingers flying across the strings so easily it seemed almost impersonal, the more she realized that she had spent so much time on the road concerned with her own routine of suffering that she knew practically nothing at all about Lara. Sofi was no closer to uncovering proof of the magic Lara was using to appear so skilled.

"Her voice was soft and fresh as snow," Lara sang, plucking the lute's strings flirtatiously as she recounted the king at the foot of the tower, calling for his lady love to show her face. *"And then the king did surely know the love he'd always hoped would grow was waiting just above."*

Around the room, the listeners' faces were soft and far away, reliving their first loves. Partners clutched hands, their linked fingers resting on the tabletops. Heads were leaned on shoulders, soft whispers exchanged with the lover sitting beside them that left both pairs of eyes bright and shining. The room seemed smaller, cozy.

But Sofi was transported nowhere. She knew nothing of romantic love. Only of sacrifice.

"Oh, lady, why are you so sure the sacrifice is golden? The colors fade, but he remains beloved and beholden."

Lara stopped playing, her voice the only instrument as she reached the final verse. The room was silent, save for the fire. The waver of nerves present in her first performance was nowhere to be found. In fact, she teased the audience, holding words just long enough that they held their collective breath, waiting for the release of the final note.

Sofi took a sip of tea when Lara finished so that she wouldn't have to clap. The applause rang out regardless, proving once again that Lara only needed Sofi for one thing: the songs.

Beyond her inability to write, Lara appeared a Musik through and through. She had the bravado, the confidence, the understanding required to manipulate an audience. She was a natural—as though she had been performing for people all her life.

Sofi ran a finger around the rim of her teacup as she watched Lara's admirers push their way toward her. Lara beamed that wide, toothy smile that always made Sofi want to punch her. She was gracious and demure as she accepted compliments. She offered a laugh when necessary and a soft blush when warranted. She was *good* with people, had a casual way of touching a stranger's arm, of brushing away a lock of her hair carefully so they could see her interested expression. Sofi watched as the villagers of Skaal warmed to her—not only could she perform, but she was *kind*. It was another reason Sofi was so suspicious of her motives. Lara was the sort of person who could be anything she wanted. So why this? Why *music*?

Just then Lara looked past the woman with whom she spoke, and her gaze caught Sofi's. Sofi turned quickly back to her teacup, accidentally sloshing hot tea over her wrist. She swore, using a corner of her long skirt to sop up the mess. She was supposed to be endearing herself to Lara, not ogling her.

Lara crossed the room with ease. "I'm so glad you both are here tonight." She swung one arm around Raffe's shoulders and the other around Cass's, ignoring their attempted accolades. "Sofi and I need help settling a bet." Her eyes twinkled. "Was Lady Wildmoore's suffering romantic or pitiful?"

Raffe cocked their head. Cass sucked in a breath.

"Romantic," Raffe said, as Cass replied, "Pitiful."

Lara giggled delightedly. "Interesting," she laughed. "The old guard versus the new guard."

"Her suffering could have been prevented by going straight to King Oleg." Cass shrugged. "It seems silly to romanticize that in any way. She could have been happier sooner."

"Thank you," Lara said emphatically. "Musik Altrew, what say you?"

Raffe considered it. "I suppose I see it as a test in patience. A commitment of devotion, if you will. How can you know that what you want is what you want without reflection?"

"Exactly," Sofi insisted, grateful Raffe was on her side for this at least. "Without the time to reflect, how could she know if her *own* devotion was pure? Declarations of intent are easy. The follow-through, well . . ." Sofi shrugged. "That tends to be the difficult part."

"I don't know," Cass countered. "It all sort of feels moot. No one should really be that devoted to a king who slaughtered half a neighboring kingdom, anyway. History really does give us the worst stories to choose from."

They all drank to that.

"I liked your play on the ending, by the way," Sofi said to Lara as Raffe turned to whisper something to Cass. "The a cappella, I mean. It worked for the small room."

Lara grinned mischievously. "Sofi, are you saying . . . that sometimes just a voice *is* enough?"

Sofi scowled. "I walked right into that one, didn't I?" She still didn't agree, not fully. Without the lute's accompaniment throughout the rest of the song, the a cappella ending would have carried no weight. But it *was* the first time she had ever found value in a lone voice.

"Oh, don't sulk." Lara flipped her hair from her shoulder. "You can't have the high ground *all* the time. It'll get lonely up there."

Sofi made a noncommittal noise in the back of her throat. She didn't like how easily Lara was able to cut right to the heart of her.

Lara rolled her eyes. "Let me make it up to you. I'll get you a drink."

"I already have a drink." Sofi gestured to her half-drunk cup of tea.

"You are," Lara declared, swiping two glasses of honey wine from the tray of a passing serving girl, "absolutely no fun at all."

"What's fun?" Sofi asked. She had meant for it to sound tongue-in-cheek, but it came out a bit stilted.

"Exactly." Lara pushed one of the crystal glasses to Sofi. "Tea is bitter. Honey wine is sweet. Let yourself enjoy something, for saints' sake. Anything. I beg of you."

Sofi pursed her lips with annoyance, but after a glance at Lara's impatient expression, she lifted her glass. Lara clinked their goblets together, then took a sip. Sofi followed suit. The nectar-like liquid coated her tongue. It was sweet and smooth and impossibly delicious. It didn't serve her in any way, but it did delight her.

"See?" Lara's expression was triumphant. "You like it, don't you? It's the best thing you've ever tasted, isn't it?"

"It's . . . yes, it's good, okay? Are you happy?" She hated that Lara was right. Again.

Lara let out a laugh, bright as a sunrise. "Never happier."

"Looks like that might change," Sofi said darkly, nodding toward the man who was making his way to the front of the room. He was of middle age, his clothing artfully shabby, reflecting the populace's implied understanding that any good poet should look both haunted and worn.

Beside Sofi, Raffe groaned. "*Saints and sheep*, is that a *poet*?" Sofi nodded glumly. "That's my cue, then." They grimaced. "Musik Hollis, it was an absolute delight to hear you perform again. We'll see you soon at Castle Lochlear. Cass, are you coming?" Raffe turned to their Apprentice.

"I have never offered a single moment of my life to a poet," Cass said darkly, "and I certainly don't intend to start now."

They pressed coins to the bar and exchanged goodbyes. Then both Musik and Apprentice bolted for the door.

At the front of the room, the poet reached for his goblet of wine. Even from where she sat in the back, Sofi could see the words scrawled across his hands: *heartbreak, anguish, angst, rhyme*. He settled himself on a stool before the hearth, a shadow falling across half his face, making him look both serious and vaguely threatening.

"Good evening," he spoke, voice like wind whipping through bare branches. "I am but your humble servant. Thank you for your presence here tonight." He put a hand to his heart. "It is the honor of my life that you would give your time to a mere poet like myself."

Beside Sofi, Lara shifted in her seat. "Is he all right?"

"No." Sofi gestured toward the words scrawled across his hands. "He's heartbroken, anguished, and angsty."

Lara wrinkled her nose. "But . . . why?"

"It's for his *art*, Laravelle." Sofi pronounced the word as though it began with an "ah."

"Oh." Lara made a soft, thoughtful sound. "So he's suffering for it. Like you."

Sofi blanched. "That is *not* what's happening." Her father's training methods and the pithy, Paper-based feelings the poet before them winced through were not the same. Sofi did not need aid, magical or otherwise, to compose her songs.

"Right." Lara sounded unconvinced. "So his using a Paper to achieve these feelings is nothing like you calling for the Muse, shouting that you'd do anything to be worthy?"

"What are you talking about?" Sofi's voice was as harsh as the storm raging outside the inn's wide window. Her whole body had gone cold, her stomach clenched like a fist.

"Last night you were crying in your sleep." A faint blush crept up Lara's cheeks.

A lump formed in Sofi's throat. "It isn't the same," she insisted, but her words sounded hollow.

"Tonight," the poet continued, "I will perform without a page, will compose right before your eyes, allowing my feelings to guide me where they may. This, dear audience, is poetry at its finest and freest."

Sofi scowled into her honey wine. She was *not* the same as this poet. Her art came from within. Not from a manufactured feeling offered by a Paper that any person could feel—for the right price. Anger roared in her ears as the poet began to recite his first poem, clutching his chest as he spewed pretty words about a love lost.

Technically, his work was good, if wholly unoriginal. Every poet who played with Papers had limited subject matter to compose with. Heartbreak, agony, and anguish were three of the preferred feelings for Paper-casters. Yet a person could only rhyme the same words so many times before all the poems sounded the same.

Still, Sofi took the most offense not to the poet's work but to his performance. The emotions written across his hand and injected into his poems did not reach his eyes. There, Sofi saw no spark, no light. Just measured, careful calculation. Nothing like the way that Lara played, her face reflecting every word she sang, every hopeful flutter, every melancholy turn. A person could watch an entire performance in Lara's eyes alone.

"What's wrong with him?" Lara leaned in to whisper in Sofi's ear, her breath warm, her curls tickling Sofi's neck. Sofi shivered.

What isn't? she started to say, but then she saw what Lara meant.

The poet had gone silent, his mouth opening and closing like a dying fish. It was as though he had lost his ability to speak.

"He started a line, and then he just . . . stopped." Lara looked concerned. "Do you think he's ill?"

Sofi squinted at the poet. He did look worrisome. His

hands fiddled with the buttons on his vest. His *unmarked* hands.

"His Papers," Sofi whispered, elbowing Lara. "They've worn off."

Lara clutched Sofi's arm, fingers digging into her skin. "What do we do?"

"Nothing?" Sofi shook her head uncomprehendingly. "He didn't time his usage right. That's not our fault."

"Isn't it?" Lara looked genuinely pained. "I'm the reason his performance was bumped. He probably timed his Paper to his usual performance slot."

Sofi grunted. She was having difficulty feeling sympathy for the poet, who was rifling through his pockets for something to recite. "Why don't you offer to go up and finish the stanza for him."

Lara shot Sofi a sour look. "You know I'm useless at rhyming. Remember Sir Stanlon?"

Sofi snorted. "Okay, fine. Don't go up there. But finish the rhyme. Right here. What was the line?"

Lara closed her eyes. "Sow the seeds of love and let them fall," she recited. "My love for Rose will bloom . . ." She opened her eyes, looking at Sofi quizzically.

"Finish it," Sofi urged.

Lara frowned, a crease forming between her eyebrows. "Above them all?" she asked bashfully.

"In the fall," the poet finally managed, shaking his head slightly.

Lara looked disappointed.

"Yours was better," Sofi insisted.

Lara made a face. "You're just saying that."

"No," Sofi said solemnly. "I promise I am not."

At the front of the room, the poet took a deep, shuddering breath. "My lady's voice is sweeter than a Siren's song," he began, the words stilted, his expression queasy. "Her smile henceforth will tell me—"

"I belong," Lara whispered quickly, her breath hot on Sofi's ear.

"I belong." The poet finished the line with a self-satisfied smile.

Lara gave a tiny nod of recognition. Her face was serious, concentration radiating from her. Despite the show the poet was putting on, Sofi kept sneaking glances at Lara. She was so entirely different from anyone Sofi had ever known. Sofi's mother was a ghost. Her father a tense, punishing man. Marie was superstitious and careful. Jakko, erratic and trusting.

But Lara was soft and caring and clever, and she *felt* in a way Sofi had never managed to, even on a fourth day. She gave so much of herself in her performances, in her interactions, in the way she saw the world. For someone like Sofi, who had spent her life carefully guarding her talent, her music, and her heart, Lara was like a howling wind, disorienting and life-altering.

"Thee, I love," Lara whispered in Sofi's ear, and it sent a jolt of surprise, cold as sleet down the back of her neck. Sofi nearly upended her teacup.

"What?" she whispered sharply, just as the poet repeated the same three words.

Oh. It had only been a part of the game.

Of course.

Strange, then, the shiver Lara's words had sent through her. The way they tapped on a door in her head Sofi hadn't realized existed. She cleared her throat and took a too-big sip of honey wine, then coughed wildly as the golden liquid trickled down her windpipe. Lara clapped her on the back as Sofi struggled to breathe.

There was a frown on Lara's face. "Was that not what you expected?"

"No." Sofi's heart was hammering so wildly she was certain Lara could hear it. "I wasn't expecting that at all."

THIRTEEN

THE NEXT morning, before following the road to Rusham, Sofi and Lara took a moment to admire the famous stained-glass window of Skaal's great cathedral. The morning sun glittered off Saint Edritch's golden hair and highlighted the beady red eyes of the Beast. The saint's flute flashed brilliantly, sending black spots across Sofi's vision.

"Let's go," she grumbled, rubbing her eyes. Sofi disliked flautists in any of their forms. She hoped that she and Lara managed to avoid Tambor on this tour.

"I quite liked Raffe and Cass." The panels seemed to have offered Lara a similar line of thought. She adjusted the strap of her lute's case where it dug into her neck. "Who from the Guild haven't we met yet?" She grimaced, looking guilty.

"I should know this, shouldn't I? Saints, they're sure to hate me if I don't even know who they are."

"Oh, I wouldn't worry about that," Sofi said darkly. Lara was so effusive that even Therolious Ambor, the prickliest man in existence, could find something to like about her.

Lara frowned at her. "What does that mean?"

"That you're irritatingly good with people," Sofi said. "How *do* you manage to get people to like you so much?"

"I don't know." Lara cocked her head thoughtfully. "I suppose I'm just delightful." She flashed Sofi a wide smile that did not entirely reach her eyes.

Sofi shook her head. "That isn't it."

"Wow, thanks," Lara deadpanned.

Sofi frowned, trying to figure out how to explain herself. "No, I mean, you have this *effect* on people. It's like you literally enchant them. They laugh louder when you're near. They stand taller when you walk away. It's . . . almost like magic."

Sofi pinched her thigh sharply through the wool of her dress, angry to have played her hand so early. But Lara didn't so much as flinch at the edge in Sofi's voice.

"I mean this with the utmost politeness, Sofi," Lara huffed as they made their way up the deceptively steep road, "but it's called being friendly. Just because you don't understand something doesn't make it *magic*."

Sofi swatted her. "That isn't what I meant."

But, of course, it was. To Sofi, effortlessness and magic went hand in hand. There was no hard work associated with spilling a drop of blood to conjure fire—no gathering of wood or sparking of tinder or careful tending to a small flame.

So perhaps what she appreciated about her own training routine was how clear cut it was. Her musicianship was proportionally affected based on her actions and her level of practice. For someone to simply pick up a lute and be able to play it without a similarly structured routine made no sense—any steps that could not be measured were surely shortcuts. Anything that came to a person naturally must be magic.

As they passed acres of frozen farmland, icicles the size of tree branches hanging from the roofs of the barns, and high fences lined with barbed wire to keep away the wolves, Sofi began to wonder if her understanding of magic was, in fact, shortsighted.

"What sort of song are you writing for Rusham?" Lara wheezed as they stopped near a circle of boulders.

"Nothing yet," Sofi panted, letting her sack drop onto the packed, dirty snow. Sweat dripped down her back, freezing as a breeze blew past, leaving her with the decidedly uncomfortable feeling of being both overheated and frigid at the same time.

"Well, you probably should start," Lara said playfully as she broke off a piece of dried meat and handed it over to Sofi. The sun had started to move the morning into afternoon.

"Hmm." Sofi made a noncommittal noise as she worked the bite between her molars. She didn't know much about Rusham—it was far enough from Juuri that she'd never taken a day trip. She consulted her father's map, her finger snaking down the main road. At the approximate place where Sofi and

Lara stood, her father had scrawled the word "wasteland" in his spidery hand.

That, at least, was accurate.

Under the town of Rusham, her father had written: *no ballads*. Sofi frowned. She was used to writing ballads—they were the easiest way to eke out the allotted performance time. Singing songs of ages past was simple enough with good source material. But it would do her well to experiment in range. She only wondered *how*.

Sofi stewed in her uncertainty until the afternoon sun began to sink in the sky, Lara trailing behind her, face contorted in thought. Sofi could hear her whispering to herself, though the wind blew in the wrong direction to make out any of her words.

"What if—" Lara began several times, falling silent as soon as Sofi turned toward her.

"Lara," Sofi finally said, keeping her voice careful and patient as if Lara were a wild creature prone to startling, "would you like to help me write the song?"

"What?" Lara blinked wildly, looking truly flummoxed. "No, I couldn't. I'd only mess it up."

Sofi stared at her suspiciously.

"It's just, after last night when I finished the rhymes, I thought—I mean, I *hoped*—that I was improving. But now I'm not so sure." Her face twisted desperately. "I don't want to do it wrong."

Sofi's heart clenched without her permission. She often felt isolated, so concerned was she about her songs and the sanctity of her sound. But Lara was becoming just as serious. Just as focused on the integrity of the music she made. It made Sofi feel like a part of something. Like she and Lara were a true team.

"No one writes a perfect song the first time. Look," she continued, gesturing down the road at a small clump of trees. "Let's stop here for the night. We'll set up camp, I'll play, and we'll both compose. It'll be like the finish-the-rhyme game but better."

Sofi missed the feeling of a lute in her hand, the sureness and certainty that came from playing with no deadline, composing without pressure or fear. Tonight she would play to her heart's content. They were alone in the wilderness, with only the stars and birds and trees to witness her art.

"Wait." There was a note of panic in Lara's voice. "Did you say 'camp'?"

"Yes." Sofi chuckled softly, grateful her father had bothered to teach her basic survival skills. "I did."

Once Lara moved past the initial shock of having to sleep outdoors, they managed to set up camp rather quickly. Sofi instructed Lara to gather firewood while she pulled the tarp from the bottom of her bag and set to work building a lean-to beneath the shelter of a thick fir tree. It wasn't glamorous, but it would keep the worst of the weather off them while they slept. Luckily, the wind had died down, and once Sofi had lit a match, she was able to coax the tinder into a merry flame. She then dragged a thick log over to rest before the fire so they wouldn't have to sit in the snow.

"I'm never getting up again," Sofi declared, flinging herself onto the log. "My body was not intended for physical labor." She held her hands out toward the fire. Her arms shook with the effort.

Lara looked up from where she was putting together a makeshift dinner of stale bread and scraps of jerky. "If I never have to eat dried meat again, it will be too soon."

"The trials of the victory tour," Sofi muttered, searching for her lute case, which she found leaning up against a tree. She groaned, pushing herself to her feet so she could collect it.

"I thought you said you were never getting up again." Lara sounded amused.

"I would do anything for my lute." Sofi didn't care if it sounded silly. Her lute was the one true constant in her life, the only thing that had ever offered her mutual respect and understanding. If she cared for it—polished its wood, changed its strings, stored it carefully—it responded to her every ask, releasing the melodies she coaxed from it, offering structured support beneath her fingers.

Sofi's lute gave her purpose. Holding it felt like home.

She settled herself on the log again, pulled the instrument from its case, and cradled it gently in her arms, brushing her fingers across the strings, letting the notes settle in her chest.

Lara watched her from across the fire. "You make the lute look as though it's a part of you."

"It is."

"There's trust there," Lara continued, her voice soft.

Sofi considered the other girl. "Do you trust *your* lute?"

Lara let out a long breath. "I do, actually," she said softly. "So much that it sometimes frightens me. It's so *powerful*."

A thrill ran up Sofi's spine. This was it. She settled her lute carefully on her lap and kept her eyes on Lara. Watching. Waiting. Urging her to finally reveal the truth behind her success.

"When Willem proposed, it felt like my life was over. I was going to lose my autonomy. Made into a wife and mother because it benefited my father. I had given up hope of ever loving anything. And then I heard your father *play*." Lara inhaled a great shuddering breath. "That night, a fire lit within me, and I knew I had to be a part of that music."

Sofi had unconsciously leaned forward on the log as she listened. But instead of her stomach clenching with excitement, her chest tightened with understanding. She knew exactly the feeling that Lara spoke of. That desperate, aching *need*.

"At the audition, when I realized I had to actually play the lute, I thought I was going to be sick." Lara cleared her throat. "Here, suddenly, was my chance to be a part of something I could truly *love*, and it was going to be taken away as soon as it appeared because I couldn't deliver the necessary performance."

Sofi nodded carefully, steeling herself for the confession that was sure to come. Lara had been backed into a corner. It was no surprise she would use magic to hold on to the life she wanted.

"But then, when I first brushed my fingers across the strings, it was like . . ." Lara glanced up at a crow swooping low in the sky. "This is going to sound stupid, but it felt like coming home."

Sofi's eyes burned with unexpected tears. "That doesn't sound stupid," she whispered. It was exactly the same way holding her own lute had always made her feel.

"I stood there, just *feeling*, and I didn't want to let go, didn't want to lose that, especially not in front of your father and the Guild. And then it was like my fingers just . . . knew what to do." Lara cleared her throat. "Do you believe in magic, Sofi?" She looked up, her eyes boring through to Sofi's soul, as though she could see the suspicion buried deep inside her. "Not Papers anyone can buy, but real, pure, deep magic? It was like my prayers were answered. I begged the saints to help me, and then my fingers flew, and I still can't explain it." She ran a hand through her hair. "And I'm so scared that one day it's going to disappear. I don't know what I'd do then. Where I'd go. Who I'd *be* without music."

Sofi wasn't certain what to say to that. It was far too close to the way she herself had been reckoning with her identity after the loss of the title of Apprentice. She refused to reopen that wound in the middle of the woods, and certainly not in front of Laravelle Hollis. So instead of responding, Sofi picked up her lute and struck a chord, merry and light. It was the high, bright sound of the sun rolling out from behind a cloud. What she imagined it might feel like to catch the first whiff of spring in the air.

Lara smiled softly. "That sounds so happy."

"Exactly." Sofi's chest loosened as Lara's expression

returned to its usual cheeriness. "Let's write something joyful for once. No longing, no . . ." Sofi trailed off, unable to make the word "suffering" fall from her tongue. She wasn't ready to give that piece up just yet. She shook her head. "Happy, I mean. We'll write something happy. Together." She patted the empty space next to her. "Let's get started."

Lara settled in beside her, kicking her feet out so the soles of her boots were dangerously close to the fire. She hummed a countermelody as Sofi plucked the strings softly, sending tiny sparks of sound shivering down Sofi's spine. She had always considered songwriting a solitary activity—words scrawled clandestinely on paper in the darkest hours of the night, melodies that folded themselves around her brain, the rhythm building inside her until it begged to be released. She had never trusted even Jakko enough to share her words before they were polished to perfection. Or perhaps, Sofi now realized, it was that she hadn't trusted *herself* enough.

But collaborating with Lara changed that. Instead of questioning every line, Lara reacted, either with glee or with a careful grimace to indicate when Sofi could do better. If her melody faltered, Lara was there to pick it up, summoning notes Sofi wouldn't have thought to include, creating a call and response like birds singing to one another in the early hours of morning. Gone was the quiet fear Lara had held before. Now she was open and free, and that made Sofi want to open just as wide. Writing with Lara did not take the act of creation away from Sofi. If anything, it drew Sofi in even closer. Together they shared themselves with the song and were better for it.

"*And tell me where the lilies lie,*" Sofi sang, glancing at Lara in her peripheral vision, "*down by the river or our corner of the sky?*"

Lara gasped delightedly, putting a hand on Sofi's arm. "Is that a reference to *me*? I've never been in a song before."

"It's a reference to the moment I knew I hated you." Sofi laughed.

"Did you really hate me?" Lara wasn't smiling anymore.

"Of course I did," Sofi answered matter-of-factly. "You stroll up to an audition without a lute, and the first time you put a hand on the instrument, it sings almost as beautifully as you?" She shook her head. "I *hated* you."

"And now?" Lara's voice was higher pitched than usual. It set Sofi's heart racing, made the place where Lara's hand was still resting on her arm burn like the lick of hot coals.

"And now it's your turn to compose," Sofi said quickly, readjusting herself so Lara's hand fell away. The bone lute still sat in its case on the other side of the fire, so Sofi offered Lara her wooden lute. Lara took it, frowning.

"Your lute feels different than mine. Lighter? Or heavier? I'm not sure." She held it awkwardly, almost uncertainly.

"No need to rub it in that your instrument is finer," Sofi said darkly, kneeling in front of Lara and adjusting her lute in the other girl's grip, tucking it in the crook of her arm. Then she reached for Lara's hand, placing her fingers on the strings where Sofi's own had rested only moments before. The brush of their fingers made Sofi shiver. She was close enough to notice the goose bumps that had cropped up on a sliver of skin that lay exposed beneath Lara's furs, right along the line of her collarbone.

"Empty," Lara finally exclaimed, as she struck a string, which buzzed unhappily. "Your lute feels empty."

Sofi raised an eyebrow at her. "That makes no sense."

Lara shrugged. "It's what I feel. Can I just use my lute?"

Sofi rolled her eyes but got to her feet to fetch the bone lute. When she returned to the log, she ran her fingers up and down its neck in a quick arpeggio. She hissed, the bone lute's strings ringing in her ear with a high-pitched hum reminiscent of the snow gnats that liked to bite at fingers and toes. Again, there was an aching in her teeth, the same uncomfortable clanging in her chest as the last time she'd touched the bone lute back in her father's study. At the time, she'd thought it was her grief. Now she was less sure.

"Here." She shoved the lute at Lara. "I don't know why you're badmouthing my lute when there's something weird about yours, too." Maybe the strings needed to be changed.

Sofi settled her wooden lute in her lap, grateful for the way her body stayed silent when she played. *"When spring did fall from winter's lips, the flowers burst from fingertips, pushing through the snow,"* she sang, picking up the line where they'd left off. She leaned into the hope of the lyric, the comfort of her lute nestled close, the soft crackle of the fire, and the warmth of Lara beside her.

"Oh!" Lara exclaimed.

Sofi looked up, frowning. The line hadn't been *that* good. But Lara wasn't looking at her. She was pointing a few feet away, where, impossibly, a flower unfurled like the bell of a trumpet up through the snow. Its petals were white with the faintest blush of pink, its stem greener even than pine needles.

"Is that . . . ?"

"A lily?" Lara finished for her.

Both girls stared incredulously at the single, perfect bloom stuck in the snow.

"What in the name of Saint Eru's sword?" Lara whispered.

That a flower had bloomed just as in the lyric was unnerving. Perhaps Lara had been lulled into a false sense of security and the magic she carried finally bubbled to the surface. "Did you do that?" Sofi tried to sound casual.

Lara turned to her, frowning. "Me? How would I have done that?"

"I don't know," Sofi said coolly. "Magic?"

Lara laughed derisively. "You made me leave behind all my Papers."

Sofi rolled her eyes. "I don't mean Papers. I mean real magic. *Witch* magic."

"What?" Lara's eyebrows practically disappeared into her hairline. "Sofi, do you think I'm a *witch*?"

Sofi scoured Lara for any telltale signs of fear or anxiety. If she had a secret that large to protect, surely she would be more defensive. But there was no anger in Lara's voice, only confusion.

"No?" Sofi forced a laugh, as though that hadn't been exactly what she'd been accusing Lara of. "Of course not. I was just taken by surprise, that's all."

"Right." Lara smiled shakily at Sofi, her eyes flitting back to the lily that had burst forth from the snow. "It's just a coincidence, I'm sure."

"Mm." Sofi made a quiet noise as she stared down at the flower. There was magic at play here. The lily offered her the clear, indisputable proof she'd been searching for.

Now she just needed to find a way to make Lara admit it.

Thanks to a poor night's sleep and an early start, they made it to Rusham before lunchtime, a kind-eyed local pointing them in the direction of the Fair Fellows. There Sofi managed to convince the innkeeper to agree to a two-hour set—the exact length of their newly composed "Song of Spring"—in exchange for two rooms. After three nights on the ground, Sofi needed a mattress.

They spent most of the day napping—the wilderness had echoed with too many unidentifiable noises for a restful slumber the night before. While Sofi had been huddled next to Lara, she'd found herself desperate for her own bed in a quiet room, away from the tension and closeness and awareness of her body pressed against Lara's. But now that she was alone, she found herself missing Lara's warmth and the comforting sound of her tiny snores.

When the sun began to slip down in the afternoon sky, there was a knock on Sofi's door. Before she could shout, "Come in," Lara had entered, looking infuriatingly refreshed. Sofi hadn't even had a chance to change. She sat up quickly.

"Did I wake you?" Lara flopped onto the edge of Sofi's

bed. "The sun is starting to set, and I want to run through the song once more." She yawned widely.

"Where's your lute?"

Lara laughed. "Still in my room. I didn't even think to bring it. Clearly I'm still waking up." She slapped herself lightly on her cheek. "Can I just borrow yours?"

Sofi hoisted her lute's case up and onto the bed between them. She pulled out her instrument and automatically tucked it into the crook of her arm. She tested the strings, tweaking the pegs until it was perfectly in tune. Then she handed it over to Lara.

"Now remember, there's that turn from the fourth verse to the chorus that repeats again after verse sixteen," Sofi said, settling back into her role as songwriter and conductor. "And don't forget that the seventh line in the bridge is '*it headed back from whence it came,*' not '*it went on back from where it came.*'"

Lara snorted. "Of course. We wouldn't want to horrify our audience with such a ghastly mistake."

Sofi rolled her eyes fondly. With Lara sitting beside her on the bed, she found herself thinking again about the poet in Skaal. His artificial talent had radiated about him like cheap cologne. But Lara's performances were subtle and sophisticated. Perhaps Sofi was wrong and there was no magic there at all. Perhaps Lara had been telling the truth that her talent was a miracle granted by the saints. As for the flower that had burst forth from the snow, well, there was surely some logical explanation there, too.

Sofi crossed her arms, drumming her fingers on the soft

skin above her elbows. A miracle was just as disappointing as magic. Either way, it proved that hard work did not always triumph the way her father had once insisted.

She glanced over at Lara, who had not yet begun the song. "What are you waiting for?" she asked, frowning as she took in Lara's look of consternation.

"I can't . . ." She worried her lower lip beneath her front teeth. "I don't remember how it starts." She scrubbed a hand over her face. "I only slept a bit. I don't know why my brain feels so fuzzy."

"The fingerpicking starts on the A string, fifth fret." Sofi sank onto her back. She was exhausted too. She closed her eyes, waiting for Lara to begin, but the room remained silent.

"The . . . A string?" Lara finally asked, her voice tiny. "That's the . . . fourth course?"

"The third." Sofi's eyes fluttered open. Usually Lara hardly had to breathe and her fingers fluttered perfectly across the strings. "What's the matter with you?" She pushed herself up again. "Did you forget to cast your secret talent spell?"

Lara's expression darkened. "I don't know how many times I have to tell you this," she snapped, "but I am *not* a witch. Frankly, it's very insulting that you can't seem to fathom a world where I'm actually a good musician."

She was right. Sofi couldn't. Not after all the years of her father's instruction, his rigid rules, and his insistence on suffering. Not after Sofi's sleepless nights practicing her playing, honing her words, calling out to the Muse. Lara's talent still did not make sense.

"I played it perfectly on *my* lute before I went to sleep," Lara continued. "I suppose I'm still waking up." She shrugged as she returned Sofi's instrument to its case. "That, or there's something wrong with your lute, like I said last night." She got to her feet. "I'm going to go splash some water on my face. I'll see you out there."

Lara left the room, but Sofi didn't move. *There's something wrong with your lute.*

Empty, Lara had called it the night before, as though Sofi's lute was lacking something that the bone lute held.

But when Sofi touched the bone lute, it made her physically ache, almost like the way Jakko's face would swell when he ate hazelnuts. His body offered proof that identified the unwelcome substance, his allergic reaction a protection of sorts.

The only thing unwelcome in Sofi's life was magic. She'd prayed daily for the Muse to protect her from its effects. To keep her clean. Surely, then, it would stand to reason that if Sofi ever encountered real magic, the Muse would offer her a sign.

Perhaps that ache in her teeth, the roiling of her stomach, was the Muse telling Sofi that there was something in the bone lute that she needed to be wary of.

Something that would cause a girl who had never played the lute before to possess technical skill that rivaled a lutenist who had been studying her entire life. Something that imbued a person with an inherent understanding of strings and notes and theory, but only when they played that particular instrument.

Something like magic.

Blood rushed in Sofi's ears, a roaring that threatened to drown her. She had been right; there *was* magic involved in Lara's ascent to Musik. Only it wasn't coming from Lara.

The magic was in the lute.

FOURTEEN

SOFI HAD never seen her father play anything but the bone lute.

Once, when she was four, ear pressed against Frederik's study door, she'd heard the strings of an unfamiliar instrument—still a lute, but absent of the sureness of tone and crisp, clean notes she'd come to know so well from her father's hand. The melody that emerged was stilted and sloppy in a way Sofi had never known music to be.

The player hit a note just the slightest hair flat. On the other side of the door, Sofi frowned when her father didn't demand the student fix it. The player cleared their throat and began a quick arpeggio. But they faltered and the final note of the scale slipped, skittering onto a different course of strings. It was then that Frederik began to shout, his anger slinking through the keyhole and rooting itself in Sofi's chest. There was a thunderous crash, the sound of wood against wood, and the dull thunk of breaking. Sofi flung herself away from the door just in time.

She cowered behind a large armoire, heart thundering as her father stormed out of the study, his face pinched like he'd smelled something foul. When his footsteps had disappeared down the long hallway, Sofi peered into the study to see which student was the subject of his fury.

But there was no one there. Just a wooden lute, broken on the floor—the same lute that he would press into Sofi's hands the following week, the catalyst for the rigorous instruction that would inform the rest of his daughter's life. The next time Sofi saw her father play, nothing was amiss. Of course, then Frederik had been playing the bone lute.

In those early days, once Sofi had tired from playing endless scales, she would run a finger across the crack in the wooden instrument's neck, wondering what the lute had done to deserve her father's ire.

Now, Sofi realized, it was what the wooden lute *hadn't* done that had angered Frederik so.

Her eyes prickled with furious tears. She had never felt so betrayed. All her life she had followed her father's training methods so that one day her talent might equal his. But now, if her father *had* no talent, what did that mean for the one truth upon which she had based her entire life?

The floor beneath her wavered as though she were skittering across a frozen pond. Perhaps she was wrong. Maybe

Lara had simply been half asleep. It was possible that when she played "The Song of Spring" for the crowd in the tavern below, her fingers would stumble, or she would forget which course her fourth finger began on. Something to reassure Sofi that the bone lute, too, was fallible.

Sofi made her way into the inn's main room and sank heavily onto the corner of a bench, her stomach sloshing with trepidation.

Lara stood at the front of the room, dressed in her gown of forest green. She tucked a strand of white-blond hair behind her ear, her brown eyes catching Sofi's. She smiled. Winked. Plucked the opening notes of "The Song of Spring" almost without thinking.

Sofi's heart sank. The instrument bent to Lara's every whim. Now that Sofi knew what to look for, it was easy enough to see the ways that Lara fumbled—but instead of dissonance, the lute responded with the correct notes anyway, almost as though playing the bone lute was solely about intention rather than execution.

Sofi had spent so much time buried in sheet music that she had not bothered to track the movements of Frederik's fingers when he played. She had simply assumed that they would follow the patterns she had committed to memory. Her father's transcription of his songs had always been impeccable. But his playing, Sofi now knew, never was.

It all made sense—the rounds of drinks he plied his listeners with when he performed in such close proximity. *Enough to take the edge off,* Frederik had said, *to make the listeners more amenable to my tunes.* But it had been to blur their attention, to distract from the way his fingers might falter even as the music did not. Frederik had explained away his reluctance for tavern performances by claiming he preferred the acoustics of large theaters. But now it was clear he had preferred the *distance.*

A wave of nausea tickled the back of her throat. The tenderness with which Lara handled the bone lute now felt like a farce. What was worse, Lara seemed to truly appreciate music and found reverence in her role as a Musik. What would happen were she to find out that the miracle she had prayed for was not a miracle at all, but deception?

"That was great, right?" Lara slid excitedly into the seat across from Sofi, who hadn't realized the performance was over. "Clearly the water helped. I didn't mess up once!"

On the table between them sat the lute, its cold, white bone glinting merrily in the firelight. Absentmindedly, Sofi brushed her fingers across the strings. The sound sent a shiver down her spine, a tense, creeping ache in her teeth, even as the notes rang out perfectly and pure. It was far less impressive now that she knew the sweetness of the lute's tone came not from mastery but from *magic.*

"Yes," Sofi answered hollowly. "Great."

"You okay?" Lara asked softly. It was the softness that put Sofi on high alert. She was used to hard people with sharp tongues and endless demands. She was less familiar with kindness. Now that she'd had a taste, she wanted to preserve it. Wanted to protect Lara's vulnerable, earnest nature. Sofi did not want to be the one to dim the joy in Lara's wide eyes, to extinguish her perfect smile.

"I'm fine," Sofi lied. "Just tired, I guess."

Sofi did not often waste time wishing for things outside her control. She tried to focus instead on achievable, attainable possibilities. But at that moment, perched glumly on a bench in a tavern in Rusham with everything she had ever known in pieces at her feet, Sofi found herself wishing Jakko were there.

The timing of Jakko's departure had been suspicious, leaving just before the audition he had been preparing his entire life for. Sofi had pushed her concerns away, believing Jakko had embraced his weakness, choosing to flee rather than fail.

But if Frederik had lied about his instrument, what else might he have lied about? He might have even been the reason for Jakko's disappearance, wanting to ensure that the secret of the bone lute was carefully preserved and passed down through the family.

It was possible that her father had never even respected Sofi's ability as a lutenist. Perhaps instead Frederik had only ever viewed her prowess as a way to protect himself. It made sense, then, why he found ways to hurt her. To keep her under his thumb.

He could not afford to lose her.

"Sofi?" Lara looked concerned.

"Don't worry." Sofi patted her hand reassuringly.

But Lara had plenty of reason to worry. With the Council of Regents so close to reopening the Gate, Aell could not afford for magic to be associated with the Guild of Musiks. And Sofi had no way to prove that it had been Frederik who had put magic in the lute. In an attempt to protect themselves, the Guild might turn the blame on Lara.

But Laravelle Hollis had not tricked or magicked her way into the title. She had stumbled and fallen headfirst into a trap. The moment her hand had closed around the neck of the bone lute at the Apprentice audition, Lara's fate had been sealed. There was nothing Frederik could have done to stop Lara from being selected without admitting the truth about his instrument.

Lara had not asked for any of this, and Sofi would not stand to watch Lara's life destroyed over a crime she hadn't committed. No, before they reached the King's City, Sofi had to find a way to clear Lara's name. She let out a deep, shuddering sigh.

I hope you can forgive me, Frederik Ollenholt had written to his daughter just before he died. Once Sofi had wondered what he'd meant. Now she wished that she had never learned what it was her father needed forgiveness for.

Sofi slept fitfully and dreamed even worse. Her father was there, towering over her. Her tongue would not move, her voice did not work, but still he demanded she play the bone lute. He used a spare string to slap the backs of her hands, cutting bright red welts across her skin. In the corner Jakko stood, mouth frozen shut, his eyes wide as he watched her helplessly.

Then, just as Sofi managed to find her footing, to follow

the melody her father had set for her, the strings began to snap. Each course broke, taking one of Sofi's fingers with it.

Snap, went the first course, taking her pointer finger. Though Sofi tried to call out, her tongue was numb, her lips clamped closed.

Snap, went the second course, taking her middle finger. Frederik stared down at her.

"Play," he demanded.

Dread worked its way through her, but in the end, as she always did, Sofi obeyed, the melody staccato and faltering as she tried to play with her remaining fingers.

Snap, went the third course, and with it, her ring finger fell to the floor. Tears poured down her cheeks, blood splattered the white of the bone lute, but still her father conducted her, eyes amused.

It was not until the fourth course snapped and took Sofi's pinkie that Frederik clapped his hands.

"That's enough," he finally said, and it was only then that she woke, drenched in sweat, sunlight spilling through the curtains. Sofi dressed quickly, though her fingers fumbled with her skirt's buttons. The dread from the dream had not lifted, as though the Muse were punishing her for having all but abandoned her routine of suffering. It had seemed so real that for a moment guilt churned in Sofi's gut at the thought of how furious her father would be were he still alive.

But then she remembered how angry she was at her father, too.

When Sofi emerged from her room, Lara was closing the

door of the one opposite. "Morning," she said brightly. "Are you feeling better today?" Her eyes swept across Sofi's face, her smile faltering slightly at the mess Sofi had made with her braid.

Sofi chewed on her bottom lip. "So-so."

A soft sound caught in the back of Lara's throat—a failed attempt to stifle a laugh. "Do you want me to fix your hair?"

"You don't have to."

But Lara had already pulled a hairbrush from the depths of her flowing yellow skirt. She motioned for Sofi to turn around and began to pull the brush through her thicket of hair, never once sighing as the bristles caught on knots. Her motions were patient and rhythmic, soothing Sofi the way a lullaby might. Sofi's left hand began to conduct a careful concerto, her wrist and fingers sweeping back and forth against the wool of her skirt.

The brush paused at the base of her skull. "Are you all right?"

"I'm fine." Sofi dropped her hand, embarrassed. The concerto quieted.

"Done." Lara offered her the reverse side of the hairbrush, which was a mirror. Sofi put a hand to her head, admiring the way Lara had tamed her tangles, her curls now effortlessly twisted into a perfect plait. "That's better."

"Yes, it is," Sofi admitted, offering the brush back to Lara. "Thank you."

"Don't mention it." Lara smiled. "Sometimes it's nice to take a moment to be kind to yourself in little ways."

Sofi narrowed her eyebrows. "Are you saying I'm not kind to myself?"

Lara let out an unrestrained cackle. "That," she said, pressing a hand to her chest, "is the understatement of the century."

Sofi's heart fluttered like a feather ruffled in the breeze. "Why are *you* being kind to me?"

Lara looked taken aback. "Why *wouldn't* I be?"

"Because I haven't done anything to deserve it."

"You don't have to *earn* kindness, Sofi." Lara frowned. "But if you must know . . . you took this trip with me. You've composed beautiful songs for me. You've taught me things I never dreamed I could learn—the difference between a verse and a chorus? It's *not* a choir?" She laughed but sobered when Sofi didn't join in. "You've helped me, and I . . . I like you. Why wouldn't I be kind to you?"

Sofi's cheeks warmed. She busied herself with her bag, head down as she searched for her father's map. They were headed for Ohre, which Sofi knew was close to the village where Denna and her wife lived. If the Musik was going to attend a performance, surely it would be there. Even if Sofi didn't yet know how to clear Lara's name, she could test the waters with Denna. Ask the right questions. Prepare her case until it was ironclad.

They bade the owner of the Fair Fellows goodbye, strapped on their wooden snowshoes, and set off south toward Ohre. The landscape was littered with towering fir trees, capped, of course, in snow, ice clinging to the needles and tightly packed branches like diamonds dripping from the neck of a noble.

The fresh layer of snow was soft as spun sugar, their shoes sinking into the banks with quiet whooshes. Sofi was going to need a new pair of boots when the tour was through.

They walked all morning in companionable silence, Sofi spinning strands of songs in her head, although she was finding it increasingly difficult to focus on composing a song for a magic instrument. She began to wonder if she was even a good songwriter at all or if the audiences of Lara's performances were only showing their appreciation for the enchanted lute.

Her father had kept so many secrets. First her mother. Then his lute.

It was beginning to seem as though Sofi had never known Frederik Ollenholt at all.

Sofi and Lara paused to eat stale bread and scrape the remaining bits of cheese from the rind when the sun took its place in the afternoon sky. Sofi stepped into a thicket of trees to relieve herself, and when she had finished scrubbing her hands with clean snow, she looked up and saw a wooden sign-post, all but hidden behind drooping branches.

Curious, Sofi stomped over and shook away the boughs and layers of snow. The sign was rather tall, and she had to squint in order to make out the letters. There was an *L* and what she thought was an *I*.

Sofi shook the sign again, kicking at the base for good measure, and a chunk of ice fell away. Her heart skipped several beats.

The sign read LAIL.

LAIL, like the name scrawled on the back of the portrait of Sofi's mother. *Lail*, like the name of a family Sofi knew nothing about. Sofi scrambled for her father's map, unfurling it to see how she could have possibly missed a town thusly named.

The yellow parchment showed a stretch of road between Rusham and Ohre. Nothing else. No town called Lail. Not even any indication that there was anything other than snowbanks and fir trees.

But there was a sign right in front of her eyes.

"Lara," Sofi shrieked, sending a bird roosting in a tree flapping away excitedly. "Lara!"

Shoes slapped across fresh snow as Lara stumbled toward the sound of Sofi's voice. "What's the matter?" She panted, bent over double. "Are you all right?"

"Can you read that sign?" Sofi asked, her finger shaking as she pointed to the wooden signpost. She needed confirmation that she wasn't simply seeing things.

"So you're not hurt?" Lara huffed, looking rather put out.

"The sign, Lara," Sofi snapped, more sharply than she'd intended. "What does the sign say?"

"What sign?"

Sofi sighed heavily, struggling with the branches to better reveal the four letters.

Lara opened her mouth, then shut it again. "I have absolutely no idea what you're talking about. I don't see any sign."

Ice flooded Sofi's veins. She wasn't imagining it. It was *right* there. "Are you trying to be funny?" She wrapped a hand around the signpost and shook it.

Lara blinked at her, completely nonplussed.

"There's a sign." Sofi spoke through gritted teeth. "Right here. It says 'Lail.' How is it possible that you don't see it?"

Lara shrugged apologetically, looking truly dismayed. Then she yelped.

"What?" Sofi shouted.

"I see it." Lara had gone as white as the snow around them. A shaking finger pointed up at the sign. "Just like you said. *'Lail.'*"

Sofi nearly sank to the ground in relief. "You *can* see it?"

Lara rubbed her eyes. "It wasn't there a moment ago. And then it suddenly . . . appeared."

Sofi frowned. Lara seemed sincere. But it made her uneasy. There was enough that didn't make sense, an itch of uncertainty. A glimmer of magic, like the flower in the snow and the power of the bone lute.

For someone who had been trained to steer clear of magic, there was quite a lot of it in Sofi Ollenholt's life.

"Change of plans." Sofi stared down at the blank stretch of map where Lail should be. "We're going this way."

"But . . ." Lara glanced over her shoulder at the main road. "Are you sure?"

"Yes." Sofi hoisted her bag and her lute case higher on her shoulder as she turned toward Lail. She had never been so certain of anything in her life.

THE FOURTH DAY

When Sofi was seven, she snuck into the South Wing with her lute. She settled herself in the corner of her mother's closet, tucking herself carefully behind the wall of voluminous dresses. It was a fourth day, and so she was free to do as she pleased. She'd already bothered Marie while the housekeeper sliced jarred beets for their dinner. She'd sat for a spell in her father's silent study. She'd wandered through the empty hallways of the manor, missing the sounds of students tapping their feet in the parlor, waiting for their lesson to begin. But there were no students due to visit until her father returned from tour.

Normally, when she was lonely, Sofi would turn to the Muse. But she'd already spent her third day calling out to the Muse, exhausting her voice and bruising her knobby knees a dark purple from rocking back and forth on the floor of her closet. The dark, her father had said, made it easier to fully focus on her prayers.

Sofi recognized the irony of choosing to spend her fourth day in a closet too. This one, at least, was larger. She plucked the strings of her lute idly. She'd been studying some of her father's sheet music, hoping to try her own hand at composing long-form songs. What she'd written up to then had been fragments: a verse here, a chorus there.

But now that she was seven, it was time to take her art more seriously.

The subjects of her father's songs ranged from saints to monarchs to knights. Each one had a clear-cut story, told in her father's own voice. It was the reason why a Frederik Ollenholt epic was identifiable from its very first line. Sofi hoped that one day her own music begged that same level of recognition, held that same level of identity.

Sofi wanted her art to be known, but because it was not a second day, she buried that *wanting* and turned her attention toward her mother's dresses and their various styles. The idea of walking outside without heavy furs, donning a dress with short sleeves or a hemline that hit above the knee, was unfathomable to Sofi, who had lived her entire life in snow.

She wondered about seasons, the enigmatic weather she'd heard of only in stories or seen in paintings. Surely that could be a subject of a song?

Conjuring a memory of the mural on the ceiling of Saint Ogden's Theatre, Sofi plucked a rolling melody that sounded like grassy green hills, like flowers with petals that turned toward the sun.

"Where the summer's sun does shine," Sofi sang softly, tucking her tongue between her teeth as she considered her lyrics, *"there the fields of green you'll find. Gentle as a careful grin, the scent of petals on the wind."*

As she sang, her chest fluttered, her heart alive and bright with dreams of green the likes of which she'd only ever seen in paintings. She let that dream bubble up to the surface, allowed it to drive her fingers as they worked their way up and down the neck of her lute. The flowers printed on her mother's dresses seemed to sway in time with her tune. If Sofi closed her eyes, she could almost smell them—the bright, sweet hint of honey and pollen usually found only on the wrists of rich ladies using the Paper for *perfume*.

So entranced was Sofi by her song of summer that she did not hear the footsteps approaching. In fact, her father's presence was made known only once he had wrenched the hangers aside to reveal his daughter huddled in the corner of the closet, tongue again tucked between her teeth.

Sofi shrank against the wall, the song falling to pieces around her. The warmth she'd felt only seconds ago had all but vanished, sucked from the room as though a window had been opened to usher in winter's icy grip. The floral scent had faded. All that remained was the lingering essence of mothballs.

She expected her father to scream. To shout. After all, she was in the South Wing, a place he usually pretended did not exist. But he didn't make a sound. When Sofi looked up from where she had fixed her gaze on the floor, she was shocked to see tears in his eyes.

Never once in her seven years of life had she seen her father cry.

Too afraid to ask if she was the reason for his tears, Sofi said, "I thought you wouldn't be home for three more days?"

"Is that why you're hiding in here? Because you thought I wouldn't find out?" Her father did not blink the tears from his shining eyes, but he did raise an eyebrow.

"No, I . . ." She and her father did not talk much about their feelings. How could she explain that she felt comforted here, enveloped in her mother's dresses in a way she would never be enveloped by the woman's arms?

"It's all right," Frederik said and, to Sofi's shock, sank down onto the floor to sit beside his daughter. "Sometimes I come in here too."

"You do?" Sofi had never heard her father speak a word about her mother. Sometimes it felt as though Sofi had never had a mother at all.

"Oh yes," her father said, wrapping his large, calloused fingers around Sofi's. "I miss your mother. When I let myself feel it, sometimes it hurts so much it threatens to swallow me whole."

Sofi blinked uncomprehendingly. That was how *she* felt when she let herself dwell on the quiet of the house, on the lack of a mother, the absence of her father. To hear her feelings mirrored was proof that perhaps Sofi was not as alone as she had always believed.

Now tears welled in her eyes, too.

"We're so alike, aren't we, my girl?" Frederik mused, leaning his head back against the wall and staring up at the ceiling. Sofi's chest swelled with pride. All she had ever wanted was for her father to recognize their similarities. It was the reason she so readily followed his instructions, why she was so grateful that his skill as a lutenist had transferred to her, too.

Music made Sofi whole, but it also allowed her to be seen. She loved it because it gave her power she otherwise did not possess, offered an avenue for her words to matter in a way they couldn't on their own. But she also loved it for how it connected her to her father. Anchored her to the family name.

The only family she had.

"I don't want that for you," her father continued, and all the hope that had taken flight sank in her stomach like a stone. If Frederik didn't want to make his daughter in his image, what was the point of her training routine? Why was he constantly testing her agility and technique? Why did he bring her into the lessons of his other students to prove a point—that these students, all Sofi's seniors by several years, weren't working hard enough if a seven-year-old could show them up?

"You . . . don't?" The tears that had gathered in her eyes now tumbled down her cheeks.

"Oh, no, don't cry," her father said, offering her his handkerchief. "You misunderstand me."

Sofi looked up from the snot-smeared fabric. "I do?"

"I don't mean as a musician, of course not," he said, and the sour of her stomach stopped swishing. "I only mean your feelings. You *feel* so much, don't you?"

Sofi bunched the handkerchief up in her fist and nodded.

"When I walked into the closet, it smelled of honeysuckle and lilies—that was your mother's signature scent. Did you find a bottle of her perfume somewhere?"

"I didn't." Sofi clung to that small kernel of knowledge, an identifier she'd never before owned.

"I see." Frederik's expression had gone hard. He didn't look as though he felt much now. "Sofi, do you wonder why I don't often speak of your mother?" She nodded eagerly. "It's because

I have learned how to temper my feelings. To keep them from spilling over into my music, where they don't belong. To become a Musik, you must be in control at all times. I believe that it is time for you to learn to stay measured. Restrained." Her father reached a hand up, awkwardly tucking a strand of hair behind Sofi's ear.

"Your craft is progressing quite nicely," he continued, and Sofi glowed beneath his touch and his compliment. "Which is why I think you're ready to progress to your next level of training. How does that sound?"

Sofi eagerly agreed. She had expected to be punished by her father but instead was being rewarded.

"Very good." Frederik nodded. "You must take note of your feelings and bottle them up, opening them only on the designated day. You must inspect those feelings so that you are ready for anything and never taken by surprise. You must ensure that those feelings do not control you—instead, you will control them. Keep them carefully contained behind a wall of your own building. It will be difficult at first," he admitted, his voice wavering slightly, "just as it was for me. But I believe in you. I just need to know that you believe in you, too."

He looked at Sofi so hopefully that she could hardly answer quickly enough. "Yes," she breathed, "of course I do."

"That's my good girl," Frederik said, giving Sofi's hand another squeeze. "Yes. The fourth day is for feeling."

FIFTEEN

SOFI'S HEART pounded with anticipation as she strode forward, snowshoes slapping rhythmically against the ground. Her ears burned with cold, and her breath was sharp, as though she had chewed on a mint leaf. Her mind buzzed wildly the way it did when she drank oversteeped tea. The name on the sign had been her mother's. *My mother's name is on the sign.*

"What are we doing?" Lara was struggling to match Sofi's pace. "I thought they were expecting us in Ohre."

"There's something I need to do here." Sofi hitched her bag higher on her shoulder, the stiff leather folio that housed her mother's portrait digging into her back pointedly.

"In a town with a disappearing signpost?" Lara's nose wrinkled the way it did when she had more to say but didn't want to overstep. It would have been thoughtful if it weren't a very obvious tell.

Sofi pushed a tree branch aside, ushering Lara forward. A crow atop the tree cawed sharply, ruffling its feathers at the interruption to its roost.

Lara yelped, putting a hand to her heart. "This is beginning to feel a bit ominous. In the stories I used to read to my brothers, crows were witches' birds. Watcher crows, I think they called them."

Sofi's stomach fluttered nervously. First the sign, now the crows. Yet it wasn't as though Sofi and Lara had simply . . . stumbled upon a witch's hiding place, had they?

The Kingsguard had been searching for witches for the better part of sixteen years. King Jovan, desperate to end winter, knew he needed to find a witch with the power to bring forth the seasons. He had offered sainthood, had publicly called for help, but none had emerged from hiding. The Kingsguard, too, had been unsuccessful in their search.

Sofi tugged at a loose end of yarn on her mitten, slowly unraveling the knitting. "Witches are magic," she mused, trying to piece the puzzle together. If the magic in her father's bone lute left no visible trace, surely its magic was beyond that of the Papers. It was old magic, deep and complex. The kind of magic that belonged to witches.

"Well, yes." Lara looked flummoxed. "That is notoriously what they are known for." She put a hand on Sofi's arm. "Are you all right? You've gone a bit pale . . . even for you."

Sofi tried to shrug her off. "I'm fine."

"Sofi." It was the way Lara said her name, as though it had always belonged on her tongue. Like she had learned how to speak for the sole purpose of one day uttering those four letters.

Sofi stopped.

Lara swiped at a strand of hair stuck to the sweat on her forehead. "Tell me what we're doing here."

Sofi tugged on the mitten's yarn again, exposing the tip of her thumb to the frigid air, fighting with herself. She wasn't sure how much she could trust Laravelle Hollis, but she supposed she'd never know until she tried. "I never knew my mother," she finally admitted. "When my father died, he left me nothing but an empty apology and a portrait of her. On the back was a name—one I'd never been told: Delphine Lail."

Lara's eyes went wide. "Lail, like the sign?"

Sofi nodded. "Lail, like the sign."

"Oh." Lara dug the tip of a snowshoe deep into the snow. "Wow. That's . . . not a coincidence."

Sofi exhaled. Hearing Lara affirm her own suspicions, confirm the creeping trepidation and excitement that cut her heart like a sled runner through ice, made her feel steadier. Surer.

The same feelings she often begged the Muse for had been granted to her by the girl standing before her.

"I . . ." Sofi was still nervous, despite having sliced open her chest to share the most secret part of her with Lara. "I have to know."

Lara wrapped her fingers around Sofi's now-half-exposed

hand, blanketing her in the warmth of her own mitten. It might as well have been a fire the way it sent impossible heat racing through Sofi's blood.

"Of course you do," Lara said. "You've only just told me, and now *I* have to know. I can't imagine how *you* feel."

"Really?" Sofi stood stock-still, afraid that if she moved even a single step, Lara would let go. If she had been the Musik, pulled off course by someone chasing a ghost, she wasn't certain she would have been as understanding.

"Come on." Lara tugged Sofi forward.

While Lara moved gracefully through the trees, Sofi— distracted by the warmth of Lara's hand on hers—was less agile. A branch scraped at her left cheek, leaving a stinging streak behind. Snow seeped into her socks as she stumbled, and once, the cawing of a crow even made her scream.

Then, the trees began to thin. A soft breeze warmed the tip of Sofi's nose. Birds trilled and tweeted, the muted colors of their feathers giving way to vivid blues and reds. Beyond the copse of firs, Lara came to a stop. Sofi gasped.

Lail unfolded before them like a dream of better days. The sky was a ferocious, unbelievable blue. The sun was so bright Sofi had to squint. The ground was not the expected white of fresh snow or even the muddled gray of dirtied foot-steps. Rather, the ground was covered in green, razor-sharp grass the likes of which Sofi had only ever seen in paintings. It bent beneath her snowshoes and rippled softly in the same breeze that ruffled Sofi's hair.

Without the haze of heavy clouds obscuring it, the sun

was positively *hot*. Indeed, Lara had let go of Sofi's hand and was tugging off her gloves and hat. Sofi followed suit, flabbergasted at the warmth spreading across her body absent of a fire or a warm bath.

The true colors of nature were so dazzling that Sofi began to feel light-headed. She had never seen anything like the landscape laid out before her.

A well-constructed pen housed several goats and a docile-looking brown cow. It startled Sofi that animals could live outdoors. But in a world without snow, it made sense. To the left of the pen was a large plot of dirt so wet it looked nearly black. From the ground grew leafy green crops, making a mockery of the limp, pale vegetables Marie spent all year canning and stewing. On the horizon were buildings, carefully crafted, each with their own structure and construction, personality apparent even in the outlines.

"What . . . ?" Sofi gasped. "What *is* this?"

"Sofi." Lara sounded just as incredulous. "I think this is spring."

"That's not . . . ," Sofi began, but the word "possible" died on her tongue. Her time on the road with Lara had taught her that *anything* was possible.

"Oh!" Lara, who was in the middle of shrugging off her furs, pointed at a hiccup of movement in the distance. "There's something there."

Sofi squinted at the horizon, the sun seeming to sparkle off the ground. She could just make out a figure, kneeling. It wasn't something. It was some*one*.

Suddenly, faced with the idea of seasons and strangers, Sofi feared she'd made a terrible mistake. She'd hoped to find the truth about her mother and the bone lute in one fell swoop, but now that she was facing it head-on, it was too much. Already she was hot, sweat dripping down her spine and between her breasts. The collar of her dress was too tight. She was having trouble breathing.

"Hey, hey, hey." Lara was suddenly in front of her. "It's okay, it's okay." Lara had flung her fur to the ground and was clutching both of Sofi's hands. Sofi had been wrong before. If Lara mittened was like a fire, then the touch of her skin was the sun.

At first Sofi couldn't understand the look of concern on Lara's face, but then she heard herself gasp—a brittle, scratching search for air. Shakily, she exhaled. Paused. Let herself want for air. Sucked in again, slowly.

It took several careful repetitions before her breathing had returned to normal.

"If this is too much," Lara said, glancing at the kneeling figure, "we can turn back. Stick to the king's route and stop here on our way home."

Home.

Sofi knew that Lara meant Juuri, but there was very little of the Ollenholt manor other than Marie that Sofi missed. Home had never been a place—that big house made empty by the absence of her father and the loss of her mother. Home had always been her music.

No, Juuri wasn't home. But a place where the grass rippled

in the breeze, where gardens bloomed, and the name of her mother was displayed proudly on a signpost rather than shoved at the bottom of a locked drawer . . . well, that place might be.

Sofi wouldn't know until she tried.

"No," she said fiercely, struggling with the metal clasp that secured her furs at her neck. "No, I don't want to turn back." As soon as her cloak fell to the grass, she felt lighter. "Let's go."

She took one unsteady step, snowshoes swishing across the grass, before she stumbled. She knelt, unbuckling those, too, and leaned them carefully against the trunk of the nearest tree. She folded her furs into a tight bundle that would have made Marie proud and left them nestled at the roots.

Sofi didn't want anything to hold her back.

At first it appeared as though the girl was praying.

What had once been a distant figure was now a girl about Sofi's own age kneeling in a bank of mud. Her hands were dipped in bright blue water that cut a serpentine line across the village rising before them. Sofi had a difficult time recognizing the river for what it was without the thick layer of ice she was accustomed to. She had only ever seen water in small doses—just enough to drink, or chunks of ice in a cast-iron pot above the fire heating up for a bath.

This rushing, roaring monstrosity was enough to take away the breath she'd only just regained.

But as Sofi and Lara drew closer, the scene grew clear. Wet clothes were spread on the bank around the girl. A large skirt was submerged in the churning water. She was scrubbing it ferociously with a bar of soap. Sofi nearly fainted at the idea of doing the washing without having to bring out the pickaxe. Surely she would have aided Marie much more enthusiastically if cleansing had been as simple as carrying a basket to a stream.

The girl's head was down, her dark braid thrown over one shoulder to keep it from the water's clutches. Her eyes were focused on her work. When the distance between the three of them shrank uncomfortably close, Sofi and Lara exchanged an uncertain glance. They didn't want to frighten the stranger, but they needed to announce their arrival.

Sofi settled on a small cough.

The girl dropped both soap and skirt into the water as she leaped to her feet. Within seconds, both were lost to the current. The stranger's eyes roved frantically over both Sofi's and Lara's faces, her fear amplified the longer she looked at them without recognition.

"Who are you?" she squeaked, like the highest note on an oboe. "And how are you here?"

Sofi held her hands out in front of her, trying to gesture that she meant no harm. "I'm sorry to scare you. I'm Sofi, and this is Lara. And the reason that we're here . . ." She tried to determine the best way to articulate both her loss and curiosity in one breath.

But the girl held up a hand. "No," she said sharply. "I didn't ask you *why* you were here. I asked you *how* you were here."

Sofi frowned at the semantics.

"We followed the sign," Lara chimed in helpfully.

The girl's face darkened like a cloud rolling across the sun. "You saw the sign?"

"Well, not right away," Lara interjected easily, carrying the conversation the way she often did. "At least, I didn't, anyway. Not until she told me what it said." She jerked her head toward Sofi. "Then . . . there it was." She smiled sheepishly.

The girl turned her attention to Sofi. It was, perhaps, the first time a person had voluntarily looked away from Laravelle Hollis to focus on Sofi Ollenholt. "Where did you learn the name?"

Sofi shook her head uncomprehendingly. "I don't understand the question."

The girl grimaced. "Goddess help me, if you don't tell me where you learned the name 'Lail,' I will *turn you into a newt.*"

Sofi's heart resumed its thundering. "Are you really a witch?"

The girl threw her hands up in the air. She looked ready to scream. "Of course I'm a witch."

Lara elbowed Sofi sharply. "Sofi," she pleaded. "Just tell her." She looked genuinely frightened.

"Okay, okay." Sofi reached for the bag on her shoulder. "I'll tell you."

As soon as Sofi moved, the girl put a hand to the charm she wore around her neck and whispered an unintelligible word. The grass at Sofi's feet burst into flame.

Sofi and Lara screamed. This wasn't fire forged by

someone following the instruction of the Papers. This flame burned white, the edges streaked with silver. It was hungry, impossibly sharp, and alive in a way embers in a hearth could never be. As the flames crept toward her ankles, Sofi swore she saw the fire *smile*.

"I'm not trying to hurt you," Sofi shouted, stamping at the flame. "I'm trying to *show* you."

The girl snapped her fingers, and the fire at Sofi's feet extinguished itself, leaving behind a perfect circle of charred grass. "Show me what?"

Sofi pulled the leather folio from her bag. "Where I learned the name 'Lail.'"

She untied the leather straps and tenderly extracted the portrait of her mother. Her heart hitched in her chest at the sight of her mother's eyes. She held the page out to the girl, signature-side-up. She wasn't yet ready to share her mother's face. "Here. See? That's the name I saw on the sign."

The girl took a step closer to examine the parchment. She gasped, hand squeezing the charm that hung from the chain around her neck. Sofi braced herself for another spell, but nothing happened.

"Where did you get this?" The witch no longer looked suspicious. She looked furious. "Who else knows this name?" Her voice hardly echoed in the wide-open air, so vast was the space. It was strange, Sofi noted, to feel the absence of that echo of snow.

"Just us." Sofi was bewildered by the shift in the witch's tone. "The person who left this to me is dead." She hadn't intended to obscure her father's identity, but as soon as the words were out of her mouth, she knew they were the right ones.

The fire in the girl's eyes dimmed, but only slightly. "And no one else knows?"

Sofi shook her head insistently. "Only the two of us."

"Okay." The witch tapped a finger to her lips, eyes on the trees from which Sofi and Lara had emerged. After a moment she nodded resolutely to herself. "Okay. But you'll still have to come with me. She'll want to see you."

Sofi's stomach twisted. Of course they would have to face some head witch who would punish them for their trespassing or enchant them into forgetting they'd ever known the name "Lail." Perhaps her father had been right to turn Sofi away from magic. To keep her mother's portrait locked in a drawer if her name was connected to this world of witches. Surely he had done it to protect not only himself but Sofi, too.

"Who will want to see us?" Sofi's nervous fingers tapped on her thigh in six-eight time.

The girl's eyes darkened as she gathered the washing into a basket, which she settled at her hip. She, too, looked nervous.

"My gran."

SIXTEEN

YOUR . . . GRAN?" Lara's voice was thick with amusement. "You made it sound as though we were headed to see the Kingsguard." She giggled a little, sounding relieved.

Sofi's chest loosened. Sure, the girl had just set the grass at their feet ablaze without lifting a finger, and certainly that meant her grandmother was a witch too. Still, it *was* a bit amusing picturing a wizened old woman chastising them with a wrinkly finger. A laugh slipped out from Sofi's mouth.

The girl shot them a withering look. "You lot won't be laughing soon." She hoisted the basket higher on her hip. "Come on."

They followed her along the twisting bank of the river, the soil soft as fresh snow beneath their feet. The sound of the water lapping against the shore was like the slurp of soup from a spoon. Ripples ran across the surface from the tiniest disturbances, whether it was a crow that dipped in its beak to drink or a stone that tumbled from the bank. The river was so *movable*, so *noisy*. It was practically a symphony in itself.

As they crossed a long bridge, the wooden slats creaked beneath their feet, lending a gentle percussion to the churning water below. On the other side, the town opened up before them.

The first thing Sofi noticed was the birds. There were crows absolutely everywhere. They roosted in trees and on roofs, their feathers gleaming blue in the sharp sunlight. There were crows that sat on open windowsills, crows that perched on fences, and even a few who stood guard on the paths to front doors.

Each house in the village was entirely unique—some cottages were squat and round, others tall and angular—but each house had at minimum two crows circling. Black feathers littered the cobblestone streets as though a pillow had exploded, its contents carried off by the wind.

The second thing Sofi noticed was the flowers. Bright blooms burst from the ground of every front yard, some flowers delicate and drooping, others with stalks taller than Sofi herself. Ivy twined its way across the front of many houses, dripping from windows and circling the front pillars.

There was not a single greenhouse in sight, which meant the soil in Lail was fertile enough for not only crops but flowers, too. Everything was so *alive*. Sofi could hardly breathe, the air was so thick with lush greenery and floral scents that did not carry the sharp bite of perfume.

A group of young children sent brightly colored sparks zooming around a yard while a large crow observed them, looking thoughtful. The children didn't seem to notice the strangers, but the crow's beady eyes clocked Sofi and Lara as they passed.

Their guide hardly batted an eye at the world around her. She was incredibly poised, all things considered. If anyone in Aell had seen a witch appear through the trees, Sofi was sure they wouldn't have offered such a polite, if cold, reception.

"What's your name?" Sofi caught up to the girl, accidentally knocking her laundry basket.

"I'm not telling you that," she said, righting it before any clothing fell.

Sofi frowned. "Why not?"

The girl looked incredulous. "Because names have *power*. How do you think you found us?" Her eyes went suddenly wide, like she'd let too much slip.

Of course. The sign had been visible to Sofi because she knew the name. Lara hadn't been able to see it until Sofi spoke the name "Lail" aloud. This girl had worried about who else might have seen Sofi's mother's portrait, because anyone who knew the name "Lail" could find the town.

The Kingsguard had stations in every village up and down the King's Road yet had never successfully uncovered a witch. Sofi had always puzzled over that absence, but now it made sense. None of the Kingsguard knew the name of the town, so none could find the witches housed by its secret. It was possible guards had even ridden their horses right through the spot where Sofi now stood, completely and utterly oblivious to the truth.

Down a short path was a small house wound with ivy, leaves clinging to every inch of its exterior. Sofi thought the roof was black until she realized that the color came not from shingles but crows crowded atop the structure.

On the porch, an old woman rocked in a wooden chair. She was dressed in a long smock the same color as the ivy that clung to her house. Her gray hair was braided in two long plaits that hung down each shoulder. A pipe was balanced between her teeth, perfect rings of smoke floating up into the air as she puffed. Her eyes were closed, her face serene.

She didn't *look* very frightening.

The girl set the basket down lightly on the porch's front step.

"That wasn't nearly long enough for the washing, Viiv." The woman's eyes were still closed. Her voice was tough like leather, but warm like a candle lit in the middle of the night.

"It's not the washing I brought you," said the girl, who was apparently called Viiv.

The old woman's eyes flew open midrock, and the pipe fell from between her teeth as her jaw went slack. But instead of it clattering onto the porch, the woman snapped her fingers and the pipe landed in her left hand. "Who in the name of the Goddess are they?"

"That one's Sofi"—Viiv pointed at Sofi—"and that one's Lara. They came in through the trees."

"No, they didn't." The old woman spoke as though Sofi and Lara were not there.

"We did, actually." Lara blushed slightly as she injected herself into the conversation. "Ma'am," she added, almost as an afterthought.

"How?" The old woman's eyes were on Lara, but Sofi found that she wished the woman's focus was directed toward her. Her face was a familiar melody Sofi couldn't quite place. "How do you know the family name?"

Sofi's breath caught. If *Lail* was a family name, that meant . . .

"I found a portrait in a locked drawer of my father's desk," she said, and her wish came true. The full force of the old woman's gaze landed on her. It was a heat not unlike the rays of the sun. Direct. Unflinching.

The woman scowled. "And who is your father?"

Beneath the woman's scathing scrutiny, Sofi balked. She pinched the inside of her wrist, trying to abate the squirming of her stomach. Trying to silence the voice in the back of her head that sounded suspiciously like Frederik telling her to cut and run—to rid herself of these witches and their magic while she still had the chance.

But Sofi had followed the sign to Lail for a reason. And even as she shook in her boots, standing before Viiv's gran, Sofi knew she had to see that reason through. She couldn't end this song too early, refused to let it linger on an unresolved note.

"His name was Frederik Ollenholt."

The old woman went pale, her eyes sharp as ice. "Is it with you?" She rose to her feet, her voice hoarse and thin. "The portrait? Let me see it."

Sofi nodded, untucking the folio from beneath her arm. The old woman swayed as her eyes fell upon Sofi's mother's face.

"Gran?" Viiv rushed forward, grabbing her grandmother's arm to steady her. The old woman clutched her heart, tears clouding her eyes. "Are you all right?" Viiv asked. "Who is that?"

"This is Delphine." The woman tore her eyes away from the portrait to look at Sofi. "She was my eldest daughter." Her gaze was like sleet, pounding against every inch of Sofi.

Beside Sofi, Lara gasped. "So that means that you're . . ."

"The daughter of a witch." Sofi could hardly believe the words that fell from her own lips.

The world began to spin, everything she'd ever known disappearing until she was left with an uncertainty so wide she thought she might drown in it. Sofi was used to losing things—her future gone, her parents gone, her best friend gone. But now Sofi had lost herself, too. Everything she thought she'd known about her identity had disappeared.

Just like magic.

The woman took a shaky step forward, placing a palm to Sofi's cheek. Her skin was weathered, but her touch was soft. "I thought you were dead," she whispered, the tears back in full force. "When I felt her die, I just assumed . . . and then the winter came, like an omen. Oh, my darling girl, I should have come for you. I should have *known* Delphine's daughter would live."

Sofi's heart raged a storm. Thunder struck her chest and throat. Lightning shocked her bloodstream, sent her mind reeling. Even as she grappled with the impossible uncertainty of who she was, the idea that she had been dreamed of by family the way that she, too, had dreamed *of* family sent shivers down her spine.

Some days, when her father had been away and the loss of her mother loomed like a shadow, Sofi wondered if she had ever been wanted at all. But the way the old woman was staring at her now sent that fear by the wayside. All she could find in the old woman's eyes was love.

She wanted to embrace the woman. She wanted to run away.

"You never told me about Delphine." Viiv pouted, turning to her grandmother. "And now she has a secret daughter?"

Her gran—Sofi's gran too—turned from Sofi to Viiv. "Our family tree has many hidden branches, Viivi." The old woman chuckled softly. "Many roots, too. Some losses hurt too much to speak of." She sighed, and in her exhale, Sofi could hear the burden of many years and even more secrets. "Why don't you all come in? It seems that we have plenty to discuss."

She shuffled toward the front door. Viiv, shaking her head, reached for her basket. Sofi made to follow, but Lara hung back. "I don't want to intrude."

Sofi began to argue, then stopped. If Lara remained

outside, Sofi might have a chance to speak candidly with the witches—with her *family*. Perhaps she might even learn the truth about the bone lute's magic.

"Are you sure?"

Lara nodded, looking relieved that Sofi didn't push her. "I'd only be in the way or monopolize the conversation."

"You don't . . . ," Sofi began, but Lara held up a hand.

"It's okay." She laughed softly. "I do. This is your family. It's your time. I'll stay out here. Maybe by the time you're through, I'll have been able to compose a halfway decent chorus on my own."

Sofi highly doubted that, but she nodded encouragingly. "If you need anything . . ."

"I know where to find you," Lara finished, dropping her bag and her lute case on the porch. "I'll be fine. And hey"— Lara squeezed Sofi's hand—"now we know why that flower bloomed in the snow. It was *you*." She grinned. "I hope you get some answers, Sofi. You deserve them."

Sofi shot her a real smile this time. "Thank you."

"Don't mention it." Lara grinned. "I already know how lucky you are to have me." She giggled again and, after a moment of hesitation, kissed Sofi quickly on the cheek.

In a day that had already been filled with unexpected moments, Sofi found it was possible to still be surprised.

The house was cluttered yet tidy, the walls lined with curio cabinets packed with trinkets—floral-patterned teacups stacked ten high, chipped saucers that displayed rings and crystals and stones. Snail shells and wings of flies filled glass jars. Sofi followed the hallway to the back of the house, into the kitchen. Large antlers were fixed to the wall above the modest table. And everywhere, there were boxes and boxes simply labeled BONES.

Viiv bustled toward the table with a teapot and three mismatched teacups. She set the pot in the center of the table, steam rushing from the spout as it steeped. She took the chair opposite her grandmother and gestured for Sofi to sit beside her. Hesitating only slightly, Sofi took the seat and claimed a willow-patterned teacup.

"So . . ." Viiv poured tea into Sofi's cup. "Why are you here?"

Sofi didn't like her tone. It was accusatory rather than curious.

"Well," she began, "if you were wandering in the woods and found a sign with your dead mother's name on it, are you telling me you *wouldn't* have followed it?" Viiv had been combative since the moment she'd seen Sofi on the riverbank. "There was no mark of it on my map. If I hadn't chosen that particular patch of trees to pause in, I might have walked right past."

"Should have," Viiv grumbled.

"Viivi," her gran snapped. "Be nice to your cousin."

"She has bad energy," Viiv whined. "I can practically feel her squeezing the life out of her power."

Viiv and Sofi sized each other up. Viiv scared Sofi. She was so sure of her magic, wielded it with such ease. Sofi wondered if her cousin saw things in Sofi that equally unnerved her.

"Considering that I didn't know my mother was a witch until a few minutes ago, you'll have to forgive me for not knowing what to do with this newfound magic." Sofi blew on her tea.

"You really had no idea?" Viiv raised her eyebrows skeptically. "I've seen toddlers turn their wooden blocks into toads. Six-year-olds can make fire spark from their fingers if they get angry enough. Surely there were signs you were just too stubborn to see."

Sofi pursed her lips. "There were a few moments, I suppose." She thought of the song that conjured church bells in her father's study, the lyric that had sent the scent of her mother floating through the South Wing. "But it all felt coincidental enough to ignore."

Her gran pulled a pair of glasses from the front pocket of her smock and settled them at the bridge of her nose. "And your father, he never gave any indication that he knew what was going on?"

"The strange things stopped once I started seriously training to become a Musik." Sofi shrugged, trying not to betray the pounding of her heart. The fluttering had only ever happened when she played the lute and sang original compositions. Back when she'd performed with reckless abandon. But as soon as her father implemented her training routine, restrained her feeling to fourth days, her wanting to second days, such occurrences ended. "My father created a schedule to help me focus. To keep me technical rather than emotional."

Viiv *tsk*ed into her tea.

"What?" Sofi demanded.

"Sounds like he knew exactly what he was doing," her gran said darkly. "Teaching you to suppress your instincts. To guard your head from your heart. To keep your power pent up, safe behind walls."

Sofi's hands began to shake. She had built a wall every time she played. Used it to hold back that fluttering in her chest. And when she broke the wall down on the road with Lara, the flickers returned. Warm wind in Trogg. Aching in Skaal. A flower blooming from the snow on the way to Rusham.

When Sofi sang, the world responded.

When Sofi played, she was magic. And her father had *known*. He had tasked each day with a new way to keep his daughter's magic at bay. To make Sofi repress the power that flowed through her veins.

"He told me it would make me a better musician," Sofi whispered. "But it had nothing to do with my talent, did it? It was only ever about keeping my magic locked away."

Her gran's face was hard. "Where is Frederik now?"

"Dead," Sofi said flatly.

"Stupid, selfish little man," her grandmother muttered. "I told her not to marry him, but she was a stubborn thing, my Delphine. When she loved, she loved *fierce*, and none could sway her, not even me." She looked up from her gnarled hands. "What he did to you is unbelievably cruel, Sofi. Making you believe that your power was something to be suppressed rather than celebrated."

"But . . ." Sofi attempted to find a way to justify her father's actions. "Music and magic cannot coexist. If one wants to be a Musik like my father was, no magic can be at play. He was only trying to protect his title. Protect *me*."

Notes floated in from the porch, the opening strain of "The Song of Summer." Both Viiv and her gran stiffened at the sound.

"What is that?" Viiv winced. "Goddess, I feel that in my *teeth*."

"That," her gran said, pursing her lips, "is proof of Frederik Ollenholt's hypocrisy."

"Is that . . . bone?" Viiv asked, grimacing. She looked accusingly at Sofi.

"What does bone have to do with anything?" Sofi had always wondered how and why her father had chosen that material for his instrument.

"Bones are the conduit." Viiv rolled her eyes, clearly irritated by how little Sofi knew. "Magic is a living, breathing thing. It exists in the marrow; it is a part of the world. But human bone is too unpredictable, too volatile to use long term. And so we turn to creatures we can train and care for to help keep us balanced. We attend to the crows, and then, when it's their time to move on, they leave us their bones as an offering and we move our magic through them." She held out the necklace she had clutched earlier. What Sofi had initially believed to be a charm was actually a tiny bird's skull.

Sofi turned back to her grandmother. "Why does my father have a bone lute?"

Her gran grimaced. "Your mother made it for him. After your father learned what she was." She shifted in her seat. "Delphine knew the Kingsguard was looking for witches. She knew how she'd be treated if captured. She was about your age when we fled to Aell, you know. We helped our coven create the Papers using the bones of our birds in exchange for the king's protection. But when Ashe turned his sights beyond his border, the coven had run low on bones. He didn't want to wait for the time we needed to forge the necessary relationships. So he asked us to pull from our own marrow."

Gran's expression darkened. "But, as Viivi said, human marrow is volatile. Violent, even. That mess beyond the Gate could have been avoided if the king hadn't been so concerned with coin. If a few angry witches hadn't been so willing to push the limits of their power. Siphoning human marrow is painful and harrowing. Most of the witches who participated didn't live past the week's end." She sat back in her seat, twirling a teaspoon idly between her fingers. "I took my girls and any others willing to leave under the cover of night, and we fled the King's City. We posted up here, hidden ever since. I fear we may never be allowed to venture beyond the trees again."

"So my father blackmailed my mother?" Sofi was clenching the edge of the table, white-knuckled. "When he learned she was a witch?"

"Nothing so simple as that when hearts are concerned," her gran said. "Delphine knew he loved her, and she, him. I'd find love songs tucked into the pockets of her skirts when I'd do the washing. He was always good with words, your father. Slick and shiny and perfect, all of them. It was just his playing that needed some assistance. By then, the new king had taken the throne and had put out a call for musicians. Delphine thought that Frederik's words were too sweet to be sung only for her. So she crafted him the bone lute."

Her grandmother's eyes flitted to the boxes of bones, her gaze far away. Remembering. "Delphine didn't tell him at first. Just presented him an instrument that fixed his fumbling, redirected his fingers, and he was arrogant enough to believe that he had improved overnight. He sought a place in the Guild and found acclaim. And then his secret was found out, and the consequences of Delphine's actions played out twofold. She had to earn back your father's trust and keep her secret safe by bribing another."

Sofi leaned forward. For so long she had believed that her mother had left no mark on the world when in fact it seemed like quite the opposite.

"She constructed another piece of magic undetectable to the human eye. But there was no time to tend to a bird, to find bones that kept her magic steady. Instead, she pulled from her own marrow to bind the magic." The old woman began to tear up. "It wasn't until the task was complete that she learned she was with child. *You.*" She stretched her hands out across the table toward Sofi.

Sofi clutched the paper-soft hand of her grandmother, a warm spring breeze floating through the kitchen, yet despite the pleasant atmosphere, she was cruelly, unbearably angry.

"Mining marrow isn't pleasant," her gran continued, squeezing Sofi's hand, "and it isn't pretty. Perhaps she pulled too much or worked too quickly. To this day, I don't know. What I do know is that had she known you existed, she never would have given in to that man's demands. She wanted to be a mother more than anything. She would have given up even your father to keep you. That, I know for certain."

Sofi's heart clenched, a lump rising in her throat. It was as though her loss, which had always been a shadow, was illuminated by light, showing her all the ways she hadn't yet begun to hurt.

Gran's face was cloudy. "But Delphine didn't know she was with child. When the spell was finished, her body was depleted, which made her pregnancy difficult. She wrote me once that she was suffering. That she wanted to come home." The old woman sniffed. "That was the last time I heard from her. When I felt her die, I assumed the Goddess had taken you with her." She cleared her throat. "For years I worried that *I* had created the endless winter, so strong was my grief. The snow started the day she died, you know?" Gran's eyes searched Sofi's.

Hesitantly, she nodded, then admitted, "When I was younger, I used to fear that *I* was the reason the snow never stopped."

Beside her, Viiv snorted. "Like you'd *ever* be powerful enough for that. It takes the power of thirteen fully grown witches and a pile of bird bones the length and width of a tree to keep the winter at bay from our village. We only have the seasons thanks to the strength of our coven. No one girl could call forth winter on her own."

Sofi scowled. She'd just bared her soul, and still her cousin was mocking her. She turned her attention back to her grandmother, fire coursing through her veins. "This man who blackmailed my parents, do you know who he was? What kind of magic my mother performed?"

Surely if Sofi found this person, she could uncover the proof she needed to absolve Lara of any responsibility for the bone lute. Sofi would also be able to give name to the person responsible for her mother's death. Without that person's greed, Sofi might have had a family. A life beyond the empty halls of the Ollenholt manor and her distant father, ashamed and overtly aware of the shortcut he'd taken. That shame had turned to anger when he saw that magic rear itself in his daughter's music.

"Oh, I've never forgotten him," her grandmother continued. "Horrible name. Made him sound like a type of slug. Therolious Ambor." She winced dispassionately. "He demanded that your mother make him a magic flute."

SEVENTEEN

WHY DON'T you offer the poor girl your lute, Frederik?

Sofi was back in the wings of Saint Ogden's Theatre on the day of the Apprentice audition. Lara trembled desperately beneath the spotlight while Sofi lurked in the shadows just offstage. Both of them listened as Tambor made a seemingly innocent suggestion.

He had known what would happen when Lara picked up the bone lute.

He had known, because his instrument was the same.

Sofi remembered Frederik's finger in Tambor's face that afternoon. Their rivalry had lasted Sofi's entire life—the snide comments and barbed line of questioning, all of it fell into place. The two of them had shared a life-ruining secret, and instead of bringing them together, the fear of keeping it had turned them against each other.

Sofi could have kicked herself. Tambor's phlegm-soaked handkerchiefs should have been sign enough. No man who coughed that frequently had lungs strong enough to play the flute without magical assistance.

Tambor's Apprentice had already been chosen: his oldest son, Barton. His secret was protected by blood. With his own legacy secured, it was no wonder Tambor had jumped at the opportunity to ruin the one man to whom he was beholden. Tambor's behavior was repugnant, but what Frederik had done was not much better.

When the truth of her father's betrayal threatened to be revealed, rather than facing it head-on, he had left a web of mystery and lies for his daughter to unravel. Had left Lara accountable for his crimes. Both men deserved to pay for their actions. But only one of them was left to face the consequences.

"How do I break the spell?" Sofi's voice was loud, the sunlight too bright as it streamed through the kitchen's small window. Her teacup rattled on its saucer.

Viiv laughed openly. "You can't *break* a spell. Unlike the Papers, our magic is lasting. Permanent."

Sofi shook her head, unwilling to be deterred. "If a spell can't be broken, can it at least be *revealed*?"

Across the table, her gran sucked her teeth. "That's tricky, that. It's only the witch who cast the spell who can alter it. But, of course . . ." She trailed off, looking sad.

"My mother is dead," Sofi finished dully. She finally had

all the pieces and was so close to being able to clear Lara's name. But without a way to prove the magic to King Jovan and the rest of the Guild, all she had was her word against Therolious Ambor's.

Sofi sank her head in her hands.

"There, there." Viiv tapped lightly on her back. Sofi turned her gaze on the girl. This close, she could see the similarities in their faces. The slope of their noses, the curl of their hair, although Viiv's was several shades darker, closer to the color of the crows she so loved.

"Gee." Sofi grimaced. "Thanks."

Viiv removed her hand and pushed her chair away from the table. "Anytime, cousin." She flashed Sofi a wide smile before disappearing down the hallway.

Sofi looked to her grandmother for guidance.

"You'll have to forgive Viivi," the old woman said, watching her granddaughter go. "She can be a bit prickly, but she's a whip-smart witch. She just gets lonely." She, too, pushed her chair back from the table. "Spends more time with birds than people these days, now that her mother's passed on. She's used to being my only grandchild. She'll get over her jealousy soon."

Sofi was flooded with guilt. It was far too easy to get caught up in her own devastations, far too easy to forget that other people were also suffering.

A loud swear came from the porch. Sofi leaped to her feet.

"Go check on your friend," her gran said, pouring herself more tea.

Sofi, grateful for the dismissal, hurried down the hall and out the front door. "Lara! Are you all right?"

Lara was hunched over the bone lute, shaking her head angrily. "What rhymes with 'orange'?" she asked Sofi, her brown eyes wide with concern. "I've tried *everything*."

Sofi began to laugh. It started as a giggle but turned into a river of mirth, large, gasping breaths catching in her throat. Before she knew it, tears were pouring down her face.

"What's so funny?" Lara looked distressed.

Sofi struggled to speak through her impossible laughter. "Nothing," she finally managed.

Lara shook her head, confused. "Surely there's something. You can barely breathe."

"Nothing rhymes with 'orange,'" Sofi clarified through peals of laughter.

"Huh." Lara started to laugh quietly, more at Sofi's amusement than her answer. "That explains it, I guess." A soft smile lingered on her face. "How'd it go in there?"

Sofi considered this. "Enlightening, to say the least." She tried clearing her throat, but the lump left by her grandmother's tale remained. She wasn't ready to share it. "So why are you using the word *orange* in a song?"

"Oh." Lara waved a hand unconcernedly. "I was trying to imagine autumn—I mean, we have 'The Song of Spring,' I thought it might be nice to write a counterpart. Perhaps even come up with a harmony that lets the two songs be sung atop each other in a round, the way the seasons are supposed to flow. . . . But that's stupid, isn't it?" She was talking very fast.

Sofi leaned against the doorframe, her heart striking a bright chord. There was something so endearing about watching Lara *try*. She was playing a magical instrument, her performances were literally perfect, and still she wanted to work harder. Learn to be a songwriter. Cultivate her talent.

All things that Frederik Ollenholt and Therolious Ambor had pushed to the side when the magic took over, Lara embraced. It set a flutter in Sofi's stomach. She loved that Lara *cared*.

She sat beside Lara on the porch step and stared out at Lail. The grass rippled in the breeze; birds flapped and cawed as they moved from perch to perch. She tried to determine the time from the placement of the sun in the sky—her stomach told her it should be nearly supper—but the sun hadn't even begun to set. It seemed that in the spring, the sun lingered longer.

Sofi sighed. "I suppose we should head to Ohre. We won't make it in time for the show, but I don't want to get us too far off course." She also didn't want to run the risk of her gran or Viiv saying anything to Lara that would give away the truth of the bone lute—not before she figured out what to do about it herself.

"Nonsense," came her gran's voice from the doorway. "You only just arrived. Spend the night here—I've already begun dinner. Get a good night's rest. Then you can carry on your quest tomorrow."

Lara grabbed Sofi's arm. "We should stay."

Sofi was torn. Of course she wanted to spend the evening with her newfound family. But already her mind was focused on Tambor and finding a way to expose him for his crimes. The longer they stayed in Lail, the longer Tambor did not suffer a single consequence.

Then her stomach growled.

"I heard that," her gran said from the doorway. "You're staying. Come help with the salad." The screened door banged shut behind her.

"You heard the woman." Lara pushed herself off the steps and settled the bone lute back into its case. "Come on." She offered Sofi a hand, pulling her up so enthusiastically that Sofi stumbled into her. She pressed a hand to Lara's sternum to steady herself, feeling the rhythm of Lara's heart beneath her palm. This close, Sofi could see the amber ring around Lara's brown eyes, the dusting of freckles across her nose. The way the corners of her lip twitched up as she stared down at Sofi too.

The front door banged open again, and they jumped apart. Viiv poked her head out into the afternoon. "Are you coming?"

"Yes." Sofi collected her things, trying to extinguish the flicker of disappointment that had settled in her chest. "We're coming."

Sofi had never eaten a carrot that wasn't boiled. In Juuri, produce was limp and wilting, and it was up to Marie to find a way to make it palatable. Most vegetables were pale and colorless, brined in salty liquid and dried herbs in hope of infusing them with a flavor beyond merely *squishy*.

Not so in Lail. Gran had whipped up a creamy dip for the

incredible bounty of fresh vegetables she'd pulled up from her garden. Dinner was a cacophony: carrots crunched, celery snapped, tomatoes dripped, and radishes crackled. Each bite was sharp and bright, and the structure of the food brought with it easy conversation.

To Sofi's relief, there was not a single mention of magic or music. Instead, Viiv and her gran had a spirited argument over the proper way to brew tea—Viiv preferred to oversteep and overhoney; her gran preferred a more subtle approach. Lara and Viiv compared notes on the jewelry they wore—Lara's earrings had been made by a man in Visc from what he claimed was a king's coin, and Viiv's armful of bracelets came from a tinker she'd met on the other side of the trees. Her gran scolded her for that one, as apparently that foray beyond Lail's border had not been approved.

Sofi sat back and watched them interact, smiling softly. Colors spilled in through the kitchen window as the sun began to sink in the sky. Bright oranges mixed with light pinks and purples, culminating in a sunset more vivid than any Sofi had ever seen. She was safe here in the small kitchen filled with voices of people she cared about. People who cared about her, too.

"Home" was a word Sofi had only ever associated with music. But here, with a soft breeze blowing through the kitchen, Lara and Viiv's laughter floating toward the ceiling, and her gran's knowing gaze, Sofi began to see how it might apply to a place, too.

Her gran reached across the table for Sofi's hand. "I'm glad you're here."

"Me too." Sofi found she meant it. "I think I'd like to come back one day. If you'll have me."

Her gran's face split into a wide smile. "You're always welcome here, my girl." Her eyes crinkled in the corners.

When the plates were emptied and drinking glasses drained, Viiv began to clear the table.

"Let me help you." Sofi got to her feet and stacked plates on her palm, hoping to gain even the slightest bit of favor with her grumpy cousin.

Viiv placed the dishes in the sink and turned on the water. "I'm sorry if I was harsh earlier." She glanced at Sofi. "It's hard for me to fathom someone who has magic in their blood but doesn't use it. Or even seem to *want* it." She used an elbow to brush her braid over her shoulder so it wouldn't get wet as she scrubbed.

"I *don't* want it."

Viiv shook her head uncomprehendingly. "Why not?"

Sofi sighed. "Because music is all I've ever known. It's what I love more than anything. I'm afraid that now I'll have to give it up."

Viiv scrubbed at a particularly finicky bit of residue on a plate. "Why can't you have both?"

"Because I can't," Sofi answered automatically. "That's the entire point of a Musik."

Viiv pursed her lips. "Why do you have to be a Musik, then?"

"Because if I want to write music, there's no other option." Sofi picked up a dish towel that was embroidered with a crooked sun and began to dry the stack of plates.

"That seems . . ." Viiv squinted out the window. "Absurd."

Sofi let out a laugh. With each step she put between herself and her old life, the more she found absurd. "Yes." She set the dry plate onto the counter. "Yes, I suppose it does."

"Sofi." Lara called her attention back to the table. "Play something for your gran."

Sofi blanched, suddenly self-conscious. "I couldn't." Playing for people she cared about, people who knew where—and who—she'd come from, people who knew that her dreams had been dashed, was too much like opening up a wound that had only just begun to heal.

"What are you talking about?" Lara got to her feet, reaching for the bone lute's case. "Show them how talented you are."

"No," Sofi said sharply as Lara opened the case, revealing the instrument to the room. Her grandmother's eyes had hardened at the sight of the bone lute. Viiv, too, had stopped her washing. It didn't look as though either of them was breathing. "No," Sofi repeated, softer this time. "Put that away. I'll use mine."

Lara frowned but mercifully obeyed. Stuck, Sofi pulled her own lute from its case. While tuning, she considered the catalog of songs she'd written for Lara on the road, but it felt cheap to play her gran a song that was not fully *hers*. Yet she had grown so much as a songwriter in that short time that none of her old work felt apt either.

Sofi could delay it no longer. If nothing in her life made

any sense, surely her music did not need to follow its usual pattern. So she abandoned her careful planning, her towering walls, and her restrictive routine, falling into a soft cascading melody she'd been saving for a rainy day, and began to sing.

"Life is not some careful thing, it's a hopeful swell, it's listening," she sang softly, eyes fixed on the antlers above the kitchen table. *"But words once spun like lyre strings make fools of one and all."*

Sofi grasped wildly for words that fit her melody, struggling to make sense of the way they fell into place. She hardly knew what she was saying, only that the lyrics were pouring out of her the way that water fell from the tap. It was as though the wall she had spent so much time sheltered behind had come crashing down, freeing phrases and feelings she'd long tried to ignore.

Now here they were, tumbling from her tongue, offering truths.

Something Sofi was not often wont to do.

"And would I hope to feel spring's touch, like a maiden's cheek so lush, languid were the days until my sorrow led to ruin." Sofi could feel eyes on her, but she refused to meet them. She kept her gaze fixed on the curve of the antlers, the way the sharp tips jutted out like bare branches on a tree, gleaming in the evening light. *"When that same maiden lay in wait, oft' I wondered, is it fate or folly that has led us to this wand'ring, wicked road?"*

Sofi sucked in a quick, hiccupping breath, still uncertain

where the song was headed. *"I may have walked this path before, but I would walk it evermore. There's none but her I'd want to tell the tales I've left untold."*

Lara let out a squeak, almost like a frightened mouse, pulling Sofi's attention from the antlers back into the sunlit room. Her concentration broken, and without her usual strict, technical attention, the melody fell apart, notes crashing to the floor like an armful of logs for the fire.

"Anyway, it's a work in progress." Sofi busied herself with replacing her lute in its case. "I haven't finished it yet. Don't judge it too harshly." *Or me*, she wanted to add. Her face burned with embarrassment as she closed the case's clasps slowly. This was exactly the reason she'd followed a strict routine, to avoid such displays of uncertainty. Such distractions. Such truths.

Saints, she had essentially shouted her ridiculous crush on Lara to the world. Even the crows roosting on the fence outside likely knew. Sofi's throat tightened. Her crush was ridiculous for several reasons, not the least of which was that Sofi had only just now realized that was what it was: a crush.

Massive and enveloping, the word reframed the flutters when Lara's skin met hers, the way her smile managed to light Sofi up like a lantern, the way she craved and coveted Lara's attention even as she convinced herself it was trivial. She was conflicted, feeling so strongly for someone who had uprooted her life so impossibly. Feeling so strongly for someone whose future she could ruin with a few choice words.

"That was lovely, dear." Her gran reached up to adjust

her glasses, very nearly hiding the fact that she was wiping away tears. "You sound like your mother when you sing."

Sofi's stomach clenched with longing. For the length of a song, she had given herself over fully to her instincts. Had forgotten how much she had lost. How hard she had to work to protect herself. But reality always left her yearning, always longing for something. She was so tired of wanting.

"Could I . . . ?" Sofi refused to meet Lara's eye. "Could someone show me where I'm going to sleep?"

"Of course." A chair scraped across the floor, and her grandmother touched her elbow. "Come with me."

She led Sofi down the hall and up the stairs, opening a door to reveal a cozy room with a large bed covered in a patchwork quilt. "All yours," her gran said, ushering her inside. "Anything else you need?"

Sofi shook her head, sinking down to sit on the edge of the bed. "I'm just so unbelievably tired."

Her gran perched herself carefully next to Sofi, petting her hair. "I know." Sofi closed her eyes and leaned against her grandmother's shoulder, giving in to the soothing rhythm of the hand running across her head. "It's okay to rest."

Sofi's eyes flew open. She sounded so much like Lara. "I can't *rest*. I have to stay vigilant. I must remain on top of my training if I want my art to matter." She hated the way that even speaking those words made her want to cry. The drive, the fire that had once burned within, had all but been extinguished. She hardly knew what her music was for anymore.

Her gran's smile faltered. "You are an incredible musician, my girl. But if you don't take care of your heart, your art will suffer too."

"No." Sofi shook her head insistently, but her voice wavered. "It's the *suffering* that makes the art."

It almost didn't matter if her grandmother believed it, so long as Sofi did. But she was having trouble even convincing herself.

"Oh, Sofi." Her grandmother's eyes were unbearably sad. "Your father was afraid, and he planted that fear in you. He trimmed your greenery away, leaving only a stump." She sighed heavily. "But you are so much more than what he made you. And *all* pieces of you are worthy."

Frederik's fear had been based on his own decision to accept help. To defy the law of the land because he somehow believed himself and his talent worthy of such a loophole. When his daughter revealed magic in her own right, perhaps some part of Frederik *had* wanted to keep her safe from an unwelcoming world. But his guilt had manifested in cruelty as he worked to suppress Sofi's power. To protect himself at any cost, no matter the price his daughter had to pay.

"I wish your mother were here," her gran said quietly. "She'd be so proud of you. Of your talent, yes. But also of your tenderness."

Sofi exhaled shakily, leaning further into her grandmother's embrace.

"I know it might not seem like much," the old woman continued, "but I want you to have this." She rummaged around in the front pocket of her smock and pulled out a silver chain. Hanging from it was a tiny white bone. "It's from the wing of my favorite crow, Petra." She motioned for Sofi to turn so she could fasten the chain around her neck. "Keep it close. It's a connection to me. To your magic. A promise of what I could teach you, if—and only if—you wish to learn."

Sofi put a hand to the bone that hung above her breasts. It was only as long as her pinkie finger and just as thin. She had never been more torn—half her heart was devoted to music, the other half to her family and, by association, to their magic. She turned back to face her gran, her hand clutching the small bone. "Thank you." Her gratitude was sincere, but her uncertainty was stronger. The two pieces of herself swirled like oil and water, the magic and the music struggling to mix.

Sofi was no longer sure which part of her would triumph.

"I'll leave you to rest now." Her gran let out a soft grunt as she pushed herself to her feet. "I know today's been a lot to handle."

Sofi sank back onto the bed as the door clicked closed. She stared at the ceiling in silence as she conjured the terrible image of Therolious Ambor and his magic flute. Tambor had been the catalyst for her mother's death. Had goaded her father into death too. The man had taken everything from Sofi.

No matter what it required of her, she would find a way to ruin his life right back.

A soft knock on the door pulled Sofi from her dreams of revenge. "Come in," she called, expecting her gran again.

But it was Lara. "You okay?" She hung in the doorway, looking self-conscious.

"Fine," Sofi said, sitting up. She wasn't, of course. She was carrying so many secrets, secrets that could burn the world down around her. But as Sofi stared at Lara's open, hopeful face, she knew she couldn't share those truths. Sofi was used to carrying hurt. There was no reason Lara should suffer too. So instead of saying anything, Sofi merely sighed.

An awkwardness lingered in the air between them, thick and unfamiliar.

"You've been holding out on me," Lara finally said, worrying her bottom lip between her teeth.

Sofi cocked her head. "How so?"

"The songs you write for yourself are even better than the ones you write for me." She smiled wryly. "I should have anticipated as much."

"I . . ." Sofi trailed off, feeling caught. Chastised. Her wall began to build itself back up, stone by stone.

Lara took a step forward. "Who was it about?" Her presence on the other side of the room's threshold, one footstep inside the doorway, left the air heavy and charged.

"I—what?" Sofi rubbed her neck sheepishly. She was having an extraordinarily difficult time catching her breath.

"Did you . . . did you write those lines about me?" Lara breathed, her voice no louder than a flower unfurling its petals in the snow.

Sofi didn't think she could say it. She didn't know if she could bear to admit it, to shatter the tentative, fragile secret that existed between them. So much of Sofi had only found the light thanks to Lara. Thanks to her gentle teasing and tugging, thanks to the way she opened up, making Sofi feel safe doing the same. The way she looked deep into the heart of Sofi and saw her for who she was instead of merely what she could do.

Instead of answering, Sofi buried her head in her hands.

A moment of silence. Then: "You know how you feel about the Muse?"

It was so unexpected a question that it pulled Sofi from her spiral. She looked up from her hands. "Yes?"

"How she fills your mind with subjects fit for songs? How she guides you? Inspires you?"

"Yes?" Sofi repeated, uncomprehending.

"That's what you do for me." Lara stared firmly at Sofi's feet. "What you *are* to me. A muse. The sort that I want to call out to. For guidance. For support. For . . ." She swallowed thickly. "You make me feel things—the way you sing, the way you play, the way you think and feel and breathe, and *saints*, when I wondered if it was possible for me to love something, Sofi, I never knew it could feel like this."

Sofi got to her feet, took one step forward. It was impossible to make Lara's words register, so Sofi just stared. Lara was so beautiful. Unbelievably, she was looking at Sofi with a similar intensity. The fire in Lara's eyes burned ferociously, but her expression was cautious as she closed the space between them.

Lara put a hand to Sofi's cheek, sending a shudder through her. Lara's thumb brushed tenderly across Sofi's cheekbone, sending hope and fear thundering through her in equal measure.

"Can I kiss you?"

Sofi stared at the girl before her. It was impossible to believe that they were perfectly aligned in their wanting. Then Sofi said "yes," and they were something else entirely.

They were wonder and inspiration and potential, and they were *kissing*. Lara pulled Sofi close, her arms wrapped around her waist as her soft lips met Sofi's. Sofi clutched at the back of Lara's dress, digging her fingers between Lara's shoulder blades. She could feel the other girl's heart beat against hers in a complementing rhythm. They were their own percussion section. Their own symphony. Their own song.

One must not love anything more than one loves the music, Frederik Ollenholt's voice warned, brassy and bold as it interrupted his daughter's first kiss.

But instead of heeding him, as she had been trained to do, Sofi pushed her father's words away and, for the first time, let her wanting speak for itself.

EIGHTEEN

THEY LEFT Lail when the sun was still asleep, buried somewhere beyond the horizon, weak moonlight rippling against the surface of the river as the sky slowly began to bloom blue.

It was hard to say goodbye—goodbye to the cluttered house, to Sofi's caustic cousin and her steady grandmother. Hard to say goodbye to family she'd only just met but felt as though she'd always known.

"You'll be back," her gran said, Sofi's face buried in her shoulder. "And should you need help on your journey, you have a piece of me." She ran her fingers across the chain around Sofi's neck. "Family first."

Even Viiv had deigned to pull herself from bed to witness their departure. "See you, then." She offered one arm for a half-hearted hug. Sofi squeezed her cousin tightly and, shockingly, Viiv embraced her back.

They waved from the porch as Sofi and Lara made their way down the path back to the trees. The town was different in the dregs of moonlight, the crows blending into the darkness so that the structures looked like living, breathing things.

Lara was quiet. Sofi shot her a few furtive glances, but she didn't appear to notice. She hoped she didn't have to add "ill-timed kiss with travel companion" to her list of things to worry about. She had quite enough to deal with, what with the truth about Tambor's flute and no knowledge of how to reveal the magic to the king and the Guild without incriminating Lara or herself.

There was also that hollow ache in her heart as she left her only remaining family behind.

They reached the copse of fir trees as the sun began to rise, colors cascading in the bright spring morning. Disappointment welled as Sofi caught sight of her furs and snowshoes propped against the trunk of a small tree. Another indignity: *choosing* to leave spring behind and reenter the endless winter. She pulled the furs around her shoulders, morning dew tickling her cheek as it clung to the edges of the cloak. She waited until Lara's shoes were strapped on, and then she led the way, watching as the bright pinks of the sunrise faded into the dull gray of a winter morning, as green turned to brown, until their feet no longer swished against grass but clomped atop snow.

Just as swiftly as spring had arrived, it was gone. Beside Sofi, Lara shivered.

"Well," Lara said rather darkly, the weak morning sun as pale as her hair, "I haven't missed *this*."

They were the first words she'd spoken all day, and Sofi couldn't help but read into them. While of course the most obvious explanation was simply that Lara, like Sofi, was sorry to be back surrounded by snow, what made the most sense in Sofi's head was that Lara was sorry to be back on the road with *her*. That she regretted kissing Sofi the night before.

Sofi couldn't blame her. Not when Lara was Lara and Sofi was, well . . . so Sofi.

She shoved her hands into her mittens, frowning as her fingers stayed cold. She'd forgotten that she'd unraveled them almost irreparably.

Beside her, Lara giggled. "Here." She offered Sofi her left mitten.

"But then *your* hand will be cold."

Lara shook her head, smiling slyly. "Not if I do this." And she closed her left fingers around Sofi's right hand.

Sofi bit back a grin. "Very clever." Her cheeks burned even as she tried to look demure.

"I have my moments." Lara squeezed her hand, sending heat rushing through Sofi that had nothing to do with furs or mittens. Sofi took a step toward Lara, breath hitching as she took the other girl in. Lara's face was open and hopeful. Sofi took another step.

"I really want to kiss you again," Lara whispered.

Sofi grinned. "So kiss me, then."

Lara did. It was overwhelming at first, longing bubbling

up and over until they were nearly breathless. Lara nipped at Sofi's bottom lip and she gasped, her mouth opening to allow for a glimpse of tongue. Sofi pressed herself against Lara, reveling in the comfort of her body, the softness of her, the safety. She had not known what to hope for the first time her heart opened itself to another, but there was a grounding to it. An anchoring.

A comfort like Sofi had never before known.

Eventually, they pulled away from each other. Lara's cheeks were flushed pink, her eyes sparkling as she took Sofi in. Sofi always wanted Lara to look at her so. Like she was worthy of being loved. Worthy of the attention and adoration she had always craved. Lara made her feel special in the way she only ever had when playing a lute. Like she had a purpose. Like she was exactly where she was supposed to be.

A squawk rang through the trees. Lara shrieked as a crow swooped low enough to ruffle her hair. She jumped away and began to run, pulling Sofi along behind her, their fingers still intertwined.

"Lara," Sofi begged, snowshoes slapping against the ground, "it's okay. It was just a bird."

Lara stopped running, her chest heaving, cheeks pink. She began to laugh. "Sorry," she gasped. "I guess I'm a little jumpy."

"No kidding," Sofi wheezed, tugging lightly at the ends of Lara's hair.

Lara rolled her eyes. "Okay. I'm fine. I'm fine." She glanced over her shoulder at the trees from which they'd emerged. "Let's go."

As they carried on, Sofi caught a melody on the breeze. The wind shook the bare branches of the trees to create a soft, percussive swishing, offset by the crunching of the snow beneath their feet. Beside her, Lara hummed flatly, the single note buzzing like a bass, snagging on something in Sofi's chest.

She wanted this girl and all of her sounds. Every swish of her skirt, every clearing of her throat, every noise that proved she was right there beside Sofi. She never wanted a chance to forget, wanted to ride out the rhythm of Lara's breathing, the clack of her nails against a tabletop. Sofi wanted every single note Lara's existence created.

She was a song Sofi couldn't wait to learn.

The road to Ohre wound its way through a thicket and over a river, whose disappointingly glassy surface glinted in the pale sunlight. On the other side of the frozen river, a puff of gray smoke floated up from a small fire, flickering next to a ragged lean-to.

Sofi and Lara exchanged curious glances. They hadn't come across many travelers on the road. The tradition of traveling on foot was much more glamorous in ideology than execution.

Movement caught Sofi's eye. A figure had emerged from the tent and settled in front of the fire. When the person pushed back a hood to reveal a head of black curls, Sofi gasped. She knew that hair. That slouching posture. Those hands.

Without thinking, she shot across the ice, her snow-shoes skidding and sliding against the slick surface. In her desperation, she fell backward, her tailbone slamming against the frozen water. She shrieked in pain, her lute case hitting the ground with a sharp thwack. The lake's surface splintered but mercifully did not crack.

"Sofi!" Lara shouted from the bank.

The camper raised his head, squinting at where Sofi was sprawled across the ice. "Sofi?"

"Jakko!" It was such a relief to speak his name aloud. Sofi had truly believed she would never see him again.

Jakko hurried toward her, skidding across the lake's surface, coming to rest at her feet. "Saints and sheep, Sofi," he panted, using his forearm to brush his curls from his face. "What are you *doing* here?" He held out a hand to her. Sofi accepted it gratefully. "Are you okay?"

"Honestly," Sofi said as Jakko hauled her unsteadily to her feet, "I have no idea how to answer that." She reached down to collect her lute case. Tears had frozen in the corners of her eyes.

"Sofi!" Lara was toddling across the ice like a baby who had only just discovered their legs. Both Jakko and Sofi watched her with trepidation. Lara nearly slipped, and Jakko sucked in a sharp breath.

"What are you doing here?" Sofi clutched her best friend's arm tightly. "Camping on a riverbank near Ohre? Why didn't you . . . ?" Her voice caught in the back of her throat. "Why did you leave?"

Jakko's eyes widened with shock. "I didn't *leave*. Your father sent me away."

Sofi's stomach plummeted. Just as she'd suspected, her father had sacrificed Jakko in an attempt to keep his secret safe. She nodded angrily. "He told me you ran away. That you no longer heard the Muse's calling." She laughed humorlessly.

"The Muse." Jakko's brown eyes clouded. "I'm starting to think she doesn't exist at all. Surely no one could be so cruel, to offer up ideas and songs that are useless. I was penning an epic about Saint Isthen, you know." Sofi had, of course. "I had to burn it to fuel the fire. It all seems a bit silly now. I was never going to be a Musik anyway."

"It wasn't silly," Sofi insisted. "Your songs are beautiful."

"Your father didn't seem to think so." Jakko swallowed thickly. "He cornered me in the stairwell and told me that I should preserve my dignity while I still had the chance. 'Love of the art is not enough,' he told me. 'It is only about owner-ship. Mastery that you will never possess.'" Jakko scowled, remembering. "He told me he was sorry. And then he told me to get out of his house. Clearing the way for you, I guess," he said a bit bitterly. "So now I'm here."

"Jakko," Sofi said urgently, unable to bear the pain that flashed in her best friend's eyes. She wanted to tell him every-thing, to assure him that Frederik's lies had only served him-self. "It wasn't true. My father, he—"

"Made it," Lara panted, dropping her bag and lute case onto the snow.

Sofi paused, torn between her loyalties. Jakko's eyes caught on the bone lute's case. "Is this your roadie?" His smile didn't meet his usually sparkling eyes.

"Laravelle Hollis." Lara held out her non-mittened hand. "Newest member of the Guild of Musiks."

Jakko's jaw dropped. He looked uncomprehendingly at Sofi. "I don't understand."

She didn't know how to answer. Her failure, magic lute aside, was something she still had not fully faced. In every town, the villagers didn't care who played the music so long as they heard it. The other Guild members and their Apprentices already knew. Sofi had not yet been forced to say the words aloud.

"Her audition was better than mine." The smile plastered across her face was painful.

Jakko's eyes narrowed, and even as bile rose in Sofi's throat, his disbelief filled her with a strange sense of pride.

"But your father would never—" There were a hundred different ways that sentence could end. Sofi finished it for him.

"My father is dead."

For a moment Jakko just blinked down at her. Then he sank onto the log, clutching his head. He peered through his hands. "Are you okay?" He sucked in a sharp breath. "I'm sorry, I'm not sure what to say."

Sofi laughed, grateful for the release even as her heart clenched. "It's okay." She exhaled. "I'm okay."

"No, you're not." Jakko reached for her hand. "But if it helps, you're not alone in being alone."

Sofi frowned. "What do you mean? Aren't you headed home to Visc?"

"No." Jakko's face darkened. "I can't go home."

"Why not?" Lara sank down next to Jakko, hand on his shoulder like they'd been friends forever. For the thousandth time, Sofi marveled at the ease with which Lara moved through the world.

"I ran away." Jakko groaned, head back in his hands. "My father didn't approve of me devoting my life to something with such terrible odds. Only one lute player would ever become a Musik. But, of course"—Jakko shot a look at Sofi— "that didn't matter to me. I only ever cared about the music. Ever since I was little, the first time I saw your father perform at a theater in Visc, I knew I had to learn from him. I had to be a part of it. And so before I left, my mother slipped me an antique sapphire brooch that belonged to my father's mother. I used an irreplaceable family heirloom to pay your father for lessons, room, and board. I can't let her know I've failed." He ran a hand through his curly hair. "Her sacrifice was for nothing. All my joy, all my *love*, my music was for *nothing*."

It was the same way Sofi had felt when she had lost the title. Like her hard work, her devotion, her love, had been for naught. Her time on the road with Lara had only cemented that idea: Music didn't belong to the people who loved it. If her father's bone lute and Tambor's flute were proof of anything, it was that the Guild of Musiks was more concerned with talent than with heart. Until recently, she'd thought the same thing. But being with Lara had taught her that music without heart wasn't really music at all.

"It wasn't for nothing," Sofi said more certainly than she felt as she pulled Jakko to his feet, "because it brought you to me. Now, tear this place down." Sofi began kicking snow onto his fire. "It's time to go home."

"I already told you," Jakko protested, "I can't go back to Visc."

"Home isn't a place, silly." Sofi squeezed his hand tightly. "It's people. You're coming with us to Ohre."

"Life is not some careful thing, it's a hopeful swell, it's listening." Lara sang the now-finished tune to a packed room at the Passing Breeze, the largest tavern in Ohre. *"But words once spun like lyre strings make fools of one and all."*

The innkeeper had been a bit put out when they'd arrived, having prepared the town for a performance the night before that had never taken place: *That's money I won't get back, mind.* But with a bit of coercing, she had allowed the Musik to take the stage. Sofi had slipped Lara the sheet music when Jakko wasn't looking.

"And would I hope to feel spring's touch, like a maiden's cheek so lush, languid were the days until my sorrow led to ruin," Lara continued, her eyes meeting Sofi's across the room. A secret smile tugged at the edges of her mouth, and Sofi shivered with delight, listening to Lara sing a song Sofi had written *about* her. It reframed the intimacy of the act and showed how personal music could truly be.

"When that same maiden lay in wait, oft' I wondered, is it fate or folly that has led us to this wand'ring, wicked road?"

Sofi forgot to breathe. Lara's performance was spellbinding. But it wasn't because of the lute, which kept her fingers on the right notes. It was because of the *performer*. Because of Lara herself and the heart imbued in her song.

Frederik had always insisted that a voice was not enough—it was the mastery of an instrument that made a musician. Yet even when Lara sang a cappella, she was captivating. The bone lute didn't *make* her. It only aided what skill and ability were already inside her.

Saints. Her father had warped Sofi's understanding of artistry in his attempt to stifle her magic. He had taught his daughter that control made a musician better when actually it had only served to suck the soul out of her performances. Of course Sofi's pained expression and detached, technical playing had been overshadowed by someone as expressive as Lara.

"She's good." Jakko rested his chin in his hands, watching Lara and the bone lute thoughtfully from his place beside Sofi on a long wooden bench. "Surprisingly good, actually. When did she study with Frederik?"

Sofi choked on her last sip of cider. "She, um, didn't." Jakko made a low noise of disbelief. "I know." Sofi leaned her head on Jakko's shoulder, inhaling his familiar scent. "Trust me, I know." She sniffed his shirt, hoping to change the subject. "You smell like the outside."

"Well, I *have* been living outdoors for the last few days." Jakko pinched her arm lightly. "So that makes sense. Saints, it's nice to be inside."

They sat together as the song finished and Lara was swarmed with adoring fans. Sofi was almost able to pretend that she and Jakko had snuck out of the Ollenholt manor for an afternoon at the local tavern, like life was still predictable. Her dreams still attainable. Yet now she was all too aware of the magic that flowed through her veins.

"A cider for your thoughts, Sofi-girl?" A strong, dark brown hand set a tankard onto the table, and Denna slipped into the seat across from them. While Jakko doled out the fresh drink between their two empty glasses, Sofi beamed at the Musik. She couldn't have been more grateful to see her favorite Guild member in the flesh. Knowing what she now knew about the lute and Tambor, it was a relief to see someone who loved music for what it was rather than for the power and notoriety it could offer.

"Always." Sofi reached for her newly refilled mug gratefully and let the warm spice spread across her tongue. It settled the churning in her stomach some.

"Thought she'd be here yesterday," Denna said lightly, but her eyes were sharp. "We were left to listen to a novelist." She wrinkled her nose, turning to share a commiserating look with the man who had settled beside her on the bench. He was white-skinned, with high cheekbones and a sharp jaw. "This is Wes, my Apprentice."

"It's a pleasure to meet the Guild's newest liar." Sofi chuckled softly, the old joke still fresh on her tongue.

"She thinks she's funny," Denna told Wes, rolling her eyes. "But tragically, she is not. So, Sofi-girl." Denna returned her attention to Sofi. "Did you lead our newest Musik off course?"

"Oh." Sofi took another sip of cider. "No, we just got a

bit lost in the woods. You know how the wilderness is." She laughed self-deprecatingly. "But we're here now. And we found a friend along the way." She pinched her best friend's cheek. The cider was making her warm all over.

Denna turned to Jakko. "We missed you at the auditions."

"Oh, I . . ." Jakko squirmed next to Sofi. "You know how it can be." Sofi squeezed Jakko's arm supportively. Frederik's bad choices had affected so many people in the worst ways.

"No shame there," Denna said knowingly. "Whatever the reason." Sofi cleared her throat loudly. As she'd hoped, Denna turned toward her. "I have to admit," the Musik said, "I'm surprised that you're traveling with Laravelle. I thought you'd be a bit"—the corners of her mouth twitched upward—"bothered."

Next to Sofi, Jakko snorted. "That's an understatement."

Sofi tapped a fingernail against the tankard. It made a hollow thunk. "I was." She shook her head. "But, I don't know. She needed someone."

"Indeed," Denna said. "I was concerned for her growth when your father passed. But I should've known you'd take the reins. She's coming along quite nicely. Excellent performer." Her gaze softened. "I voted for you, Sofi-girl." Her eyes were sad. "I know how talented you are, how hard you work, how much you love music."

Sofi's stomach churned at the words Denna wasn't saying. "But not because of my performance that day." It wasn't a question.

The Musik looked pained. "There was a bit of a disconnect

with your audition. Your technical skill is unparalleled. But . . ." Her eyes flitted to Lara at the front of the room. Denna cleared her throat. "Lara's doing well. In fact, I heard a lot of you in her song."

Sofi froze, ice flooding her veins. "What?"

"Laravelle's song." Denna frowned at her. "Why did it make me think of you?"

Sofi shook her head, trying to come up with an acceptable lie. "I'm not, I mean, I haven't . . ." She was getting sloppy. Of course Denna would have noticed Sofi's influence in songs Sofi herself was composing. She had seen Sofi play many times, had talked to her about music theory and song composition so frequently she could likely recite Sofi's songwriting philosophy by heart. Sofi had been so focused on keeping the bone lute's secret that she'd forgotten to keep her own.

Denna started to laugh triumphantly. "It *is* about you! Who'd have thought—Sofi Ollenholt, the subject of a song."

Sofi was extraordinarily confused at the turn the conversation had taken. Her heart was still pounding, but the twisting in her stomach was for an entirely different reason. "We kissed," she finally admitted, smiling sheepishly.

Jakko bumped Sofi's shoulder. "I *knew* there was a thing. You were watching her with the most lovesick expression I've ever seen." He *tsk*ed softly. "I'm gone a fortnight and you become an entirely different person."

Sofi rolled her eyes, biting back a grin even as she felt her face flush.

"Ah." Denna clapped her hands excitedly as Lara

approached their table. "And there she is, the woman of the hour."

"Musik Mab!" Lara offered Denna both her hands.

"Denna," Denna said quickly. "Please call me Denna."

Sofi sat back, watching Wes and Lara and Jakko and Denna talk. Earlier that morning, Sofi had thought she'd left her family behind, but now, as she clutched a mug of steaming cider in the front room of a cozy inn, she realized she'd been wrong. Viiv and her gran weren't the only family she had left.

"I'm so pleased you came tonight," Lara was telling Denna and Wes. "It's been so nice to meet the Guild. There's just Tambor . . . and his son left, right?" She looked to Sofi for confirmation.

"Barton." Wes rolled his eyes. "Word of advice"—he turned to Lara—"put that meeting off for as long as you can. He's foul."

Jakko snorted. "I mean, his name *is* Barton."

Wes laughed, sending a flush across Jakko's face that had once been reserved only for mentions of Prince Jasper. Sofi couldn't wait to tease him about his newest crush.

"You know, Tambor *has* been strangely scarce since your father's passing." Denna leaned forward as Lara slipped onto the bench beside Sofi. "Normally he'd be here coughing up a storm. But the room is silent." Wes snorted. "If he was going to show face, I just assumed he'd be here. But he wasn't here last night, and"—Denna glanced theatrically over her shoulder—"he isn't here now."

Sofi perked up at Denna's tone. The hint of clandestine

ridicule tempted her to pull the Musik aside and reveal the truth about Tambor and his flute. But when her eyes fell on Lara, she hesitated. Sofi still didn't know how to prove Lara's innocence. No, Sofi needed more information before she could set the truth free. And who better to get answers from than Tambor himself? If Denna expected to see Therolious Ambor in Ohre, surely that meant he was local. "Does he live around here?"

"Right on the outskirts of town." Denna raised her eyebrows at the excitement in Sofi's voice. "Giant mansion on the top of a hill. You can't possibly miss it."

"Perfect." Sofi rubbed her hands together. "Make sure to get some sleep tonight, Musik Hollis."

Lara looked bemused. "Why?"

"We can't send you to Castle Lochlear without meeting the entire Guild first." Sofi nudged Lara with her shoulder. "Tomorrow we're going to pay Tambor a visit."

Tomorrow Sofi would finally come face-to-face with the man who had ruined her life.

THE FIFTH DAY

Sofi was eight the first time she met Therolious Ambor's son, Barton. The Musik and his offspring had come to the Ollenholt manor before Musik Ambor was set to perform at Saint Ogden's Theatre. While their fathers spoke in the parlor, Sofi and Barton stared at each other awkwardly in the kitchen. Sofi was settled on a stool by the fire, lute in her lap, working on the fourth verse of a song about Saint Hilde's flock, the ever-multiplying fold of lambs she shepherded from town to town.

Barton was eleven, gangly, freckled, and floppy-haired. His lips were incredibly chapped, the skin white and flaking, which Sofi found concerning considering that he used his mouth to play his instrument. But then again, she supposed she used her hands to play the lute, and the pads of her fingers were calloused and firm from practice.

She assumed it was the same for Barton. But when she asked about his training routine, he raised his pale eyebrows and laughed at her like she was a fool.

Sofi did *not* like feeling foolish.

"I don't *practice*," Barton said snidely.

But that didn't make any sense. Sofi knew that Tambor was grooming his son to one day take his place in the Guild of Musiks. "Then how do you intend to win your Apprenticeship?"

Barton blinked at her blankly. "By being the best."

Sofi frowned down at her lute. That logic went directly against everything she had ever been taught. "I don't understand." She struck an errant string, the discord of the note mirroring her uncertainty.

"Well," Barton said, shrugging disinterestedly, "you wouldn't, would you?"

Sofi's temper flared as hot as the flames crackling in the hearth. "What does that mean?"

"*My* family was smiled upon by the Muse. We don't have to do anything so common as"—Barton held up his fingers to emphasize the quotation marks—"'practice.' Anyone who *does*"—he looked Sofi up and down, disgust plastered across his pale face—"clearly won't ever become a Musik. But . . ." He considered, squinting at her. "Maybe if you get prettier, one day I'll marry you." He shrugged again as though it didn't matter either way.

Sofi scowled, her knuckles white as she clutched her lute to her chest. She wanted to spit on him. She wanted to smack him. Instead, as she knew she ought to do, she stayed measured and turned her attention back to her song.

In this verse, Saint Hilde's flock was in the city of Visc, where a fire had broken out in the local chapel. *"Then the saint began to call,"* Sofi sang, trying to ignore her anger, *"as the town crier's mouth did fall."*

Barton snickered. The sound was sharp and rough, like the slice of a knife. Embarrassment ran a small shiver up Sofi's spine, turning to rage as it reached her tongue.

"The saint, she sent her gentle ewes," Sofi continued, as her fury settled in her chest, *"right to where that fire grew."*

The flames in the hearth crackled and hissed. Barton made

another sound. This time, it was a noise not of amusement, but of pain. Sofi stopped her song just in time to see the ends of Barton's blond hair bright with fire.

Sofi shrieked. Casting aside her lute, she dove for a bucket of water, which she dumped unceremoniously all over Barton. The boy's eyes went wide, his face twisted with fury.

"DAD!" he roared, smacking open the kitchen door and stalking through the hallway to the parlor, leaving a puddle in his wake.

Sofi reveled in the silence before the storm. She did not shrink away or try to run. She stayed fixed to the floorboards until, just as she knew they would, her father's footsteps echoed down the hall.

Frederik stared down at his daughter with an impassive expression. "Come with me."

Dread pooling in her stomach, Sofi followed her father to the parlor, where Therolious Ambor and Barton stood, their faces in identical scowls. The small patch of facial hair that rested beneath Tambor's bottom lip quivered.

"Sofi." Even though his tone was firm, her father didn't sound nearly as angry as Sofi had expected him to. "What happened?"

"His head was on fire," she said incredulously. Even from here, the ends of his pale hair were visibly singed.

"And who *set* him on fire?" Tambor snapped.

"*I* didn't." Sofi held her hands out, placating. "I was only playing my lute."

"Singing about flames," came Barton's accusation back.

The room fell silent. Frederik paled.

Tambor's face split into a wide grin. "Oh ho," he said, studying Sofi with much more interest than he had a moment ago. "Frederik, it seems that your daughter has inherited some of your wife's more . . . indelicate traits."

Sofi didn't like the way the Musik was looking at her.

"Don't you *ever* speak about my wife, Therolious," Frederik said, his voice deadly quiet. Sofi shivered at her father's tone. "Now," Frederik continued, "as a measure of my good faith and fraternity, I'm going to ask my daughter to apologize. In return, you and your son will put this moment from your mind. Do you understand me?"

Tambor and Frederik stared at each other icily, the cold between them sharper than the storm raging outside. Then Tambor nodded. Just the slightest dip of his head.

"Sofi, apologize to the boy," Frederik snapped. "Now."

"Sorry," Sofi said flatly, dropping the apology on the carpet in front of her. Then she turned on her heel and went to dress for that evening's performance.

Her father let her go, but Sofi knew he wasn't done with her.

And indeed, on the carriage ride home from Saint Ogden's Theatre, after three hours of sitting through Therolious Ambor's good albeit uninventive performance, Frederik finally spoke.

"That wasn't wise, what you did today."

Sofi, sensing a test, stiffened. "Oh?" She stared down at her hands, folded demurely in the lap of her midnight-blue dress. She was tempted to fidget.

"You showed him your anger," Frederik continued, "which in turn showed *the world* your anger." He paused. Sofi worried her bottom lip between her teeth as she waited for the other shoe to drop. "Anger is a dangerous emotion." Her father fiddled with a button on the sleeve of his crisp white shirt. "It should have been suppressed on the fourth day." Sofi's stomach plummeted to her toes, already pinched in her too-small leather boots. "Yesterday," Frederik said pointedly, although Sofi needed no reminder.

Her palms were still swollen from the way her fingernails had dug into the flesh of her hands. In the year since she'd taken to sequestering her feelings to fourth days, she'd progressed past containing, measuring, and tamping down temper tantrums or loneliness or hope and had started experimenting with another level of feeling—the physical.

She'd begun to test herself in tiny ways to see what she could stand. What she could endure. She had been excited to share this new victory with her father. To be praised for her dedication and ingenuity.

Instead, she had only illustrated the ways she had failed.

"Kneel," her father said, nodding toward the floor of the carriage, which was wet with melted snow and other debris. Sofi did. "I'm disappointed, Sofi," Frederik said as Sofi hissed, a tiny twig pressing itself through her dress into the soft corner of her knee. "I expected more from you. I certainly never expected you to show such weakness in front of another Musik."

"But I didn't—"

"Do not interrupt *me*." Frederik's eyes were fixed on the opposite wall of the carriage. "It isn't *me* who I've created this training routine for. It isn't me who will benefit from control and careful precision. I'm only trying to help *you*, Sofi." His gray eyes finally met hers, and even though they were cold, the knot in Sofi's chest loosened slightly. At least he was looking at her. "Unless that *isn't* what you want?"

His question seemed earnest, which *only* served to frighten Sofi further. Surely her father had to know that becoming a Musik was, in fact, the only thing she wanted.

"Of course it is," she whispered desperately, hands clasped in front of her like a brother during a sermon. The carriage hit a bump, and Sofi went flying, her shoulder slamming against the seat where she'd once sat.

"Then prove it," Frederik said once she'd rightened herself and blinked back her tears. "Repent for your oversight. Tell the Muse exactly how you failed so that she might see you redeemed."

"Repent?" That made it sound as though she had erred seriously enough to require redemption. Surely she was not nearly that far gone for one flare of anger. It had only been a little fire.

"You want the Muse to deem you worthy of becoming my Apprentice, don't you?"

"Of course."

"That's my good girl." Frederik almost smiled as the carriage swayed back and forth. "I can't say the little brat didn't deserve it, but just because he might have deserved it doesn't mean you had to do it. Restraint, my girl. Careful walls will keep you safe. You know this, don't you?"

Sofi nodded eagerly, glowing with her father's measured praise.

"Of course you do." This time Frederik did smile. "I see now that I may have been too lax with you. I think this reflection will do you well. Let us add it to the routine. Yes." Frederik put a hand on the carriage window to steady himself, his fingers leaving a violent streak down the foggy glass. "The fifth day is for repenting."

NINETEEN

THEROLIOUS AMBOR lived in a sprawling estate atop the tallest hill in Ohre. In the early-morning sunlight, the stone turrets cast long shadows across Sofi's and Lara's boots as they stared up at the Musik's fortress.

"Is that"—Sofi squinted to get a better look at the stone figure settled in the alcove above the second-floor balcony—"a gargoyle?"

She was beginning to envy Jakko, still tucked into bed in their warm room at the Passing Breeze. *Tambor looks like the kind of man who'd slice off your arm and serve it up for tea,* he'd mumbled when Sofi asked if he wanted to join them. *Don't know why you would put yourself in his path willingly.* Then she'd rolled her eyes at his dramatics.

Now, though, Jakko's assessment felt frightfully apt.

"Well." Lara ran her hand across the iron gates like a harpist to her instrument. "This is certainly a spectacle."

"Says the daughter of the king's second cousin fifteen times removed." Sofi snorted.

"He's actually a fourth cousin twice removed." Lara snickered. "But don't tell my father I told you so. Anyway." She stuck her nose through the gap in the iron bars. "I've seen the house you grew up in. This isn't much bigger, if I'm honest."

Sofi leaned against the gate, the cold metal shocking against her cheek. It was true that physical comforts were something she had always taken for granted. It hadn't occurred to her how privileged a position that truly was.

"May I help you?" Sofi and Lara jumped away from the gate at the sound of the brittle voice. They had not heard footsteps approach, yet there was a man on the other side of the fence, sizing them up with hawkish yellow eyes.

"I'm Musik Laravelle Hollis." Lara smoothed her hair with a white-gloved hand. "Here to call on Musik Ambor."

The man frowned. "Musik Ambor is not expecting you."

"Tell him that Sofi Ollenholt, the daughter of the late Musik Ollenholt, is also present," Sofi said darkly. "Surely he would not turn away the grieving daughter of a former Guild member?" She offered the man her most withering stare, daring him to walk away from her.

The man pursed his lips dispassionately before pulling out a thin, spindly key, which he fitted into a lock. The gate opened with a squeal like a bird call, high and shrill. Sofi

winced as she led the way forward. The clang of the gate closing echoed in her chest like church bells. For a man who so
delighted in delicate sounds, Therolious Ambor's home was
quite cacophonous.

The black-clad servant paused outside the giant wooden
door and grabbed the round iron knocker. Instead of banging it against the door, the man lifted it delicately upward,
which sent a tinkling melody echoing through the inside of
the house, alerting its residents to their company.

They waited at the door, the man's back stiff, his gaze
never turning toward them. Sofi glanced at Lara, who was fidgeting with her gloves. Sofi wanted to fidget too.

She had distracted herself all morning with incessant
chatter, listening to Lara talk about the next sort of song she
wanted to play—*something upbeat; honestly, you act like writing
something happy might kill you*—and discussing music theory
over breakfast with Denna and Wes. That conversation had
loosened the knot constricting her heart. Had quieted the part
of her brain shouting that the entire Guild was made up of
impostors.

But now, as she drummed her fingers against her thigh in
the opening rhythm of "The Ballad of Sir Ellis," that piece of
her mind was shrieking again.

Sofi had only ever known one thing: that to be a Musik
meant a person had achieved the purest form of artistry. But
two members of the Guild had magic fueling their instruments. Not only had they continued to profit off their deception, but they had reveled in it. Pulled other people, innocents

like Sofi and Lara, into the trajectory of their storms.

Everything Sofi had known was shattered. Her life upended. Her dreams uprooted. Her family broken. And now that Frederik was gone, Sofi had only one man to blame.

Footsteps echoed behind the door, sharp soles slapping against stone. The sound paused. Beside Sofi, Lara stiffened. Then the door opened with a tremendous squeal to reveal Therolious Ambor, tall as the doorframe, with tiny spectacles resting on the top of his nose. A gargantuan mustache rested beneath, and a small patch of whiskers sat below his lower lip, both the same color as the hair on his head, dark brown streaked with gray. His blue eyes narrowed suspiciously.

"Sofi Ollenholt?" Tambor frowned at her, and then his eyes flickered to Lara. He coughed indelicately into a handkerchief. "Mistress Hollis?"

"*Musik* Hollis," Sofi corrected him automatically, frowning. His refusal to address Lara by her title seemed pointed.

"My apologies, *Musik* Hollis." He smiled sanctimoniously. "It's nice to see your face again. I'm sure the songs you pen are just as lovely."

Lara stiffened. Sofi struggled to keep her expression neutral even as her skin crawled like her sleeves were stuffed with spiders.

"She's a prolific songwriter," Sofi replied tersely.

"Quite the compliment from Frederik Ollenholt's daughter." Tambor turned to Sofi as though she were an afterthought. "Terrible shame, what happened there." He shook his head somberly. "Terrible shame." But the glimmer of relief in his eyes said otherwise. "Oh, now," the Musik said, coughing again, almost delicately, "I'm forgetting my manners. Let me show you to the parlor. Mads"—he turned to the birdlike man—"please go find my son. He'll want to say hello."

They followed Tambor down a long midnight-blue hallway that offered not even a glimpse of sunlight. Sofi ran her fingers along the wallpaper, glossy and smooth as the silk of Lara's dress. Sofi kept expecting her calluses to catch on the smooth surface, but the tips of her fingers, usually sharp as knives, had gone soft from disuse. Before her father's death, Sofi had played the lute incessantly, hour upon hour until her arms went wobbly and her fingers weary. Since she'd taken to the road with Lara, she was lucky if she eked out even half an epic. Her calluses had softened from lack of wear.

Yet another loss to face.

Tambor waved them into his parlor, leading Lara to a long couch.

"Oh, I'll just sit here." She tugged herself free from his grip and settled on a small settee by the roaring fire. "I run cold."

Tambor coughed into the crook of his elbow, looking slighted. "You do seem rather frigid."

It took every ounce of patience Sofi had garnered on second days to keep her fury to herself. She settled herself daintily on the edge of the sofa Tambor had intended for Lara. Tambor sank furiously into an armchair instead, coughing wildly. Sofi toed the rug, brown as the mud in Lail. Tambor's taste in decor left much to be desired.

"So, Laravelle," Tambor said, when he'd finally regained his breath, "I'm honored you chose to visit me. I'm so eager to hear about your travels." He leaned forward theatrically.

"You could have come to a show," Sofi interjected, trying to pull his prying eyes away from Lara. "Every other Musik has."

"Yes, well." Tambor's expression was sour. "I find performances so *tedious*. When you've attended as many as I have, music all begins to sound the same. There are only so many notes in the end. Isn't everyone merely playing the same song in a different order?"

Sofi was speechless, so loud was the perfect plane of fury that rang through her.

Lara frowned. "There are only so many letters, yet storytellers manage to spin them into endless combinations of words." She shifted carefully on the settee. "I certainly haven't noticed a repetition of the notes I've played."

"Well, now." Tambor eyed her pointedly. "You wouldn't, would you?"

"What does that mean?" Lara cocked her head, looking truly curious. Tambor's gaze flitted to Sofi searchingly. She turned her attention to her hands folded in her lap, nails digging into the flesh between her thumb and pointer finger, praying for some way to move Tambor away from the subject of the bone lute.

"Mads said you wanted me?" A tall boy leaned against the doorframe, his arms crossed sulkily over his chest. Although Barton had aged, his lips were still chapped, his hair was still floppy, and his face was still plastered with a scowl.

It was the only time Sofi had ever been pleased to see Therolious Ambor's son.

"Barton," his father barked. "Sit. We have company."

Barton Ambor scowled at Sofi and Lara. "Who are you?"

"This is Laravelle Hollis." Tambor gestured to Lara. "She will be joining you in the Guild of Musiks." He coughed. "On the lute." Sofi searched Barton's face for a flicker of recognition but found none. He didn't know the significance of the bone lute. That, Sofi supposed, was something. Better that the newest class of Musiks were not pitted against each other from the start. "And that's Sofi." Tambor waved dismissively at her.

Barton sank onto the sofa next to Sofi. He squinted at her suspiciously. "Didn't you set my hair on fire once?"

"Yes." Sofi scowled at him. "Don't get too close, or I'll do it again."

Across the room, Lara stifled a giggle as Tambor lifted a bell from the side table. Servants descended upon the room like a flock of crows, bearing silver trays with a teapot, mugs, and plates loaded with pastries. As quickly as they'd come, they were gone.

The parlor was filled with the clinking of silver against porcelain.

"So." Tambor leaned back in his chair. "Sofi." He set his teacup down on its saucer. "I was sorry to hear of your father's passing. We were childhood friends." He smiled wryly. "Neither of us knew then what we would one day become."

Sofi pursed her lips. "And what was that?"

"Great musicians." Tambor's smile was all teeth. "I was so inspired by him. As soon as he met your mother, his playing changed. Almost like *magic*. He always chalked it up to love. But I did wonder if it had something to do with his beautiful instrument."

Sofi blinked, trying to keep her expression carefully blank. She refused to let Therolious Ambor ruin Lara's life too. "I don't know what you mean."

"Only that he was always quite protective of it, your father." Tambor set his teacup onto the saucer with a soft clink. "Wouldn't even let anyone touch it. I never saw him play another lute."

Sofi bit back a snarl. "That's funny," she said. "I've never seen you play anything but your flute."

"Both of us loyal." Tambor dodged Sofi's hit. "Runs in the blood of Musiks, I suppose."

"Did you always love music, Musik Ambor?" Lara asked, her intention so pure it made Sofi unbearably sad. She shouldn't have come here. Facing the man who had ruined her life wasn't inspiring her to seek vengeance. It only served to make her feel more helpless.

"Music isn't about *love*, Mistress Hollis." Tambor sounded affronted. "Although if it was, I imagine you would be the most prolific of the bunch. I'm sure your clamoring fans have less to do with your musicianship than with that face of yours." Sofi couldn't help but notice how sharp Therolious Ambor's incisors were when he smiled.

Lara giggled in an overperformative way that signified she

didn't find the Musik's remarks the least bit funny. "That's what my father said when I was chosen as Apprentice." Her words were careful. Precise, like a pick through thin ice.

"I'm not surprised." Tambor put down his spoon with a resounding clink and stared across his folded hands at Lara. "It seems a shame to waste a face like yours on *music*."

Lara fluttered her eyelashes dangerously. "What could you possibly mean by that, Master Ambor?"

Tambor coughed. "Men have time. But, Laravelle, you are in your prime—you shouldn't be wasting it on what I'm sure are very proficient attempts at songwriting, not when your talents could be used . . . elsewhere."

Lara looked stricken. Sofi shifted uncomfortably in her seat. She had come into this meeting expecting to hate Therolious Ambor for his smug attitude and the knowledge of what he had done to her mother. She had not expected him to turn his beady eyes and lascivious grin on Lara, giving Sofi another reason to despise him.

"Can I use your washroom?" If she didn't get out of this room, she was going to explode, speaking words she would no doubt regret. Lara made a soft squeak of distress as Sofi leaped to her feet. "I'll be *right* back," Sofi promised her firmly before turning her steely gaze on Tambor.

"To the left, miss." The butler had appeared out of nowhere. His voice was clipped with resignation.

Sofi hurried down the hall, tapping a steady rhythm on her sternum, trying to coax her racing heart back in time. She needed to splash some water on her face. Take a breath. Cool down.

But before she reached the washroom, she came upon an open door. The room beyond was purposefully decorated, all cool blues and shiny silver threads through the tapestries that decorated the walls, giving the room a lived-in feeling she would not have thought possible from a man as calculating as Therolious Ambor.

But then, Sofi supposed, cruel men still craved comforts.

She slipped inside, closing the door carefully with a soft click. The room was small but familiar. A large desk took up most of the space before the window; a leather chair was tucked in the corner beside a tall bookshelf. A silver music stand was assembled in the center of the room, sheet music spilling from a leather folio.

It was Tambor's study. And while she knew the seconds were ticking down, that the length of her absence would soon be suspicious, Sofi couldn't tear herself away from the room. When Sofi had walked through Tambor's front door, she'd tried to put her own emotions in check. But watching Tambor hurt Lara had made Sofi want him to hurt, too.

To hurt someone, one needed to locate the thing they cared for most. Tambor had made it clear that he did not care at all for people. He only cared about power and acclaim.

At the root of that success was his flute.

Sofi moved across the room and ducked beneath the desk, hands grasping about the shadows. Her fingers closed around something hard, and she dragged a black leather case across the carpet into the light. Heart hammering, Sofi flicked the gold clasps open to reveal Tambor's silver flute.

Quickly, she pulled the pieces of the flute from its case, fitting the head joint into the barrel of the body covered with keys. The flute's mouthpiece, which she'd never been close enough to see, was unmistakably made of bone. She fitted the foot joint onto the end of the flute, resting the assembled instrument carefully in her lap before closing the case and returning it to its hiding place. She fumbled with the clasp on her skirt, loosening her petticoat to slip the flute into the waistband, retying it tightly so it would not slip.

She moved carefully to the study door, her steps odd and stilted as she tried to protect the flute, its cold body pressed against her hip. She pulled her long hair over her left shoulder, in hopes of disguising any bulge that might be visible through her thick woolen garments.

Sofi peered down the empty hall. She moved as swiftly as possible, nodding demurely as she reentered the parlor. Three sets of eyes were on her as she moved toward the sofa. She began to sit, then remembered the flute pressed against her side. There was no way to reclaim her position on the sofa without revealing the instrument stuck down her skirt.

She gripped the arm of the sofa dramatically. "Apologies, Master Ambor," she said, voice shaking, "Barton. We must depart early. I'm afraid I am unwell."

Tambor waved away her words. "Nonsense. I'll have the servants bring you a digestif."

Sofi's eyes flitted nervously to Lara, who was watching her warily. "No, that isn't it." She grasped wildly for an explanation that would let them escape unquestioned. Across the room, Lara pressed a hand to her lower abdomen and feigned a wince.

"My monthlies." Sofi mirrored Lara's posture, putting a hand to her stomach and groaning. "There is just so much blood." The wince on her face was not false. It was uncomfortable to speak about her bleeding aloud in this strange, brutal house.

Tambor coughed so ferociously his face turned puce. "I see. Go, then." He pushed his chair backward toward the wall as though he was afraid Sofi's condition was contagious.

"I wouldn't want to ruin your lovely chairs." Sofi smiled sweetly. "Thank you for your hospitality, Musik." She turned toward his son, who was using a pocketknife to clean his fingernails. "Barton." Barton grunted.

Lara swiftly got to her feet. "It was a pleasure," she said, her voice chilly. Her eyes did not meet Tambor's.

Sofi led the way to the door, her steps still stiff and careful. She could feel Lara's eyes on the back of her neck. It wasn't until the front door had closed firmly behind them that Sofi let out a deep sigh of relief. Still, she did not speak until the iron gates were far behind them. She kept a hand pressed against the flute at her side as the snow crunched beneath their feet.

"Thank you." Lara's voice and eyes were dull. "I couldn't stand to breathe the same air as him for one more minute." She sniffed, tugging the sleeves of her dress over her hands. "All those things he said, do you think . . . ? Is he right? Am I fooling myself?" She stopped walking, tears streaming down her face.

"Of course not." Sofi put a hand to Lara's cheek, trying to wipe away her tears with her thumb. But even as she said it, a lump rose in her throat. If Lara ever learned the truth about the bone lute, it would break her heart.

"My father always said I was nothing but a pretty face." Lara's mouth wobbled, and she scrunched up her nose. "I wanted to prove him wrong. When I found music, I just thought . . ." She descended into sobs.

"Shhh, shhh." Sofi pressed a finger to Lara's lips. "That isn't true, and you know it. Your value is so far beyond the physical. Your heart is enormous, and your voice is sweet as a lark's. Come on." She took Lara's hand. "Let's get back to the inn, and I'll regale you with all your positive qualities."

Lara finally smiled, albeit weakly. But they had taken only a handful of steps before she narrowed her eyes. "Why are you walking like that?"

"Like what?" Sofi put a hand to her hip, trying to keep the flute carefully tucked in the folds of her skirt.

"I can see you holding something." Lara laughed, reaching for Sofi's waist. Sofi darted away, but she wasn't fast enough. *"Saints and sheep,"* Lara whispered almost reverently. "Sofi, what did you do?" But she didn't sound angry. She appeared positively delighted. "Let me see it."

Sofi had no choice but to pull the flute from her petticoat. As soon as it was freed, Lara tugged the instrument cleanly out of Sofi's grip and turned it over in her hands. "Which side do you even blow into?"

"Lara, don't—" But Lara put the flute to her mouth, its

body extending out to her right side. Her lips formed a delicate O. She puffed a breath into the mouthpiece playfully.

When a novice tried to play the flute, it usually stayed silent and still. Instead, Lara played a perfect arpeggio, her fingers flying across the pads, the magic guiding her up and down scales. The wind howled, kicking up a flurry of snow, circling around them like a cyclone, clinging to Lara's eyelashes and crowding Sofi's nose. Lara removed her mouth from the flute, looking alarmed.

"What was *that*?"

Sofi opened her mouth, then promptly shut it. She had absolutely no idea how to explain this. "Are you secretly a trained flautist?" She tried to sound playful, but it came out like an attack.

"Sofi," Lara whispered, her expression as dark as a moonless night. "You know full well I've never played a flute in my life." She swallowed thickly. "That day at Saint Ogden's Theatre, I thought my prayers had been answered because I *wanted* it enough. Because I loved the art. But . . ." She paused, her voice no more than a whisper. "But that isn't really what happened, is it?"

"We need to go." Sofi's eyes darted wildly about for an escape. "It's a crime to steal a Musik's instrument."

"Is it a crime for a Musik's instrument to be *magic*, too?" Lara's eyes were steely. "Sofi." She grabbed Sofi's wrist roughly, her brown eyes wild like a house on fire. "You don't look nearly alarmed enough, which means you *knew*." Her breath hitched. "I'm not a true musician, am I?"

When Lara had first been named Apprentice, Sofi had spent hours imagining the way it would feel when she revealed the truth about her rival's incredible, falsified musical prowess. Had dreamed about the day she would finally expose the girl who had stolen her future as a fraud. But now that she was faced with the moment, Sofi felt no joy, no glee.

She was hopelessly, desperately sad that it took but a single syllable to ruin Laravelle Hollis's life the way Lara had ruined hers: "No."

TWENTY

LARA HOWLED like the wind, her usually bright eyes dull. "You *knew*."

She looked so pitiful, so broken, that Sofi wanted to sweep the girl into her arms. But she knew if she tried, Lara would push her away. So instead of being rebuffed, Sofi turned her anger outward.

"Come now," she scoffed. "This can't be *so* surprising. You can't honestly have believed you could play the lute perfectly with no training whatsoever?" Sofi's voice scraped the back of her throat. "Life has been easy for you. You've been able to get things because you're pretty and nice and polite, but everything isn't that simple, Lara." She ran a hand through her tangled curls. "Do you even realize what it has been like for me, watching you perform *my* songs on a tour that was my

destiny?" She flung her arms out wide. "All of this was supposed to be *mine.*"

Lara gaped at her like a fish. When she managed to
regain her voice, her words were frighteningly level. "I know
this might come as a shock to you, Sofi," she said, each word
clipped like an eighth note, "but I *know* life isn't fair. It's *you*
who seems to have this fantasy in her head, this idea that the
world rewards people duly. That just because you *wanted*
something so singularly, because you hurt yourself for it, that
it would be yours. But look at your life. Your wanting makes
you selfish. Cold. Falsely superior. You only care about yourself and what you think *you* deserve. You don't care about
other people at all."

Sofi had steeled herself, donned armor thick enough to
withstand the insults she lobbed at herself. But hearing that
same sentiment from Lara's mouth cut deeper than she'd prepared for. Sofi sucked in a breath, the sting of the truth sharp
against her skin. Then she laughed.

"That's rich, Laravelle." At the sound of her full name,
Lara recoiled. "Without me, you wouldn't have had songs to
play. You would have wandered the road alone, your shoddy
lyrics and simplistic melodies disgracing the art form." The
words were sour on her tongue like an underripe berry.

"There!" Lara waved a finger in her face. "That, *there*, is
exactly what I mean. You're so concerned with what music
should be that you forget who it's for. People don't care about
the syncopated rhythm or your rhyming conventions. They
want to listen to a song that makes them *feel* something. Be

transported by a performance. Find escape. They don't care about that superiority you love so much. But it's no wonder you're so misguided, considering the Guild is a sham." She threw her hands up in the air, looking helpless. "A magic flute? A bone lute that lets anyone play like a master?" Lara's bemusement was evident. "I don't understand why you want this so much, when all your heroes are frauds."

"Not all of them," Sofi said softly. "Not Denna. Not Yve or Raffe." There were still people like Sofi who respected music, who cared for it, who loved it. Who had dedicated their lives to the pursuit of something *great*.

"But they chose me." Lara's eyes were steely. "Not you. *Me*. The magic tricked them, too. So tell me, is there *anyone* who's as discerning as you?" Lara raised her eyebrows, waiting. She looked so incredibly tired. "I thought what we had was different, but I see now that I was wrong. You don't know how to love something you didn't create." A single tear clung to Lara's lower lashes. "I know you love music, Sofi, but saints, at what expense?"

When Sofi didn't answer, Lara turned on her heel and made her way down the path back toward town, the snow crunching beneath her shoes, leaving Sofi clutching Tambor's flute.

She didn't want to follow Lara. Didn't want to stumble through the snow, snot and tears freezing to her face as she begged for forgiveness, bending to Lara like a bow to the strings of a violin. Sofi knew all too well what it was like to suffer at her own hand. She would not give that power to another.

So instead of heading down the hill toward Ohre, she turned back toward Tambor's front gate, her knees shaking from the cold, and rattled the iron bars angrily.

"Come out," Sofi hollered, her voice fading into the afternoon. "Come out, you coward."

She shook the gate furiously, the way she wished she could shake her father's shoulders, yelling the way she wished she could yell at him. For all of Tambor's horrifying qualities, his actions that had inadvertently led to the dissolution of Sofi's family, Frederik Ollenholt had chosen deception first. He had given life to the illegal magic that was now a living, breathing creature residing in the Guild of Musiks.

"Can I *help* you?" The hawkish butler was back. Sofi hadn't even heard the front door open. His eyes caught on the flute in her hand, his irritation shifting from surprise to horror in an instant. He pulled the key from his belt and unlocked the gate, pulling Sofi roughly inside.

"Hey," she shouted, trying to squirm out of his grip, but his hand was like an iron clamp. "Stop it." She jerked wildly about as the butler dragged her toward the house. "You're hurting me."

"I don't have patience for thieves," the man snapped, hauling Sofi through the front door. "Master Tambor," he screeched, like a bird of prey. "Your presence is required in the parlor."

He released Sofi, sending her sprawling onto the sofa where she'd been perched daintily only a short time before. He jerked the flute away from her, holding it triumphantly above his head.

"Mads?" Therolious Ambor had returned, his eyes darting from the flute in his servant's hand to Sofi on the couch. Barton trailed behind him, looking sleepy. "What is the meaning of this?"

"I found her at the gate." Mads peered down at Sofi as though she were a bug he'd successfully squished beneath his shoe. "With your flute."

Tambor's eyes narrowed. "My *flute?*"

Sofi stared defiantly up at him. "Under your desk is not an inspired hiding place, Master Ambor. You should keep your secrets closer to your chest. Wouldn't want someone to *blackmail* you."

"Barton." Tambor's eyes flashed with fear that quickly turned to fury. "You're not needed here. Save yourself from the ramblings of a madwoman." His mustache twitched as his expression rearranged itself, watching as his son shrugged and wandered from the room.

Once they were alone, Tambor began to laugh. "You poor, useless girl." He clutched his waistcoat as he chortled, his laughter punctuated with coughs. "You can't possibly believe I'm in any real danger of discovery."

Sofi frowned. Lara had uncovered the truth in seconds. Merely raising the instrument to her lips had been enough to reveal its magic. "What do you mean?"

"When you make a deal with the devil, girl," Tambor said, sinking heavily into the settee Lara had previously occupied, "you must protect yourself. I was warned about the devil by my first instructor—the devil who tempts men away from the Muse, wreaks havoc on songs, mixes up stories. That woman your father married, well, she was tempting enough."

Sofi rose to her feet, fingers curling into fists. But before she could lift a hand, she was intercepted by Mads and a length of rope, which he used to bind her wrists together.

"Thank you, Mads." Tambor nodded his head almost reverently to the man, who swept away as silently as he'd come. "Now"—he refocused his attention on Sofi—"are you ready to speak civilly?"

"I will do no such thing," Sofi snapped, baring her teeth. But Tambor merely chuckled.

"Youth," he said, almost fondly. "Wasted on the foolish. Your father and I were about your age when we met, you know. We were both musicians, albeit middling at best. When the king announced the Guild, we both wanted it, more than we'd ever wanted anything before."

"Why?" Sofi shook her head. "You said it yourself—you never loved the music."

Tambor's face split into a nasty grin. "But I loved where it could take me. Do you know how rare the air beyond the Gate is, knowing you're one of only a handful of Aellinians to have access to it? To have seen the cities beyond, the way their villages are constructed, to taste spices I have no name for, to touch fabrics I have never seen spun? The world was *mine*. Of course," he said derisively, "you'll never understand that. Considering."

"Considering you used your knowledge to ruin my

father's life and grant my title to another?" Sofi spat.

"My apologies." Tambor did not look very sorry at all. "But sometimes a sacrifice must be made."

"I spent my entire life eschewing magic. Preparing to take over my father's legacy. But he's gone, thanks to your meddling. I'm an *orphan* because of you."

Tambor looked affronted. "Your father took his own life, and I certainly did *not* kill your mother. Your accusation has no grounds."

"My mother drained her magic to appease your threats!"

Tambor rolled his eyes as though Sofi were nothing more than a yapping dog. "It isn't my fault your father was too proud to admit he wasn't talented enough to hack it on his own."

"Neither were you."

"But I never claimed to be," Tambor said, self-satisfied. As though that was enough to absolve him of his sins. "See, that's where your father went wrong. He tried to take credit where it wasn't due."

"Your flute is *magic*!" Sofi shouted. "You are due nothing either. You don't even care about music. You only care what it can do for you."

Tambor looked at her carefully. "What is my crime here, Sofi? Is it that I don't respect music, or that I used your family's magic to do the disrespecting?"

"I . . ." Sofi hated the way that Tambor's eyes flashed knowingly. She didn't know why she was angry anymore, only that she was so impossibly furious that she wanted to break Tambor's flute and the magic it contained. But as Sofi still didn't have the faintest idea how to do that, she decided to change tactics. "When you said you protected yourself the way my father didn't, what did you mean by that?"

Tambor sat up straighter, looking smug. "I ensured that *my* instrument would keep my secret. That none but my blood could play it. Something that your father should have thought of. Certainly would have saved *you* some heartache."

Sofi frowned. She was no expert in family trees, but surely if Lara was descended from Tambor's family line, they both would have known about it. "Is that so?"

"Of course," Tambor snarled. "I am no fool. Not like your father, so enchanted by that witch that he forgot to protect himself."

Sofi was furious at her father too, but there was something in Tambor's tone that set her blood boiling. "That witch," she said coolly, "was my *mother*. And she was much cleverer than you."

Tambor snorted indelicately, his mustache vibrating. "I highly doubt that."

"Well." Sofi struggled to rise from the depths of the sofa without the use of her bound hands. She crossed the room swiftly, fumbling awkwardly for the flute, which Tambor had left resting on the arm of his chair. "I suppose there's only one way to find out."

Before Tambor could stop her, she brought the flute to

her dry lips and blew. Her heart pounded. Her body froze. There was a high-pitched ringing in her ears that came not from the instrument but from within.

Then her fingers jerked across the flute's keys, like a coach behind a team of dogs, and she began to play a melody she had never even considered before, almost as though the flute had willed the tune into existence.

Sofi had never played the flute, let alone with bound wrists and a hammering heart. It shouldn't have sounded so pure. It shouldn't have been so easy. As she continued to play, the ringing in her ears making her cringe, the flames in the parlor's hearth flickered and sputtered out. A pile of snow dropped from the chimney onto the ashes, suffocating the remaining sparks with a sharp hiss. The temperature indoors dropped immediately, and every candle and lantern was snuffed with a soft whoosh. Snow pounded against the window, like a child smacking the keys of a piano, like mallets against a drum. An endless racket of ice.

Sofi shivered, lowering the flute from her lips. Tambor had gone pale, eyes darting from Sofi to the fireplace and back again.

"You little witch," Tambor snarled, lunging for Sofi. She stepped aside, but she wasn't fast enough. Tambor grabbed her elbow and she stumbled, dropping the flute. Tambor howled, lunging for the instrument, his fingers closing around the foot of the flute before it hit the ground. The Musik cradled the flute in his arms like an infant. Sofi was sure he had never looked upon another human with such tenderness. The love that he had was only for himself or for things that served him.

While he was distracted, Sofi crept toward the parlor door. She was unnerved by the avalanche that had unleashed itself when she'd played the flute. Usually, when her magic pushed itself to the surface, it had to do with her lyrics. But this cold was bigger than anything Sofi had ever called forth. It was almost out of her control.

"Where do you think you're going?" Tambor's voice was vicious. "Mads has already sent for the Kingsguard. They're on their way to collect you. Surely you *do* know that stealing is a crime. Especially from a Musik. *Especially* when you're just some common girl. Because that's all you are, Sofi Ollenholt." Therolious Ambor's eyes danced wildly. "Your father was a fraud, and you are *nothing*."

"You're lying," Sofi tried to convince herself. The Kingsguard only presided over the most heinous of crimes. Thieves were usually dealt with by the mayor of a town, and even then punishment was often nothing more than the price of the item. There was enough in Frederik's account to cover the cost of even the finest instrument.

"I'm not." Tambor grinned wickedly. "King Jovan is my patron, and therefore, my protector. And so you will *wait*."

There was nothing to be done, with Tambor watching her and Mads standing guard at the parlor's entrance. Sofi waited, her throat dry, her hands fidgeting with her bindings. The longer she sat there, the more time Lara had to stew over the harsh words they had exchanged. The longer Lara considered Sofi's selfishness, the more difficult it would be for Sofi to earn Lara's forgiveness.

Finally, when Sofi thought she could bear the waiting no longer, there came a ringing through the large house. The doorbell's melody was soft and lilting. It set the hair on the back of Sofi's neck standing up straight.

Chain mail clinked and rattled as two men swept into the room behind Mads, the king's colors of red and gold peering through their armor. The towering men made Sofi feel even smaller than usual, their thick fingers clutching spears tightly, their expressions stoic. When their eyes fell on Sofi, they frowned.

"Really, Tambor?" The man on the left looked irritated. "A teenager stole your flute?" He exchanged a weary look with his companion. "This is what we came here for? To arrest a child?"

"She's not a child." Tambor looked affronted. "She's a witch."

"We've spent twenty-five years searching for witches, and the first one we find just *happened* to steal your flute?" The other Kingsguard cast a wary glance at Sofi. "If she's a witch, why doesn't she magic herself out of those bindings?"

The first Kingsguard chortled. Sofi began to relax. The Kingsguard appeared to have about as much respect for Therolious Ambor as Sofi did, which was to say, none.

"If you do not take her out of here in chains and throw her in the dungeon of Castle Lochlear, I will send a bird to King Jovan himself and let him know his own staff is undermining his most important project." Tambor's voice was dangerously calm. "The Guild of Musiks is working to create unity and harmony throughout this saint-forsaken earth, and *you would do well not to forget that.*" Tambor's face had gone scarlet, his fury so overarching that his entire body trembled.

The Kingsguard exchanged looks of irritation. "Fine," said the first one dully, "but I'm warning you, Tambor. If you continue to call us here to take care of children, one day, when you really need us, we'll be nowhere to be found." He reached for Sofi's elbow, guiding her gently forward. "Come on, then."

Sofi's fear overtook her confusion, and she began to struggle, trying to slip away from the guards with their spears and swords. The second guard clamped a giant hand on her shoulder, gripping so tightly she could already feel the bruises begin to form.

"I'll tell the king," she shouted at Tambor in one last, desperate attempt to free herself.

Tambor turned on her, his quivering mustache so close to Sofi's face she could have counted the individual hairs. "You will do no such thing," he said, "or I'll make sure that pretty little friend of yours gets Redlisted. As I said, she's far too lovely to be wasted on music."

Sofi spat in Therolious Ambor's face.

"None of that, now." The second guard sighed, scooping Sofi up and over his massive shoulder. Sofi pounded at his back, but his armor was so thick it only served to bruise her knuckles. "We're just doing our jobs." Outside, Sofi was thrown onto the snow. Her hands were untied, then rebound behind her back with a chain. She was shoved into a small carriage that smelled of soup. The first guard took the reins, and the second joined Sofi in the cramped space.

"You can't be serious," Sofi said as the carriage began to move. "He's lying. I didn't steal anything. You know as well as I do that he's a ridiculous man."

The Kingsguard shook his head. "You picked the wrong one to anger, girl. Now be quiet. We've got a long way to go, and I need a nap."

He leaned his head against the carriage wall and closed his eyes. The coach flew down the hill, the sled runners slicing through the snow with a sharp swish. As the dogs raced through Ohre, Sofi caught a glimpse of white-blond hair outside the Passing Breeze.

"Lara," she shouted, pressing her face against the small window. Lara wouldn't know where Sofi had gone. She would only know that the two of them had exchanged angry words, and then Sofi disappeared, leaving her to face her final town and the king's performance alone.

It would validate all the awful things Lara had said about Sofi—her selfishness, her superiority complex. She had to let Lara know that she wouldn't abandon her.

"Lara," she shouted again, struggling with the carriage door. She needed to warn her about Tambor.

"Please be quiet," the Kingsguard grumbled, unfolding his arms and wrestling Sofi back into her seat.

"Lara!" Sofi shrieked, but it was too late. The Kings-guard stuffed a handkerchief in Sofi's mouth to muffle her yelling. Sunlight reflected off the spears in the corner of the carriage.

Sofi knew when she was beat.

She spat the handkerchief onto the ground as the coach hurtled forward, leaving Ohre—and the girl Sofi cared for most—behind.

TWENTY-ONE

S OFI HAD not expected to enter the King's City in chains.

She had expected to stride confidently through the towering iron gates, wind at her back as she moved through the wide streets, trampled by so many feet that the snow melted in patches to reveal gray cobblestones underfoot. She had expected to wander through the dizzying alleyways, laughing with Lara as they strolled arm in arm, waving away the smoke that poured from hundreds of chimneys like the steady puff of bassoons. She had expected to duck beneath laundry lines and avoid the heavy feet of city dwellers all while keeping her eyes on the turrets of Castle Lochlear.

Instead, the Kingsguard's coach skipped the city proper altogether and was waved through a side gate. The dogs hurtled down a dark tunnel. Without the snow, the sled's runners scraped against the stone like a feral cat howling along to an out-of-tune oboe solo. The guard in the coach clapped his hands over his ears. Sofi clenched her jaw so tightly her teeth ached.

Then the carriage came to a violent stop, sending Sofi slamming against the wall, her arms nearly jerking out of their sockets. "Worms eat your eye," she swore to no one in particular. The guard chuckled softly.

"Come on, then." He exited the carriage first, using a thick arm to pluck Sofi from the carriage to the floor of the tunnel as easily as if she were a feather. She stretched her neck and wished her hands were bound differently so she could brush her skirt flat. She didn't want to look too rumpled before King Jovan. Even so, the king had always been kind to her. Sofi was certain that she could find a way to explain herself, even if she couldn't offer him the whole truth.

The other Kingsguard swept snow from his shoulders and cap and flanked Sofi's left side. But instead of leading her to the castle proper, the two men escorted Sofi down a circular staircase, the air around them growing colder and darker the farther they descended. At the bottom of the stone steps was a small door. The first Kingsguard pulled a key from his belt and unlocked it.

"Wait." Sofi's voice was urgent. "Where are you taking me?"

"Home sweet home," the first guard grumbled, pushing the door open to reveal a tiny dungeon. Weak afternoon light poured in from rectangular windows that lined the ceiling, too high for a person to reach. Snow and ice clung to the metal bars. Wind whipped through the small space. Sofi shivered.

"In you go," said the second man, opening the cell nearest the door and pushing Sofi inside. He locked her in with a nearly silent click. She peered into the other cells. They were all empty.

The first guard noted her gaze. "It's been a quiet week. You'll have some privacy, at least."

"I want to see the king." Sofi stood up straight in an attempt to look authoritative. "Please, tell him Sofi Ollenholt needs to speak to him. He knows me. He'll want to see me."

The guards exchanged a look. Then they both began to laugh. "He'll want to see you?" gasped the second guard. "Of course he will. Isn't like he has a country to run." His laughter echoed eerily throughout the dungeon, reverberating from the far wall so that it sounded like he was behind Sofi.

The tiny bubble of hope Sofi had been clinging to burst. "You don't understand." Her voice caught on the lump in her throat. "He's been to my home. He *knows* me."

"I don't care what you think he knows," said the first guard. "I'm telling you the king won't come down here for the likes of you."

Sofi blinked back tears. "Can I have my wrists back, at least?" She turned around, holding out her chained wrists. She looked at the guards desperately over her shoulder. "Please?"

The second guard, the one who had been in the carriage with Sofi, reached for his belt loop. "Give it here, then." As he freed Sofi from her chains, she began to weep in earnest. It was a relief to no longer feel the cold metal burning her skin.

Once, Sofi had wandered willingly into the snow without shoes, letting the ice consume her bare feet as she watched her toes turn blue. She had found strength in that *feeling*. But now, with a frozen nose and a body that ached from the rattling and jostling of the Kingsguard's carriage, Sofi didn't feel strong. She didn't even know what day it was. Which suffering she was supposed to submit to.

She supposed it didn't matter either way. Tambor had won. Sofi couldn't reveal the truth about his magic without incriminating Lara. Without incriminating her father. Her mother. Herself.

That knowledge only made her cry harder. The Kingsguard exchanged looks of alarm. "No need for all that," the first guard said.

"We'll tell the king," the second said placatingly. The first guard elbowed him. "Just in case," he said defensively as they left the dungeon, the door slamming shut with a sharp finality.

Sofi sank to the floor. She couldn't believe what her impulsivity had wrought. If only she had kept her calm, if only she had taken a deep, measured breath, she wouldn't be in this mess. If she'd splashed the water on her face instead of sneaking into Tambor's study, she would have been able to steady herself. She'd be with Lara and Jakko on their way to Elgan. She would be planting kisses on Lara's rosy-pink cheeks, twirling her silky hair between her fingers. She would be commiserating with Jakko as they watched their broken dreams fit Lara perfectly.

Lara wouldn't know about the lute and would play her newest song with blissful ignorance.

Saints and sheep. Her *song.* Without Sofi there to compose, Lara would have nothing to play. It would feel like a pointed insult—Sofi had gone on and on about being a good person because she had stepped up to help Lara, even though her intentions had never been sincere. She had expected to learn the truth about Lara and revel in her downfall. She hadn't expected to fall in love with her.

And then Sofi had ruined everything with her angry words. She should have listened more carefully to her father. Sofi was only good for wanting, for repenting, for praying.

Not for caring, or guiding, or loving.

Night fell, the darkness seeping through the bars of the tiny, high windows. Sofi wrapped herself more tightly in her furs. Every time she closed her eyes, all she could see was Lara's disappointment as Sofi's polished veneer had given way to reveal the waste of a person she truly was.

So Sofi kept her eyes open.

The night passed, cold and unrelenting, as Sofi huddled in a corner of her cell. The floor was stone, the walls were stone, the metal bars were frozen, and yet despite that fact, everything was still somehow wet.

As weak sunlight began to creep into the morning sky, Sofi repositioned her furs. The dungeon door opened with a clang, rattling the keys that hung beside it. But the guard who entered did not reach for them. He wasn't one of the Kingsguard who had chaperoned Sofi. This one was shorter, with fiery red hair and a blond beard. He carried a sliver of bread and a plush velvet stool. He flung the bread through the bars and set the stool daintily outside Sofi's cage.

"Who's that for?" she shouted, ignoring the bread, which had landed in one of the incomprehensible puddles and was growing soggier by the moment. But the guard didn't answer, merely closed the door with a whoosh. Seconds later, the door opened again, and in strode the King of Aell.

"King Jovan." Sofi threw off her furs and ran to the bars, clutching them even as her palms screamed with cold. "It's so good to see you. I thought you wouldn't come."

The king settled himself on the velvet stool, his thick, fur-trimmed robe billowing out around him. He looked even older than he had the last time Sofi had seen him only a few weeks prior. The bags beneath his eyes were nearly black. His dark hair was run through with patches of silver. He did not look Sofi in the eye; rather he looked everywhere *but* at her.

"You stole Therolious Ambor's flute." King Jovan's voice was grave. He heaved a heavy sigh.

"Yes . . . but I brought it back." Sofi willed the king to look at her. He was a man who'd embraced her more warmly than her own father had. Surely if he saw her desperation, he would understand it was not she who was at fault.

"He can be a prickly fellow," the king said, "but of course, you know that. Which is why I want to know the reason you chose to anger him so." His brown eyes were like the night sky, endless, wide, and sad.

"I . . ." Sofi bit her lip, considering. She knew that Tambor's threat was real. He would expose Lara, wouldn't even blink as the Kingsguard branded her skin. Sofi couldn't tell King Jovan the truth, no matter how desperately she wanted Therolious Ambor to burn.

"I know it must be difficult." King Jovan leaned forward, elbows resting on his knees. "What with your father's death. I'll admit, I expected it to be *you* who joined the Guild. I can see that both of these losses have hit you hard." He sighed. "But dreams can change, Sofi. Loss is not a reason to also lose hope or faith. Nor is it a reason to stoop to the level of theft. Against one of the Guild, at that."

Sofi wanted to roll her eyes. "You know me, King Jovan. You must know that I would only have done what was absolutely necessary." She raised her eyebrows, willing him to understand without having to speak the truth.

"I'm afraid I don't know anything other than your word against Musik Ambor's." The king rubbed a hand across the back of his neck. "You've been accused by a Musik, which means this will go to trial. You'll take the stand day after next, before the celebration of your father's career. Until then, I'm afraid you must remain here."

Sofi gripped the bars of her cell so tightly that her knuckles went white. "You're going to leave me locked up?"

King Jovan looked at her sadly. "I have to keep the Musiks happy. It's for the good of Aell, Sofi, you understand. This program *must* work. We need the Council to open the Gate."

"But the Guild is passing along their titles. Tambor is almost retired."

"Musik Ambor," the king corrected her sharply, "is almost retired, yes. But not yet. And considering it is his son taking his place in the Guild, I'm afraid that retirement doesn't eliminate your problem. In fact, that the instrument is being passed down to Barton Ambor only amplifies the crime. You would have prevented him from heading out on the road."

"But I gave it back," Sofi screeched, her own voice ringing in her ears.

King Jovan got to his feet. "It's too late, Sofi."

Sofi nearly spilled all her secrets there and then. But King Jovan was too focused on keeping his Musiks happy to believe anything Sofi had to say. And locked in the dungeons, she had no way to prove her accusations. Anything she claimed would look like conjecture.

Tambor had been right. Sofi *was* no one.

She pressed her forehead to the cold bars of her cell. "Please," she begged, her tears freezing on her cheeks, "don't leave me here alone."

King Jovan put a hand to her face. Hope bubbled in her chest at his tenderness, until . . . "I'm so sorry, Sofi." Then he swept away, taking her last shred of hope with him.

She slumped to the floor beside the slice of soggy bread. There weren't even any sounds in the room, no shifting or sighing, no clinging or clanging, just one endless quiet punctuated by her own breaths. There was no music to be made, not there. Sofi closed her eyes tightly, folded her hands, and whispered the Muse's Prayer. Surely she had done enough to garner a response. Some guidance from the deity she had spent her life worshipping.

But there was no reply. In fact, the Muse's silence was so loud that Sofi began to fear the voice she had once heard, that whisper of her destiny, had merely been in her own head. Another way that she had forced herself to suffer.

Sofi opened her eyes to her dank, dark surroundings. She scooted back against the wall, her head meeting rough stone. As she considered a life without it, she began to wonder if she had ever truly loved music at all or if she had merely loved the escape it offered her. The way it connected her to her father, the only parent she had been allowed to know. The only way to prove to herself that she had worth, a little girl in a big, empty house. A reason to hold on, to dream, to *hope*.

If Sofi didn't even love music, then what *could* she love?

Maybe Lara was right, and the answer was nothing at all.

TWENTY-TWO

SOFI SLEPT even worse the second night.

Although the king had sent a serving girl to deliver Sofi a thick woolen blanket, a dry pair of socks, and a bowl of warm stew, those physical comforts did little to ease her inner turmoil. Her dreams were filled with frozen figures: icy Laras and static Jakkos, glacial King Jovans and glistening Dennas. While everyone around her was made of ice, their faces all frozen in perfectly chiseled surprise, Sofi, alone, was on fire. Orange flames sprang from her fingertips, burst from the ends of her hair, but no matter how hot she burned, no matter how close she pressed herself to the icy forms of the people she loved, the frozen figures stayed perfectly preserved.

Entirely lifeless and utterly empty.

When Sofi woke, her ears burned from the cold. Her fingers were stiff, and the horrible mood she'd fallen into the day before had molded like a potato, turning black and foul-smelling overnight. Sofi was thoroughly rotten.

Lara would be on her way to the King's City by now. While she walked the cobblestones of the city above, Sofi would remain locked up below. Lara wouldn't know how close they were. How desperately sorry Sofi was for hurting her. For withholding the truth.

And she was. Truly. When she'd learned that Frederik had worked so hard to suppress Sofi's magic while possessing a spell of his own, it had been a blow so crushing that Sofi feared her heart might never recover. She'd felt not only angry but foolish, too.

Of course Lara was upset. Sofi had subjected her to a similar betrayal.

For so long, Sofi had wanted to be just like her father—to garner the same respect, showcase the same level of talent, create work of the same value—but now she feared she had only inherited his darker parts. The parts that prioritized herself at the expense of others.

Lara had been right. Sofi *was* selfish. Their time on the road had always been about what Sofi had expected, what Sofi wanted, what Sofi could do. All the while, she had completely ignored Lara's own hopes and dreams and fears. Lara wasn't a practiced lute player, but she did hold talent, that much was true. Her voice was sweet and captivating, her charisma was undeniable, and her eagerness—the effort she made to understand the songs Sofi had penned for her, to contribute and understand the compositions—showed that she *cared*.

Music, Sofi now understood, wasn't just about technical skill and precision, but about emotion, too. Lara had that in spades. But Sofi had been too busy building mental walls and chasing perfection to reveal the careful corners of her heart.

What a mess she'd made. In an attempt to reclaim her father's legacy, she had ripped it to shreds. After a lifetime of eschewing magic, she'd stumbled into the arms of her grandmother and Viiv, who were proof that magic wasn't what Sofi had to fear. The lies of men were much more dangerous.

If only she had taken advantage of her time in Lail, had asked her grandmother more about her own magic. Had she been brave enough to embrace her own abilities as Viiv had suggested, maybe she wouldn't be trapped in a jail cell while the kingdom prepared to celebrate the legacy of her fraudulent father. If she'd been willing to learn about the blood in her veins and the magic in bones, she might have discovered a way to reveal Therolious Ambor's crime without putting Lara in danger.

Instead, as always, Sofi had been too focused on herself.

And because of that, she was completely, utterly alone.

She fiddled with the chain around her neck, remembering her grandmother's soft fingers brushing her skin as she secured the clasp. Sofi was often so focused on the things that came next that she forgot to exist in the present moment. While in Lail, she'd been so consumed with taking down Tambor, worrying about the next song, the next town. Thanks to her lack of focus, all she had from the time with her family was a single bone, no larger than her smallest finger, hung on a silver chain. And because she hadn't bothered to reckon with the magic that was a part of her, that bone was useless.

"I'm so sorry, Gran," Sofi whispered, clutching the bone tightly in her palm, squeezing her eyes shut. "I didn't know . . . I don't know what to do." She began to cry in earnest. The dams she'd constructed to hold back her sadness, anger, and resentment broke, and she was flooded with her failures. She'd had no sympathy for Jakko. No understanding for Lara. No time for her gran and Viiv.

"*Hollow God.*" Sofi slapped the floor with her hand, and the shock of it radiated through her palm. She couldn't have ruined her life more perfectly if she'd tried.

A pebble of snow tumbled down from the window high above her, plunking her on the top of her head. She clapped a hand to her scalp and squinted up at the tiny window. She scooted aside as more snow tumbled down and narrowly avoided an icicle to the face.

There was a rustling. A ruffling. Then a sharp black beak poked through the bars of the window. Above her, a bird cocked its head, considering her. Its beady black eyes blinked. Then it wriggled its way through the gap in the window's iron bars and landed at Sofi's side, its talons clicking against the stone floor.

"What the . . . ?" Sofi hurried to sit upright, casting a cursory glance around the dungeon, but of course there was no one else to bear witness. She wasn't due the company of a guard until lunchtime.

Sofi pressed her hands to the ground so that she was eye level with the bird. She was almost certain it was a crow, which seemed like a good sign considering the bone she wore. Crows were drawn to witches, after all. Maybe this one had heard her plea. Then again, the bird might be a raven. Sofi had never thought she'd need to know the difference.

"Are you a raven or a crow?" she asked, feeling remarkably stupid.

The bird opened its beak, and Sofi's heart leaped. If it was a crow, perhaps it understood her. Maybe it could even answer. She braced herself for a caw or a croak. Instead, there came a voice: "You're even more hopeless than I thought."

Sofi shrieked, scrambling backward. She hadn't expected the bird to have a voice, and certainly not one so irritated. In fact, it possessed a level of annoyance so familiar that Sofi couldn't help but whisper, "Viiv?"

"Yes, Sofi," came her cousin's flat voice. "Obviously."

Sofi darted a glance around the empty dungeon despite herself. If this was obvious to Viiv, Sofi didn't want to know what her cousin found strange. "I don't understand. . . . Are you *in* a crow?"

Sofi could practically hear Viiv roll her eyes. "I'm not *in* a crow, you idiot. I'm speaking *through* a crow. I talk through a beak on my side the way you're talking through a beak on yours. It's the easiest way to communicate across long distances. Letters take too long to arrive." She sighed. "Honestly."

"What? I . . ." Sofi shook her head, feeling like she was losing her mind. "So you're still in La—" Viiv hissed as Sofi nearly spoke aloud the secret name. "Still with Gran?"

"Yes," Viiv snapped. "And while this has been a lovely albeit pointless conversation, it's feeding time, so if you'll excuse me—"

"Wait," Sofi shouted into the crow's beak, feeling beyond foolish. "I really need your help."

"Yeah," Viiv said, "hence the crow."

Sofi squinted at the creature. "*You* sent the crow to me?"

"Of course I did." Viiv sounded proud. "I can communicate with birds anywhere. I've transcended borders. I simply rerouted this one when I heard you cry for Gran."

"Okay . . ." Sofi didn't understand a word her cousin spoke. "But what's a crow going to do for me?"

The crow ruffled its feathers indignantly. Viiv sounded affronted too. "What *wouldn't* a crow do for you? Sofi, have you not been paying any attention at all? These birds are the conduits of our magic. They're whip-smart, caring, and endlessly devoted. That's why one witch can't break the spell of another. Only a witch known by the bones is able to offer the sacrifice necessary to break the spell."

"Sacrifice?" Sofi asked, confused. "What sacrifice?"

Viiv made a soft clucking sound with her tongue. "That's why you need a relationship with the bones, isn't it? The sacrifice is different for every spell, just as every bird—every bone—is different."

"So there's really nothing I can do?" Sofi asked, a pit

forming in her stomach. "I stand trial against Tambor, and if he wins, he gets to play his magic flute forever and I just have to accept that, knowing what I know?" She sighed, hanging her head helplessly. "I played it, Viiv. His flute. Snow came crashing down through the chimney. It was weird."

"Well spotted, Sofi," Viiv said darkly. "Magic is super *weird*." Sofi rolled her eyes. "Anyway, I suppose it's not entirely surprising that the flute might react differently when it was played by a witch. Your magic probably amplified its usual reaction." Sofi pictured her cousin shrugging.

"What, like it always brings snow when it's played, only slowly?"

"Could be," Viiv said dismissively. "There's consequences to using a human as a conduit. We've been over this."

Sofi stared up through the tiny window at the top of her cell where, outside, the winter raged on. "Consequences like snow falling in the middle of summer and then never stopping?"

"Hmm?" Viiv sounded distracted.

Sofi sat up straighter. "Viiv, my mother used her marrow to make Tambor's flute. What's more volatile than snow in the summer? What if every time he plays it, he reinforces the winter? What if it's spreading the icy fury my mother felt being trapped by his blackmail?"

On the other end of the crow, her cousin was silent.

"Viiv?" Sofi prodded.

"I'm thinking," Viiv said sharply.

"Viiv, when I played his flute, it was like I called the

cold forth," Sofi continued, unable to restrain her thoughts. "Tambor has been playing that flute every day for the last sixteen years. What if that's why the winter never left?"

"It's highly improbable," Viiv mused, "but . . . not implausible."

Sofi's heart stuttered. "If it *is* true, if that is what's been happening, how do we stop it? How do we end the endless winter?"

"You can't," Viiv replied flatly.

"What do you mean, I can't? Others have changed the seasons before. Saint Evaline brought forth the harvest. Saint Brielle brought winter back."

Viiv snorted. "Sofi, you are *not* a saint. And I know you don't seem to want to hear this, but you can't break another witch's spell. If this winter curse belongs to your mother, she's the only one who can end it. But"—Viiv sucked in a breath— "she's dead."

Sofi clenched her jaw. "I *know* that, Viiv." She knew that all too well. "But if we don't do something, Tambor is going to pass the title of Musik to his son, and once the flute is out of his hands, it will be much more difficult to stop him. This country will bury itself in snow. We have to do something." She got to her feet and rattled the bars of her cell furiously. Unsurprisingly, they did not budge.

"I'm sorry, Sofi," Viiv said, and she sounded it. "But there's nothing you can do. Just focus on winning your trial. Come back to Gran's. We can put our heads together. It might take time, but we can work something out."

"We don't *have* time." Sofi's jaw throbbed from her clenched teeth.

"Sofi." Viiv's voice was patient.

"What?" she snapped.

"You can keep the crow," Viiv said. "Get to know him. Give in to your magic a bit. You have to start somewhere."

"Gee." Sofi stared at the bird, which blinked blankly back at her. "Thanks."

"Just focus on the trial," Viiv repeated. "Then we can look to the world, okay?"

"Fine." Sofi's stomach was sour from hunger and anguish, her mood growing fouler by the minute.

"I'll see you soon, Sofi." The crow snapped its beak shut. Sofi's cousin's voice was gone.

"Well," Sofi said to the crow, who continued to blink up at her, "that sucked." She held out a hand to the bird, and after a moment of suspicious examining, the crow got close enough to allow Sofi to pet his soft feathers. They were smooth and slick as oil.

"Do you see that there?" Sofi pointed to the ring that held the key to her cell. "Right there, just grab that." She gave the crow a slight tap on the tail. "Go on." She gestured at the dull metal. "Shoo." She tried to urge the bird forward, but it merely ruffled its feathers. Sofi jumped, removing her hand. The crow shot her a withering stare.

Who was she kidding? Who was *Viiv* kidding? It didn't matter if Sofi embraced the magic within her or not. She couldn't even maintain good relationships with living things.

How could she possibly build relationships with bones? No bird would ever want to reveal its full self to her. Sofi would never know a creature from its beak to its marrow.

Marrow.

Sofi sat up so suddenly that she startled the crow at her side. It cawed sharply and settled on the other end of the cell. Sofi might not have a relationship with birds. But she did have a relationship with the marrow that fueled the magic of Tambor's flute. It was her *mother's*.

Sofi got to her feet and began to pace, heart racing, blood roaring in her ears. *A sacrifice*, Viiv had said. A sacrifice was required to break the spell. A sacrifice that would mean something to the one who had provided the bones.

Sofi didn't have much left. So much had already been taken from her. Her future as a Musik. Her father's life. Lara's trust in her.

The only thing Sofi had left to sacrifice was herself.

Through everything, Sofi had clung on to a desperate certainty that she could still become a Musik. Whether that was by taking on Lara's Apprenticeship or revealing the bone lute's magic to dethrone Laravelle Hollis. Until now there had always been a way forward.

But in order to take down Tambor and clear Lara's name, Sofi was going to have to tell the world the truth about her mother and claim the magic that existed within herself. This truth would, at best, ensure she was Redlisted. At worst, it would imprison her forever.

Sofi flexed her fingers. If she did this, she would never

be allowed on the other side of the Gate. She would never become a Musik.

But if that was what it took to save Lara, to take down Therolious Ambor, to preserve the truth and honor of the art form she loved beyond measure, and to end the howling winter, well, then it was what she would have to do.

Sofi stopped pacing and began to compose, fingers striking imaginary lute strings, lines tripping off her tongue. It was how she thought best, after all: in lyrics and notes.

She would compose one final song to perform at her trial. A song that told the truth about everything—about love and magic and failure and deceit and snow.

And Sofi.

A song about Sofi, too.

As the verses fell into place, she prayed to the Muse and the saints alike that it would be enough to save her. If it was to be the last song she would ever write, Sofi wanted it to be a masterpiece.

THE SIXTH DAY

Sofi's first epic was a three-hour composition entitled "The Care of Saint Claudette." Most musicians didn't complete a song of that length until they were well into their teenage years.

Sofi was nine.

The morning the ink dried on the epic's final verse, the manor was empty. Marie had gone to the market to procure jarred beets. Frederik was away. Again. So it was a surprise when there was a knock on Sofi's door. It held more weight than the rap of Marie's bony knuckles, more flesh to pad the sound. Sofi stiffened as Frederik Ollenholt opened the door without waiting for her response.

"You're back early." Sofi sat up from where she'd been lying, feet on her pillow as she idly plucked her lute's strings. She moved to put her instrument back in its case, but her father held out a hand to stop her.

"I don't recognize that melody." His nose was still red-tinged from the cold. "It isn't one of mine, is it?"

Sofi shook her head. She had been experimenting and perfecting the twists and turns of this tune for almost the entire month her father had been away. Frederik was away far less these days, no longer spending stretches of time with the rest of the Guild beyond the Gate. Instead, Sofi found him more frequently underfoot, always at the dinner table, always right behind her, as though waiting for her to falter. To fail. She had started silencing her thoughts as she passed him in the wide hallways of the manor, so eager was she to prove to him that she was dedicated to her routine.

But for one blissful month, Sofi had allowed herself to make noise, to tease out a melody note by note. She listened, wanted, prayed, felt, and repented.

And then she wrote.

Like Frederik had promised, the Muse rewarded her handily for her suffering. Sofi had heard Musiks complain of the time it took to compose, yet after obeying Frederik's training routine, notes poured from her fingers and lyrics burst to life on her tongue. Sometimes Sofi's hand could hardly keep up with her brain, so quickly did the ideas flow onto the page. But until now she had not shared the fact of her bounty with her father.

"Play it for me," Frederik insisted, seating himself in the chair beside her desk.

"Oh, no," Sofi said, even as her heart swelled with hope. Wasn't this exactly the situation she had wanted to find herself in—an opening to prove to Frederik that her training routine was not only adhered to, but *working*? "It's rather long."

Frederik leaned back on the chair, which emitted a short creak. "I've the time."

Sofi hardly dared to believe it. For so long she'd been forced to beg for even a scrap of her father's attention, had been granted his focus only when she'd failed. Could it be possible that he might finally bear witness to her success?

"I've only just finished, so it might need more work—" she began as she got to her feet, but a *tsk* from her father interrupted her.

"Don't apologize before you've even begun. A Musik would state the title of the piece, nothing more." He nodded at her, almost encouragingly, but Sofi knew it was not so simple as that. Her father hadn't said it aloud, but this was a test.

The last time she'd been tested, she had *felt* on a fifth day and had been made to repent. There was no telling what a sixth day might become if she erred now.

"Right." Sofi rolled her shoulders back and tucked her lute securely in the crook of her arm. "This is 'The Care of Saint Claudette.'" She inhaled deeply. Set her left hand. Exhaled. Began to play.

It had taken her the better part of six months to compile the full story of Saint Claudette. There wasn't much in the history books, and while Marie claimed to know all her saints, even she had some gaps in knowledge. It had taken a carefully penned letter to Denna, first to identify the tale Sofi wanted to tell, then another handful of restless months before that letter was returned, accompanied by a book from Denna's father's collection, bound in black leather, its pages yellowed and dusty with age.

It appeared there wasn't much interest in keeping a record of the miracles Saint Claudette performed. The way she wandered the world, healing those with unfamiliar ailments, even offering preventative care. The tales of knights who slew creatures made perhaps for more exciting fodder, but Sofi had taken great care to infuse her melody with the sort of surprise that kept the listener on edge. So different were each of Saint Claudette's healings that it only stood that the verses of her ballad should be too.

And indeed, Sofi could see her father, who was staring idly at his hands when the song began, had leaned forward almost unconsciously, his left ear tilted toward his daughter as he tried to figure out where the melody would take him next.

As Sofi played, excitement rising at her father's rapt attention, there was a fluttering in her chest, a warmth that began to spread throughout her body, from her blood to her bones. But before it got too far, Sofi called forth the Muse to help her build the necessary walls. Carefully, as her fingers moved from course to course, the warmth began to retreat, snapping back behind the careful stones of restraint she had worked so hard to place perfectly around her heart.

Sofi played, and each time her fingers flew from note to note, she reeled in her feelings, swallowed her hope, and instead focused only on that which she had first learned to control: the music. The technicality of the transitions. The shape of the words on her tongue. Sofi sang of Saint Claudette's care, and she, too, was careful. Her edges were hard. The fluttering ceased.

Now when she sang there were no strange sounds or scents or feelings or objects that appeared unbidden. Now when she sang Sofi was strong enough to ignore the shaking of her knees, the weariness of her fingers, the urgency of her bladder.

Now Sofi simply sang.

When she struck the final notes, Frederik sat for a moment in silence. Then he spoke: "I thought so."

The certainty in his voice set Sofi on edge. He *had* been expecting her to fail, and she'd proven him right. Only she wasn't sure how.

But when she looked up at her father, his expression was open and hopeful in a way that was almost alarming upon his usually frowning face. "The Muse has smiled upon you, my girl," Frederik said. "Your suffering has made you an artist the likes of which the world has never seen." He got to his feet, a heavy hand clasping Sofi's shoulder. She let her father's praise flow through her like the hot spiced cider she loved so much from the King's City, even as uncertainty twisted in her stomach. She had never been given reason to trust Frederik's good moods.

"If you maintain your training this well," her father continued, eyes blazing bright as the small fire crackling in Sofi's fireplace, "the Ollenholt name will go down in history. None will be able to deny us or defame us."

Sofi hadn't known that was something she needed to fear.

"You've been so patient." Frederik began to pace, deep in thought. "It's time that you were rewarded. Time to take an entire day to do exactly what you love." He stopped moving, eyes meeting his daughter's, and he looked so sincere that Sofi couldn't help but release the tiny giggle that had bubbled up within her.

"You love music, don't you?" her father asked, suddenly concerned.

Sofi stammered her agreement. Of course she loved music. It was, perhaps, the only thing she *did* love, not that she could admit that to her own father.

"That's my good girl." Frederik pulled his daughter in for a hug. It was awkward, his arms tense, Sofi rigid with surprise at the unfamiliar expression of emotion, but it wasn't long until she allowed herself to give in and take one small sigh of relief. "You're such a good girl," he said.

Relief, Sofi now knew, smelled of leather and pipe tobacco.

"Yes," her father murmured tenderly into Sofi's hair, "the sixth day is for music."

TWENTY-THREE

THE KINGSGUARD came for her before the sun rose.

Sofi was pulled from her fitful slumber by the scraping of the dungeon's main door. She groaned, pushing herself upright, her neck stiff from the stone beneath her head. Her crow companion squawked indignantly at the interruption to his roosting. At the unexpected noise, the guard dropped his keys with a musical clatter.

"What the . . . ?" He peered into the cell, frowning. "Is that a raven?" He raised his lantern to get a better look. It was the guard from Sofi's carriage ride, his dark hair swooping over his left eye artfully.

"It's a crow." Sofi stared up at him. "Obviously."

The Kingsguard frowned. "Right," he said, still fumbling

with the keys. "There we go." He inserted a small silver key, turning it with a loud creak. "Hands where I can see them." Sofi sighed, getting to her feet and sticking her wrists out in front of her. "Thanks." The Kingsguard expertly wrapped her wrists in chains. "Come on, then."

"Isn't it a bit early?" Her furs slipped from her shoulder, and she struggled to right them with her bound hands.

The guard glanced up at the window and the sliver of still-dark sky. "The king does his best thinking before breakfast." He shrugged.

Sofi's stomach soured. She had factored in the morning to put the finishing touches on her song. It wasn't ready yet.

"Can't I bathe first?" That would buy her some time. And she really was disgusting. Her dress was frozen and dirty, and she could practically feel the grease emanating from her scalp. As far as first impressions went, hers would not do her any favors.

The guard sniffed, making a face. "Sorry." It sounded like he meant it. "No time."

Sofi chewed her chapped bottom lip. It was the first time she wished she owned a Paper. The glamour for clean hair or a fresh-looking dress. Anything to endear her to her audience. She'd watched Lara capture crowds with merely a deep breath and a kind smile, but Sofi needed all the help she could get today.

The Kingsguard led Sofi up the circular staircase and back into the stone chamber from which she'd first entered the castle. But instead of turning left toward the carriages, the guard took her right, up another set of circuitous stone stairs and down a long corridor. They ducked through two low doorways, emerging in a bustling corridor.

"What's your name?" Sofi asked the guard as they walked down the white stone hallways, footsteps echoing against the polished floors. Despite the early hour, the castle was a flurry of activity, tailors passing scullery maids chatting to errand boys trailing the Kingsguard. No one even batted an eye at Sofi. A young girl passed them, balancing a tray longer than her torso that smelled of grilled sausages and fresh eggs. Sofi began to drool.

"Sir Ilya," he replied, tipping his hat to the young maid, who giggled brightly.

"Ilya." Sofi tried his name on her tongue the way she wished she could try the sausage.

"*Sir* Ilya," he chided good-humoredly. "You seem in awfully high spirits, considering." He squinted at her.

Sofi frowned. "Considering what?"

Sir Ilya's face flashed darkly. "Considering that you're going up against Therolious Ambor. The last two men he brought to trial lost their toes and life, respectively. It might behoove you to be a bit more nervous."

Sofi exhaled sharply. "Someone lost his *toes?*" She wiggled her own in her boots to remind her of what she still possessed. "But King Jovan knows me. My father was a member of the Guild of Musiks as well. I really don't think—"

"That's your problem, right there," Sir Ilya interrupted. "Musik Tambor doesn't care about logic. He'll just throw things at you and pray something sticks. Usually," he added thoughtfully, "it does."

"Hmm." Sofi made a soft noise in the back of her throat. She had never been one for nerves, had always thought that the fear before a performance was proof that the performer was not ready. But there was a creeping sense of dread that spread slowly through her like thick jam atop a roll.

Saints and sheep, she was hungry.

Sir Ilya led Sofi through two more arched doorways. Doors along the corridor kept opening and closing with a percussive rhythm, a backbone beat of the household. More happened in Castle Lochlear before sunrise than took place in some villages all day.

"Didn't mean to scare you," the Kingsguard said after a moment.

"Didn't you?" Sofi ran her fingers through her hair, hoping to make herself look more presentable, anxiety gripping her throat so that her voice came out sounding like a croak.

"I only want to prepare you. This whole ordeal feels blown out of proportion, which means Musik Ambor is afraid. He will strike to kill."

Sir Ilya paused in front of a nondescript wooden door. Inside, there was nothing more than a straight-backed wooden chair and a mug of water. No window. No sound. "Wait here." Sir Ilya looked as though he wanted to say more, but he merely gave Sofi a small nod before exiting, closing the door firmly behind him.

She tried the doorknob, but of course it didn't budge.

There was nothing to do, Sofi supposed, but sit and appreciate the change of scenery. But the small stone room didn't feel very different from her cell in the dungeon. A bit warmer, perhaps, but only just.

She reached for the mug of water, a difficult feat with chained wrists, warring between giving in to her dry tongue or her dirt-streaked face. In the end, she forced herself to take a small sip of water, then dumped the rest of the cup's contents over her head.

She gasped at the shock of cold, blinking the water from her eyes, using her hands to wipe at her face in the closest approximation of cleanliness she could garner without a mirror. She did her best to gather her hair into a bun at the nape of her neck, a mockery of the hairstyle she'd worn for her Musik audition.

Then, she'd had every single moment planned down to the breaths she would take between verses. She'd prepared her whole life for a performance that had been technically perfect but empty-hearted. Today she hoped that even if her performance wasn't perfect, it would be enough to right the wrongs of her family.

Sofi closed her eyes, running through the notes she'd penciled onto her brain the night before. She wondered if she ought to swap the second and third verses to ensure the narrative was building properly. She was running through the chorus, fingers flying silently through the air, when another Kingsguard flung open the door.

He raised an eyebrow at Sofi, who had frozen with her fingers in an approximation of the position of the third line of the chorus. She was so attuned to her lute that she could play it even when it was not there. "Come with me," he grunted.

Sofi got shakily to her feet and followed the new guard down another busy hallway, up a long marble staircase, and through a set of double doors that opened up to a small theater, a bright performance space with a tall stage rivaling the one at the Saint Ogden's Theatre. The walls were sky blue, dotted with wispy white clouds, covered in portraits of people laughing, dancing, reclining, relaxing upon bright green grass that Sofi recognized from her time in Lail. Spring.

The main floor held no seats; instead, it was a sprawling open space that could likely accommodate nearly one hundred people standing. Private boxes lined the second floor—ten at Sofi's initial count—each separated by velvet curtains. The sort of box she would have occupied on any other occasion. In fact, Sofi had once, nearly six years before, when attending one of Denna's performances. Sofi still remembered weeping as the Musik sang about the First Lovers and their Sorrow. It was then that Sofi had decided the sort of songwriter she one day hoped to become.

Then the stage had been empty, waiting for the Musik's brilliance to fill it. Now it was set with three plush chairs.

"What are we doing here?" Sofi looked at the Kingsguard with confusion.

The guard grunted. "It's a public trial, isn't it? So"—he pointed to the chair on the left—"get up there and wait for your public."

It certainly wasn't the way Sofi had hoped to one day take

the stage of the King's Theatre. Her dreams of performing at Castle Lochlear had always been much grander. For one, she would have bathed first. For another, she wouldn't be fighting for her freedom.

"Can't I wait in the wings? I don't want people to see me like this." Sofi gestured awkwardly at herself.

The Kingsguard laughed hollowly. "If you don't wish to be perceived, don't commit crimes. At the very least, not against someone like Therolious Ambor. Now, up you go." He gave Sofi a gentle push forward.

Sofi trudged miserably up the stairs and perched on the edge of the plush chair with as much dignity as she could muster. The Kingsguard leaned against a column, looking bored. Sofi crossed her legs, her right foot shaking wildly beneath her wide skirt. There was something about a silent theater that didn't sit well with her.

She began to hum her melody softly, hoping to ease the racing of her heart. She trailed off as the double doors swung open to reveal Therolious Ambor and his son. The two were dressed in formal garb, the sharp cuts of their black suits more appropriate for a performance than a trial.

"Miss Ollenholt." Tambor nodded as he took the stage, settling deeply into the chair on the right. "You're looking"—he swept his eyes up and down her ragged appearance—"well."

"Oh, worms eat your eye," Sofi snapped back.

Tambor giggled delightedly at her profane language. "Prison certainly seems to suit you. Your father would be *so* proud."

Sofi leaped to her feet, the chain around her wrist rattling dangerously, but before she could reach for Tambor, the Kingsguard was there, wrestling her back into her seat.

"That's right." Tambor looked happier than Sofi had ever seen him onstage as the guard held her by her shoulders. "You'll need to behave."

"May the Muse steal your soul," Sofi spat, trying and failing to evade the guard's grip.

Tambor merely smiled serenely. "Oh, I don't think we need to worry about that."

Sofi sank back into her seat, resigned, as people of the court began to filter into the room. Finely dressed courtiers crammed themselves five to a private box, craning their necks and leaning over the balconies to get a better look. The main floor was crowded with bodies dressed in bright silks and other fine fabrics, everyone's face powdered, their hair in perfect Paper styles. It served only to make Sofi more self-conscious about her own appearance.

Sofi scanned the crowd for white-blond hair or a mop of dark curls, but despite the continued influx of audience members, neither Lara nor Jakko appeared. Sofi thought she caught a glimpse of Denna, but when she blinked, the Musik's familiar face was gone.

Seeing the audience assemble made the moment feel even more like a performance. The tips of Sofi's fingers had gone numb with panic. Once, performing had been her lifeblood. Now she wanted to run away. But before she could give that option the thought it deserved, the entire theater fell silent. King Jovan, flanked by his advisers, swept into the room, parting the crowd with a simple wave of his hand.

The king ascended the steps to the stage, looking weary despite his perfect appearance. He nodded his head to Tambor in acknowledgment, then turned to Sofi. His face flickered.

"The trial of the accused, Sofi Ollenholt, versus Musik Therolious Ambor is about to begin," King Jovan's deep bass boomed through the theater. "Miss Ollenholt faces the accusation of stealing Musik Ambor's flute, an item which is intrinsic to his position as Musik, a liaison between our country of Aell and the rest of the world." The king turned to face Tambor. "Musik Ambor, in your own words, please state the details of the crime and the punishment you seek."

Tambor got slowly to his feet, his chest puffed out confidently. His shoes had silver buckles that glittered in the light. "I am a musician first," he pronounced loudly, "and a man second. I serve the Muse and the king. None other."

His words were as saccharine as licorice dipped in honey sprinkled with sugar. And just like that concoction, they served only to make Sofi sick. Tambor, of course, held none of those beliefs. Therolious Ambor had only ever served himself.

"This girl"—Tambor pointed a shaking finger in Sofi's direction—"this ungrateful girl tried to ruin my livelihood, out of anger for not voting her into the Guild of Musiks. I know she lost her father recently, and of course, grief does make fools of us all." His voice dripped with pity. Tambor was giving the best performance of his life, all without his flute. "I only wish she had known when to stop. Her decision to hurt me could have put all of Aell in jeopardy."

Sofi could take his false accusations no longer. "I brought it back," she interjected. "You didn't even know it was gone until I brought the instrument back to you."

"Miss Ollenholt," King Jovan said sharply. "Please wait your turn. You will soon have a chance to speak."

Sofi exhaled sharply, pursing her lips, but fell silent.

"Because she stole with malicious intent," Tambor continued, "she put the transition of title to my son in jeopardy. Any intent to dismantle the Guild of Musiks deserves punishment. I therefore recommend that Sofi Ollenholt be Redlisted."

There was a murmur of shock from the crowd. Redlisting was a well-enough-known punishment, but the idea of getting to witness it sharpened the audience's attention. As Sofi scanned their eyes, she began to feel the deck was stacked firmly against her.

"Why couldn't your son purchase another flute, Musik Ambor?" She rose to her feet, her voice as shaky as her knees.

"Miss Ollenholt." King Jovan looked furious. "I will not warn you again. However"—he turned his attention back to Tambor—"it is a fair question: How would this have affected the transition of the title? Why could your son not simply procure another flute?"

For the first time, Tambor looked flustered. Sofi couldn't help but smile.

"Barton," Tambor called sharply into the crowd. "Bring it here, Barton."

His son hurried the black flute case to the stage. Tambor accepted it and carefully fitted the pieces of his instrument together. He lifted the flute to his lips and played the opening lines to his most famous tune: "The Helpless Heart of Sir Theodore." The crowd in the theater seemed thrilled to witness a free and impromptu performance by a Musik.

"As you can see," Tambor said smugly, once the applause had died down, "the craftsmanship of this flute is unparalleled. The person who constructed this instrument is long deceased. There will never be another like it. While of course Barton could procure a new flute, the question isn't could he, but why would he?" Tambor turned toward Sofi, feral glee flickering in his eyes. "Because Sofi Ollenholt stole from him. She took the finest instrument in the land and stuffed it down her skirt like it was nothing more than a candlestick or an iron poker.

"If this crime is something we punish with a mere slap on the wrist, what stops future musicians from tampering with the Guild of Musiks in a larger way? What would stop them from, for example"—Tambor caught Sofi's eye, and the smile he broke out into was chilling—"beginning to use magic?"

The murmuring in the audience grew louder. Sofi looked desperately at the king. Surely King Jovan wouldn't take Tambor's threat seriously. The logic didn't make any sense. But of course, just as Sir Ilya had warned her, Tambor would make any argument in an attempt to save himself. To Sofi's horror, King Jovan looked shaken.

"I know how important this transition of power is, Your Majesty," Tambor continued. "As we prepare to induct a new class of Musiks into the Guild, I fear that if we do not make an example of Miss Ollenholt, there will be more of this foolishness in the future."

Sofi watched a storm brew in King Jovan's mind. She knew that he cared for her, but there was a limit to that care. The man who offered her embraces in her parlor also presided over an entire country. And when the future of that country and the borders between Aell and the rest of the world were at stake, Sofi realized that unless she was able to prove the flute's magic, she would not—*could* not—emerge victorious.

"Musik Therolious Ambor demands that the accused, Sofi Ollenholt, be Redlisted for her crime and stripped of her right to ever perform again." He turned to Sofi, his eyes unbearably sad. "Now, Miss Ollenholt." The king's voice was tender enough that Sofi knew she was right—he believed he would have to make an example of her. "It is your turn to speak."

Sofi took a deep breath as she got to her feet. There were so many people, so many unfamiliar faces looking up at her with pity and distrust. She swayed as she took a step forward. She couldn't believe it had come to this. Couldn't believe how impossibly, completely alone she was.

Despite knowing what she needed to do, Sofi couldn't seem to make a sound. Her bound wrists clanked out of rhythm. Her hands felt empty without a lute. Her plan, which had seemed so bold and brilliant in the dim light of her prison cell with only a crow for company, now seemed like the half-baked ramblings of a sleep-deprived girl.

King Jovan frowned at her. "Miss Ollenholt?"

Sofi's heart hammered louder than Raffe's largest drum. She opened her mouth.

Nothing.

Where once Sofi had been a confident, careful performer, she was now as frightened as the mice that would skitter across the kitchen floor at the first hint of Marie's footsteps. She had spent her entire life training to be a Musik, yet now, during the most important performance of her life, she could not make herself react.

"I really can't allow this to drag out any longer," King Jovan urged. "There's a performance that my staff must prepare for." He looked down desperately at her. "Speak now, or I will be forced to make my ruling."

"She doesn't seem to want to speak." Tambor shrugged. His smile was all teeth. "Let's put all this to rest; there's a good girl."

The ice that had overtaken Sofi turned to fire.

My good girl, her father had called her each time she took one of his punishments in stride. Each time she opened her arms to another one of his hurts.

I am good, Sofi had convinced herself, *so long as I'm quiet. So long as I listen. So long as I do what I'm told.*

Now, as Sofi stood on the stage of the King's Theatre, those words ringing in her ears, she saw the truth: She had suffered because her father was a coward. He had plucked the heart and soul right out of her because he was afraid of her power. Of the consequences of his own choices. And it was easier to silence his daughter than to take the steps to silence himself.

That routine he had so carefully crafted and which Lara had dissected so sharply had been created to suppress Sofi's magic further. To hide her better instincts behind a wall of her own making.

Frederik had turned his daughter into a weapon and then used Sofi against herself.

Now Sofi would take those carefully sharpened skills, that expert precision, and she would tear down the wall around her heart. For too long Sofi's magic had been suppressed in the name of her music. It was time to release her instincts and let the other half of her take hold.

"This is 'The Bone Song,'" Sofi said, the way a Musik would.

She closed her eyes and focused on feeling all the way down to her bones, the way a witch would.

And then she began to sing.

TWENTY-FOUR

HEN SUMMER'S heat still roved the land, a woman felt her love unfold." Sofi's voice wavered in the small theater. As expected, the acoustics were exceptional. *"How she fared is hard to guess; her story then was left untold."*

Before, the crowd in the King's Theatre had appeared dense as berries in a bucket, many but contained. Now that Sofi had only her voice to support her, the audience seemed to expand, the way Marie's sourdough starter left to proof overnight would inflate until the dough grew too large for the bowl. There were so many witnesses to her potential failure.

Sofi had never thought much of her singing voice. It was as small and mousy as she herself had always felt. With a lute, Sofi's voice was supported, her words bolstered by a tender or tenacious melody. Singing unaccompanied left her feeling too vulnerable. But there, in the King's Theatre, her voice echoing like a bell atop a cathedral, her power pulsed. The flutter in her chest turned into a flickering fire. If this was to be her final performance, she would strip away every restriction, each lasting piece of damage done to her heart, soul, and magic.

Sofi sang, bound not by her father's fear, but her freedom.

"But when at last her love she found, his talent was not much to sway. When words he wrote and spells she spoke, she knew that they would find a way."

The words were thick as syrup on her tongue. She was still grappling with the secrets her parents had kept. The truth of the bone lute. The cruelty to which her father had turned after her mother's passing to ensure Sofi never gave him away. The coarse, casual certainty that Tambor held, the way he acted as though success was owed to him.

"Her love and magic overtook, and thus his songs were played by rook."

Sofi's fingers itched for strings to pluck. The chains around her wrists rattled out of time. She winced. The small slip of concentration caused her to waver. The faces that stared up at her were unflinching but not unfriendly. Instead, they were focused, concentrating deeply, the way the audiences were enraptured by Lara's performances in the taverns of Aell. Music inspired people, intrigued them. Even now, despite her wavering voice and lack of accompaniment, Sofi had control of the crowd. Because she was offering them her heart.

A performance.

"And then, one day, the truth unveiled, by a man most tall and pale. To save her love, the woman gave a flute that sent her to the grave."

She chanced a glance at Tambor, whose face was satisfyingly red. "This is blasphemy," he bellowed, voice floating wildly around the room. But his anger only served to grant Sofi more confidence. His fury was proof of his fear, his fear proof of his guilt. Surely the king could see that.

"Silence, Therolious," the king snapped. "It is Miss Ollenholt's turn." He offered Sofi a soft smile, emboldening her to continue.

"A flute, a lute, a truth set free," she sang, *"a girl whose blood won't let her be. A mother's curse, a daughter's cure, when summer turns to winter, sure. Steady is the song of breaking bones to season's end."*

Sofi was especially proud of the chorus. The chorus was a song's only constant—the piece that reached every corner of the verses and tied them all together. Which was why in this song about her mother, the chorus was about Sofi. *She* tied the tumultuous story together. Her fear and frustration and uncertainty was the song's through line.

"And when a girl who loved the sound found herself her soul unbound, tied to what the magic found, it left her all alone." Sofi's voice wavered as she began to sing about Lara. She wished that Lara were there to witness her performance, to see what Sofi was facing, what she was sacrificing. But then, that defied the point of a sacrifice. If Sofi sang the truth for the wrong reason, what was the point of revealing it at all? No, this truth was

for her mother. For the flute. For Therolious Ambor and King Jovan. For the country of Aell. For spring.

"They made their way from town to town, where the roots go way, way down. Oh, lover, why are you so sure? When all these tunes the bone lute bore." Sofi laughed slightly, the lyrics catching on her lips. The time Sofi had spent on the road with Lara had been some of the most exhilarating days of her life. Composing for someone else, entrusting her songs to another, was freeing in a way Sofi had never before known. There was an understanding between them, a partnership, creative and otherwise. Lara had changed the way Sofi saw not only music but the world.

"And then when one turned into two, one learned a truth few seldom do. Two offered love that seldom few would choose to leave behind."

Sofi had fallen for Lara, but her heart had betrayed her in the end. Sofi had chosen music when she should have chosen Lara. Music had betrayed her. Lara had been nothing but kind and loyal.

"With that the knowledge raw, untamed, oh, how was one to run the game? Face the facts on lists of red? Deny the father surely dead?"

Sofi's voice was stronger now. She let herself taste every word, let each one ring resolutely through the theater. Lara was right. Sometimes all a person had was their voice, and Sofi had finally found a way to use hers. To reignite the love for music she had feared was gone for good. Sofi sang, to the bone lute, to Tambor's magic flute, to the face of her mother seared upon her memory, to the ghost of the father she'd once worshipped, to the endless snow falling to the ground.

"A flute, a lute, a truth set free," Sofi repeated, and as she did, a warm wind enveloped her in an embrace. Like the shadow of her mother's arms around her, holding tight. But instead of shying away, Sofi leaned into her magic. Drew forth its warmth. Let it envelop her. Protect her.

"A girl whose blood won't let her be." Sofi gave herself fully to the music the way she had always wanted to. *Saints*, how she *felt*, how she *wanted*, how she *prayed*, how she *listened*, how she *repented* all in one lyric.

Those pieces of her had never needed to be separate from her songs. In fact, they made her performance whole. They made her music powerful. Without those restrictions, her heart was open. Exposed. Without a routine to suppress her instincts, it beat steadily in the background, keeping her magic in tune and in time. Offering proof that Sofi was—and had always been—worthy of anything she set her mind to.

"A mother's curse, a daughter's cure, when summer turns to winter, sure."

The warm hold of the wind spread beyond Sofi and enveloped the room. Hats were blown from heads, skirts were ruffled, the audience shrieked and shouted as the air around them continued to whip like a snowstorm, only it did not carry bitter cold but gentle warmth. A lump rose in Sofi's throat as she caught the scent of honeysuckle and lilac.

For too long Sofi had not been allowed to speak her wants, but that was exactly what "The Bone Song" was: a wanting.

Every word was a wish. Every syllable a reclamation of the power Sofi always should have been allowed to possess.

"Steady is the song of breaking bones to season's end."

End, Sofi urged her mother's spell, and the word echoed through the theater like a church bell. Sofi had never known she could make so much noise. Take up so much space. And as her own plea, her own wanting, reverberated in her chest, the final levee broke. Tears poured down Sofi's face, a garish display of emotion never before present in her performance.

She could only hope it had been enough. As she fell silent, the wind died down, though the sweet, floral scent remained. Sofi turned toward King Jovan, veins full of fire. But the king wasn't looking at Sofi at all. He was staring out the wide windows that lined the second floor.

Throughout the trial, snow had pelted the glass with the incessant *tap-tap* of fingers on a tabletop. The gray sky had hung low and close, like the aftereffects of a nightmare. But the light had changed. The heavy clouds were gone, as though blown away by the same strong wind that had whipped through the theater. The sun's rays used their newly found freedom to spill onto the balcony's carpet, illuminating its red undertones.

Strangest of all, there was no snow.

Certainly, it still clung to the ground, to the white-capped firs and hedges, held desperately to the turrets and the shingles that roofed the castle. But it no longer fell from the sky, which had turned a crisp, clear blue, the color as rich and deep as it had been in Lail—in the season of spring.

"Can it be?" King Jovan whispered reverently. In the new light cast from above, he seemed to glow.

The audience still had their backs to the window. But at the wonder of their king, they turned to take in the scene, gasps and murmurs billowing through the high-ceilinged theater. Several people fell to their knees, sobbing.

It was a miracle the likes of Saint Evaline, who'd brought the sun to stop the endless ice and snow. The likes of Saint Brielle, who had sent a windy chill to free the country from the sweltering heat.

Sofi, who had always loved songs of powerful women, now found herself among them.

"What did you do?" The king had turned to Sofi, his hands clutching her shoulders. Even though his words were not angry, Sofi's first instinct was to recoil. She was so used to being blamed for her magic that it was difficult to believe she might be celebrated.

"I . . . ," Sofi stammered, feeling every set of eyes in the audience. Now that her song had ended, she was rather lost for words. "I *think* I just ended winter." She exhaled sharply, hoping to drive away her nerves. "I'm a witch, Your Majesty."

She winced as the truth fell so plainly from her lips. Yet there were no gasps of horror; nor did the king shrink away. Instead, he began to laugh, the great, beautiful sound of unbridled joy. He laughed so hard that tears began to pour down his face, and he swept Sofi up in an embrace, the fur and velvet of his cloak tickling her cheek. The flicker of dread in her stomach was replaced by a glimmer of hope. If she had truly spoken to her mother, had ended Aell's sixteen-year winter, perhaps that meant she had broken the spell of Tambor's flute, too.

Sofi pulled away from the king's embrace and searched the stage for Therolious Ambor, but he was nowhere to be found. "Guards," Sofi shrieked, but her voice barely made a dent, so cacophonous was the noise inside the theater. Several audience members had pressed their cheeks against the glass. Several more had exited the theater altogether and were standing in the gardens, their faces turned toward the sun.

Sofi sprinted to the edge of the stage, rising on her tiptoes to survey the crowd. She spotted Barton's silver-blond hair moving swiftly toward the door. "Stop them," Sofi shouted, pointing to Tambor and his son. This time the king heard her and motioned to his guards, who barred the door just in time. Sir Ilya was the one to seize the Musik by the arm and bring him roughly back to his place onstage. As he passed Sofi, Sir Ilya winked.

"Where were you headed, Therolious?" The king's brow was furrowed as the crowd settled down, the better to overhear the Musik's potential downfall. "This trial is not ended."

"I . . . ," Tambor wheezed, trying to catch his breath, "only wanted to bear witness to the sun."

"He was running away," Sofi insisted, "unwilling to take responsibility for his part in all this."

The king's brow only furrowed further. "I don't understand what my flautist has to do with anything."

"She's rambling, Your Highness," Tambor said scathingly. "Doesn't know what she's saying."

"Tambor's flute is the reason for this country's winter," Sofi told the king. "My mother was a witch, and he blackmailed her to make a flute that played perfectly every time. But she used her own marrow to channel the magic, and it turned volatile, the way the Papers did on the other side of the Gate. Each time Tambor played, the winter's hold on our country grew stronger."

The king turned to his Musik. "Is this true?"

Tambor, whose face had gone a particularly vivid shade of puce, stammered, but he could not seem to formulate the necessary words.

"Ask him to play," Sofi urged the king. "And you'll see."

"I do not answer to your whims, you ridiculous girl," Tambor sneered. "I am not your jester."

"No, Therolious," King Jovan said. "But you *do* answer to me. And your king demands that you play." Tambor glowered, but even he did not dare disobey the king. He bent down to retrieve his flute and then lifted it to his lips with such confidence that for one heart-stopping moment, Sofi was afraid she would be proven wrong.

The Musik exhaled sharply, but the flute made no sound. He blew into the mouthpiece again like a small child blowing into a paper bag but was met with silence. Tambor's face turned redder as he huffed and puffed to no avail. He readjusted, looking flustered. Blew again. But still there was only silence. A titter escaped from the audience.

Tambor was flustered. He shouted for his son. "Barton. My lips are too dry. Play. Prove her wrong."

Barton Ambor sauntered onto the stage with his patented look of disinterest. He accepted the flute from his father, then frowned. He turned it over in his hands uncertainly. Sofi recognized that confusion. Had seen it on Lara's face that night in Rusham when she'd picked up Sofi's lute instead of her own.

Barton lifted the tail end of the flute to his mouth, casting an uncertain look at his father. Tambor shook his head sharply, and Barton turned it over, blowing into the mouthpiece with a shallow breath. The flute did not respond to his attempts. It huffed and wheezed like an old man but did not produce a single note.

The whispers in the crowd turned to shouts. Order had flown out the window. As the king motioned for his guards, Sofi placed a hand on his arm, nodding to Barton.

"Please don't punish the son for the sins of the father," she pleaded softly. "He didn't know. He didn't choose this."

The king hesitated, then nodded once, gesturing for Sir Ilya. "Take Tambor to the dungeons, but leave the boy."

The Kingsguard frowned but nodded. "As you wish."

"Speaking of fathers . . ." Sofi wrinkled her nose, dread pooling in her stomach as the king's attention returned to her. "I think it's time I confess to the sins of mine."

TWENTY-FIVE

I T WAS a relief to be led to a chamber with a bathtub and a bed. A gift to be given time to prepare for her meeting with the king, a meeting that would tear her family's legacy to shreds the way Marie used to rip out every crooked stitch Sofi sewed.

King Jovan had invited Sofi to his chambers for supper, and so, with an afternoon to waste, Sofi climbed into the bath and stayed, soaking, until the water turned tepid, until she was as wrinkly as a raisin, until her skin had been scrubbed red and raw and she finally, *finally* felt clean.

Hair dripping down her back, Sofi pulled herself from the tub and shrugged on the gown of soft purple silk that had been delivered by a girl with hair a shade darker than Lara's. Sofi rolled up the long, flowing sleeves and padded barefoot toward the bed. She had only just flung herself across the mattress, which was like reclining on a cloud, when there was a knock on her door.

Sofi groaned. She had been craving the sweet relief of sleep, had been hoping to pause the worry still ricocheting around her head. She had done something incredible—impossible, even—but she didn't feel accomplished so much as she felt entirely and completely worn down and weary. Entirely aware of how alone she was.

She hadn't spotted Jakko or Lara at the trial. Had Lara even played her final show in Elgan, knowing what she knew about the bone lute? Was she worried about Sofi? Did she care that they were apart or was she grateful for the space? Sofi scrubbed a hand across her face. Lara was likely glad to be rid of her.

The knock came again, louder this time. So instead of closing her eyes and floating blissfully away to a dreamscape, Sofi pushed herself to her feet and went to open the door.

"I cannot believe you didn't tell me you were a *witch*!" Jakko shouted, flinging himself on her so wildly that she nearly toppled over. She staggered backward into the room, reveling in Jakko's warmth, in the sweet smell of spring that lingered on him. "And not just a potion-brewing one but a bona fide spring-bringer like Saint Evaline herself!"

"You heard 'The Bone Song'?" Although she'd searched the crowd desperately, she hadn't been able to locate his mop of dark curls.

"Even if I hadn't, I heard no fewer than twenty-five people

talking about you in the corridor. You're a legend, Sof." Jakko grinned, pulling back to pinch her cheek.

"I noticed you didn't need an instrument to make music worth listening to," Lara said quietly. She stood hesitantly in the doorway.

Sofi wanted to go to her, wanted to clasp her hands and kiss away her uncertainty, but she held back. The hurt from her angry words was still raw on Lara's face. Sofi hadn't earned the right to comfort her.

"You were right," Sofi said softly. "As usual."

Lara very nearly smiled. Behind Sofi, Jakko huffed contentedly as he flopped onto the long orange settee, running a hand tenderly across the velvet. "Nice place you've got here," he said. "If this is sainthood, I want in."

Sofi blanched. "Sainthood?"

"That's what the scullery maid was saying to the page we passed on the staircase." Jakko shrugged. "The king told the chef to pick the finest produce from the greenhouses for his feast."

Sofi caught a glimpse of herself in the looking glass hung on the wall beside the bed. Her wet hair had soaked a giant spot in the silk of her purple dress. "I can't be a saint," she moaned, raking a hand through her hair, which had begun to dry in a frizzy pouf. "I'm barely adept at being a person."

From the doorway, Lara snorted. "I've got it." She dropped her bag and rifled through it until she had located her hairbrush. "Sit," she commanded, directing Sofi to an overstuffed chair across from the settee where Jakko was settled. Sofi obeyed, trying to breathe through her rising nausea. This was all too much.

Lara's hands were less gentle this time as she yanked her brush through Sofi's tangles. She swiftly separated the strands, expertly twisting and smoothing and pinning until Sofi donned a braided crown.

"Honestly," Lara said once she'd finished, running the brush through her own hair and gathering it at the nape of her neck, "I don't know how you ever survived without me." A strand of hair slipped out of her intricate bun, pulling Sofi's gaze down the long line of Lara's neck.

"I . . ." Sofi trailed off helplessly. She had too many things to say but none of the right words.

"Hollow God, Sofi," Jakko said from the settee, sounding bored, "you are completely and utterly useless. Apologize to the pretty girl for lying to her. *Repent*, but to the people in your real life rather than your Muse." He pushed himself to his feet as Sofi gaped incredulously at him. "Now, if you'll excuse me, I'm fairly certain I saw Wes in the gardens. Watch my things." Jakko shrugged off his coat and headed for the door, stopping only to give Sofi one last, patronizing look.

Jakko was right. Sofi *was* useless. She had lied to Lara, and even though she'd done so in an attempt to protect her, intention was not more important than impact. But Lara wasn't the only one Sofi's actions had hurt.

"Excuse me one moment." Sofi hoped that Lara had one more minute of patience left in her as she ran after her best friend.

She caught Jakko in the hall, fingers closing around his wrist before he turned a corner. Jakko blinked at her, bemused. "What are you doing?"

Sofi bit her lip. "Lara's not the only one I need to apologize to." She took a great, shuddering breath. "I'm sorry that I was never the friend you deserved."

Jakko's gaze caught on the carpet. "You were a bit . . . single-minded."

"Intense and self-obsessed, you mean?" Sofi countered. That coaxed a smile from Jakko, which loosened the knot in her chest. "Well, I did learn from the best," she said dryly, thinking of Frederik. "I wish I could make my father apologize for what he put you through. I'll have Marie find the brooch and return it to your family. You should be able to go home, wherever that home might be."

"Thanks, Sof," Jakko said, squeezing her hand. "I needed that." Then he cleared his throat and pushed her away. "Now go apologize to Lara. She's the nicest person I've ever met, *and* she somehow still seems to like you." He shook his head. "I don't understand it."

Sofi rolled her eyes but couldn't contain the warm reassurance that flooded her. "Fine," she snapped playfully. "I'll see you later."

"As you wish, Saint Sofi," Jakko said, offering her a mock bow.

Sofi shook her head. "I *really* don't want to be a saint," she grumbled as she reentered the room.

"Then don't be a saint." Lara had settled herself on the

settee, Jakko's jacket carefully folded beside her.

"Brilliant. Thanks for that," Sofi said darkly, sinking back into the chair across from Lara. The good humor between them faded back into awkwardness. She might as well come out and say it. "I'm really sorry that I lied."

"I'm sorry that you lied, too," Lara said softly.

"I didn't always know about the bone lute," Sofi added quickly. "I suspected there was magic at play, but I thought it was *you*. I never suspected my father's talent was fraudulent. I didn't realize until Rusham—"

"When I tried to play "The Song of Spring" on your lute," Lara finished, nodding slowly. "Of course." Her eyes flashed up to Sofi's. "That was incredibly unnerving, by the way. Like trying to recall a word that's on the tip of your tongue, but no matter how hard you try, you just can't find it." Her hesitant smile faded. "But you didn't say anything once you knew."

Sofi's stomach soured. "I was trying to protect you. You said it yourself. You didn't know who you'd be without music. I didn't want to be the one to ruin you."

Lara frowned. "You think that if I'd known the lute was magic I would have given up music altogether? You think that if something isn't easy, I won't love it? Won't work for it?" She looked unbearably sad. "Sofi, why don't you believe in my ability to *try*?"

Sofi didn't have a good answer. Only that she had always been trapped by her own reliance on hard work, by the punishment she inflicted on herself, the constant berating and insistence that everything must always be perfect. In all honesty,

Sofi had assumed that anyone who moved so easily through life wouldn't *want* to try to love something that did not always love them back.

Then again, Lara had always been up for a challenge. And if Sofi's performance of "The Bone Song" was any indication, perhaps there were times when she was not perfect but her efforts were still enough. Her voice had been shaky, but her lyrics were still sharp. Her knees had been weak, but her mother's magic had still responded. Because Sofi's heart had been open, her magic bright and bold. Because she had accepted that she wasn't perfect. That she didn't need to suffer to create something worthwhile.

She only had to *try*.

"You're right," Sofi said, and the words were sticky on her tongue as she tasted their truth. "I made so many assumptions, all of them false." She fell to her knees on the plush carpet, and it was emboldening, repenting at the feet of the girl she loved. Taking responsibility for her actions rather than flinging falsehoods at the Muse. "I'm so sorry, Lara. I should have trusted you. I should have confided in you. I should have done a lot of things differently."

"You're not the only person who has ever suffered, you know," Lara said dryly. "And not everyone's suffering is of their own volition."

"I know that." But had she truly? Her own father, although disappointing, had never offered her to the highest bidder. Her family had never turned their backs on her dreams. She had never faced a suffering she herself had not inflicted in the name of the Muse or her art. "I hope I can make it up to you one day."

"You'd better," Lara said softly, slipping off the settee to join Sofi on the floor. "Because I hated not having new material for Elgan; I had to play "Lady Wildmoore" again. I tried writing something, but I need help with the lyrics." Sofi stared at her as Lara rifled through her pocket and came up with a scrap of paper. "Now I'm trying to rhyme this stanza"—she pointed to the top line—"with this one, but I'm worried that the rhythm is all wrong."

Sofi hardly even registered the words on the page. She just stared at Lara's bright eyes and hopeful expression and in the flip of her stomach found that she had a brand-new definition for "wanting."

"What?" Lara noticed Sofi staring and turned bashful, her cheeks blooming pink. "Did I do something wrong? Is it awful?"

"No," Sofi said, not bothering to disguise her wonder. How could she ever explain the love that bloomed in her heart at the soft curl of Lara's hair, at her crooked letters penned in a hurry? She would never be able to put it into words. So instead she reached for the parchment, her fingers brushing Lara's, sending a shiver down Sofi's spine. "It's absolutely perfect."

The sun was still in the sky when Sofi sat down to supper with the king.

The king's chambers were larger than the entire ground floor of the Ollenholt manor. The room was draped in royal red, the carpet so plush Sofi sank into it the way she would a snowbank. The long table was laid with gilded finery, vases boasting artfully displayed bouquets of sticks and pine fronds. Heaping plates were loaded with thick slices of rye bread, freshly churned butter, and pickled quail eggs. There were dishes of salted fish and fresh radishes, cabbage and beet soup. Sofi toyed with a gold-plated fork as the king speared a slice of fish.

"Strange, isn't it?" he asked, eyes fixed on the floor-to-ceiling windows at the far end of the room, where the sun sank slowly, offering a spectacular showing of oranges and golds. "I'm so used to dining in the dark."

"It's nice," Sofi said weakly. She was overwhelmed by the light, by her surroundings, by the impossible truth of what she had done.

"It's a miracle," King Jovan said plainly. "Sofi, you have saved us."

Sofi pushed a quail's egg around the perimeter of her plate. "I only did what was necessary. Paying for the sins of the father and all." She offered the king a small smile, her stomach churning. "I didn't know about the bone lute. Neither did Lara. You have to believe me."

The king furrowed his brow. "Of course I do, Sofi. But I'm not entirely sure that matters now. You have brought the seasons back. Spring is a time for renewal. Rebirth. Something our country is in desperate need of. There will be stories about you for years to come." He smiled. "Our very own Saint Evaline. Known not for her music, but her magic."

Sofi swallowed thickly. "I want to write songs about saints, Your Majesty," she said, "not *be* one."

King Jovan considered her. "I see. I wouldn't force you to accept such a title, of course. But I don't know that we can keep the truth of your magic quiet. There were so many witnesses."

Sofi's stomach plummeted even as she nodded. Her final glimmer of hope had been extinguished. She would never bear the title of Musik. Never travel beyond the Gate. "That's it, then? Even after all of this, my music means nothing because I hold magic? Because my family are witches?"

The king frowned. "Of course it means something. You ended our winter."

"With a song I can never perform in public again because I am not a Musik," Sofi challenged.

The king opened his mouth to argue. Made a face. Put his fork down with a soft clink, looking perturbed. "I suppose," he spoke slowly, choosing his words carefully, "that there is a bit of a flaw in our current system of limiting art to a select few. But the Guild still serves an important purpose. We cannot eliminate their positions to allow access to all."

"Why does it have to be one or the other?" Sofi directed the question at the king, but she was also asking it of herself. Why did her music only matter if she held the highest title, achieved the furthest end goal? Why couldn't each one of her words simply matter as much as she wanted them to?

"It would be enough for you to play in taverns and inns?" the king asked, eyebrow raised.

Sofi would perform on empty streets, in the frigid snow, in the blistering heat, so long as she could *play*. "Music should be for everyone," she insisted, "not hoarded by the few. I was lucky enough to be surrounded by music my entire life. To find purpose and meaning in notes and lyrics, and for that I'll be forever grateful. But my opportunities were not everyone's. When I took to the road with Lara, I saw the way music was embraced by the citizens of Aell. For some, Lara was the first musician they'd ever heard play. If you loosened your restrictions, music could become an art for the masses. Let anyone play who is offered a stage. Let all instruments be heard, even if they are not one of the five that belong to the Guild. Let performers stumble, fail, and love music without consequence."

What she wanted to say but didn't was: *Let* me *play*. This was bigger than Sofi now.

The king exhaled heavily. "Considering that I am currently at your service for freeing my kingdom from the icy grips of winter, I suppose there's no harm in the trying. I will draft up an edict. But I will ask you one favor in return." The king scowled. "I do hate asking for favors."

"Anything, Your Highness." And she meant it. Sofi would do anything so long as she could continue to play the lute.

"I was hoping you might help me arrange a meeting." King Jovan grimaced, sucking in a breath through clenched teeth. Sofi frowned. Surely the king had attendants to do his scheduling. "For years now, I've been trying to get in contact with Aell's witches," he continued. "I know that they may not trust the monarchy after what my father did, how he mined them for their power and then sold it to profit himself." He scrubbed a hand across his face. "But I'd like to meet with them and beg forgiveness. Broker peace, even."

Sofi idly touched the bone that hung around her neck. She couldn't imagine her gran here, in the King's City, but she could picture Viiv gleefully negotiating the future of witches in Aell and the world beyond.

"Perhaps you could pass on a message from me?" the king continued, mistaking Sofi's silence as refusal. "If you have the means to contact them? I'd like to ease our tensions and find a way to exist together."

Sofi nodded. "I think they'd like that."

"Very good." King Jovan turned his attention back to his plate. But he had only just picked up his fork when he frowned again.

"The Council of Regents still expects the new Musiks to come through the Gate any day now," he said, looking put out. "Now that the season is changing, opening the borders is less urgent, but Aell still needs allies. And I'm now short a flautist and a lutenist."

"Well," Sofi said, stirring her tea with a soft smile, "while I think you may be out of luck with the flautist, I have a sneaking suspicion you may be able to find someone here who plays the lute."

TWENTY-SIX

THE NEW Musiks went through the Gate on a sixth day.

Sofi and Lara woke early to see them off. The morning air was rich with the wet, earthy scent of soil. Not all the snow had melted, as there was still sixteen years of ice to thaw, but the scent of flowers on the breeze was warm with possibility. Sofi had even dared to don short sleeves—she proudly wore the blue flower-print dress she'd smuggled from her mother's closet the afternoon that now felt so long ago. As Sofi reveled in the warmth of the sun on her skin, Denna, Yve, and Raffe joined them on the steps of the palace.

While Luk, Cass, and Wes bade farewell to their mentors, Jakko and Sofi embraced.

"I'm so proud of you," she whispered into his shoulder.

Jakko's audition had been a triumph, and the remaining Guild members had voted unanimously for him, just as Sofi had known they would. "And I'm not even the slightest bit jealous."

"Liar." Jakko pulled back and clapped a hand on her cheek, grinning broadly. The clasps on his new lute case glittered in the morning sun. The bone lute had been destroyed at King Jovan's request and a new one had been constructed especially for Jakko.

This lute was made of spruce.

"Okay," Sofi admitted, forcing her smile wider than was entirely comfortable. "I'm a little jealous. But that doesn't make me any less proud."

Jakko laughed, planting a wet kiss on her cheek. "I love you."

"Come back and visit soon." Sofi's throat tightened. "I'll make sure Marie gets your favorite cheese." She couldn't believe she had to say goodbye to Jakko again. "I love you too. Make us proud."

Lara threw her arms around Jakko. "Thank you," she said, tears gliding down her nose, "for everything. Really."

"Anytime, 'Velle." Jakko kissed Lara on her cheek.

"No thanks for that nickname, though." She wrinkled her nose.

"Jakko," Wes called from the bottom of the steps. "The coach is here."

"Better go." Jakko ruffled his hair artfully. "Don't want to miss my chance to squeeze in next to him."

"Don't worry," Sofi said, trying not to laugh at the giddy expression on her best friend's face. "There are plenty of opportunities to fall in love on the road." She cast a glance at Lara, then back at Jakko. "Go on, then." She gave him a nudge in the direction of the Guild's newest lyrist. "He's waiting for you."

"Oh, *they* get a carriage?" Lara pouted as the four new Musiks clambered into the coach.

Sofi leaned against Lara's shoulder. "Don't worry, I got us a carriage too."

Lara's face lit up. "A carriage to where?"

"You'll find out tonight." Sofi grinned.

Lara fanned herself dramatically with a gloved hand. "How romantic."

"But until then"—Sofi wrapped her fingers around Lara's—"we're due to breakfast with the king. And my grandmother and cousin."

"Less romantic," Lara sighed, "but I'll allow it."

Sofi pulled Lara back inside Castle Lochlear, making a quick left and darting up a long marble staircase. "Don't trip," Lara chastised through a laugh as Sofi nearly stumbled in her excitement.

Sofi had called to Viiv via crow. At first her cousin, ever the skeptic, had been unconvinced. But she'd finally agreed to travel with their gran to the King's City. Sofi couldn't wait to see Viiv's face when she had no choice but to accept the truth of Sofi's spring.

And she had come to think of the season as *hers*. King

Jovan had said that spring was a season of rebirth, and wasn't that what Sofi was due too? A chance to plant the seeds of her dreams and to bloom a brand-new hope?

She burst through the doors to the king's chambers and found an impossible tableau—the King of Aell pouring tea for her grandmother. To Gran's right sat Viiv, hawkishly observing the room.

"Sofi!" Her cousin pushed back her chair and ran to meet her, pausing before Sofi almost nervously. "You really brought the spring." She frowned. "How?"

"Thanks to you." Sofi pulled her cousin into a hug. Viiv, who was stiff at first, relaxed into Sofi's embrace. "It was about the relationship with the bones."

"I still have a lot to teach you," Viiv said, squirming out of Sofi's grip. "Don't think that you're some prodigy just because you banished a season."

"Certainly not." Sofi bit back a smile. "I will defer to you."

"Sofi," her gran called from her seat in a plush velvet chair. "Come say hello to your grandmother. I can't seem to get out of this chair, so you'll have to come to me."

Sofi hurried to greet her gran, offering a kiss to the woman's leathery cheek. "There's my girl." Her gran squeezed Sofi's hand, her papery skin and knobby knuckles much stronger than they looked. When the words came from her gran, Sofi did not feel owned the way she felt when her father called her *my good girl*. Rather, Sofi felt accepted. A part of something, rather than an outlier made to claw her way back to acceptance.

When they had all taken their places around the table, King Jovan raised his goblet. "To the future," he said, and Sofi appreciated the way that he looked to her grandmother for confirmation.

"The future." Sofi's gran nodded.

"And the dissolution of the Papers," Viiv huffed under her breath.

"Viivi," her gran chided half-heartedly. Sofi smiled into her goblet. The king had no idea who he was up against.

"I want to apologize," King Jovan said, expression grave. "And express my deepest gratitude for the trust you have instilled in me by showing up today. I do not take that for granted."

"Yes, well," Gran said, "we seem to have a certain girl in common. It's easier to trust someone who cares for my Sofi." She winked at Sofi. Under the table, Lara squeezed Sofi's fingers.

Sofi had never realized how freeing it was to be loved. How the warmth that flowed through her, a warmth that felt like magic, cleared the fog from the windows of her heart.

"I hope that we can move forward together," King Jovan continued. "That I can be a resource for your coven and that you can trust me enough to be a partner in your endeavors. Our country needs magic—careful, safe, controlled magic," he clarified. "I do not condone the decisions of my father." He turned to Viiv. "The Papers have twisted your gift." His eyes flickered to Sofi. "Have replaced the backbone of our art. I wish for us to start anew. With your support, of course."

Sofi's gran took a bite of eggs. "You will not lay a hand on my coven." It wasn't a question. "Even if that means your Papers are all used up and your treasury runs dry."

The king nodded. "Of course," he added. "If your coven wanted to take over the crafting of the Papers entirely, I would defer to you and compensate your efforts accordingly. . . ." He trailed off, looking hopeful. "I want witches to feel comfortable living freely in Aell."

Gran pursed her lips, but Viiv's eyes had gone bright. "I could try it," she said, turning to her grandmother. "We have all those boxes of bones."

Her grandmother considered this. "No harm in the trying, I suppose."

Across the table, Sofi beamed at the lot of them. "To trying," she said, raising her goblet.

"To trying," came the reply, just off tempo, just out of time.

To Sofi, it was the most beautiful thing she had ever heard.

Sofi called for the carriage at sundown. It was only a short ride from Castle Lochlear to their final destination. But still, she *had* promised Lara a coach.

"Where are we going?" Lara breathed, nose pressed against the glass as she watched the King's City roll past.

"Oh, now," Sofi said, bending down to ensure that the lute case she had tucked beneath the seat that afternoon was still in place. "It's no fun if I spoil the surprise."

"I'm not so sure I like your surprises," Lara teased,

flicking her hair over her shoulder. She looked positively radiant in a gown of gossamer silk, silver like moonlight with elaborate white beading down the bodice. It should have been illegal, how good she looked. But instead of reaching for her, Sofi simply stared. "What?" Lara put a hand to her face, self-conscious.

"Nothing," Sofi promised her, then recanted. "Everything. You are everything."

"You're just trying to butter me up, aren't you?" Lara dismissed her compliment. "That means I should absolutely be worried." Just as she finished her sentence, the carriage slowed, coming to a halt in front of the Lonely Lover, one of the finest inns in the King's City.

Lara frowned out the small window. "What are we doing here?"

"We're here for the show," Sofi said, ushering Lara out of the coach first, then tugging her lute from its hiding place.

"Oh!" Lara exclaimed. "Who's performing?"

Sofi bit her lip, trying to contain her laugh. "Well, *we* are."

Lara's eyes went so wide Sofi feared they might pop out of their sockets. "No," she said, shaking her head and giggling nervously. "No, we're not."

"You still remember that fingering pattern I taught you last night, don't you?"

Lara blanched, but Sofi wasn't worried. Lara was an exceptionally good, albeit rather distracting, student. She had picked up theory quickly and, of course, understood the structure of a song better than most beginning players. There was something inherently comfortable about the way she had begun to navigate the strings of Sofi's wooden lute. She was still a gifted performer. And even though she sometimes hesitated, although her transitions were sloppy or her fingers struck errant strings, she never flinched.

More importantly, she never gave up.

It was her tenacity that Sofi loved most. Well, that, and the nimbleness of Lara's fingers, which came in handy in a multitude of ways.

Sofi had been tutoring Lara for less than a week, but already she had mastered simple melodies. The bone lute might have been magic, but the muscle memory and calluses Lara had gained on the road were real.

"You can't be serious," Lara said, her eyes filled with a bright, erratic panic as Sofi led the way through the front door of the inn. As she'd hoped, she was met with the sharp, sweet scent of cider and spiced wine, a loud echo of bright laughter, a light haze of smoke from the fireplace.

"I'm afraid I am," Sofi said, beaming as she reached into the pocket of her vest. "I've got permission, courtesy of the king himself."

"But . . ." Lara shook her head quickly. "We haven't written anything."

"Yes, we have." Sofi pulled a stunned Lara through the packed crowd toward the bar. "We wrote 'The Song of Spring.'" When first they'd penned it together, it had seemed like a frivolous escape. Now it felt like a prophecy.

"Sofi," Lara whined as Sofi passed the permit to the man

behind the bar. "I don't know how to play that."

Sofi frowned at her, feigning confusion. "You've played it before."

"Not really." Lara looked pained. "The bone lute did. *I* didn't."

"No." Sofi shook her head, smiling. "You played it last night. I just didn't tell you."

Lara frowned. "I only played that simple run."

Sofi grinned mischievously. "I simplified the melody somewhat, but the integrity of the song is the same. Besides"—she tucked an errant strand of hair behind Lara's ear—"even with only a few days of study, you're already a better lutenist than anyone in the audience."

The bell chimed as the inn's front door opened again. "Well . . ." Sofi reconsidered as she waved to Denna and her wife, Ari, a brown-skinned woman with red-painted lips. "Denna *might* be able to give you a run for your coin," she admitted. "But don't worry about her."

Lara's eyes went wide. "How am I supposed to do anything but worry?" She wrung her hands desperately. "I changed my mind." Her voice was high-pitched and frantic. "I don't want to be a musician."

"Liar." Sofi squeezed Lara's hand. "Just play what I taught you, all right?"

Lara took a deep breath. "I can do this?"

Sofi grinned, tugging her forward to the empty space before the hearth. "Of course you can, Musik Hollis." She bent down to pull her wooden lute from its case, plucked the strings to ensure the instrument was in tune, and handed the lute to Lara.

Hesitantly, Lara struck the song's opening chord. The bright hope of spring, both as Sofi had once imagined it and then again as she had witnessed it rang out through the packed room. Lara moved on to the next chord, thinking just a moment too long, and the room fell into silence. But then the next sweep of sound came, louder than the last. Lush. Languishing. And as Sofi opened her mouth to sing, to enter into a duet with this girl who had almost been her downfall, she realized that for the first time she knew not what her future held.

Her knees were no longer bruised from praying to the Muse. These days Sofi had eyes only for Lara, who was a muse of another kind entirely. Sofi's stomach no longer churned with hunger or guilt; instead, she spoke freely, dreaming of ways to use her unique blend of music and magic for good. Singing songs of harvest during barren winters. Penning songs of healing amid hurt. Even though she would never be a Musik, she would effect change all the same—her existence would still leave its mark.

When they reached the chorus, Lara's sweet soprano swept up to meet Sofi's steady alto, the lyrics tumbling from their tongues in tandem. A warm glow spread from Sofi's chest all the way to her fingers, which were moving through the air the way that Lara's were beginning to dance upon the strings of the lute.

The audience was smiling. Sofi located Viiv and Gran hovering near the bar in the back of the room. Gran's eyes sparkled. Viiv frowned with concentration. Then, when she could stand the anticipation no longer, Sofi caught Denna's eye.

Denna winked, and the final knot of fear in Sofi's stomach dissipated. Denna loved music the way Sofi did. She had performed for that love, had written epics because she had to, notes pouring from her fingers, lyrics tripping off her tongue. She had played for smiling parents and dancing children in taverns, for lovers who sang their words softly to partners as they drifted off to sleep, for people who needed stories, who were looking for a way to fill the ever-present ache in their chests that could only be sated by song.

Denna was—and had always been—on Sofi's side. A mentor the likes of whom she'd always desired. Someone who loved music for music. Someone who loved Sofi for Sofi.

With the ban on performing lifted, with a tentative peace forged between the monarchy and witches, with Frederik Ollenholt's memory returned to dust just like his ashes, Sofi was finally free. Free to play, to write, to sing. To love, to dream, to *want*. Free to be as loud as she could scream. Free to become whatever she wanted, whether that was musician or witch or some balance of both.

For so long, Sofi's life had been dictated by fear. But now Sofi would choose safety over suffering. She would be patient with herself. She would be kind. There would be moments when she might fall back into the shadows of the past, moments when she would hurt more than she would heal.

But whatever Sofi did, it would be *her* choice.

In the spring of her life, Sofi Ollenholt, too, would be reborn.

When Lara struck the song's final chord, the room burst into a round of enthusiastic applause, as loud as it had ever been when she'd performed with the bone lute. Lara threw her arms around Sofi. "I did it," she squealed.

Sofi squeezed Lara back. "I knew you could."

And she had. After all, it was a sixth day.

And sixth days—like every breath Sofi had ever taken, like every dream she'd ever dreamed, like every future she'd ever imagined—had always been for music.

ACKNOWLEDGMENTS

Everyone says writing your second book is hard. Writing your second book during a global pandemic is even harder. This book (and I) would be worse off were it not for the following folks:

My editor, Sarah McCabe, who connected all my dots. Thank you for getting me to the heart of Sofi's story, and for pointing me towards spring.

My agent, Jim McCarthy, who is without a doubt the best advocate an author could ask for. Thank you for all you do.

The entire McElderry team, including Justin Chanda, Karen Wojtyla, Anne Zafian, Eugene Lee, Tatyana Rosalia, Lauren Hoffman, Caitlin Sweeney, Alissa Nigro, Lisa Quach, Savannah Breckenridge, Anna Jarzab, Yasleen Trinidad, Saleena Nival, Emily Ritter, Annika Voss, Nicole Russo, Jenny

Lu, Christina Pecorale and her sales team, and Michelle Leo and her education/library team, as well as artist Mona Finden for bringing Sofi to life, and designer Sonia Chaghatzbanian, who gave me the cover of my dreams. When I say I fell out of my chair when I saw it, I am not being hyperbolic.

The countless readers, booksellers, bloggers, booktubers, bookstagramers and booktokers who supported both this book and my debut—for your tireless work, your heartfelt messages, and your kind words. Without you, I wouldn't be here, so thank you, thank you, thank you.

Kelly Quindlen, Jen St. Jude, Kiki Nguyen, Carey Blankenship, Rey Noble, Emma Warner, Meryl Wilsner, & Mary E. Roach who offered eyes on early drafts, eternal support, late night texts, pep talks, and memes. I love you all beyond measure.

The authors whose books and friendships helped me survive debut year: Courtney Gould, Leah Johnson, Kalynn Bayron, Morgan Rogers, Jas Hammonds, Allison Saft, Ava Reid, Ciannon Smart & Ashley Shuttleworth. Honored to be in your company.

Pat Buchanan, Charmaine Lindsay, Dylan Tooley, and Rosa Villalpando whose love and support know no bounds.

My mother, who read every single draft, who woke up to emails with scenes out of order and stream of consciousness panic paragraphs all beginning with "what if . . .", and who somehow always knew the right answers to my questions. Thank you for being my second set of eyes.

My father, who bought me my first guitar before I even

knew I wanted to learn to play and who always kept me in music.

My grandfathers: Roy, who left me his sheet music, and Tony, who left us his poems. I hope the melody lingers on.

And last (but not least), my wife Katie. You already got the dedication, but just in case it needed to be said twice: this one—like everything, really—is for you.

ADRIENNE TOOLEY is the author of *Sweet & Bitter Magic* and *Sofi and the Bone Song*. She grew up in Southern California, majored in musical theater in Pittsburgh, and now lives in Brooklyn with her wife, eight guitars, a keyboard, and a banjo. In addition to writing novels, she is a singer/songwriter who has currently released three indie-folk EPs.